# EAST
## TO LYDIA

### MARK J. MOE

CEDAR FORGE

For permission requests, please address:

Cedar Forge Press
7300 West Joy Road
Dexter, MI 48130

Published 2019 by Cedar Forge, an imprint of
Publishing Services @ Thomson-Shore
Printed in the United States of America
21 20 19    1 2 3 4
978-1-943290-88-8 (hardcover)
978-1-943290-89-5 (paperback)
978-1-943290-90-1 (eBook)

Library of Congress Control Number: 2018958554

To my wonderful family.
Your patience with me is extraordinary
And my love for you remains unconditional.

IBERIAN PENINSULA
CANTABRIAN MOUNTAINS
PYRENEES MOUNTAINS
MASSILIA
DOLOMITES
ROME
ADRIATIC SEA
MACEDONIA
BLACK SEA
BYZANTION
EPIRUS
THESSALY
GREECE
ANATOLIAN PENINSULA
SARDIS of LYDIA
MILETUS
ATHENS
SPARTA
CARTHAGE
SICILY
IONIAN SEA
ASPIS
SABRATHA
MEDITERRANEAN SEA
TYRE
JERUSALEM
ALEXANDRIA
EGYPT

TYRRHENIAN SEA
AEOLIAN ISLANDS
LIPARI
ERYX
STRAIT of MESSINA
LILYBAEUM
SICILY
MOUNT ETNA
SICANI MOUNTAINS
AKRAGAS
ECNOMUS
SYRACUSE
MEDITERRANEAN SEA

Praise for *East to Lydia*

"Mark Moe is a gifted author who has used his expert knowledge of ancient history and geography to vividly describe characters and settings for his novel, *East to Lydia*. His characters emerge from the violent era of the Roman and Carthaginian Empires, each walking, marching, or sailing the fragile edges of life and death. As from an ancient theater, they bring with them their blood and chains, their swords and armor; their fears, their love, their hate, their cruelty. *East to Lydia* is a masterpiece in merging story with names, terms, and places dug from ancient history. Readers may, on one page, recoil at the unfurling imagery of ancient wars, then on another reflect upon civilization's humanitarianism. With the unusually detailed descriptions of landscapes and early life around the Mediterranean Sea, we will ponder our own past and our own destiny."

—Ren Holland, author of *The Edge of Itasca* and *The Early Resorts of Minnesota*

"Those who love historical novels will find *East to Lydia* a very satisfying read. This sequel to the author's debut novel, *The Crucible of Man*, continues the story of a simple fisherman turned gladiator caught up in the world-historical events of the ancient Near East. The depth and breadth of Dr. Mark Moe's understanding of the political, economic, social, military, and religious contexts of the Mediterranean world some 250 years before the birth of Christ is impressive and he skillfully weaves that knowledge into a compelling story that will keep the reader turning page after page. The stories of strangers traveling trajectories of convergence lead to a satisfying climax that begs another sequel."

—Rev. Dr. Henry French, retired Lutheran pastor and professor of historical theology and author and editor of seven books, including *Lenten Journey Book of Faith, Prayer – A Primer,* and *It Came Upon the Midnight Clear*

"That the most acceptable service we render to Him is in doing good to his other children. That the soul of man is immortal and will be treated with justice in another life respecting its conduct in this. These I take to be the fundamental points in all sound religion, and I regard them, as you do, in whatever sect I meet with them."

— Benjamin Franklin, 1790

# Prologue

This is the continuing story of a warrior, once forged within the crucible of the Mediterranean basin, and the special individuals responsible for saving him from his own inimical destruction. It is also a story about how man can change; how outside forces, pressing in upon them, can drive men to become something altogether different from how they began. Such a pressure, as it is within a crucible, can take a seemingly innocuous set of ingredients and fuse them together, as if by magic, into one substance capable of poisonous effect and far-reaching harm. Or capable of great loyalty and far-reaching change.

And so it was that, in such an environment long ago, an innocent Greek-born boy (as well as so many like him) became molded into a warrior full of hate, eager for revenge. Yet, within each man there also exists something much deeper. Some inherent property, presumably placed there by his creator, is capable of righting wrongs and strong enough to resist permanent and evil change. A fire, acting as one additional force, applied through an inexplicable power that man does not truly have the capacity to comprehend, is capable of igniting that inherently worthy property and steering it into something good and true—thereby helping that man and the others whom he touches become the individuals they were meant to be.

All one must do to evoke such change is allow that fire to ignite, burn, and glow inside as an ember flashes into a flickering flame, catching its breath before engulfing its fuel in white-hot light. Such potential has always been there, waiting for us to accept it, although so many fail, and have failed, to accept that truth.

In 1816, in reference to "the dogmas of religion," Thomas Jefferson wrote, "As distinguished from moral principles, all mankind, from the beginning of the world to this day, have been quarreling, fighting, burning, and torturing one another, for abstractions unintelligible to themselves and to all others, and absolutely beyond the comprehension of the human mind." Indeed, more than two millennia before these aptly written words appeared, the winds of change encircling the Mediterranean basin were fanning the same quarreling, fighting, and destruction of its people. The same will be said of our time, although there is hope for those willing to allow that light to shine.

A mere two and a half centuries before Christ walked the earth, the Mediterranean basin was awash in man's passion for control and conquest. In the western half of the basin, the Romans and Carthaginians struggled to control the vast territories surrounding the great sea as well as the sea itself. To the east, the trusted generals of Alexander the Great had fought continuously to maintain control of his vast empire, defending their kingdoms from invaders attacking the perimeters and usurpers from within. His vast empire stretched from the Balkans in the north to Egypt in the south and from Sparta in the west to what is now India in the far east of their known world.

By the middle of the third century BC, the Roman Republic was a tenacious war machine just beginning to stretch its limbs into the neighboring lands and waters near the Italian peninsula. The republic embarked on a long and costly battle against the widely spread nation to its south and west—Carthage.

Rome had evolved into a system of government that employed the ideals of people from different backgrounds and cultures. It relied on its citizens for its laws and its soldiers. The people voted for the members of the Senate and the ruling consuls to lead them. The men, women and children of the many villages and tribes on the mainland, which Rome had conquered, became Roman themselves in many ways, assimilating the new culture and its rules. The able-bodied men who survived the grip of Rome's often violent and ruthless acquisitions were trained for battle in its citizen army. Their farms and forests fed the expanding republic. Resistant peoples were massacred or tortured, and their once fertile soil poisoned for decades to come. For all of them, however, their religion remained untouched. In fact, Romans were very religious—to many gods. They were also a very superstitious people; they might forego a military advance for a day based on such omens to guide them as birds in flight. Early in the life of the new republic, citizens were left to their own devices with respect to their gods, for Rome had little interest in enforcing such things until much later.

At this time in history, Carthage was a major sea power. She controlled the waters with a brilliantly successful navy. Her merchant ships traded goods throughout the Mediterranean, while her warships patrolled the shipping lanes, savagely protecting her interests. Carthage had established control of much of the Iberian Peninsula and had taken much of the North African coast for its own, stretching from the sandy border with Egypt in the east through the Pillars of Hercules to the west, and beyond. The various Berber tribes of Numidia and Libya, who were sandwiched between the brutal Sahara Desert and the grip of Carthage along the coast, were temporarily subdued. Their cooperation was their survival.

Carthage also had a senate of leaders who were influenced by the large landholders and wealthy aristocrats like Hanno the Great; their personal desires influenced the decisions of the less powerful. Like the Romans, the Carthaginians practiced polytheism, a belief in more than one god, but their religion was perhaps more structured than the Romans' and followed their ancient Phoenician past. Child sacrifice was their burden for trust in the gods.

Rome and Carthage shared one other important interest: land. Peace treaties between Rome and Carthage from 509, 348, 306 and 279 BC all disappeared like a flash in a hot pan when the two sparred over Sicily, the focus at the start of the first Punic War between the two nations. This rich landmass triggered the Carthaginians' war with Greece and this rich landmass now attracted the attentions of Rome.

On the eastern end of the island, near the Grecian city-state of Syracuse, the city of Messina was conquered by a mercenary clan from Campania on the Italian peninsula. These peoples were the Mamertines. After squabbling with, and eventually losing a battle to, Syracuse, they looked to the Carthaginians for support. In response, Carthage established a garrison in the city. The Mamertines, however, had also sought Roman support. The Romans were able to convince the Mamertines that they could help them win their independence, so the Carthaginian garrison was ejected. Soon the Romans established a foothold on the island. From Messina, they defeated the local armies of Carthage and Syracuse, which had briefly allied against this Roman newcomer. However, this bond between Carthage and Syracuse was soon broken when Syracuse, under siege by the Romans, pledged a new allegiance to Rome. In retaliation, Carthage sent a new army to the island. Thus, the First Punic War was incited. Over the course of three separate wars and the next one hundred years, Rome and Carthage battled fiercely.

Other conflicts also engulfed the great sea. For centuries before the existence of Rome, the land to the east of the Mediterranean changed hands repeatedly, displacing or scattering whole cultures and eliminating others from the earth. Once, a great Persian empire stretched from Turkey to India and from what would become Europe to Egypt. The benevolent King Cyrus gave Jerusalem back to the Hebrews after Nebuchadnezzar had enslaved them in Babylon. He also returned their sacred belongings and let them rebuild their temple. Some of his grateful Jewish followers fought for him. When Cyrus's son Cambyses extended the Persian reign into Egypt, many Jews returned to Egypt behind him, filing back into a land that once held them hostage.

Later, in 331 B.C., Alexander the Great conquered nearly all the same lands, including the great Phoenician city of Tyre on the Mediterranean shore and Gaza to its south. He was feared because he exterminated the residents of conquered lands and repopulated the cities with his own Greek culture and people. When he reached Jerusalem, however, for some unknown reason, he allowed it to remain, temple and all. For this he was considered a messiah and therefore he, too, was followed into Egypt by the Jews.

Upon his death, Alexander's body lay entombed on the shores of the great sea near the mouth of the Nile, within the beautiful city he founded, Alexandria. His generals would struggle to maintain his vast empire under their control and, in the end, they fought bitterly with one another. By 262 BC, Macedon and much of Alexander's great empire had fallen into chaos as it shifted back and forth between the hands of the descendants of his great generals and outside forces hoping to gain control amid the chaos. Only the lands held by the families of Generals Seleucus and Ptolemy maintained some degree of stability.

General Ptolemy survived to control Egypt and the Syrian lands. Like the Persians before him, he accepted the role of pharaoh and adopted the gods of the Egyptians. By 260 BC, his son, King Ptolemy II Philadelphus was in power. He did not neglect his Jewish contingent, but by this time, the Jews spoke Greek and the few elders who knew how to read the Hebrew Torah were gone. To give the Jews the rules for living and governing themselves, and to fulfill his desire to amass the largest collection of important written works known to date, King Ptolemy II commissioned the translation of the Hebrew Torah into one Greek text, the Septuagint. He requested that the High Priest in Jerusalem send him the men necessary to complete such a monumental task, a task with far-reaching consequences.

This resulted in one, perhaps unintended, consequence: altering the path and molding the soul of one Greek-born warrior. Only combustible ingredients and a flame, appropriately applied, would be needed to affect his life, molding him within that great crucible.

Herein lies the continuing story of a vengeful warrior, once forged within the crucible of man in the Mediterranean, and how he may once again be changed within that volatile and violent milieu by the power and light of a legend—as well as the precious yet unsuspecting people who will help fulfill its promise.

The warrior's childhood began on the island of Leros, one of the most distant and secluded of the Greek islands. The son of a fisherman, his story began on the water, appropriately, and so must it continue….

The warrior pushed forward through a driving rain that rode on a wind like none other he had ever felt, pushing his craft over the swells and billowing the sail as if the gods were blowing the wind. Several days earlier, he had set sail from the shore of Ionia and was making his way west, stopping at Crete for supplies and food. Rome was the destination. There, he would search for the man he believed to hold the answer to the bitter question that consumed him.

The air on this particular morning had been clean and clear. A breeze from the west was soft and warm, carrying with it a sweetness of the sea. The sky was a pale blue and the warmth of the morning sun soothed his sore muscles as he rowed the boat against the subtle disturbance of the water. On and on he rowed, driven by a hate so deep and dark it alone could have been the great sea on which he steered his craft.

By midday, the wind had switched to the east and his progress became easier. The wind slashed at the sail's fabric, making it billow out like the massive ears of an elephant. He secured the lines as the large sail scalloped open, drawing the lines so tight the knots groaned against their wooden placeholders, squeezing the moisture from the twists of rope into a skin of white froth along its surface. His boat raced hard toward the horizon in the west, giving him a much-needed chance to rest his body, which yearned for sleep.

He awoke to the sensation of cold air and the splatter of raindrops upon his flesh, chilling him and startling him from a deep slumber. As his mind cleared, he could feel the vibration of the old wooden hull as it shuddered each time the bow collapsed onto the water after the wind drove it over another massive swell. He sat up to find the fabric of the sail stretched to capacity, beginning to tear around the lines holding it in place.

The sky around him was dark and gray, with a deep greenish hue that blended with the surface of the sea, obscuring his orientation on the water. The sounds of thunder were continuous and came from all directions as the swells of open water now threw him about in his craft like a child's doll. Between swells, the crests of water behind and in front of him dwarfed the height of his mast and, on top of the swell, the wind dragged upon the sail, pushing the craft on its side, nearly tossing him into the water. The man pulled himself to the lines to free them, but they had been drawn so tight even his powerful hands failed to undo them.

The howls of the wind made the lines sing an eerie song; a song that could unsettle the nerves of even the most experienced sailor. He clung to the plank-sheer with one hand and reached for his knife to sever the taught bindings holding the sail. The muscles of his forearm strained to hold him in place, keeping a grip upon the wooden rail until the acid burned inside the sinews of his arms and hands. He would need to move quickly or the boat would spin out of control.

Applying the sharp blade to the first of the tethers, the line frayed and snapped, like the slashing end of a charioteer's whip. Launching himself to the next line and then to the next, the sail ripped from the mast and disappeared into the dark green water far ahead of him.

Without the sail, the craft slowed, but only slightly. The boat no longer mounted every swell on its side. The minutes passed as he hunkered down at the base of the mast, clutching at the timber as tightly as he could until the rain began in earnest. A torrent of rain slapped at his face and pounded on the bottom of his boat. His grip on the wood became tested as the once dry fibers swelled into a slippery mass. He slid within the hull with the passing of each massive swell; he had no means to wedge himself firmly within the bow or stern. He fought to his knees and wrapped an arm over the plank-sheer near the starboard side of the stern and watched in awe as the boat dropped off the peak of the last crest.

This time the top of the swell overturned in an arc like the strike of a cobra, dropping down in a wall of water on top of him. The swells had now grown into massive waves, each standing high above him before crashing down in an avalanche of eerie green power. He realized that he now had no idea where he was. Drifting off course without the light of the sun, he had lost his bearings completely.

With nightfall, he was surrounded by total darkness. He could no longer see the bow of the boat from its stern and the rain had filled the boat to his crotch as he knelt on the bottom. He could not see the waves that threw his craft. Every fall from the peak of a cresting wave rattled the structure of the boat, popping and straining the joints. The deluge of every collapsing wave practically submerged the entire vessel, the power of the water slamming forward and driving him hard into the bow. He was at the mercy of the water. Blinded by the pummeling rain and the darkness of night, he slid back and forth along the bottom of the boat, propelled by water that could easily pick him up at any moment and hurl him into the depths of the sea.

At the top of the next surge, a gale of wind caught his craft, spinning it sideways and driving it over the water into the air. For an instant, everything seemed to stop. There was no shake of rushing water. There was no weight pressing down on him. A brief sense of weightlessness came over him as he dropped out of the sky. Then he landed with a crash upon the water, his body smashing against the wooden timbers. His head cracked against the unforgiving ribs of the boat. A flash of bright white light shocked his senses. He struggled to draw back the breath that had been knocked from him by the sudden conclusion to his fall.

The sailor's mind was foggy, but he reached out for anything to cling to, his fingernails digging into the wood beneath him—but that grip was lost as fast as he had found it. He was suddenly beneath the surface of the water, jostled and spinning out of control as the boat overturned on top of him, driving him deep into the sea.

The noise of the storm above was silenced by the deafening darkness of the water. The last sensation he felt was the splintering bolt of lightning that shot through him as the mast of his boat slashed through the dark water, striking him. While one last flash of light faded from his mind, he escaped from the wickedness around him into a peaceful darkness he had never before enjoyed.

# PART I

# Chapter I

---

ONE PERTINACIOUS WAVE after another, each one trying to outdo the one before, invaded the warm golden sands before failing and sliding slowly backward into the sea, leaving only the foam and sediment behind. The high African sun on its daily migration across the clearest of skies baked the exposed shoreline down to the limit of the waves' reach, where the sand turned cool and forgiving.

The coastline sloped gently here, unlike the jagged and rough terrain to the east and west, where large rocks and boulders made the waves work much harder for their precarious gains. A gentle wind carried the smells of the sea over the top of those slowly rolling waves and mixed with the smells of fish and kelp. Gulls circled and squawked and darted along the sand and water. Against this inimical environment, a lone tufted ghost crab made its way along a perilous line. Scalding hot sand covered the high ground to its left and to the right rose the successive clingy hands of the surf as it came in, wave upon wave.

The small brown creature had been displaced the prior evening by a torrent of wind and rain and the sudden invasive arrival of an overturned and battered fishing boat. He had abandoned his home, looking for a new place to settle, away from the danger of the birds overhead and the inevitable return of the tide. Carefully working his way to the south, the crab's path was impeded by yet another strange obstacle. He approached slowly and tentatively, flaring the bluish tufts above his eye stalks and tapping his outstretched arm against the formidable structure. He found it softer than stone, but no easier to circumnavigate. He sidled along a limb of this massive creature, which had also invaded his territory the night before, careful to stay out of the sight of the predators circling above.

Working her way toward the beach, Yzebel Gisgon never imagined such a spectacle as the one she was about to find. She had been considering the tasks of the day and the people involved with those responsibilities while walking along the dirt road that separated the grain fields from the coast. She sang softly to herself, paying attention only to the bird song emanating from the wind-swept date palms and oleander trees along the beach. The young children working in the wheat field had called and waved to her as she strode by and she had broken from her songs to wish them a good day and to thank them all for their hard work. The elders, too, acknowledged Yzebel as she strolled each morning. Now, as she combed the beach for displaced crabs or any fish that may have gotten stranded within tide pools by the storm, she thought about these people and how they treated her as one of their own. She celebrated the thought of it proudly.

Yzebel had been a young girl when she came to live on this coast, some twenty years ago. The only child of a soft-spoken, simple man, she was her father's trusted confidant and informal captain, helping him run the farms and lead the laborers. She had also assumed her late mother's role after her untimely death from fever, which the mother had contracted days after a storm such as the one that pounded the coast yesterday. Yzebel had grown up to resemble her mother, which reminded her father every day of the precious woman they had lost.

Like her mother, Yzebel was tall and dark, although her father's contribution to her appearance was her lighter skin tone. Her bones were long, her hips were narrow. Her eyes were a deep brown, her lips full and pleasant. Her hair was long and dark and tightly curled; she allowed it free reign over her head, shoulders, and beyond. She had also inherited her mother's love for her people and a tenacious desire to fear and love the god of her father's family.

Jabnit Gisgon, Yzebel's father, moved to this place from Tyre, an ancient city situated on the eastern shore of the Mediterranean Sea. He was not the first of his family to relocate in the wake of war. His parents had chosen Tyre to escape the unrest of civil war between the feuding generals of the late Alexander. Living among the Phoenicians in Tyre offered the family a new way of life, though they retained their belief in God and their language. When Jabnit learned of the agricultural opportunities in Carthage, however, he left his parents and sailed to Africa. There he met and married a young Numidian girl and they had one child, Yzebel. When Yzebel was just five or six years old, her father was hired as the caretaker of a collection of farms owned by the man known only to her as Hanno.

She had never met or seen the landowner, but she learned that he was a powerful and wealthy man who owned many such farms, covering an unimaginable expanse of land. Every month, at Hanno's command, soldiers from the nearby outpost near Sabratha came to inspect the farms, observe the tenants, and discuss business with her father. Although Hanno was not a general, as a wealthy politician, he was able to command the soldiers and employ them to ensure his own success and the food necessary to feed Carthage's large population.

Today, Yzebel thought nothing about Hanno or his soldiers and she harbored no desire to see them. She carried a woven basket in which she hoped to collect some of the fallen dates from yesterday's storm, as well as a few berries from the plants that grew tenuously in the sand near the water's edge. Slinking quietly over the raised dune onto the beach, she bent over, staring hard at the ground for small crabs that often scurried about after a high tide or powerful storms.

As she searched across the ground at her feet, she thought about the storm that pounded the shore. It had brought with it a wicked wind and driving rain, which relentlessly pelted the walls and roof of her father's home for much of the day and night. The wind ripped off the large glossy leaves from the line of oleander trees that separated their house from the sea, and on that wicked wind, those leaves were hurled through the air to slap at the thin walls of the modest home. This day was so much quieter, she thought, as she reached down to catch a small fish trapped in a tide pool and hidden by a patch of tall, thin canary grass. Timid and alone, it had made the mistake of splashing at her shadow as it passed over the water.

As she pinched its head, she looked up the beach and froze in place. She saw an abandoned fishing boat ahead of her, looking as though it had been pitched and toppled and thrown onto the sand by God himself. The side closest to her had been torn away, leaving a large gaping hole in the hull. Had it not been for the driving wind and waves last night, the rocks surely would have sunk the little boat straight away, instead of carrying it so high up the shore. The crew must have perished in the churning, unsettled waters, leaving only this remnant behind to speak for them, she thought. She passed the fish into her basket and advanced down the gentle slope of sand, weaving between the small clumps of tall brome grass and short, woody tahara bushes dotting the upper beach where the tide rarely reached.

Just a few meters away from the boat, she caught a glimpse of the thing she had hoped she would not find: a man, lying prone on the sand.

She stared at the body for many moments, but it didn't stir. Yzebel glanced around for something to throw in his direction. Seeing a small piece of driftwood, she picked it up. Damp and cut with square edges, it was a piece of the boat's hull, she surmised. She took aim and carefully lobbed it near the body of the man. Again, he didn't stir. Setting down her basket, she closed the remaining distance to the man and quietly knelt at his side to inspect him. He was breathing!

Stretched out before her, he must span two meters, she calculated. His skin was tanned a golden brown and his hair was dark brown and wavy.

Small cuts and shallow abrasions covered his legs and arms, but the hair over his right temple was matted with dark maroon blood. She didn't part the hair to look at the wound. Instead, she leaned over his back to find his right hand lying along his thigh. As she pulled it by the wrist, a small ghost crab darted free into the thick clump of grass just out of reach. The man appeared to have no weapon. His large hands were well worn.

Sitting back on her haunches, Yzebel glanced at his back. Perplexed, she ran her fingers gently over the network of scars that ran from his neck to his waist. The reality of what they represented lifted her to her feet. Yzebel backed away slowly, watching and listening for any sign of the man awakening. She turned and sprinted up the beach and through the tree line to the road. Driven partly by fear, yet mostly by her urge to help him, she ran toward the fields.

Approaching the wheat field, Yzebel called, "Jugurtha! Jugurtha! Come quickly, I need your help!"

A strong, dark-skinned man straightened up from his position behind an ox. He had been using the animal to pull a heavy wooden plow along the edge of the field, making a trench for water to run from a freshwater swamp nearby. Seeing the master's daughter calling to him, he dropped the rope harness from his shoulders and stepped forward, raising his hand to signal that he had seen her. She beckoned anxiously to him once again, so Jugurtha jogged forward to meet her.

"There is a man on the beach. He is hurt. Bring help!"

Running hard, Jugurtha overtook Yzebel as she headed back to the beach, beckoning to several other men in the nearby field to join them. At the top of the dune, Yzebel pointed in the direction of the wrecked boat and gripped Jugurtha's arm. "Bring him to the main house, then send Vermina with water and rags. Take care with him. We cannot know how he may respond if he awakens." She ran to the house to prepare for their arrival.

Within minutes, the men came through the doorway with the unconscious stranger held between them. They struggled through the narrow doorway, suspending the large, limp body by its arms and legs. "Bring him here. Gently!" Yzebel gestured to the table in the center of the main room. "Place him on his side so that I can clean the wound on his head." Carefully, the laborers laid the stranger on the table. Staring at the limp figure, they awaited Yzebel's next order. Soberly, she thanked them and excused them back to their work.

Before leaving, Jugurtha asked with concern, "Yzebel, should I stay close by if he should wake?"

Yzebel smiled at her friend and servant. "Please send your wife to help me. I will be all right, Jugurtha." Jugurtha nodded and Yzebel stared at the tall man as he walked out of the house. Her uncle's graying hair reflected a wisdom and confidence she wished her father possessed.

Yzebel closed the door and prepared to examine her new charge. She took a long breath and sighed deeply, trying to calm her nerves. When Vermina arrived, they set to work cleaning the man's wounds and applying age-old remedies of bitter root, honey, and herbal anodynes to speed his healing and lessen his pain.

Hours later, her father arrived home to find an unconscious man on his table. This wasn't the first time, in fact. Yzebel had a habit of helping injured or sick laborers. As he stared at the unconscious stranger, Yzebel noticed the confused look spreading across Jabnit's face.

"Who is this man?" His voice sounded nervous.

"He washed ashore last night with his boat. He hasn't awakened yet to tell us anything," Yzebel glanced at Vermina. "There was nothing in the boat and he had only the clothes you see."

"Is he going to be all right?" Jabnit asked.

"I don't know for sure, but he looks better than his boat. The injury to his head is now clean, but there is no telling what damage has been done within."

Jabnit studied the man more closely and then rolled him farther over onto his stomach. As he did this his face turned sullen and he stepped backward. "I do not like this man here, Yzebel. These whip scars on his back are a sign that we should not ignore. This man has a history that could bring to us irreparable harm. When Kanmi Zimrida comes on his inspection, this man must not be here."

"He needs our help, Father. If he is not ready to travel, then we will hide him. He will eventually tell us his history and we can help him go where he needs to go."

"Perhaps he is a deserter from Carthage's army. We should turn him over to Kanmi," Jabnit argued.

"And what if he is an innocent man?"

"Then he can be trained to fight for Carthage. Look at his muscular build and the scar on his shoulder. He is not a simple laborer."

"At least let me help him heal his new wounds," begged Yzebel. "Promise me that you will not tell Kanmi anything when he comes. Promise me, Father!"

Jabnit grunted. "You have a heart of gold, my lovely daughter. There is much of your mother in you." He studied the man on his table before looking back at Yzebel. "Very well. Do what you must and then send him on his way."

That night and throughout the next two days, Yzebel tended to her duties, but checked on the stranger frequently, changing the blankets under him and praying to her God to either take him or wake him.

Yzebel woke the next morning to find the stranger still on the table, but this time he appeared to be dreaming and restless. His head rocked back and forth and sweat wept from the pores of his face and bare chest. Sitting on a stool next to the table, she quietly observed him. Gradually, his limbs began to stir. His thin lips drew into a grimace, tightening the skin over his strong, square jaw while his nostrils flared beneath a long, straight nose. He looked to Yzebel like a stone sculpture magically coming to life before her eyes.

She put her hand on his, to calm him. When his eyes flickered open, he gasped as if he were still captured within a terrible dream. His light hazel eyes seemed fixed on the terrible image that must be haunting his mind. After a brief moment, his breathing slowed and he looked around silently. Sensing someone at his side, he abruptly sat upright, fear and anger in his eyes. Instinctively, he drew his fist back to strike out, but he paused when she whispered gently to him. He relaxed his assault. The throbbing in his head caused him to squeeze his eyes closed and he placed his palm over his right temple.

Yzebel spoke softly to him in the Punic tongue, but he didn't answer. Without thinking, she repeated her words in the language of the Numidian natives who worked the farmland. Again, he didn't respond. In desperation, she spoke in the language of her childhood, Koine Greek, the old language of her father and his parents when they first arrived in Tyre, before accepting the Phoenician tongue. She had not used it since she was eight or nine years old. "Be calm, stranger. You are all right."

This time the man understood. He cleared his throat. "Water," he requested in a raspy, quiet voice. Yzebel lifted a cup to him, which he sniffed suspiciously, then he emptied the cup and handed it back to her, gesturing for more. "Where am I?" While he waited for an answer, he put his hands to his head and pulled at the bandages in order to feel for the devastation that he was sure was present, given the throbbing pain he had.

"I found you on the beach. This is my home. My name is Yzebel Gisgon. You have been here for several days." She paused and noticed his blank stare, then added, "There was a boat."

The man stared into Yzebel's dark brown eyes and spoke sternly. "You will take me to see it."

Yzebel nodded and helped him to his feet. He swayed. Yzebel clutched his torso then helped him down to the floor and offered him more water to drink. "I think we are rushing into things. Please drink more and sit for a while to regain your strength. Your legs are weak. Are you hungry?"

He nodded. She handed him several figs from a basket nearby and opened a pomegranate over the table. He ravenously consumed all of it and then drank more water after she filled the cup once again. They sat quietly for a few minutes as he looked around the room, inspecting its contents. Yzebel held out her hand to offer him help to stand. Once he was upright, she led him out of the house and down the dirt path toward the beach.

They walked slowly. When he paused to rub his eyes, as if to coax them to adjust to the bright sunlight, she walked on. After surveying the house and then the field and then the rows of trees in the orchard beyond, he took several large steps to catch up to her and asked, "What is this place? What do you do here?"

As they walked, she waved to a little girl pulling weeds from among the crop in the field and then answered him. "My father manages the farms in this area for a wealthy man named Hanno. The laborers are from the local tribes of Numidia. They are forced to work in these fields as slaves of Carthage. My father and I treat them well, not like the slaves on other Carthage farms. Here they are family."

"What does one man do with so much grain and fruit?"

"All of this goes to feed the army and the navy and the people who live in the cities of Carthage. The other farms raise different crops, such as cotton and barley. My father's job is to ensure that all the farms in his charge run smoothly and that they have successful harvests."

As she finished speaking, they walked over the dune and down the beach toward the disabled boat. They stopped briefly at the site where she had found him before he stepped to the side of the boat.

"Is this Hanno at war with someone?" asked the stranger as he stared at the boat.

"Yes, but not just Hanno. Carthage has many strong leaders. Hanno is but one. Carthage fights Rome for control of Sicily."

"How did this war begin?"

"I can only repeat what I have been told by my father and travelers that rarely pass this way, and it may be incorrect. I believe it started with a people called the Mamertines who were mercenary fighters for Agothicles. They settled on the big island in the north and then sacked the city of Messina. When King Heiro of Syracuse tried to push them out, the Mamertines asked Carthage for help against King Heiro. Unknown to Carthage, the Mamertines had also asked Rome for help. Soon the Romans came to Sicily seeking a foothold to further their own expansion."

Listening intently to Yzebel's calming voice, the large man ran his hardened hands along the side of the weather-beaten hull of the old wooden boat. Squatting, he placed both hands on the plank-sheer and lifted the waterlogged boat with a groan. It was very heavy. The muscles in his arms and legs strained under the weight and its awkward shape. When the lip of the hull was at his chest, he shoved it forward and the craft swung over, right side up. Yzebel watched the man as he scanned the bare patch of sand on which the boat had rested and then as he leaned over the side of the hull to see what, if anything, may have clung to the inside. She walked up beside him and looked in as well. It was completely empty.

The boat had capsized during the storm and lost whatever this man carried with him. She looked at him curiously as he stared off into the distance, over the gentle waves of the Mediterranean.

"It is hard to believe that such calm water could become so violent," offered Yzebel.

The man didn't respond. He looked at the sun and mumbled, as if to clarify in his own mind where he was. "We stand on the south side of the sea."

"We are near Sabratha, a trading post and sea port east of Carthage, on the north coast of Africa. Where did you come from?" asked Yzebel, as she stepped to his side and placed her hand on his shoulder. "What is your name?"

The man turned around slowly and faced his questioner, looking solemnly into her eyes. "I do not know."

# Chapter II

———

AN INTENSE EGYPTIAN sun shining through the small, square window illuminated only one corner of the dusty little cell. It was just after midday when the young scribe alone in the cell, seated at the foot of his grandfather's bed, leaned forward with his elbows on his knees as he studied the work that had consumed his days and nights. The sunlight came in at such a sharp angle that it forced him to lean deeply into the corner in order to read the words he had written the night before. Balancing precariously over the jagged hole in the floor, designed for the expulsion of body water and excrement, he studied the words carefully, trying to understand their meaning. Growing weary, he slid the papyri under the straw mattress and stood to peer out the lone window.

Resting his chin in the lower corner of the opening, he strained to see a narrow sliver of the city. For many weeks he had looked into that part of the city, hoping to glimpse even one more meter of it. He yearned for a window on the south side of this dark, drab room, which would have let him see the city in its entirety. Instead, he and his grandfather shared a cell on the western end of this long stone building, far removed from the famous city of Alexandria.

The scribe wondered if the other cells had windows facing south or if they had any windows at all. Perhaps, he thought, he should be thankful for the view he had. After all, he could look over the bay and watch the occasional merchant ship drop anchor and observe small fishing boats mingle with one another before heading out to sea. To him, it was far more difficult to see this city and not be a part of it, like he was looking at a picture in which he couldn't move or touch or feel anything beyond his room.

Sometimes the waves coming into shore met the rocks lining the Island of Pharus with a thunderous commotion. When that happened, the spray from those waves nearly reached his window, but during the two months he had been in this cell, he never felt it. He longed to experience the coolness of the mist, rub it into his skin and taste the brine that smelled of fermenting algae and old wine. Before his prolonged sequestration in his cell, he had never seen the sea and only briefly did he catch a glimpse of the most famous city on the Mediterranean, to which he had journeyed with the oldest member of his family.

The small island where he lived stood out in the water more than a kilometer from the city of Alexandria. It was connected to the city by a long, slender mole, an earthen pier made of dirt and stone that had been hauled in and dumped into the sea over many years. The building on this island, previously a prison, now housed men like this man and his grandfather, who needed to complete a task in solitude. This solitude was Elijah's prison. But his captivity would soon be over—or at least that is what his grandfather had been telling him.

Much of the time when he was left alone, which happened once every day for several hours, he talked to the birds. Seagulls danced and jumped from rock to rock and sailed over the waves, picking out small, unsuspecting delicacies riding the surf into the shore. Occasionally, one of these gulls would seek respite on the ledge of his window, seeming to find the rest valuable and the threat of the cell's inhabitant minute. As he gazed out the window this afternoon, he let the words he had written and just read again sink into his mind. Doing that relaxed him. It was only a matter of time, he thought. Soon the job that brought him here would be completed.

When he was just fourteen years old, Elijah had walked to the temple in Jerusalem with his grandfather, at the request of the high priest Eleazar. He explained that the pharaoh of Egypt, King Ptolemy II, the one they called Philadelphus, had written to Eleazar requesting his assistance to assemble and forward seventy elders to Alexandria to translate the Hebrew books of Moses into a Greek text. Eleazar sent six elders from each of the twelve tribes of Jews. Elijah's grandfather was one of those learned men. Elijah and his family, including his grandfather, had descended from the tribe of Zebulun, one of the twelve sons of Jacob. They lived in Jerusalem. All of that seemed so long ago. He sighed just before the heavy wooden lever outside his door revolved and swung out of the lock.

Slowly, the door swung open. Light from the hall spilled into the dimly lit room before it was suddenly extinguished by the shadow of his daily visitor. "Here is your meal, Elijah," said Dorotheos with a smile. "I am sorry I am late today." The tall man ducked through the doorway, stepped forward, and set the wooden bowl onto the low table at the side of the room near the door. "The sage should be ready to come back soon. I will bring him with the others when they are finished speaking with the pharaoh's high counselor. They should be finished with their meal by now."

Elijah smiled and thanked Dorotheos for the food. "Dorotheos, do you think it would be possible to see more of the city?"

The courtier thought for a moment and then looked back to Elijah. "I do. Perhaps when the sages share their next meal with the high counselor, I will come for you and give you a short tour of our great city."

"I would love to see Alexandria very much." Elijah spoke as if he had been separated from a best friend.

"Then you will, Elijah. The king owes you that and more," Dorotheos said with a kind smile. He looked at the delicate young man, sensing the frustration. "Take heart, Elijah. Soon the task will be done and you will be free to live in this place and enjoy all it has to offer." The courtier stepped out of the room and swung the heavy door shut, once again locking Elijah in.

Elijah stared at the door and sighed. "Have faith, Elijah," he said out loud then he picked up his bowl of food and walked back to the window. He pushed the small portion around in his bowl with his thin finger and ate some of the roasted lotus seeds. Then he pinched one of the pieces of meat and held it out the window to feed his favorite gull while he watched the large orange sun begin its rapid descent into the horizon.

At dusk the door opened again, heralding the return of Elijah's grandfather. Elijah jumped up and met the weary old man in the doorway, taking his hand from Dorotheos and guiding him to the wooden chair at the table. Dorotheos waited in the doorway for Elijah's bowl and to light the candle Elijah handed him. He held it up to the torch he carried, ignited it, and handed it back to Elijah before locking the door and departing for the night.

Elijah liked Dorotheos, although he wondered if he might have liked anyone who came with his food every day and spoke nicely to him. Dorotheos was a soft-spoken courtier assigned to the needs of all seventy-two Jewish elders. His kind smile and wise eyes, coupled with his royal robes, made it easy to trust him. Elijah recalled the confused look the courtier had given him when Elijah had first arrived with the elder sage. The reason soon became apparent, and later Dorotheos told him that he should be proud of his grandfather, for he was a great man, doing a great thing for his people, and that Elijah served as his eyes. Recalling Dorotheos's encouraging words, Elijah returned to his grandfather's side with candle in hand.

"What did they say, Grandfather? What did you eat? What was he like?" asked Elijah in rapid succession as he set the candle down on the middle of the table. He was starved for any news of the outside world.

His grandfather held up a hand. "Be patient. All of this I will share with you in time, but first we must do our work together. Sit at your candle, Elijah," said the old man with a sigh. He sounded tired but ready to proceed.

"Yes, Grandfather." Elijah went to retrieve the roll of papyri he had hidden under the mattress and then pulled forward the ink and quill sitting at the back of the table near the wall. He sat down on the other chair, found his place on the papyri, and pulled the candle more closely to his work. The candle had been given to his grandfather by Dorotheos when the old sage requested a candle for use with evening prayer. It was to be used for the purpose of Elijah's transcription after dark, but that was not the reason they had given to acquire it.

By the light of day, Elijah used the ink and the papyri to write down everything his grandfather said, word for word, letter by letter, as he recited the books of Moses. By candlelight, they did the same thing, only this second copy had a different destiny. Each night, the old man and the young scribe secretly repeated everything they did during the day. Elijah never questioned his elder, trusting that one day it would all become clear to him. Their work remained a secret even to Dorotheos, because they did not know if such a copy would be allowed. "I am ready, Grandfather."

"Then we shall begin." Stroking his long white beard, the sage hesitated for a moment, then asked, "Where did I start this morning, Elijah?"

"We were counting the men in the tribes of Levi, Grandfather."

"Oh yes, thank you."

And so, came and went the days and the nights. Elijah obediently served his grandfather and, in turn, learned the stories, the message, and the guidance of the Hebrew Torah, dutifully transcribing it in Greek for a king and a people he had not yet met.

On another day, which had started out much like all the rest, one of the sentries came with a bowl of food for Elijah. Instead of handing it to him immediately, however, he held onto it and said sternly, "Eat while you walk. I will take you to meet Dorotheos near the library. He wants to meet with you."

Elijah was surprised and excited at the change of routine. He accepted the bowl and followed the sentry out of the building and down along the slender mole. He couldn't eat. In fact, he carried the bowl at his side as he gawked at the city spreading out before him, leaving a trail of rice and stewed fish to mark his path. At one point, the scrawny young man was so mesmerized by the landscape before him that he nearly stepped off the path into the water. The alert sentry clutched Elijah's arm and yanked him back onto the mole's narrow walkway so he didn't walk off the edge into the bay. This was followed by a gruff warning to pay closer attention because there wouldn't be another helping hand.

Trying harder to control himself, Elijah followed the man up a narrow street where he soon saw Dorotheos waiting for him. Relieved, Elijah ran up to him, leaving the sentry with the empty bowl. "Why is the sentry so harsh, Dorotheos?"

"He is Egyptian. You and I are Jewish. It is easy for Jews to gain high position in the royal court here. The common ones have developed a dislike for us over the years."

Elijah looked surprised. "Don't worry, Elijah," Dorotheos told him. "There has been no violence yet. I suspect they are jealous of our standing with the Ptolemy family, but I think the dislike ends there. As a rule, the Egyptians are treated most fairly by the king."

"What is this place?" asked Elijah, staring up at the partially constructed façade of a massive stone building behind Dorotheos.

"This will be the library!" Dorotheos said. "In it will be the grandest collection of great works from all the world. King Ptolemy has a place in his heart for all these things."

"And the Books of Moses?"

"Especially those, Elijah."

"But why? Why go to so much trouble to have a Greek copy of the laws of the Israelites?"

"There are many Jews in Egypt," Dorotheos said. "As you know, once the Jews were captive here and Moses brought them out of bondage to Canaan, but over the centuries that followed, many returned. Jewish mercenaries fought with the Persian king named Cyrus after he liberated them from Babylon and then they joined his son, the next great king of the Persians when he took Egypt."

Seeing that he had Elijah's undivided attention, Dorotheos continued. "For a long time, a Jewish force on the island of Elephantine, far up the Nile, protected the king in the city of Memphis from the dangers in the southlands. Many more Jews followed Alexander here as well. The Jews are a part of Egypt and Egypt is a part of the Jews. It would be wrong to exclude the books of Moses with such a long and valued history."

"But why bring the seventy-two elders all the way from Jerusalem and keep them separated for months while they translate the Torah from Hebrew to Greek? Why all the secrecy?" asked Elijah.

Dorotheos contemplated the question and nodded. "It is important to get it right. King Ptolemy wants it to be as accurate as possible. The King and Demetrius of Phalerum, once the high counselor to the king's father and now in charge of this library, agreed that if they could get it translated by so many men independently, then, in the end, the works could be consolidated to the most common interpretation. Then this book would be written a final time onto the kosher skins." Dorotheos smiled and looked at the thin young man's prominent features, his thick dark eyebrows and wavy brown hair, his thin torso and gangly limbs. "These men are almost done. You are almost done, Elijah. I hope this helps you feel that your work has been worthwhile. Come, let me show you Alexander's tomb and our monument to him."

Together, they set off along one of the two main thoroughfares of the city, which sat perpendicular to each other, meeting in the center of the city and dividing it neatly into quarters. The path was very wide, perhaps sixty meters, and it was lined with colonnades holding up stone arches running parallel to the path and alternating with small groves of palms. Approaching the intersection, the crowd of people became thick and frenzied. In each of three corners sat a busy market. Each market looked much like the other two, although, based on the scents wafting on the breeze, it was apparent that a variety of different items were for sale or barter at each. Nearing the corner, Elijah noted the penetrating power of incense and myrrh, their volatile perfumes mingling within his nares, overpowering the pervasive mix of fried food and tantalizing spices that hovered over the streets like a cloud.

As they passed a side street, Elijah couldn't help but notice the activities of men and women sharing their bodies with one another, some for a price. He watched more closely as he walked, gradually falling farther behind Dorotheos. Men were playing games and betting money on the outcomes. He saw fights and blatant drunkenness. The openness of such sinful behavior surprised Elijah and a pit formed in the hollow of his stomach. Shaking off the vision of what he had just witnessed, he surged on ahead to catch up to his guide.

In the other corner of the intersection stood a prominent stone structure whose broad limestone shoulders rose from out of the ground and were adorned with elaborate carvings representing Alexander's large armies. The center of the structure was rounded like a dome. Tall columns on two ends of the building held up the stone roof on the sides opposite the broad shoulders. These arches matched the colonnades along the wide roads through the city.

"Is that where Alexander is entombed?"

Dorotheos nodded. "Ptolemy I had Alexander's body brought here. He is buried deep within the center." Dorotheos looked perplexed for a moment, then added, "Elijah, your grandfather's name is Alexander, isn't it? Four other sages of the seventy-two have the same name. Do you know why that would be?"

"The year after Alexander marched through Jerusalem, when he promised to leave the city unharmed, many newborns were named Alexander in his honor. My grandfather was one of those babies." Dorotheos smiled and nodded.

After retracing their steps and turning back toward the bay, which was filled with merchant ships and the island of Pharus in the distance, Elijah stopped abruptly, once again stunned by another of Alexandria's construction wonders. A massive stone tower was situated on the eastern end of the island of Pharus. It stood on the opposite side of the island from Elijah's cell. "How did I not notice that when I came here?"

"Your attention must have been consumed by something else upon your arrival. Perhaps you were describing things to your grandfather and missed the tower altogether," Dorotheos said.

"I also didn't see it when we left the island today, but I think the large sentry blocked my view as we walked along the mole. What is it, Dorotheos?"

Beyond the bay before them, jutting out of the easternmost portion of the island of Pharus, a limestone tower rose more than one hundred meters tall. Men were still working at the top.

"That tower was started by King Ptolemy's father, Soter. Philadelphus will now complete it. It is in the eleventh year of construction. They say that there will be a cauldron at the top for a giant fire to burn and light up the sky. It will guide ships to port and alert them of the land during storms. It is the first of its kind, they say."

"I would not wish to be the man charged with keeping the fire burning!" Elijah stared at the distant sight.

Dorotheos laughed and escorted Elijah back to the island of Pharus. They discussed how busy and important this port city had become. Before stepping into his cell, Elijah thanked Dorotheos. "You are a good friend to me, Dorotheos. I thank you for your kindness."

"There is no need to thank me. It is I who should be most grateful to you." As Dorotheos slowly closed the door to the cell, he added, "Remember, Elijah. Your duty here will be over soon."

The next day brought an ominous difference to their quiet little cell. "I do not like that cough, Grandfather."

"It will be all right. I think it must be the sea air. Soon I will be able to return to Jerusalem and this cough will be gone," reassured the sage.

Gradually Elijah and his grandfather finished their copy of the five books of Moses, but on the day they turned in the last portion of the same document for the library project, Alexander's health was much worse. He seemed fatigued and coughed more often and more deeply. Elijah hugged his grandfather when they finished their copy of the translation and then each slept hard, earning a long-needed full night of sleep. Over the next two days, they waited for word that the documents from all the sages were complete and that they could go. Elijah wanted to take his grandfather to the new synagogue that was being constructed in the northeast quarter of the city. While they waited for word, Elijah tried to describe the city in as much detail as he could, so his grandfather could visualize it, at least in his mind.

On the third day, Dorotheos came to them with alarm in his voice that he could not suppress. As he let them out of their cells, he announced that all the old men were free to leave the island, but they were required to stay in the city. "There is something strange within the writings. You all must stay in the Jewish quarter, where we can find you if you are again needed."

"What could he mean, grandfather?" Elijah worried it could mean more time in confinement.

In response, Alexander barked a rumbling, rattling cough, flooding his mouth with rancid, thick sputum, which he spat onto the ground. Elijah examined the vile brown fluid and found it streaked with blood.

Alexander waved off Elijah's concern over Dorotheos's words. "Everything will be all right, Elijah. They have discovered that we old men have made it easy for them to pick out the most common interpretation. I think they will find it all in order."

Later, the word of confirmation came down to them through the new synagogue where they were staying. All seventy-two of the massive texts were the same. Even Elijah's grandfather had recited, from memory, a document exactly like the others. "This was a miracle from Yahweh and the best sign King Ptolemy could have hoped for," Dorotheos said.

"This means that the translation can now be put on the kosher skins earlier than they had expected. Just in time to save these people," Alexander said.

"What do you mean *save* them, grandfather?" Elijah looked up from his grandfather as the sound of a fight in the street broke out. He moved to the window to find two grown men pushing and shoving one another. Both men swung their fists wildly, spinning themselves off balance. These men were drunk and raucous. Other men now crowded around them, chanting what must have been the men's names. Elijah was struck by the aggressiveness of these men and then he thought about the other things he had seen in the city, first, during the tour with Dorotheos and later, when he and the older men had moved to the Jewish quarter.

Sinful acts seemed pervasive here. As Elijah pondered these things, he knew exactly what his grandfather was saying. Moving away from the window when the fight ended, he came back to his grandfather's side. He found the elderly man worse than he had been moments earlier. Beads of sweat were gathering on his brow and he was coughing and shaking with rigorous convulsions. He was struggling for breath.

"It is time for me to explain to you the true nature of our great endeavor," stuttered the grandfather as he reached for Elijah's hand. "It is also time for me to tell you what you must do, Elijah."

"Yes, Grandfather."

"You remember that I explained how King Ptolemy wanted a copy of the Torah in Greek for his library?"

"Yes. Yes, I know how much it will mean for the Jews here to have their history in his great library."

Alexander coughed and tried to sit up, pulling at Elijah's arm for help. He expectorated more phlegm and gasped several more times. As a few of the elders moved in closer to begin to pray for him, Alexander continued, "That is not the reason, Elijah. Yes, the king wants to collect the most famous literature from all the world, but more importantly he needs to rule his people. There is much unrest here and the Jews struggle with nothing to guide them. During the great migrations, first with Cyrus and then with Alexander, the Jews lost their Hebrew language. By giving them the rules of Yahweh in their new language, he has given them a way to live, rightly and justly. Now with God's words before them, they can rule themselves and Ptolemy can be assured that they will follow him. It is the greatest gift he could have given."

"And what of our copy, Grandfather?" Elijah sensed the urgency in the old man's voice.

"That brings me to the next great gift—and you are the special one to deliver it, Elijah." Profoundly weak, Alexander slumped back down on the bed, taking several minutes to gather the strength to continue. "Many Jews also fled to the north to escape the wars of Alexander's generals, as your parents did with your younger brothers and sisters. They are in faraway places now, like Lydia, Ionia, and Greece. They, too, have landed in places ruled by men of all sorts of character, though I fear none as benevolent as King Ptolemy. Those Jews need guidance in a language they can comprehend in order to persevere. You must travel to Corinth in Greece."

"But how can I do this? How do I help you? I promised my mother and father that I would stay with you!"

"And you have, Elijah! You have honored that promise and I have been able to complete the greatest task of my life. I have served my God and done my great task. Now you must do yours." Alexander sensed Elijah's discomfort, but let the words take hold. "I will wait here for my end, but this is where our paths diverge, Elijah."

"But what of Passover? It comes soon. We must go home!"

"I will deeply miss participating in the vigil in my home, my dear Jerusalem," the old man said, his voice betraying his melancholy. Then suddenly, he stirred, "Elijah, you must remember not to eat the bread during the week of the Passover. It is very important, Elijah." Refocusing his attention on the books of Moses, he added, "Elijah, my boy, you are Yahweh's messenger. I feel it. I know it. Take the Septuagint, as they refer to it here—our Torah— the stories and laws of Moses, and find your way to the rest of our people.

Teach of it all you can. Touch and change lives with it. It is the light. It is a flame. You know its power and its message. Guard it. Protect it." Alexander's voice trailed off, too weak to continue.

As the elders prayed, Elijah stayed by his grandfather's side. Alexander slipped into a deeply peaceful sleep and Elijah watched his breath gradually become irregular, first rapid, then pausing, then rapid again, and so on, until the old man blew his last breath.

Staring at his grandfather's lifeless, expressionless face, Elijah's eyes filled with tears that tumbled down his cheeks. He gripped the old man's hand tightly and sank to his knees from the short wooden stool on which he sat, praying to God and answering his grandfather's final wish for him.

"I will, Grandfather. I will."

# Chapter III

———

THE MYSTERIOUS STRANGER who had occupied so much of Yzebel's days and nights for the last six weeks plodded through the tan mud of the nearly completed irrigation ditch as he wrestled to remove debris from the intended path of the water. He and Jugurtha were working on the project, and although they didn't share the same language, they did appreciate one another's strengths. Together they struggled to cut through the thousands of winding roots that extended from the woods through the earth where they were working.

Yzebel watched them from a distance. She had become mesmerized by the stranger's strength and stature and captivated by his rare smile and deeply probing eyes. She felt her face flush as she thought back to the way he stared at her when she changed his dressings or the way he watched her lips move when she talked to him or prayed. Only a short time had passed since she found him on the beach and already she was feeling a pull toward him, as if he had been a part of her life all along. She thought often about the life he may have lived before arriving so unexpectedly on her beach. She was glad that he could not remember whatever evil he had escaped, but at the same time she felt guilty knowing that somewhere there must be a lonely woman who missed him.

Early on, she had insisted that he stay in her father's home until his wounds healed. The smaller abrasions and cuts to his body healed very quickly with her help. She wished, for his sake, the wound to his mind would heal just as quickly. He had absolutely no recollection of his past. She knew that he walked to the beach every morning to study the wreck of the boat that crashed ashore with him, yet every day he walked back with the same frustrated look scrawled across his face.

After one month passed, he moved into the longhouse where other unmarried male laborers lived. This long wooden structure contained a dozen beds spaced evenly around a raised platform made of stone. The center of the stone was hollowed, forming a shallow depression in which a fire burned on cooler nights. Metal pots balanced on the uneven surface around the fire pit for cooking meals for the men. The smoke from the fires built on this stone escaped through a hole in the center of the roof, which was otherwise kept covered with a heavy woven palm mat. The men from this barrack, as with the two others on the property, ate their meals together and worked the fields together. In the stranger's case, however, Yzebel had arranged for him to work with Jugurtha to help complete the irrigation ditch more quickly. In the end, it was an easy decision for everyone, save for Jabnit, to allow the stranger to work on the property.

The stranger had insisted that he stay on to work off the debt he owed Yzebel and her father for the care he had received and the food he had eaten. Yzebel argued that there was no debt to be paid and he was free to leave, even though she knew he had no idea which way to go. As time went by, however, she hoped he wouldn't want to leave. So far, that was the case. Jabnit argued that the man should be sent away, but, as was often the case where Yzebel was concerned, he relented. The stranger was allowed to stay and work. Jabnit made it very clear, however, that he was to vanish at the first sight of Kanmi, the inspector and his men, and that day was coming very soon.

Kanmi generally came to the farm once every one or two months. He inspected many farms in a rotation, and that rotation, including the riding time between each farm, kept him on the move for most of each month. He kept close tabs on the progress of crops and maintained detailed notes about the activities at each farm, the supplies that had been rationed to each caretaker, and how those were used. After all, Carthage was at war with Rome, and therefore it was important to manage its supplies carefully and ration them throughout the territory. In addition, Kanmi knew that if he could pinch the caretakers enough, whatever surplus was leftover might find its way back into his control and make him a profit when he sold it on his own.

Whenever Kanmi came to inspect Jabnit's territory, he and his men stayed for one or two nights while they walked through the orchards and grain fields, rooted through the buildings, and shuffled through Jabnit's documents and accounts. Yzebel hated him, but held her tongue for her father's sake, knowing that her father's position was dependent on Kanmi's positive reports to the landowner.

Kanmi was probably a few years younger than Yzebel. He grew up in Utica, a small city-state recently consumed by Carthage. He was a favorite of the landowner for his successful leadership of the caretakers and for his unswerving obedience, but his arrogance and brutality were well known to the slaves and caretakers.

Yzebel always tried to avoid being alone with him, for she knew he would take advantage of her if he could. In fact, he had a very difficult time keeping his hands off of her, groping her, often in front of her father, whenever she strayed too close. She loathed the way he ran his hand down her back, letting it linger over the small curve at the base or when he ran it down along her side and over her hip. Thinking of him coming soon gave her a chill. Every month, in the days leading up to his expected arrival, she became anxious.

Today, Yzebel was making final preparations for his anticipated visit.

She and a group of the women were mending the fences with which to keep the horses that Kanmi and his men would be riding. They gathered fresh green grass, which was now cut and drying, and hauled water to fill the large vessels in the pen. Yzebel kept a fire burning near the beach where the children disposed of the nettle weeds they removed from the grain fields. The softer velvet-leafed weeds, on the other hand, were reserved for the horses and brought to dry along with the grass.

Late that afternoon, Kanmi and his men appeared in the distance, riding through the barley southeast of the farm. The red tunic and gleaming bronze helmet that Kanmi wore contrasted with the dull brown tunics and round white shields of his men. He had been born of a different breed then they and he was proud for them to know it. Nine men rode with Kanmi and all ten chestnut-colored horses galloped through the field side by side, trampling a wide swath of precious young grains into the ground.

Yzebel shouted toward the house for her father, who promptly joined her outside to greet the riders. Yzebel moved to open the side of the wooden corral to tend the horses Kanmi trotted into the center square of the farm. Sitting high atop his tall brown stallion, he circled around Jabnit several times, looking for Yzebel. When he spotted her, he drew his steed to a halt and dismounted with an energetic hop, handing Jabnit the reins without so much as a brief acknowledgment as he lurched by.

The stranger, waist deep in the ditch near the trees, watched the men ride in with awareness. Jugurtha nodded to him, indicating that he should depart, thus confirming that this was Kanmi. The stranger bent low and took cover in the grove of tall trees and thick underbrush that separated the nearest wheat field in the foreground, which ran along the beach path, from the orchard behind Jabnit's house to the east. From here he could still observe Kanmi and his men and hear some of the conversation when the wind was still or blowing in his direction.

"Wipe down the horses, Jabnit. Then we will begin the counts," ordered Kanmi while he stared at the older man's daughter.

"As you wish." Jabnit, bowed to the young man.

Squatting down behind a prickly thicket of gray, cork-like bark and shiny-green leaves, the stranger watched Kanmi move about, dividing his small band of men with casual yet firm direction. Leaning in to focus more clearly, the stranger inadvertently bumped one of the round, yellow fruits, which exploded in a puff of air and fine powder, covering him in a thin layer of organic dust and testing his ability to suppress a cough. Struggling to remain silent, the stranger watched the men as they headed off in different directions. When they moved away, he could no longer see what they were doing or where they were going.

Kanmi walked quickly toward the fencing laid out for the horses and stood proud as he watched Jabnit's laborers walk the horses into the corral in front of him. Jabnit waddled a pace behind him and was speaking quickly and nervously. The women with Yzebel ran to collect more water for the horses, while Yzebel spread some of the drying grasses for the horses to eat.

Ignoring Jabnit's attempts to enlighten him with news of their monthly progress, Kanmi approached Yzebel as she stood near the gate allowing one of the horses to pull grass from her hand. She bowed her head and turned toward him as he stepped close to her side. Kanmi put his thick fingers on her chin and lifted her face up to his, forcing her to look at him. He had wide-set eyes with deep green irises, within which tiny streaks of light brown discoloration zigzagged around the periphery. They appeared like tiny winding roads encircling green pastures. Above the eyes, his forehead sloped sharply backward from a tall, horizontal ridge of bone on which two thick, black brows stretched in either direction, nearly joining in the center and at the ends, wrapping around toward his temples.

Kanmi smiled at Yzebel, exposing his large, widely spaced row of bottom teeth, which stood out of his broad lower jaw like a row of dead tree trunks lining the edge of a marsh. Surprising her, he made a biting gesture with his mouth and then he turned and walked quickly into the adjacent wheat field, pulling out a handful of the grains with their roots still attached.

He held them up to Jabnit and pushed them hard into the older man's chest while complaining bitterly.

"These plants are only half as high as they should be by now, Jabnit. That is very disappointing. The roots are dry and the stems lack turgor. You must force your men to haul water to this field every day."

"Yes, of course I will. I mean to say, we will water them as you say, Kanmi." Jabnit bowed.

"I better not find your other fields so far behind, Jabnit, for your sake. Hanno remains very confident about achieving the yields he predicted this year and we don't want to let him down. Do we?" His voice was threatening.

Later that night, after the sun set, Kanmi and his men sat about the fire on the beach and laughed raucously. In his hiding place, the stranger could not see the men, but he stayed in place near the front of the small forested patch, waiting for Kanmi and his men to leave. By now, he knew it would not be until morning at the earliest. While waiting, he thought about the confidence of Kanmi, as if he had known him in the past. And then he saw Kanmi emerge through the line of date palms near the beach and walk up the lane to Jabnit's home. The stranger saw him enter without knocking or calling out.

Like a vivid dream, but only lingering as long as the duration of a rumble of thunder, an image arose within his mind and shocked the stranger to attention. In it, he saw a man dressed as a soldier, a man as confident as Kanmi, but hardened and older. The soldier was marching toward him on a broad sandy beach with a vile grin on his face and a weapon in his hand. Another soldier with a bow lurked in the background.

The stranger shook off the image and realized his hands were trembling and his breathing was rapid. As he calmed himself with a few deep breaths, he realized that Kanmi reminded him of someone from his past.

Within the small house, lit only by a few candles spaced evenly across the room, Kanmi sat at Jabnit's table and waited to be served. He asked about the deserted boat on the beach and Jabnit told him that it had washed up on shore after the recent storm and evidently there had been no survivors. Yzebel momentarily froze in panic, worried that Kanmi or his men had found the blood-stained sand on which she had found the unconscious stranger's body. She feared that Jabnit had just walked into a trap. When Kanmi made no further comment, however, Yzebel realized that the darkness had hidden the evidence. With her back to the table, she closed her eyes and quietly expelled a sigh of relief, making a mental note to herself to cover the bloody sand during the night.

Taking two calming breaths, Yzebel finished preparing the meals for Kanmi and her father. Trying not to make eye contact with Kanmi, she reached across the table and set down a short drink made from fermented apples and oleander flowers and pushed it in front of him. Beside it, she set a sparse plate of food, which contained only a thin slice of bread, a few pieces of fish that had been cooked in goose fat, and a small pile of pomegranate seeds. She glared at the top of his head as he studied the meager meal and then she stepped to her father's side. To Jabnit she placed a similar cup and another plate of food. By design, Jabnit's cup was only partly filled so that he wouldn't slop it all over the table with his nervous hands, which trembled uncontrollably whenever Kanmi was around. The plate she put in front of her father was more heavily filled, which was her way of thumbing her nose at Kanmi.

Kanmi and Yzebel's father discussed the property and occasionally Kanmi asked for specific details about how Jabnit used his laborers and how much they were being fed and if any had run off. He also asked for details about some of the other farms under Jabnit's supervision. Yzebel stood behind her father against the wall and quietly stared at the floor. She could feel Kanmi's eyes on her. When he heard enough, he slapped his palm on the tabletop to interrupt Jabnit. As he stood, sliding his chair back along the hard-packed earth, Yzebel glanced up at him and found him once again smiling at her. He didn't say anything as he turned to leave. Perhaps he was tired from the day's long ride.

In the morning, the stranger was startled awake by men's voices. Kanmi was walking along the irrigation ditch with Jabnit once again trailing behind. The stranger was fatigued by his night vigil in the woods, but watched them closely from his dense cover. Without warning, as Kanmi raised his voice to Jabnit in a flare of impatience, came another flash of memory. The same sequence of events played through in his mind's eye: the same soldier he had envisioned the night before sneered his vile smile and approached him. The other man in the dream was moving behind to take up a position near a tree line and was nocking an arrow to his bow. Held captive on this dreamlike beach, he caught a glimpse of a beautiful woman in despair. She was in tears and clutching a small knife between her hands while standing ankle deep in the water.

The voices of Kanmi and Jabnit penetrated into his mind as the two men edged ever closer to the trees, and the flashback ceased, releasing the man to his current uncomfortable reality. The stranger stayed low to the ground and listened closely to the conversation, but he could not understand any of the words until Kanmi said "Roman."

Kanmi had been telling Jabnit what he had heard about the battles on Sicily with the Romans. When the stranger heard the word *Roman* something forged a union in his mind and he could put a face to a name, a Roman name. The man in the flashback was named Octavian.

Jabnit and the inspector moved too close to the woods, forcing the stranger to crawl farther south through the woods and then beyond the edge of the marsh that separated the near field by the road and a larger wheat field on the southwest of the property. He found more seclusion amidst another dense stand of trees and sat there, trying to bring back the images to his mind. He wanted all their names—Octavian, the archer, and the woman. He tried to concentrate as he looked out over the field of heavily sown green grain.

From his position in the woods, he could see a young girl pulling weeds by herself. She was singing softly as she worked. He knew she belonged to the farm, as he had seen her around the others, but he did not know her name. The stranger studied her small frame and surmised that she must be only twelve years old. He thought that she must have looked much like Yzebel when she was a girl. He hoped, for her sake, that she would not be tormented by such a man as Kanmi.

Near the outbuildings, Kanmi and Jabnit were completing their discussions, but they weren't going pleasantly for Jabnit. Kanmi was upset again and, from Yzebel's vantage point, it sounded as if Kanmi was yelling at Jabnit over some discrepancies he found in supplies and the current state of the grain.

Yzebel was brushing the horses in the corral while three young girls carried more water to them from the ditch. Presently, Jabnit ran into the house and then emerged again carrying the loose leaves of papyri on which he kept documentation to justify his expenses. While Kanmi waited for Jabnit to return, he looked around the central square for Yzebel. Peering through the horses, he caught sight of her as she disappeared behind the house. Kanmi marched briskly after her, passing Jabnit along the way. He followed her around the house and cornered her against a small table that sat next to the back of the house which was used for preparing food, cleaning fish, and shelling clams.

Placing his hands on her waist, he startled her. She tried to break free. Pressed against his body, she resisted his affections ferociously. Somehow, she managed to get a leg up on the table and she used the leverage to slip out from under his mass, but he grabbed her upper arm forcefully, yanking her back to him. He pawed at her roughly, but she scratched his neck with her free hand. As he twisted around, trying to smother the burning singe of pain in the side of his neck with his hand, she ran toward the central square of the farm. Whirling around the rear corner of the house as he chased her, he reached for her again to arrest her escape, but he missed. He fell behind as she maneuvered around the front corner of the building. He slowed to a walk when he saw Jabnit standing in front of the house staring at him.

Disgruntled, sweating, and in a fierce state of mind, Kanmi snatched the papyri from Jabnit while he rubbed his sore neck. Several of his men, standing near the horses, looked up when he started ranting. They moved closer, anticipating something more to come. He began to query them about the conditions of the fields that they had visited without him and the number of men working in those fields.

"How fat are they?" he asked his men. "Are the men fat like these women?" He gestured to the laborers now gathering near the outbuildings and gawking at the scene he was creating. In a burst of hate and rage stemming from Yzebel's rejection of him, Kanmi shouted orders to his men. "Round up ten women and any children you can grab and lock them in the males' quarters there!" he shouted, pointing at the longhouse nearest them. "Quickly!"

While his men went to work herding the women and young girls into the longhouse, Kanmi ran to the beach. He kicked around at the ashes from last night's fire, disturbing the soft grayish flakes over the top to reveal a few glowing orange embers underneath. Exposed to the air, they hissed and sputtered to life, snapping and glowing in surges near the center of the pile of ashes. Hurriedly, he stepped to what remained of the pile of weeds and grasses the girls had stacked up by the fire to destroy. Grabbing a handful of the weeds, he twisted the clump tightly with both hands, grimacing as the nettles from a few of the plants found a hold in the softer skin between his fingers.

His grimace was replaced by something far more sinister when he held the end of the clump to the embers and watched it ignite. Carefully holding the clump of burning grasses and weeds, he marched back to the others and spoke directly to Jabnit. "Next time you will be more careful, Jabnit. Now you will have to make more progress with fewer mouths to feed."

Kanmi marched to the longhouse as Jabnit, stunned, looked on. His men moved to restrain Yzebel as she tried to block his path. Holding the flickering flames to the locked door of the longhouse, the weathered old wood quickly caught fire. Yzebel, along with the women and children within the frail structure, cried out in horror as the wind from the sea fanned the flames into an inferno. The women banged at the door until the heat pushed them from it. The gaps between the wooden slats of the walls ushered the flames and smoke into the building.

Yzebel cried as she tugged and pulled against the two men holding her. Jugurtha, the only male laborer not in the fields, ran toward the longhouse, but was tackled by Kanmi's men. He fought loose of his captors but was quickly overtaken and beaten to the ground. Unconscious, he could no longer interfere.

As the flames engulfed the front of the building, Kanmi smiled at Jabnit and then reached out to touch Yzebel's cheek, and asked, "She will be mine someday. Won't she?" Jabnit looked down, unable to respond.

Kanmi mounted his horse as it was brought to him by one of his men and the others followed suit, mounting their horses to leave. Jabnit and Yzebel ran for the back of the longhouse to try to free the women from their impending death. Men from the fields had noticed the smoke and started running toward home, not yet able to hear the increasing pitch of the women's cries and calls for help. Nearing the main road, just beyond the last outbuilding, Kanmi turned to one of his riders, ordering him to ride to the west to meet with the next caretaker and survey the crops there.

"Find out if that man is faring any better than poor Jabnit. If not, I may have to pay him a visit as well," Kanmi said with a grin. His men all laughed, looking back at the smoke billowing high into the air from the longhouse.

Coughing and choking, Yzebel and Jabnit pulled and pounded at the walls of the longhouse, trying to pry the boards loose. The thick smoke now filled the end of the building, making it hard to see and breathe. The desperate women and girls gulped at the air as they pressed their mouths into the gaps between the boards. Yzebel's eyes stung in the hot, dry smoke as it swirled and twisted around her head.

Jugurtha came to his senses, perhaps jarred to consciousness by the cries of terror and the roar of the flames. He shook off the pain in the back of his head where the soldier had struck him. Limping, he joined Yzebel and her father, and with his added strength, they were able to snap one of the vertical planks free from its hold at the top and bottom of the wall. Jugurtha threw it down on the ground behind them and went to work on the next plank, opening a tall vertical space in the wall. Yzebel reached in to pull the women and children out. It felt like an eternity, helping them squeeze through the narrow gap one at a time. The women stretched out in a line as they escaped, each clinging to the woman or girl ahead of her until they could finally open their eyes.

On the road alongside the south field of Jabnit's place, Kanmi's lone soldier was pushing his horse hard and riding fast. Racing into a clearing to his right, he caught sight of the young girl in the open field and realized that he needn't be in such a hurry. He slowed his horse to a trot and looked back in her direction, before circling around and guiding the horse into the field toward the girl.

From his hiding place, the stranger smelled the first hint of smoke as it drifted slowly toward him through the trees. He looked up and back through the trees as if looking for confirmation of it. He stood to run back to the buildings to investigate, but when he did, he saw Kanmi's soldier riding his horse through the field toward the girl. He watched the girl look up and realize the rider was racing toward her. The stranger suspected that the smoke meant something horrible was going on, yet he couldn't leave this young girl alone to fend for herself.

The girl turned to run, but the horse was moving so much faster. Its hooves pounded against the ground as it closed the distance to the fleeing girl, throwing clumps of moist dirt into the air behind it. She ran toward the marsh as fast as she could, but the ground beneath her feet became soft and slippery, the soil saturated by the water leaching from the edge of the marsh. The rider pulled up alongside her, leaped from his horse, and knocked her to the ground. He rolled over the top of her and then jumped to his feet.

The girl gasped, trying desperately to draw air into her chest. She tried to sit up, but he stepped in front of her and slapped her back to the ground with his open hand against the side of her face. Kneeling over her legs, he gripped her wrists in his hands and pressed her into the mud. She screamed and spat at him, but he knew no one could hear her. He laughed at her as he clenched both of her small wrists within his left hand and then he reached for the skirts covering her legs.

Silently, the stranger hurried from the woods into the clearing behind the soldier. With the smell of smoke lingering in his nares and the cries of the girl piercing his memory, another image snapped into his mind. In this image, an older woman on a different beach was being manhandled and kicked by soldiers, soldiers wearing the same uniform as the other men in his momentary flashbacks.

Unleashing an offensive as swift as a lion, the stranger ran up behind the soldier and yanked him off the terrified girl by the back of his neck. Surprised, the soldier reached for his blade, but his attacker was upon him too quickly. As the soldier struggled to pull his knife free, the stranger grabbed him by the front of his dirty brown tunic and threw him into the air toward the marsh like a cat plays with a mouse.

The man landed on his back in the mud and his knife disappeared under the surface of the murky water. The girl stood up and clutched at her torn clothes to cover herself. She backed away, but she couldn't run, held captive by a state of shock and the flurry of fighting. She watched the stranger step to the man and grab him once more, as her attacker felt around for his weapon. The stranger lifted Kanmi's man partly out of the mud before slamming him back down into it more deeply.

The stranger appeared consumed by anger. There was to be no mercy. He placed his large hand over the man's nose and forehead and pressed him into the mud as the water began to fill in the gaps around his cheek bones, chin, and over his eyes. Kanmi's soldier kicked and flailed as the muddy water flowed over his head. The girl watched, trembling, as air bubbled out in columns from the soldier's nostrils and gaping mouth. His gurgling scream diminished into a haunting silence. Quickly his swings grew weak and his limbs went limp.

When the stranger stood up, the girl looked upon his face and saw an anger, a hatred, she had never seen before. She backed away from him, turned, and ran into the woods. The stranger watched her run away and then he looked down at the body of the soldier. He reached down and pulled on the arms. As the dead body came up, slowly breaking away from the vacuum in the mud, it created a sickening, sucking sound within its muddy grave. The stranger dragged the body farther into the water, where it was deeper, dropped it, and then walked back into the woods to find the large stone he had seen near the place where he had been sitting. He hoisted it up against his chest and carried it back to the marsh. Struggling between the mud and the excess weight of the stone, he waded out to the body, which was slowly sinking back into the shallow water, and he dropped the stone onto the body to submerge it.

Remembering the smoke, he ran along the tree line back toward the farm, being careful to watch for any sign of Kanmi or his men. He reentered the small woods near the north end, to find the fire raging through the entire longhouse. From here, he watched the girl run into the open ground of the central square and look for the elders. She spotted them near Jabnit's house and ran to the women, to find her mother among them. The girl sobbed uncontrollably and pulled at her torn clothing as the women gathered around her.

While huddled over her, the girl told them about the attack by Kanmi's soldier and the stranger who appeared out of nowhere, pulling him off her and drowning him in a most horrific scene. She shuddered and shook uncontrollably, terrified by what she had seen and been through. Yzebel listened to the girl's account and then straightened up. She looked at the women, who stared back at her.

A wild storm of emotion surged through Yzebel. She didn't know what this could mean for all of them. She tried to predict the magnitude of Kanmi's retaliation and she struggled to know what she should feel for the stranger who had struck so violently. Had God send the stranger to help them or to test her? As she stared at the billowing column of smoke encapsulating the longhouse, the wind parted it, spinning one new column off in a whirling funnel across the central square. Her eyes followed it absentmindedly. And then she saw the stranger in the distance through the smoke, staring at her.

# Chapter IV

———

ROLLING CLOUD FORMATIONS stretched high into the heavens, far above their dark and ominous foundations. They crawled with turbulence over the ragged peaks of the Cantabrian range. These high clouds shielded the red rock formations from the late day sun and those same long shadows colored the scarred, serrated edges of the long acclivity a deep maroon. Thunder rumbled through the valley to the west, heralding the rains that would follow, and each successive roll of thunder edged ever closer, attempting another ascent into the headlands and shaking the ground beneath.

The first few drops of rain that came merely tickled the rock face, each drop deflected by the sun-warmed stone without deliberation, but then, as the storm rose high into the mountains, the surface cooled, forcing the stone to accept the deluge without choice. At first, the droplets collected, one by one, until together they flowed over the solemn face of the mountain, gathering speed and volume in ever-expanding sheets of water. Coalescing in vast quantities, the water pushed its way down the slopes, growing muddier and heavier when they merged with the red dust. Small streams overflowed, suddenly overwhelmed by the spate. Small plants, clinging to life within the cracks and cervices of the range, surrendered to the power of the surging water, instantly relinquishing years of effort in the snap of each expended radicle.

Halfway down the mountain, the expanding volume of water split, as it had done for centuries, and a portion of that river was directed along a different path. An irregularly shaped and gaping aperture in the face of the mountain accepted the water funneled into it, sending it deep inside the dark, cold stone within the belly of the mountain. Within this mineralized adit, the water polished the stone all around it, forcing its way forward by weight and power through a slowly widening passageway before it once again angled to the surface, redirected by stronger stone below it. There the deluge rejoined the torrent from which it had separated near the summit. This added quantity of water swelled the descending inundation once more, creating turbulent and violent rapids that clawed and tore at the earth. In time, the slope of the land finally gave way to the placid foothills below, where the frigid water slowed and the tumescent river deposited its red-brown dregs onto the Iberian flatlands.

Here, too, was where the Romans used their knowledge of the power of water, employing their skills at hydromechanics to redirect the flow of water, thereby unlocking the stone walls of the earth in order to harvest her hidden treasures. Initially, the Romans scoured away the taiga forest near the peaks of this mountain range, exposing the red hue underneath and rinsing away the matter that held it in place. They washed away the sediment placed there eons before and harvested the precious gold they found underneath.

Once they decimated the system of life from the surface of the range, they redirected their mining procedures toward the inner margins of the highest of her mountains. This was dangerous work, for controlling a tool that could wash away the slopes of a mountain in often unpredictable and profound ways could take many lives along with it. Such loss required a steady influx of manpower, which was scarce in the highlands of northern Iberia. Consequently, the republic maintained her fascination for mining gold upon the backs of Rome's scoundrels.

The prison at Las Médulas, in the northwest region of the Iberian Peninsula, stood out from its counterparts as a creation of opposites. This was the joint venture of the Lusitanians, rugged warriors who clung to life along the far oceanic coast of the Iberian Peninsula, and the Romans, their unscrupulous partners. With the quickly expanding hordes of Carthaginian soldiers now occupying the inner plains of Iberia, the Lusitanians stood to lose everything they held dear. Out of desperation, they sought an alliance with Rome, hoping the new republic would help them conquer Carthage and restore peace in the western Mediterranean.

As things stood in the early years, Rome had no desire to fight in the wilderness to the west, but it did agree to support Lusitania with troops and arms in exchange for the opportunity to mine gold and silver from the Lusitanian-held territories. Later, in an entirely different theater, Carthage and Rome entered what would one day be a series of long wars. The gold from the mines high in the Cantabrian Mountains became vital for Rome's survival in her war with Carthage.

The mines required men to control the water that drilled deep inside the mountain range and to unearth the precious metals inside and harvest them. Consumed in battles with Carthage, Rome could waste no warriors, no highly trained and honorable men, so Rome used slaves and criminals to harvest the gold. The desolate mountains beyond the wilderness whose gold and silver would fund the Roman war machine became a prison to house Rome's worst and most despicable criminals. This was Las Médulas.

Housed deep beneath the side of a mountain, Rome's worst criminals slaved away the remainders of their lives, mining gold from the bowels of a prison. For most, Las Médulas would become their tomb. The burly, war-hardened soldiers of Lusitania watched over the prison, but with little support from Rome in their own efforts to fight the Carthaginians, the Lusitanians did very little to ensure the health and safety of their charges.

This was a horrid place. Dark, wet, and cold, the myriad small passageways and narrow rooms were filled with disease, pestilence, and rancor. With little to eat and an abundance of darkness to haunt men's minds, many of Las Médulas's slaves either wilted away in their own squalor or wandered aimlessly through the tunnels and shafts, their minds and memories long absent from the walking corpses their bodies had become.

Hidden away, high above the beautiful stands of chestnuts and the thick forests of tall oaks, the greens of which played harmoniously against the red rock formations of the mountains, one would never suspect evil lurked within such a serene landscape. Yet as a seed germinates well below the surface of the soil before springing forth into the light, so does the evil of man. From Las Médulas such evil was about to find its way out from beneath the stone walls.

As the rain washed over the mountain from the storm high above, one of the prison's more interesting characters leaned quietly against one of the damp, cold walls in a small hollowed-out room tucked deep at one end of a long quiet mine shaft. Adding to his already festering temper, he chipped away at the flaccid lower limb of his deceased chain-mate, trying to sever the dead man's foot at the ankle with the only tool he had at his disposal: a dull miner's ax. The older man had succumbed to some disease of the body. Sorian wasn't sure if it had been from the foul purulence the man frequently coughed up or if it had been from the rancid-smelling wound created by the gnawing edges of the sharp metal shackle that he wore about the ankle. Either way, the man breathed his last and Sorian was free of him, at least as soon as he could remove the man's foot and slide the shackle off the severed limb. He smiled at the thought of it, although, as he looked at the fallen man's features in the dim gray hues of darkness, his smile turned into a sneer. He suspected that he would be partnered with someone else soon enough, perhaps someone even less tolerable.

All the prisoners in Las Médulas had a partner. There were no cells or prison doors to hinder their movements. They were free to move throughout the prison, though the safest locations were typically those closest to the jets of water being used to tear apart the rock. The small avalanches of rubble and collapsing passageways were generally considered by the inmates to be a much safer alternative to the Lusitanian guards that patrolled the entrance and the ever- branching network of tunnels. Shackled together in pairs, these men could only move as fast as the slowest man of the team, and the guards at the mouth of the prison were well prepared to destroy any man who attempted an escape.

The guards occasionally patrolled the inner parts of the mine, dictating where the search for gold should take place, directed by the Romans charged with channeling the water. The guards enforced their will with wrath, using a variety of mining tools and weapons at their disposal. Whips and short lengths of chain were the commonly used tools of the guards, though wooden clubs and iron mauls appeared to provide them with more entertainment. The ankles and lower extremities of the prisoners were a favorite target for the guards. Troublemakers were hobbled, which served to slow down a pair of men considerably, although most of the time there was little need for any motion. After all, digging or chiseling away at stone walls for hours at a time required very little ambulation.

The guards had broken the ankle of Sorian's elder partner in just this way before Sorian arrived at the prison. After the old man's previous partner succumbed from his wounds, which the pair acquired trying to sneak from the mouth of the mine, Sorian was teamed with the older man to form a new pairing. Now Sorian was preparing to free himself from the only portion of this prison under his control.

Crouching low under the wet, dripping ceiling, Sorian whacked at the dead man's tibia with the dull, flattened blade of his pickax. He paused from his task to wipe his brow, thinking that the man's bone was stronger than he had expected. He soon realized that it bounced when he struck it because it was held off the ground by the odd angle in which it had regrown. Clumsily,

Sorian got to his feet and stepped down on the lateral side of the dead man's limb, forcing the bone down to the ground. Lifting the ax, he looked above his head to see how much room he had to swing the ax freely. He then studied the wound he was creating and realized that only one or two more good swings would complete the task.

Preparing to make the next throw of the ax, he heard a low-pitched roar surrounding him. It sounded like thunder, but it never ceased. He hadn't noticed it earlier when he had been in this small, dark chamber, but he had been focusing all his attention on the dead man's leg. In his weakened state, everything took longer than he anticipated, and he welcomed the brief rest as he listened to the reverberations within the stone chamber. This new feature stimulated his sluggish thoughts and senses. Most of the time, the only sounds he heard consisted of the constant dripping of water, the squeals of rats, or the occasional scream of a lost mind. Usually anything this loud would signal another cave-in, but that always came and went quickly. He paused. What could possibly make such noise within stone so thick? After all, he was nowhere near the tunnels currently being mined. Flummoxed, he returned to his bittersweet task.

Aiming carefully, he held his breath, swinging the ax down hard. The blade smashed into the gnarled limb and careened to the right, sending small bits of bone and tendon into the air. Beneath the limb, and out of his sight, a small stellate crack formed in the stone of the floor. The bone chipped and cracked unevenly but hadn't come completely apart. Instead, and much to Sorian's dismay, it cracked longitudinally, like the splitting of a tree's limb in a strong wind. Sorian took another couple of breaths and took aim for one final swing. This one would do the job, he hoped. Summoning all the energy he could muster, he swung the ax down as hard as he could. The limb jumped in reaction to the force he had applied, and the bone jerked away, leaving only the tendons and a patch of skin linking the two parts. The collision with the stone was louder than he expected, although he assumed the noise had come from the metal shackle and chain bouncing against the stone. What he had not known was that the impact made the stellate crack grow larger, exposing itself from beneath the dead man's ankle, like the legs of a crab.

The stellate's strange lines caught his attention. Curious, Sorian shoved the man's leg aside and was startled to see a hole underneath, about the size of his palm. The hole exposed this enclosed space to the loud roar of rushing water and a refreshing spray that rose up to him at an angle. He placed two fingers through the hole and felt the jagged lip of the opening. The whole floor was thin. As thin as ice. Instinctively, he lowered himself, spreading his weight evenly on his hands and legs.

Excited, Sorian grasped his ax near its head, trying to release the shackle from the corpse. The tissues resisted the dull blade much the same way sinew and tawny connective tissues resist the gnashing of one's teeth. Finally, he managed to slide the retched foot away and slip the bloody shackle from the stump. Smiling, he rolled over onto his stomach, pushed away the mass of his matted and soggy hair, and peered through the hole in the floor. But it was too dark, dark as night. With care he chipped away at the edge of the hole until it was large enough to push his arm through. As he did, he felt water within a few centimeters of the opening. It was frigid and moving quickly. He reached into the rushing water, whose power pushed at his extended arm, making it hard for him to reach straight in front of him. Turning and twisting his arm, he extended his fingertips as far as he could. He could feel no rock to the sides or straight down. If this was an underground river, it was at least as wide as a man's body, he realized.

He pulled his arm, numb from the cold, back through the hole, sat up, and pushed himself back to the far wall of the little stone room. Alone in the darkness, he considered his options. The idea of climbing into the water seemed insane. After all, what if he got stuck? He would surely drown. And what if it just keeps going down?

In time, he noticed the noise gradually lessening. Temporarily, he focused only on its sound. Within a few minutes, the water was only a trickle and the world had gone quiet, which made his little room seem suddenly larger and made him feel more alone. He sat back up with a start and slid on his belly toward the hole in the floor. Reaching down into the chasm, Sorian again tried to feel for anything to help indicate the size of the passageway. All that remained was an empty void filled with cool air that moved along his arm, drying it as he dangled his limb in the empty space. Twisting his hand back and forth, he rested his head on the floor and let his imagination take control of his thoughts. The air moving past his hand reminded him of a cool breeze. He pictured himself standing in an open field, the sun shining on his face and the cool breeze of the sea ruffling his hair.

The thought of a cool breeze awakened his mind, which began to stumble out of its imaginary surroundings and back into his harsh reality. He thought about wind under the ground. Then a thought surfaced. There was an opening in the mountain to his left—somewhere. If going down led to a dead end, then maybe he could climb up and out! His heart pounded at the prospect, driving hope through his body as powerfully as the blood flowed in his veins. He hadn't experienced excitement like this since serving in a Roman legion.

Wafting into the tiny room, the distant shouts of guards ripped him from his celebration. He pulled his arm back out and felt around for a small rock or flat piece of stone to cover the opening he had discovered. Sliding his hand against the wall, his fingers slipped under a flap of stone. He reached back for his ax and slid the blade under the flap to pry at it. Brittle from previous mining in this shaft, the slag-like mass cracked and separated, dropping to the floor of the tunnel in a shield-shaped disc about as thick as his fist.

Fighting for a foothold against the slippery stones, he slid the disc over the open hole in the floor. He moved to his partner's head and grabbed the old man's shoulders. Dragging the corpse to the corner of the room, which was out of sight from its opening and the tunnel, Sorian gathered up the short length of chain and the empty shackle. Satisfied that his hiding place was sufficiently arranged, he stood up, hunched over, and started walking along the tunnel back to the central cave where all the men would be gathering for the daily chance at food. Tonight, he didn't even notice if he had hunger pangs—he was too excited to eat.

The central chamber of the expansive mine was a massive cave at the side of the mountain from which numerous tunnels stretched out in rays. Its opening from the outside was an irregularly shaped doorway that was heavily guarded. The chamber itself had started as another small hole in the stone of the mountain until the Romans forced water through the opening. As the water caused it to enlarge, workers carved and scraped and sprayed the walls much the same way, creating the tunnels. Carrying the loose end of his chain in one hand, Sorian moved carefully along the back wall of the chamber, far removed from the mouth of the mine.

The large room was already crowded with other prisoners hoping to find a meal there. On rare occasions, the guards captured or killed more game than they could consume, and they offered the extra meat to the prisoners. They never provided any plant matter to eat and often the meat the prisoners were offered was not fresh. Occasionally, when the Lusitanians killed a deer found roaming the forest too close to the mine, this game was ample to feed the guards and at least some of the prisoners.

After the soldiers consumed what they desired, the remaining carcass was thrown into the central chamber. A portion of this offering was certainly done to nourish the labor force, but the clear majority of the food was provided as sport, as the guards found pleasure in watching these starving men fight for food. Generally, only the strongest men got something to eat, making the remainder fend for themselves over what remained of the carcass. On this day, as Sorian entered the chamber, the men were gossiping about a kill. Sorian listened to the rumors as he sidled in more closely to the others. Their excitement over a partially consumed deer was tangible.

Making his way toward one of three large fires burning within the chamber, Sorian spotted two men with whom he shared a common background. They too were Romans, sent to this prison for theft, one within Rome and the other in Brundisium. Ordinarily, such a crime was managed with swift deliberation and even swifter punishment, but because of the war with Carthage, both men were permitted to retain their hands. Unfortunately for them, however, it was decided that their hands would be put to good use digging for precious metals in Las Médulas. Both men had been chained together after leaving Rome and had arrived at the mine only a week or so after Sorian.

As he sat down on the ground beside them, warming his chilled body by the fire, both men looked at him, and then around him, and then at the chain he clutched in his hand. Before they could inquire about his missing chain-mate, Sorian silenced them with a glare and quick shake of his head. Curious, they slid closer to him and, in doing so, men sitting farther from the fire edged closer too, filling in the space the two had left vacant. Sorian tolerated the intrusion because by sitting closely in this way, no one would notice that he was no longer paired.

"When did it happen?" whispered one of the men.

"Never mind him. Finally, he rests and is free of this place, and I am free of his rotten stench," answered Sorian quietly, a scowl distorting his face. "Now listen to me, I have found a way out of here, but I need your help to move rock."

Both men stared at him, unable to speak. Finally, Gallus, the larger and younger of the two spoke. "Where? Did you dig a tunnel?"

Sorian stared at the fire for a moment, reluctant to share more news with them in case they were prone to talking too much. Silently, he considered the unknowns, like the stones he might have to move to get to freedom and how weak his body was and if he would need help to scale some high place he might encounter. He realized that it had taken every bit of strength he had to drag the old man's body across the small chamber and prop him against the wall. He sighed and turned to look at Gallus and Cato, who stared back at him as if they had been frozen by his words.

"The rain showed me the way," whispered Sorian. "I believe there is a small passageway that leads to the mountainside. If it is wide enough, we can climb out of there."

"How will we climb through a wet hole in the ground chained together like this?" asked Gallus, clutching the middle of the strand of chain that connected him to Cato.

Cato caught Gallus's arm to silence him as two guards walked nearby. When the guards moved away, Cato responded, "Never mind the chain. I will crawl backwards if it means getting out of here."

Sorian smiled wryly at his two new partners and proceeded to explain his plan. "Somehow we must watch for the storms. I don't want to be trapped in the passage when the water comes. The best time to go is at the end of a storm and just before night, so we can follow the light to the surface and then exit the mountain as darkness comes."

"How will we know which way to go in the dark?" asked Gallus. "The forest is unforgiving and very large."

"Leave that to me. I spent enough nights with Rome's legions to know how to march at night. I need you to find us extra clothes, as the nights may be very cold for a while," explained Sorian.

The men sat quietly, contemplating this chance at freedom and the many risks that stretched before them. Suddenly, they heard cries near the front of the large chamber. Two guards threw a dead wolf onto the fire closest to the mouth of the cave. The prisoners surrounding the fire clamored and fought for a hold on the animal and, gradually, the mob tore the flaccid carcass apart as the guards watched with enjoyment. Slowly, a few of the men farthest from the wolf began to shuffle out of the chamber, despondent. Soon the other prisoners would follow. The time had come to find a place to rest their weary heads for a few hours before the digging of dirt and chiseling of stone began all over again.

Cato sighed and mumbled to his partner, "Looks like it will be rat again for us, Gallus. If we are lucky enough to find one."

"I just want the hind quarters this time."

"If you catch it, you get them," said Cato dryly.

The three men stood and joined the mass of men as they migrated from the chamber into the tunnels that billeted them. The fire had felt good, but soon the guards would let two of them burn down to nothing, and they alone would occupy the third for the night. There was no good reason to stay in the large chamber with the guards, and for the three young Romans, the thoughts of escape would keep them warm through the cold, dark night.

# Chapter V

---

CLEANING UP THE remains of the longhouse took many days, but everyone, including Jabnit and Yzebel, pitched in to help. Since the fire and the incident involving one of Kanmi's men, there had been a certain suspicion of the stranger. Many of the laborers whispered that his presence was a bad omen, yet his efforts to assist with the cleanup project were viewed as genuine. Gradually, their suspicions subsided.

Taking a rest from chopping the charred posts out of the ground, the stranger stared at the few smoldering sticks of the longhouse, still too hot to be moved. Jugurtha and a few of the men were talking nearby, but the sounds of their voices were drowned out as the stranger resumed his quest into memories.

He recalled running through a small village, finding the huts ablaze and many dead men scattered along the beach. In his vision, he searched for survivors, but found none. What he did find were several long javelins and a bright red scutum, or shield. A Roman shield. This discovery jolted his memory forward in time.

He found himself standing in the center of a massive arena, blocking the swings of a madman who hid behind another Roman shield. Surrounding the two of them, a massive crowd of people shouted vociferously and threw their fists in the air, as if each one had become a flickering of flame within a great conflagration. Their voices were loud, blending in a cacophony of chants and roars, making it impossible for him to recognize any specific language.

Deep within the midst of this recollection, he was shaken awake. Immediately, the din of the crowd ceased and Jugurtha's lone voice replaced it. The stranger looked at Jugurtha, surprised to see him within his dream. And then he realized that the remnants of the vision had gone. Not yet able to connect all of his recent visions, he and Jugurtha rejoined the men as they finished their break and resumed working on the rubble of the longhouse. Glancing to the side, he noticed Yzebel approaching them. She greeted Jugurtha and then stood near the stranger, suggesting that the stranger would be excused so she could speak to him alone.

"Will you walk with me?" Yzebel asked.

Nodding, the stranger gestured for her to lead the way. They walked slowly along the eastern edge of the grain field and then turned at the corner to walk toward the drainage ditch that he and Jugurtha had built. They followed its course back toward the marsh.

"No one has gone this way since you fought Kanmi's man here," Yzebel observed. "They are all scared that seeing the body will bring bad fortune. Perhaps it is the same for me."

The stranger walked quietly by her side, listening. She seemed nervous, her voice more timid than in the past. "I am sorry if I have done wrong," he said, waiting for Yzebel to turn around. When she did, he continued, "I would do it again, however. I could not watch what was about to happen and do nothing while the soldier tore the girl apart."

Yzebel looked into his eyes for a moment and then smiled softly, unable to completely erase the look of concern that she knew was on her face. "I thank you for trying to protect us. We all do." Yzebel gestured back toward the laborers working on the longhouse. "But Kanmi will be back and we will need to explain to him what happened here. He will never believe that we alone killed his man, so he will do unspeakable things until we give him the information that he wants—namely, who did kill him. Even then he will retaliate."

"Then don't tell him anything. Kanmi may assume the man ran away or was lost elsewhere. You owe him nothing, much less the need to explain the loss of his man."

"And how do we explain his horse?" Yzebel countered. "It has been standing in the square eating grass for two days. No one will go near it."

"Do you see the horse today?"

"Of course!" said Yzebel irritably. "It is . . . ." Her voice trailed off as she scanned the farm for the chestnut stallion. She didn't see it.

"During the night I rode it away from here," explained the stranger. "I walked nearly all night, returning before anyone knew I was gone."

Yzebel stared at the man. "And I suppose you threw the dead man's carcass over its back as well?"

"He will never be seen again. I made sure of that the day I killed him."

Yzebel shivered. "I do not like this. Yahweh has seen all of this and He does not tolerate such deception. We must be truthful to Kanmi when he comes and asks about his missing man."

The stranger walked passed Yzebel, shaking his head in disgust. "I do not know this God about whom you speak. Does he prefer the brutal destruction of an innocent girl to the punishment of the man who would destroy that innocence? My gods do not chain me with such fear!" As he spoke, he stopped abruptly. Another flashback pounded through his head like the galloping hooves of a warhorse.

He was chained to a wall in a dark room while men and women stared at him, talking quietly amongst themselves. And more missing pieces of his past flooded his mind, filling the recesses as the rising tide spills into the cracks and crevices of boulders in its path. He dropped to his knees as the images flew by, one after another in some particular order, creating a foundation on which the story might be told.

Yzebel ran to him and dropped to her knees in front of him, putting her hands to the sides of his face. "What is it? What is wrong?"

"I have seen some of my past," whispered the man. "It comes like lightning strikes, brief but sudden and unannounced." Agony was written on his face.

Yzebel ran her hands over his powerful forearms and held his hands gently. "Will you tell me what you see?"

The man looked into Yzebel's dark brown eyes and caressed her cheek with the palm of his hand. He wondered why she cared so much for a man without a future and only splashes of a past that scared him. "Soon."

Very early the next morning, the stranger woke and exited the second longhouse before the faintest pink glow of dawn made any impression on the blackness of night. A massive round moon glowed in the western sky, only now beginning to find cover behind the highest trees of the property. Was the moon trying to hide before the sun rose over the other end of the world to capture it? He mused. Breathing in the cool air and appreciating the silence of night, he set out down the beach path toward the wreckage of the damaged boat.

He was now more determined than ever to fit the last few pieces of the puzzle into place. He knew the fishing boat still held the answers to the questions he had about his past. As he ambled, he made careful note of the sound that the wind made as it filtered through the palms. It reminded him of Yzebel's soft voice when she whispered to him. He would miss this place. He would certainly miss Yzebel's kindness.

Nearing the irrigation ditch, which ended abruptly near the side of the path at the end of the wheat field, he stopped in his tracks when he heard splashing water. It came from the irrigation ditch toward the stand of trees where he had hidden himself days before. For weeks the children had played in the water here, because it was free of salt and made clear by the rushes that surrounded the marsh. He hadn't expected to find any of them out at this time of the morning.

He scanned the length of the ditch, following the reflection on the surface of the water as the moon's final brightness illuminated the ground. Yzebel was kneeling in the water. She poured it over her head, washing her hair. As she rose from the knee-deep water, her wet hair swung down the length of her back and the water dripped from her bent elbows. The moonlight glistened on her body. As she turned, the light danced over the curves of her breast, hip, and the long gentle line of her thigh. She shimmered in the light. He stared at her, mesmerized by her beauty. He had noticed it before but, seeing her in this way, all his concerns seemed to melt away, if ever so briefly.

Sensing that she wasn't alone, she turned in his direction. Squinting, squeezing the water from her eyes, she could identify the man who was watching her. For several moments, neither moved. She didn't seem embarrassed, but when she lifted her hand to greet him, he looked away. Awkwardly, he turned and walked briskly to the boat.

The image of Yzebel challenged his concentration. He shook his head and muttered, trying to refocus on his objective. He hoisted himself into the boat over the damaged hull. He squatted down in the center and reached out to the plank-sheer on each side. He ran his hands along the top edge and then tipped onto his knees, making his way toward the front of the boat. He drew himself into a seated position on the floor of the bow and leaned back to rest his head. The ocean was now turning from gray to blue in the first light of dawn. Relaxed, he drifted off to sleep as his mind passed through the years into his childhood, to a day when he was helping his father build a boat.

The boy lay in the bottom of the boat, gazing at the sky while he listened to his father hum as he shaved the sides of the hull with an adze. Contemplating how best to ask the question, he fingered a small knot in the wood to the right of his hip. It was perfectly round, with a triangular edge jutting into the center from the side of the circle.

"Father?"

"Yes, what is it?" His father paused in his work. He looked over the side of the boat at his son.

"Do you think we will ever return to the mainland? I mean, to live?"

"No. This is our home now, Carpathimos." His father spoke bluntly. "Your mother and I, you and your sister Parma, our friends in the village… We are all here to stay. Why do you ask this?"

"Don't you tire of walking the same sand every day or fishing for the same fish all the time?"

"Don't think of it in that way, son. To me, this is paradise. We are all here together and we are safe. I have no desire to restart our lives anywhere else. Does that make sense to you?"

The boy looked at his father's gentle eyes and careworn face and nodded.

"Good, then jump out of there and help me smooth out this curve," his father said with a grin.

The stranger awoke to the image of his father's grin and the sun peeking over the lip of the bow, shining on the side of his face. He pressed his eyelids together tightly, sat up, and rubbed his neck, remembering the knot in his dream. Scanning the wood along his right thigh and just beyond his hip he saw it—the round knot hole. It resembled a broken wheel with one missing piece, the terminal ends of the broken circle held to the axle by two spokes. Stunned, he poked his index finger into the hole and felt the edges. In doing so, his whole life marched forward before his eyes. *This* was the boat where he fished with his father for hours and hours and days and days. This was the boat he mended after the Romans destroyed his village and massacred his father. This was the boat he used for fishing after he returned home with Myridia, his pregnant wife, after enduring years of captivity under Roman rule. This was the boat in which he set sail for Rome after leaving his sister Parma with his son Lucia on the shores of Ionia.

"Carpathimos," he said to himself.  "Myridia!" he cried out in anger, beating his fists against the hull at his sides before burying his face in his hands and weeping.

Jugurtha watched him from the tree line, concerned about his young friend but not knowing how to console him or help him in any way. Jugurtha left the stranger on the beach to go find Yzebel and tell her what he had seen. She was his niece, but he respected her as an equal. He had seen how she looked at the stranger and how she cared for him. He also knew that this stranger seemed kind-hearted but was plagued by the memories he kept to himself.

Jugurtha hurried into Jabnit's house. No one was inside. He shut the door and ran around the back of the house. Still no Yzebel.

Jabnit had been away at a neighboring farm, supervising the first harvest of grain. As was typical, the men of the village had gone with him to assist with the harvest, as the men from that farm, in turn, would work on this one when it was time. This left only Jugurtha and Yzebel to watch over their farm. The stranger remained with them to avoid arousing any suspicion.

Running into the orchard, Jugurtha saw Yzebel behind a butter-fruit tree. He nearly missed her as she stood behind the dense crown of dark green leaves, but her smooth brown legs next to the pale gray trunk gave her away. She was splitting open one of the large, oval, lavender fruits.

"Jugurtha! Look. These are almost ready to harvest. After father and the men return, we will need to begin picking and pressing these for the oil. Are the vessels ready?"

"Never mind these fruits, Yzebel." Jugurtha ripped the melon from her hand and tossed it to the ground, surprising her in the process. "We must go to the stranger. He is not well. I found him sitting in the boat, so I watched him from the trees. I thought that he was sleeping until he started screaming, beating his fists in anger on the boat and shouting in his own tongue. I worry for him. Please go to him now."

Startled by Jugurtha's story, but appreciating his empathy for the stranger, Yzebel reached for the old man's hand to pull him with her. Together, they ran to the beach. Climbing over the dune, they looked west along the shoreline. The man had left the boat. Running, Yzebel and Jugurtha searched the wheat field, the marsh, and then the woods. Finding nothing, they circled back to scour the beach, trees, fields and outbuildings. Before they went any farther, however, the stranger walked out from the trees carrying several of the charred wooden planks from the longhouse.

"What are you doing with those?" Yzebel asked breathlessly as she approached him.

"I must repair the boat." The stranger abruptly asked Yzebel and Jugurtha, "Will you help me?"

Hesitating, Yzebel glanced at Jugurtha. "Yes. Yes, we will help you. How?"

"I need extra hands to hold these in place to fit them. May I borrow tools?" he asked. To Jugurtha he said, "Is there an adze or a sharp blade from an ax?"

Both men looked to Yzebel to translate. She nodded and told Jugurtha to go with the stranger to the beach. "I will get the tools you ask for."

Dropping the boards onto the sand, the men studied the hole in the hull. A jagged section was missing from the starboard side of the bow; it must have met with some force against a large boulder. The hole measured nearly a meter in both directions.

The stranger began separating the best of the burned boards, looking for those long enough to span the gap and overlap the hull at both ends. Jugurtha tried to understand what the man was thinking. He surmised that he wanted to fasten them using the sticky resin from the butter-fruit trees and then bore a hole through the ends of each board. That way, he could force a wooden peg into corresponding holes in the hull. Jugurtha suspected that it would leak, but it might be sound and strong enough in mild seas.

With Jugurtha's help, the stranger measured the boards he needed and then began scraping off the charred wood to make sure that each plank still had the thickness necessary to hold strong. They quickly realized, however, that the dry boards would not bend without splintering. Jugurtha could sense the stranger's growing frustration. When Yzebel joined them with more tools, he offered a suggestion.

"Yzebel, please tell him that he must slow down. These boards will not hold against the sea. We can cut down one or two trees. New planks will be stronger and much more flexible. Young wood will bend to fit the curve of the boat and will withstand the power of the waves. I understand how he wants to fit them, but he must be willing to take the time to build it right."

Yzebel knelt beside the stranger and put her hand on his shoulder. She explained to him what Jugurtha had said and stepped back, waiting for his response. Almost feverishly, he continued his struggle, trying to mold the wood under his knee with the blade of an adze, ignoring her words. When she stepped on the board he was working with, he was forced to stop. He leaned back on his haunches to look up at her. She crossed her arms and stood her ground, unwilling to step off the board and give in to him. Finally, he relented and sat back onto the sand, setting aside the tool and wiping the sweat from his face. Jugurtha smiled at Yzebel and patted the man on the back.

# Chapter VI

———

SITTING ALONE IN the darkness of the longhouse lit only by the light of a small fire, Carpathimos tried to find some tolerable place to rest his mind from the horrible images that haunted his wakefulness and ruined his sleep. He tried inexorably to concentrate on his coming voyage. Now that his memories were restored, he knew why he had set sail and he knew why he had to continue his journey. He approached a reckoning to confront with the men responsible for destroying the life he had known and taking from him the woman he loved.

Although his past had become clear, he still had one question. What role did General Lucius, a man he had respected, play in the death of his friends and his woman? When Carpathimos left his sister Parma and his son Lucia on the shores of the Anatolian peninsula, he promised himself he would find these men and avenge Myridia's death. He needed to be on his way, which meant rebuilding his boat. The longer he stayed in this place, the more he feared he would be unable to fulfill that promise. He couldn't let these people, these beautiful people he had come to know and care about, into his life for fear they would change him.

Shifting his weight, he leaned back against the wood wall and closed his eyes, trying to picture Myridia in his mind. He carefully recalled each feature: her emerald eyes, her full and sultry lips, and the long dark hair curling around her face in cascades of shining strands. She had been beautiful in so many ways. He longed for the sound of her voice and the way she looked at him. Lucia had inherited some of his mother's appearance. Carpathimos yearned to go back to his son once again.

Slipping through the doorway, Yzebel tiptoed toward Carpathimos, carrying two bowls of food, one for him and one for her. He was concentrating so deeply that he didn't hear her. The smell of the food brought him around. His eyes snapped open, surprised to find Yzebel standing so close.

Yzebel smiled. "I am sorry to surprise you. I came with food, but I thought you were sleeping. I can leave if you would rather be alone."

"Please stay," Carpathimos said. "I am grateful for the food. It smells very good."

For several moments, the two ate quietly. Yzebel broke the silence. "Jugurtha came to get me when he saw you in the boat earlier. Are you all right?"

The stranger looked up from his food. "I do not know. I suppose it seemed strange that I needed to fix the boat and depart so suddenly."

"I knew that one day your memory would return and you would know where you were needed." She avoided his eyes. "I was hoping that when you realized what you were running from, or running to, you would decide it wasn't so important. I was both selfish and wrong."

"You have been very good to me—all of you." Carpathimos said, "Part of me wishes that I could remain here with you."

"Part of you?"

The stranger corrected his course. "Part of me wishes that I could stay here and work, making a difference one harvest at a time."

"Then why don't you?"

"First, it is not the will of your father. Nor would I wish to hide whenever Kanmi or his men come here. I would only cause more trouble if I stayed."

"I am certain that my father will change his mind. We can make some arrangement with Kanmi." Yzebel tried not to plead with him.

Carpathimos could see no way in which Kanmi would leave Yzebel alone as long as he lived here. He knew he would always pose a threat to Kanmi. "I have a debt to pay," he added.

"After so much time, perhaps the man, or men, you owe won't believe that you will be returning to pay your debt."

"You don't understand, Yzebel. This debt is called revenge. I owe it to myself and others to pay it to them," Carpathimos said sternly.

Yzebel stared at him. As she pondered what the man could possibly mean, Jabnit walked into the center square with his horse in tow. Stiff and tired, Jabnit went into his house to find Yzebel, but the house was empty and dark. He called for her but there was no answer. He left the house and walked toward the beach were sometimes she tended a fire at night. He turned back when he found no fire. Perplexed, he walked back toward his house to wait for Yzebel but as he crossed the central square, he glanced over at the second longhouse and decided to check for his daughter there. Approaching, he slowed when he heard voices.

Yzebel set her food aside. "Please help me understand what makes you hate so much. What did these people do to deserve your anger?"

Carpathimos searched carefully for the right words. "Before I came here I was trapped in a storm much like the storm that brought me to you, only it has lasted much, much longer. It came to me when I was a small boy and no matter how hard I try, I cannot escape it." He searched her eyes for a sign that she was following him. "I left my home on Leros, an island in the east, and took my sister Parma and my son Lucia to Anatolia. I was sailing west when the wind came."

Yzebel listened with an ache in her heart when she learned he had a son. "Why did you leave your sister and son there?"

"Lucia is not yet three years old. I sent him away with Parma to our mother's family in Lydia while I am gone."

"And where were you going before the storm changed your course?"

"Back to a place I never wanted to see again." The man sighed and stared at his hands.

Yzebel sensed the topic was becoming difficult for him. "Take your time. Perhaps telling me will help you feel better. Please explain this storm that won't leave you alone."

"Then I must start at the beginning." The stranger took a deep breath and then began. "When I was a boy, my father and I did everything together. We were very close. He taught me everything I needed to know about life on our island. He brought us to that place to hide from the wars fought between the families of Alexander's generals. He always told me that the world was becoming too small, that we were not as secluded as he had hoped. He was right. One day troops came by boat and decimated our people. They killed my father."

Yzebel gasped. "That must have been so frightening to a young child," she said.

The man nodded. "Years later, the troops returned to repeat what they had done earlier. This time, they left with my mother and sister and others in chains, slaves of their republic. I did not hide. I chased them. When I tried to rescue my mother and sister, I was captured. They took us to Rome, where they trained me to become a soldier. I never saw my mother alive again."

"How did you get your sister back?" Yzebel asked.

"As a soldier, I was singled out to fight in their games. They called us *gladiators*. Gladiators fight one another to the death in a large arena for the entertainment of Rome's people."

"That is awful!" gasped Yzebel.

"It was," he agreed, "but several good things occurred that never would have happened had I not been chosen to fight."

Yzebel raised her eyebrows.

"Under their whips and rods, I became a great fighter, an animal in chains, tormented and fighting for its life. It is not something of which I am proud. I had no feeling for those who fell. My life was full of three things: death and hatred and cruelty. The people of Rome who came to see us filled an arena that could cover the wheat field outside this door. They came with a lust for blood. They came to watch men slaughter one another while they cheered." His voice was harsh.

"You mentioned good. What good could possibly come from such a brutal thing?" she asked.

"While I was a gladiator, I met a woman who helped me survive. She was the inspiration I needed to wake up each day, to defend myself in order to see a future. She saved me. She saved my sister. And when I was no longer forced to fight, she left Rome with me."

"What was her name?"

"Myridia."

"And you have a son with her named Lucia?" she asked.

"We raised a son together on Leros. I love him as my own."

When Yzebel looked perplexed, he continued. "Myridia was the daughter of one of Rome's great generals, Lucius Myridias, and the niece of Emperor Tiberius. Myridia tried to free me, but Tiberius prevented that. He raped Myridia and instead of freeing me, he sent me to battle alongside the Romans in the mountains." He added in a wooden voice, "Lucia is not mine."

"How were you able to get back together?" Yzebel was mesmerized by the story. "Did you run away?"

"Myridia's father was a kind man, or so I believed. Myridia begged him to help me and, as a result, after the fighting season ended, he let me return to Rome to get her. We left for Leros soon after, where we lived very happily for two years."

"And then something terrible happened?" Yzebel surmised.

"The men who had been sent with us to watch over Myridia killed her." He struggled to keep the emotion out of his voice. "They attacked one day, murdered my friends, and tried to kill me. Myridia was killed by an arrow that I think was meant for me. I went after them and killed all of them. I hunted them down one by one. Only three of us survived—Parma, Lucia, and me."

"And you believe that Myridia's father had something to do with that attack?"

"I know someone knows the answer to that question, and I know that someone must pay for her death."

Yzebel shuddered at the words. "So, you intend to kill more people, as savagely as the man you smothered in the mud here!"

The stranger raised his voice. "The Romans have taken everyone that I have held in my heart! Not even my son is truly mine! Only Parma is alive, yet she cannot be free of the nightmares that have haunted her from the day they came to take her. I will not hide from them any longer. I, Carpathimos, will seek out everyone who had something to do with her death. I will take away from them everything they took from me—and more!"

Yzebel watched until the temper faded from his face. The amber light the small fire cast upon his head and rigid frame made him appear as menacing as the wicked beasts in the stories her father told her when she was growing up. She felt small and timid in this man's presence. Looking into his eyes, she saw someone altogether different from the man she thought she knew. This was a wild animal that had once been tame and peaceful, gentle and loving. He had been harmed by man. She hoped that she, with God's help, could mend his heart and soul.

As his temper cooled to a smolder, Yzebel slid close to his side and touched the back of his hand. What he needed was compassion, empathy. Gradually his breathing slowed and she placed her left hand on his shoulder. When he looked at her, his face softened. She rested her cheek against the firm muscle of his shoulder and he opened his fingers as she slid hers between them.

Jabnit had heard everything. He backed away quietly and mounted his horse. Kanmi must know about this man, he thought, for in Rome they shared a common enemy. Yzebel and Carpathimos sat quietly together while Jabnit rode away from the farm.

Carpathimos shifted and placed his arm around Yzebel's shoulders, pulling her close to him. When she looked up, he smiled. Yzebel returned his smile and raised her face to his. Tenderly she kissed his cheek. He made no movement. He didn't pull away, but he didn't return the affection. She realized that his heart wasn't ready for hers.

They held one another quietly in the dark until she repeated his name, "Carpathimos," and rose to collect the bowls. She stood still, unsure of what to do next. She placed her hand gently upon his head, feeling his thick waves of hair and whispered, "I hope that you find what you are looking for, Carpathimos. I hope Yahweh can lead you away from this destiny you have chosen."

As she moved away, Carpathimos reached for her hand, but caught only her fingers. She pulled them away without looking back and ran out the door.

The next two days were quiet and cold. The laborers began trickling back to the farm and the men filled the longhouse once again. Carpathimos began working on his boat in earnest after enlisting Jugurtha and some other men to help him cut tamarind trees and render them into planks. The red wood needed to be thin enough to mold to the curve of the hull, yet thick enough to withstand the pounding of the surf. The tamarind would tolerate the salt water for years and be more forgiving of the force sustained on choppy seas.

Yzebel avoided him. Perhaps she was too busy to see his progress, but he suspected by the way their last meeting ended that she wasn't too busy, just disappointed in him. He thought of Yzebel unceasingly. She had become the best thing in his life, but he could not let her dissuade him from his journey. Still, he hoped all was not lost with her.

Nearing the completion of the hull repair, he heard a commotion in the square. Concerned, he dropped the mallet he was about to swing and hurried up the beach. When he saw Kanmi's men scouring the property, he ducked down low, but several of the laborers, directed by the javelins of Kanmi's men, led the soldiers straight to the beach to apprehend him.

At knife point, the soldiers surrounded Carpathimos on three sides, indicating that they wanted him to walk into the center square. He complied. The soldiers had him outnumbered, but he calculated the moves necessary to overcome them. Yet he didn't have a burning urge to fight them. Perhaps his last conversation with Yzebel give him pause.

Crossing the central square, Carpathimos and his escort approached Kanmi and Jabnit. Yzebel was approaching Jabnit from behind, her lovely face stricken with anguish. "What is the meaning of this, Father?"

"Be still, Yzebel," Jabnit pleaded, then he turned back to Kanmi. "Remember our discussion, Kanmi, Please. I beg of you."

Kanmi looked at Carpathimos, who was now completely surrounded by his men, then he looked at Yzebel and smiled. "I will honor our agreement, Jabnit. I will leave Yzebel alone . . . for now." Yzebel looked at her father. Jabnit couldn't bear to look at her face. He cowered, as if expecting Yzebel to erupt like a volcano.

"Chain him in the cart!" commanded Kanmi.

His men tightened the circle around Carpathimos while two of them approached him from behind with chains and shackles.

"What are you doing to him?" cried Yzebel. "What have you done?" she shouted at her father.

Like an animal senses a trap closing in, so too did Carpathimos. He was outnumbered, but he was not willing to be taken without inflicting some pain of his own. He struck with a speed that left watchers awestruck. Spinning on his heel, he grabbed the chains dangling from a soldier's hands and whirled them over his head. They knocked two stunned men to the ground. He then pulled his knife from his tunic and lunged at a third man, severing the man's arm at the wrist. As the other soldiers came to their senses, they grasped their shields and trained their lances at Carpathimos, but he grabbed a fourth man and held him as a shield before the wall of javelins. Slowly he stepped backward, dragging the soldier by the neck.

Carpathimos found himself cornered. He looked toward the woods to determine if he could make it into the tree line before the javelins hit him, but he couldn't be sure how experienced Kanmi's men were with the weapons. He glanced back when he heard Kanmi's voice and Yzebel's cries. "How much is the woman worth to you, warrior?"

Kanmi held Yzebel tightly from behind, his hand clenched over her mouth while the tip of his long knife pierced into the skin under her chin, forcing her face upward. Kanmi and Carpathimos glared at one another. No one made a sound. Kanmi twisted his blade slightly, just enough to make Yzebel squeal. Defeated, Carpathimos released the tension in his arm, setting his captive free. He threw down the knife.

Humiliated by their costly lesson, the soldiers took extra care to ensure that Carpathimos would not strike back at them. They beat him to the ground before shackling his hands and ankles together. The lot of them struggled to hoist his battered body onto the back of a small cart pulled by one of Kanmi's horses. As he wobbled forward, one of the men struck him hard in the forehead with the butt of a knife, splitting the skin and releasing a trickle of blood over his brow and down the bridge of his nose. Dazed, he shook off the blow, but bright red blood continued to flow over his right eye and cheek and down the angle of his jaw.

Fighting her way out of her captor's hands, Yzebel ran to Carpathimos, wrapping her hands around his shoulders and pulling his head to hers to get his attention. Amused, Kanmi and his men mounted their horses. She had very little time to speak to Carpathimos, but she said what was important. "Do what you must to survive. I know you will be free again and, when you are, please release the rage that consumes you, Carpathimos. Someday our paths will cross again. I beg you to let Yahweh into your heart to show you the path to peace."

Carpathimos tipped his head to her shoulder. She kissed his head as the cart lurched away. Running behind the cart for a short distance with tears streaming down her face, she struggled to keep up. Carpathimos looked back at her as the horse pulled him beyond the last outbuilding and onto the road.

Trembling with fear and anger, she put her hand up in the air to bid him farewell.

# Chapter VII

—

IN THE DAYS following his discovery of the underground river, Sorian found no need to defend his small chamber. Few men bothered to fight him for the space, since the smell of rotting flesh was more powerful than their own quest for solitude. What's more, the Lusitanians seldom ventured too far into the network of small passageways, fearing retribution by the prisoners or becoming trapped behind a cave-in.

The rats of Las Médulas, however, felt no such conflicting emotions. The numbers that followed Sorian and his elder partner around the mine had grown considerably. Within a few short days of his partner's death, the voracious scavengers had scoured everything from the dead man's bones, but had not bothered Sorian. In time, however, with the tender bits devoured and the little remaining tissue failing to pacify their large numbers, the rats grew emboldened and more aggressive—so much so, that, at times, Sorian needed to remind them that he was not a corpse. His length of chain struck down one of the largest rodents, but he needed to react quickly to nab the dead prey for himself. He found their meat sour and stringy, but he ate, hoping to maintain enough strength to see his plan come to fruition.

Sorian stood at the mouth of his small tunnel, illuminated only by the dim light of a flickering torch he had stolen from the main chamber. It stuck out from the wall at an angle, perched in a hole in one of the support beams. The fire kept the rats at bay and the light helped to keep his mind from playing tricks on him. As he studied the sores on his skin and the depressions on his body where muscles had once been, his two Roman acquaintances rushed to him.

"It is time, Sorian!" announced Gallus, glancing behind them to make sure they were still alone.

"Yes," added Cato, "the rain comes again soon. We saw the guards begin to move into the mouth of the mine with some of their equipment. They will be off the mountain soon. The rain should be upon us before night comes."

"Good," replied Sorian. "I hope it will be a short storm."

Gallus was carrying a small bundle under his arm, which caught Sorian's attention. "Three tunics are rolled up inside this skin," said Gallus.

"Resourceful" whispered Sorian, lifting his eyebrows. The bag looked like a patchwork of various animal hides, wolf fur on one side and a combination of deer skin and rat hides on the other.

"Gallus and I made fur bags for our feet, too," added Cato. "They might not last long, but they should keep our toes warm until we get down the mountain."

"You have done well," Sorian assured them. "Hide that bag and come back after the rain begins. You will be able to listen to it with me here, but for now we should not bring more attention to this place."

The two men shuffled off, leaving Sorian behind with his rats. He paced back and forth under the torch, listening to the irritating sound of forty or fifty small sets of teeth as they scraped and gnawed against bone. Frustrated, he tried to drown out their noise by humming a favorite cadence that he had learned on a military march. At first, he thought the humming was working until he paused to take a breath. He realized it was actually the sound of rushing water returning to the underground river that had quieted the rats. As the sound escalated, he noticed the rats seemed torn between the corpse and their fear of the water beneath them.

That gave him an idea. He swung the length of chain he carried around what was left of the neck of the corpse and hooked the rim of the shackle to the chain, forming a loop. He dragged the corpse along the floor toward the mouth of his tunnel and the rats followed eagerly. When he reached the next room, which was merely a widened and abandoned section of the shaft in which others had previously extracted gold, he brought the corpse to a halt. This widened space was an area considerably larger than his own tight chamber at the end of the shaft. It had deeper corners and a higher ceiling. He peered through the dim light into the room's corners to see if any were occupied. He had never seen anyone in this space before and he walked through this room nearly every day during the call for food, but this time he was delivering an unpleasant burden to anyone who could be sharing his tunnel. Finding no one, he propped the dead man's corpse into a corner and slipped away as the rats reassembled on top of the body.

This limb of tunnel, and the series of empty rooms spaced out along its course, had not offered a successful harvest of gold. Those working this shaft never found a vein of gold to follow, so the narrow shaft was abandoned long ago. Other men might become uneasy in such a dark and small space, but Sorian seemed to prefer this tomb over the company of the foul men found elsewhere in the prison's shafts. He was a hermit within Las Médulas.

Bending and backing into the distal end of his tunnel, Sorian looked at the writhing mass of rats and the faint, yellow glimmer of bone that reflected the torchlight behind him. Briefly, he imagined hungry vermin consuming his own body. He shivered, remembering how they often started chewing on flesh before the man was dead.

Such a vivid imagination had always been one of Sorian's favorite attributes as a child, he recalled. He could always picture in his mind anything his brain conjured up. Being the only child of abusive parents, he learned to play games by himself and he often invented the most elaborate places in which his mind could escape the frequent punishments and thrashings that his body endured. Later, he used his acute abilities to ascend the ranks of the Roman legions, finally ending his short career as the trusted right hand of an emperor. He had the ability to imagine the outcomes of military strategy and suggest alternatives to avoid disabling failures. He had become an expert in geography and manipulating large numbers of men over insurmountable terrain. When he began hearing the voice of another within his head, he sometimes struggled to control his innate ability for organization and to separate right from wrong.

After smashing the lit end of the torch into the ground and smearing out the remaining embers in the damp, muddy silt that coated everything, he threw the extinguished torch aside and made his way back into his chamber at the end of the shaft. He just needed to wait for his partners and the end of the storm. While he waited, he chipped away at the sides of the opening in the floor with his ax, creating a hole through which even Gallus, the largest of them, could slip through.

As the minutes passed, he turned his attention to the passageway just beyond the mouth of his little room. A series of wood beams stood erect along both sides of the tunnel, each set holding a cross member that supported the low ceiling. With only scant light reaching him from the next torch along the passageway, he squinted at the support beams nearest him. For a moment he hesitated, concerned that if he proceeded to do what had occurred to him, he could become trapped by a wall of rock, permanently entombed within the mountain. Then, the concern subsided—he realized that he already was entombed.

In a flurry of activity, he began chipping away at the foot of one of the wooden pillars, flailing his ax as fast and as hard as he could. The soggy bottom of the beam splintered easily and by the time his counterparts returned to him, he was nearly through its girth. The two younger men looked puzzled, but Sorian reassured them that this was the correct course of action, preventing anyone from following them.

"Rest easy!" he declared. "This will hide our escape and motivate us to push forward." The two men nodded, accepting his challenge. "Now help me pull this beam free," Sorian directed.

With a few more chops, Sorian severed the last bit of wood from the base of the beam and it came down hard, pinning his ax to the floor. The top cross member fell with it, leaving a triangular gap between it and the stone ceiling. Cato pushed on the vertical beam while Gallus lifted the cross member out of position, carefully nudging it to the side. This caused the vertical beam on the opposite side of the tunnel to twist out of position. The weight of the cross member, some of the rock, and the lone supporting vertical beam collapsed with a loud rumble, freeing Sorian's ax and cluttering the narrow passageway. Chunks of stone the size of fists fell from the ceiling amidst a cloud of dust. Sorian smiled.

"When the water slows, place a few ax blows in the center of that ceiling. More rock will pile up and separate us from our captors, although I do not believe they will bother looking for us, as cave-ins are too common." Gallus nodded, but Sorian sensed the man's concern. "Do not be afraid. We will not be trapped," he said. "Trust me."

The three men sat and waited for the water to slow, staring down through the darkness at the hole near their feet. Only the sound of the moving water and the spray from its turbulence could illustrate to them the location of their escape. Sorian looked across the nearly black space at his two chained counterparts. He could barely make out their features. Each had very long dark hair and long shaggy beards. He knew he looked much the same, yet he felt more alive than he had in a long time. Cold, damp, bruised and scarred, Sorian took inventory of his feeble body, suspecting that the coming sprint to freedom might inflict an even greater toll. He tried to understand how long it had been raining and how long they had been waiting at the side of the hole, but time seemed meaningless in the darkness.

The rain fell for an eternity—or had it just been an hour? Sorian tried to estimate the length of time he had been slaving within Las Médulas. Two years? Three? It really didn't matter now, he concluded. His hatred of the men who incarcerated him here was just as strong as it ever was, like a broken arrowhead plunged into his body, festering deep within. He savored the moment to come, the retaliation he had planned for them each and every day since his arrival in prison. All he needed was a break in the storm and safe passage to Rome.

As the minutes turned to hours, the men waited, shivering in the darkness. Growing alarmed, Cato slid over toward Sorian. "What if night has come? Will we still be able to find our way, Sorian?" Sorian didn't stir. "Sorian!" Cato tapped Sorian's leg to get his attention.

Sorian startled at the intrusion into his fantasy. "There will still be light," he grumbled. "We need only dusk to make it to the trees. If the clouds pass over, the stars will light our way."

"Listen!" cried Gallus. The men stiffened and leaned over the opening, witnessing the gradual and steady decrescendo of the water's force below them.

"The end comes now!" announced Sorian, directing Gallus to the fallen timbers. Gallus and Cato slid back to the feeble barrier they had created hours earlier. Gallus gripped the ax handle tensely and took aim at the low ceiling. He took a slow practice swing, starting the ax head from between his ankles and guiding it up to a spot on the ceiling.

Cato patted his shoulder. "Hard—like you mean it," he encouraged. Gallus swung the ax with a grunt, slamming the blade home into the crack in the ceiling. Dust and gravel showered the two men, but nothing else of significance. They peered up at the rock again after clearing their eyes of dust. "Look! There!" Cato exclaimed. "That crack is new."

A long crack had formed nearly perpendicular to the one running where the cross member had been. Gallus took aim again, rocking the ax back and forth between his outstretched ankles. He took a deep breath and blew it out through his clenched teeth as he thrust the ax head upward. The ax hit home between the two cracks and again debris collapsed around them, but this time, it kept falling. The two men hustled backward along the wall as the ceiling began to crumble, chasing them as they shuffled.

The clatter of pebbles grew to a rumble of stones and the tunnel filled with dust, choking their breath. The men pawed their way in the darkness toward Sorian, who met them with outstretched arms, guiding them to the floor near the hole. The little room shook and echoed as the tunnel collapsed behind them. Fear gripped the men as they felt for the hole in the floor. Quickly the rumbling subsided but was instantly replaced by the high-pitched squeals of frantic rats running for their lives toward the men.

"Hurry!" shouted Sorian as he coughed and sputtered from the dust in his lungs. "Follow me into the hole."

Sorian slid into the hole, his feet just touching the bottom of the waterway as he hung from his elbows. The surface felt slippery, but the slope wasn't insurmountable. He dropped in and curled down against the side wall of the watery passage. Cato's head and torso were right behind him and then Gallus dangled his own feet over the ledge, letting the chain connecting them go slack. By now, the swarm of terrified rats were clawing and biting their way down the hole, using Gallus and Cato as a bridge into the passageway. The men swatted and writhed as the rats flooded through the hole over them. Choking for air, Gallus dropped in, landing on Cato in a heap. The rush of rats, some tangled in the mass of limbs and clothes, scratched and clawed their way free, disappearing into the passageway in one direction.

While the dust settled, the men surveyed their bodies. Aside from a few bleeding nips and scratches, each was all right. "Now where?" asked Gallus.

Sorian pointed down the slope of the passageway. "Follow the rats."

A scant bit of light illuminated the long, narrow channel. It could have been coming from either direction. Briefly, Sorian crawled up the slope. When he reached a bend in its course, he discovered that a few meters away, the channel looked like it turned straight up and down. He realized that would be a difficult climb with shackles and wet stone. He hoped they wouldn't find a similar drop in the other direction.

Turning the other way, Sorian guided the men down the slope after the rats. Together, the men slithered along on hands and knees, and sometimes bellies, in single file for nearly one hundred meters, until the walls of their river-carved channel became far enough apart for Gallus and Cato to limp along side by side. The going was slippery and at one point, Sorian slid on his back for several meters before colliding with a bend in the stone.

Slowly, painfully, they made their way along the course. Gradually the light within the channel became brighter, illuminating their way and speeding their descent. For a time, the intensity of the light caused them to blink painfully, but slowly the light began to fade. The men guessed that nightfall was approaching. With it came the sound of more water. Sorian felt panic growing within his chest, making him push forward at a faster pace. He guided them, always keeping three limbs in contact with the wet sides of the channel, to avoid slipping. Exhausted, he paused to take a breath and realized that the sound of water was in front of him. Gallus and Cato came from behind him and they listened together to the sound of the water.

In a final scramble down the last few meters, the men reached the mouth of the channel at the riparian of the river. They ducked their heads out of the opening to glance at freedom in the distance. Peering over boulders and the remains of past avalanches, Sorian studied the river's rapids, the writhing and twisting of its rapidly flowing water. Spray rained down on them. It felt cold, but blissfully clean and fresh. The three men let it saturate their clothing and hair, washing their faces and bodies almost frantically as they tried to remove years of stagnant filth deposited from their tomb.

Feeling remarkably invigorated by the fresh water and the smell of freedom, the men gathered the courage to attempt a river crossing. Scrutinizing the river bank along its course, each of the men tried to detect signs of someone on patrol along the river or above them on the mountain slope while they discussed the possible outcomes of crossing the river in this location. They were still reviewing plans to cross the river and link back up, if separated, when the sun set and the last glimmer of twilight signaled that their time had come.

Hand in hand, the men made their way into the torrent of rushing water, their feet feeling carefully for the bottom. They did not move until each had a solid foothold. The process became more difficult as the river became deeper. As they fought for every step, the water pushed hard against their legs and bodies. Angling across and down the river, they reached the midpoint of the span. Here the water was nearly head-high, and the river bottom was flat, without stones or boulders on which to hold. The current was much too strong and the river too deep.

Sorian was the first to give way to the will of the water. Letting the river carry him, he grasped his chain and held it tightly to his body so it wouldn't catch on some hidden obstruction in the river. Gallus and Cato clung tightly to one another as the power of the river spun them around and threw them forward. Gallus felt below the water for the chain that shackled him to Cato. He held it high above his head to take up the slack, pulling his foot and Cato's foot out of the water, nearly tipping them over. Just meters ahead of them, Sorian fought with the current, trying to claw and kick his way toward the far bank.

At a narrow neck in the river, the water's grip on them tightened, yanking the men down. Their bodies spun in somersaults within the twisting rapids before the water suddenly expelled them into a gently circling pool at a bend in the river. Choking and panting for air, the men kicked and thrashed toward the shore. It was within reach of their spent limbs. Sorian was the first to grab hold of a net of tree roots that reached out over the water. Here the river had chewed out the ground beneath a few towering spruce trees, exposing their roots as the bank eroded away. Squeezing the roots firmly, Sorian reached out and caught Gallus's outstretched hand. He, in turn, pulled Cato to shore. With a few remaining sparks of energy, the men crawled on their bellies up the bank, collapsing on a bed of dry needles on the forest floor.

"Where now?" questioned Cato, struggling to regain his breath. "We can't stay here tonight or we will freeze to death."

"We must put distance between us and the mountain," Sorian said, "and then make a fire." He paused to look up through a gap in the trees at the darkening sky above them. "Come," he commanded. "Let us go this way."

Sorian got to his feet and stumbled before regaining his balance. Cato and Gallus helped each other up and then stabilized their leader. Slowly, they picked their way through the underbrush in the dark following the river to a clearing. For the first time in countless months, Sorian could see stars. After exalting in his freedom, he shook his head and reset their course to the east.

Marching into the night with chains rattling, the men plodded away from Las Médulas. Gradually, the evergreens gave way to oaks and groves of other deciduous trees while the undergrowth became less dense. Able to move through this terrain more quickly, the men made enough progress that eventually Sorian stopped them. "Let us bed down here tonight. Gather what you can to make a fire, enough to last all night. I will find some branches to make a small shelter and something to hang our clothes on so they can dry," said Sorian. "Hurry! Now that we are not moving, we will get cold very quickly."

Naked but finally dry, Sorian crouched into the tiny structure he created out of branches and twigs. Gallus and Cato had done the same. They stared at the snapping and crackling flames and watched the steam billow up from the wet tunics hanging from a tall pyramid of long oak sticks that straddled the flames. Gallus drifted off to sleep at Cato's side. Cato was still trembling from the cold. Sorian also shook with bone-rattling chills, but they were getting fewer and less intense as heat from the fire probed into the little shelter.

The men had started the fire just in time; a few minutes more might have marked the end of the shortest escape from the Cantabrian Mountains ever attempted. Racked with cold, their weakened bodies felt increasingly feeble and helpless. Not even the exhilaration of freedom could have warmed them enough to withstand the cold of night.

Sorian stared at the flames and slid his body closer to the wall of the shelter. As much as he had hated the prison, the walls of his tiny tunnel had created a source of protection for him, secluding him from the hideous companions imprisoned with him. It had been a place to hide from the guards as well as the other prisoners who, at times, could be just as cruel. Feeling the wall of the stick-made shelter against his back eased his mind and calmed his nerves.

Tired but unable to sleep, Sorian let his mind wander between dreams and reality, as it so often did within the prison. As he stared into the fire, he focused on a glowing ember that seemed to wiggle and dance in the orange glow. It was about the size of a sword's pommel. He gazed at its shape and imagined a man's face staring back at him. The man's name was Lucius. Standing to the side and just a pace behind was Lucius's vile friend, Tacitus.

General Lucius, the man under whom Sorian had served for so many years, and Tacitus, the gutless emperor who unraveled everything his predecessor had achieved, stood before him now. For years, under the order of his friend and leader, Emperor Tibirius, Sorian had observed and reported on Lucius's every move. He grew to hate the man who so stubbornly defied his emperor's calls to action. Lucius had stood down when he was to attack the Gauls in the Dolomites. He had moved south when he should have been confronting them again in the north. Lucius defied his brother and emperor's orders, and Sorian loathed him for it.

For the promise of advancement in Rome, Sorian dutifully spied on General Lucius for Tibirius. However, without a triumph down the Via Sacra in Rome under a victorious General Lucius, Sorian was unable to climb those political steps any higher. In time, he arranged for the death of Lucius's only daughter. He loved the way it made him feel to carry out the bidding of his emperor, hand-picking the Roman soldiers he sent to kill her. Imagining the way those men would attack and slaughter the general's daughter and her lover made his remaining time in Lucius's service tolerable. He could look upon the general's face and know that he, Sorian, had been the one to cut out Lucius's heart.

After Tibirius's death, Sorian believed the murders remained his secret, but then the wind changed. One day, soldiers brought him back to Rome, where he was accused and sentenced by Lucius, now a senator, and his friend, Emperor Tacitus. Death would have been simpler, but they sentenced Sorian to grind away the remaining years of his life in the Las Médulas prison.

Now he was free. He would have those men groveling at his feet. Staring intently at the fire, Sorian tormented them in his mind. He attacked Tacitus and then Lucius, each in turn, cutting apart their bodies, finger by finger and limb by limb, as each man struggled beneath his blade. Enthralled by the picture of torture, Sorian was startled to awareness by the faraway howl of a lone wolf. The piercing cry hung in the air before it died down, replaced by the rustle of the wind in the trees. Sorian thought about the wolf, the hunter, and his plans for retribution evolved. He glanced over at his two unsuspecting and dependent partners, both naked and out of place in the world. At first, he felt sickened by their battered forms and lack of military training. When he stood up to throw more wood on the fire, that old sinister grin of his returned.

# Chapter VIII

———

**B**OUND, THIRSTY, AND miserable within the confines of the small cart, Carpathimos rolled into Carthage, now and then managing to sneak a glance at his surroundings when the cart wobbled to a halt. The long journey from Sabratha in a small wooden cart, lined only with a thin layer of straw, did little to ease his mind about the trials in store for him. Unable to stretch his long legs out the back of the cart, Carpathimos shifted his weight back and forth from one buttock to the other, trying to restore sensation to his feet. Quickly, the prickles of thousands of sharp imaginary pins spread down along the backs of his legs and wrapped around his feet. The act of moving his toes was practically unbearable. Gradually, the sensation subsided, as if the small pins had themselves escaped from captivity and somehow disappeared into the air without a trace. Furious at his capture, he rubbed his forehead at the spot where he had been hit by Kanmi's men, feeling the firm lump that rose out of the bone above his eyebrow.

He had no idea how much time passed before the cart stopped and five men arrived to fetch him. Four of them held him down while the other unlocked the end of his chain from the front of the cart. He collapsed on the ground, his legs temporarily useless. One of the soldiers grabbed the end of his chain and started up a curving stone path, pulling on it to make him rise on shaky knees and follow, like a trained bear. The others surrounded him, restricting his movement by spear point as he followed the leader up the long stairway.

The stone path was wide. Every few meters, it rose in elevation, following the contour of the hill towards the summit. The right side of the stairway clung to an alabaster wall that Carpathimos presumed was the outer wall of the military citadel that overlooked the city. After marching for nearly one hundred meters, the group approached an entry of sorts, on the opposite side of the walled structure from where the stairway had first started. Here, the path of flat, smooth stones levelled off and made a turn through the open gate, which was several meters wide.

Stepping through the gate, Carpathimos noted that he was within an area that was more secluded and private than a citadel would be. This looked like someone's home in Rome, but it was much more sprawling and had a much higher outer wall. High atop the hill, it overlooked the city and the other buildings surrounding it. Presently, Carpathimos was not able to look back to see any of that panorama, but the dwellings in front of him captured his interest.

Like the walkway under his feet, the buildings were masterfully constructed, the stone uniformly shaped and stacked. One large structure stood in the center, with two smaller, equal-sized buildings flanking it closely on either side. The center building was surrounded by a row of large columns. That was where Kanmi's men were leading Carpathimos. Glancing to the side between the columns, Carpathimos surveyed the open spaces of the compound. They were rich and colorful, lavishly filled with flowering plants, shrubs and trees. Birdsong filled the air. So did the sweet perfume of the brilliant red and orange flowers that dotted the landscape. The setting contrasted fiercely with the chain that linked his wrists together.

Interrupting the serenity of this place, Carpathimos grew curious about the random grunts and pounding noises made by creatures that Carpathimos had not seen before. One of these small furry creatures threw a smashed red fruit toward their entourage, hitting one of Kanmi's men in the back of the neck. Carpathimos looked up to find another of these man-shaped creatures smiling at him, then hissing before it swung gracefully out of sight through the high branches of a stately acacia tree.

Walking into the center structure, Carpathimos was handed over to several large men who escorted him down a flight of stairs into a dark corner of a long underground room. Unlike the scene above ground, this room was dank, musty smelling, and cool. At knifepoint, they shackled him to the back wall and then retreated from the room, leaving him alone. As his eyes adjusted to the darkness, objects within the room began to take shape, each item contrasting from the others by its texture and form. He saw crates of fruit and large round containers with lids. The stone floor around these containers was wet, which explained the dampness in the air. The odor of fermenting juice was so sweet it sickened him.

Allowing his muscles to relax, he leaned back against the wall which felt cold against his sun-darkened skin. He rolled his head against it and let the coolness soothe the lumps and bruises he had acquired from the wooden cart and Kanmi's men. Inexorably, exhaustion came upon him. He surrendered to it, allowing himself to slide slowly to the floor until he was seated, his legs stretched out in front of him and his hands clasped together by the side of his face, held there by the wrist shackles. Straining his ears, he could hear a songbird outside the room. The rhythmic repeating message soothed his mind. He drifted off to sleep.

Leaning over a short section of the wall, the landowner cast his gaze over the harbor below. He had been standing at the north end of the property when Kanmi approached him through the garden. Moving quickly, Kanmi called out to announce himself.

Hanno turned and smiled, "Kanmi! Welcome! I trust you bring good news or you wouldn't have come all this way."

Kanmi smiled broadly as he approached, stopping just a meter away from Hanno so he, too, could gaze over the wall at the many ships in the harbor. "I think you will be very pleased with your harvests this year. The farmers have taken care to ensure that all the bounty will reach Carthage in the best condition. The grains are plentiful, and the animals and fruits are growing nicely as well." Removing a thick roll of parchment from a sack he wore on his shoulder, he added, "I will leave the values in your room for your review, but they are much better than the last, I assure you."

The landowner studied Kanmi carefully, inspecting his eyes and posture before chancing a grin. He turned and motioned for Kanmi to follow him as he began to probe the outer boundary of one of his flower gardens. "Personally," he said as they ambled along, "I would give Sicily to the Romans and forego such bloodshed. We control much of Iberia as well as most of this southern shore. Actually," he continued, stopping to pinch off the dead heads of a few waist-high flowers, "I own land in both places and believe we can support our way of life without sacrificing so many over Sicily. Truthfully, there are still places within our reach that would cost far less to maintain. But the *One Hundred* have decided to fight for Sicily, and so, fight we must."

Kanmi stepped carefully between the tender plants, trying not to crush them with his large feet as he followed Hanno a pace behind. "Have you received word from the inspectors in your other territories about the farms they manage?"

The landowner paused to listen to the question and then started walking again. "I remain confident that the quantity and quality of the harvests from all of the territories will be better this year. I made it quite clear last year that they would be," reminded the landowner wryly. "If your numbers come out satisfactorily, as you claim, Kanmi, then I can only assume that you have met my challenge, pushing the farmers to achieve their goals. And, if you met the goal I placed on you, then you will be rewarded, as I promised."

Again, Hanno stopped walking and turned to face Kanmi with a quizzical look. "It was the daughter of the farmer in Sabratha you wanted, correct?"

Kanmi flushed, surprised that the elder man knew what had been shared between the young inspectors working for him. Kanmi cleared his throat and answered in the affirmative.

"Rest easy, Kanmi," Hanno said. "I have every intention of rewarding my men when they achieve. I treat success as aggressively as I treat failure—as you know." Kanmi nodded, not so subtly reminded of his place within the order of things. "Now, I believe you have something else to tell me before you go, Kanmi, since I saw your men leading a man in chains into my home."

Kanmi took a deep breath then smiled nervously, hoping that his offering would bring good fortune. Providing every detail, and embellishing the story where he felt comfortable, Kanmi explained to the landowner what he had learned about his captive from Jabnit Gisgon, the farmer who had found the man named Carpathimos hiding on the property. He understood that the man came ashore in a storm with his boat, the very boat that Kanmi had seen abandoned on the beach. The stranger was later found trying to make repairs by stealing tools from Jabnit's outbuildings.

While Kanmi delivered his rehearsed tale, his captive lay chained in Hanno's home, unaware of the metamorphosis his life would soon experience.

Carpathimos's slumber had been fitful. He awoke with a start when something wet and soft splattered against the wall near his left ear. He opened his tired eyes and found three pairs of young eyes staring back at him from across the long room. Two children giggled, while the smallest of the three poked at one of the others with his finger, seemingly trying to prompt another round of attacks with half-eaten plums. The largest of the three cuffed the other two on the back of their heads and then proceeded to uncover one of the large containers near the wall.

The largest boy must have been about eight years old, the other two perhaps four or five, Carpathimos estimated. The older boy took a small loaf of bread and broke it in half, dunking each of the exposed middle ends into the container. Letting the pieces soak up the liquid, he stared at Carpathimos momentarily. Then, as he pulled them out, each piece dripped vigorously, sending streams of the dark liquid running down his wrists. He sampled one of the halves then handed it to his small partners, who divided it carefully between them, squeezing out some of the liquid onto the floor. Cautiously, the older boy moved closer to Carpathimos by sliding his feet across the cold stone floor. He stopped short of Carpathimos's feet, signaling that he was about to toss the bread toward the man. Carpathimos cupped his hands together and the boy tossed the bread to him, hitting the mark before scampering from the room with the two smaller boys racing to catch up.

The bread was still warm and smelled wonderfully rich and inviting. Nearly half of it was drenched in the liquid from the container. It smelled fruity and a bit like the sweet aroma of a spoiling pile of wet grain. He put it to his lips and inhaled, sniffing the fruit-filled morsel with a long, slow draw of air. At first, the air he smelled was soft and pleasant then it suddenly burned his throat making him cough unexpectedly. He smiled briefly, guessing the children probably made regular visits for this treat. Then he took a bite, savoring the best warm meal he had had in days.

He must have fallen back asleep, for he was jolted awake, this time by the sounds of his captors approaching through the darkness. One lit a torch and slid the handle into a small metal ring in the wall. The brightness of the flame made Carpathimos shield his eyes with his chained hands while he swung his legs beneath him and rose to his feet.

Three men surrounded him in a tight circle while a fourth extended a long spear toward his chest, its tip touching the skin beneath his left nipple. The guards, all with shiny dark skin and dressed in plain tan robes, gestured to him using their hands in an up and down sweeping motion. They repeated the motion over and over until he understood. To Carpathimos, it looked as if they were trying to tell him to sit back down and extend his hands in the air. He eventually complied. As he sat, he studied the men closely. They each wore polished gold wrist bands and they all had bare feet. Each man wore his hair closely cropped and colored with a dust or powder, which made it look nearly white against their skin.

While he stared at the men, one of them tapped Carpathimos on the arm and repeated the gesture of lifting his hands in the air while sliding in closer to his left side. The man reached for the chain and pulled up on it gently, pushing a few of the slackened links back through a hole in the wall from which the chain extended. He then backed away, but kept a hand on the chain, holding Carpathimos's hands in place.

Carpathimos could hear someone behind the wall. He felt the chain moving slightly before he heard, or felt, a large thump on the ground behind the wall. Immediately, the man to his left pulled the chain through the hole, freeing it completely. The three men then beckoned Carpathimos to stand and follow them. The fourth, holding the spear, stepped aside as his partners led Carpathimos out of his cell.

Night had come and gone, replaced by a dawn filled with the power of the rising sun. Carpathimos squinted in the bright light as he followed his captors up the steps and around the face of the main building, skirting between it and one of the smaller structures. Once again, the smell of blooming flowers and the antics of the playful tree-swingers captured his attention. Rounding the back corner of the main house, he was stunned to see a huge striped cat lying in the grass just meters from the path ahead of him. Carpathimos observed its long body and massive paws. The cat seemed to follow him with its deep green eyes, flipping the end of its tail in the grass impatiently as the men walked by. It paused to lick its thick, orange fur and then yawned, exposing a set of yellowish-white teeth. Carpathimos had once seen lions in Rome and had heard stories of these similar beasts as well, but he never imagined them being this large.

Descending a second set of steps, the landscaped gardens spread out in front of him like one of the fields on the Gisgon farm. This field, however, was crisscrossed with stone paths and dotted with fruit and nut trees. It lay completely within the confines of the wall that encircled the property.

Bisecting this field of luscious foliage, another stone path stretched the width of the property. The men turned onto this path and followed it to its conclusion at the wall. Arranged smartly along each side of the path stood old-growth acacia trees, which stretched their long, yellow-flowering branches over the path, shielding the men from the intense summer sun. Approaching the wall, Carpathimos saw the waters of the Mediterranean glistening under the light of day. Peering over the wall, which was lower here than anywhere else on the property, he saw the great city of Carthage and its famous harbor extending before his eyes into the sea.

Sitting on a low bench with his back to the wall, Hanno quietly observed the warrior in his possession. After studying the city, Carpathimos looked at the man, perhaps in his fifth or sixth decade of life, who sat with his arm around one of the children who had visited Carpathimos inside his fruit-filled cell. The two men stared quietly at one another until Hanno tapped the child's shoulder, prompting the boy to scurry away into the garden.

Carpathimos watched the boy dart away until he disappeared amid the various bushes and flowering plants. Then Hanno stood and spoke to Carpathimos in the Roman tongue, introducing himself to the warrior before shifting quickly to Greek, to match his first question. "Perhaps you would prefer we speak in Greek, Carpathimos?"

Carpathimos refused to answer. Unwilling to join the conversation as a slave, he lifted his hands to draw attention to the chain. Hanno gestured to the men guarding Carpathimos to free him, but they didn't move. He repeated his gesture with a look of disgust and they immediately responded, unbinding Carpathimos's wrists and freeing him from the chain.

Carpathimos glanced at the men as they cautiously stepped back out of reach. He rubbed his wrists and flexed and extended the fingers of each hand repeatedly while staring at Hanno. Hanno spoke again while he walked over to the wall, turning his back to Carpathimos, indicating, perhaps, that he did not fear the warrior behind him. Instinctively, Carpathimos followed him, head tipped and turned slightly to hear what Hanno was saying over the whoosh of the gentle but steady breeze coming over the wall.

"The great sea is restless today," Hanno said. "It has seemed unsettled for years, but worse these last few months as the war rages on Sicily." He laid his hands on the top of the low wall in front of him, bending forward to put some of the weight of his upper body upon outstretched arms. "The Romans have been marching west, trampling all in their path. They now encircle the walled city of Akragas, along the southwest coast of Sicily. For nearly five months they have laid siege to the city. No one goes in and no one comes out. We must stop them before they reach Drepanum and encircle the island."

Carpathimos joined Hanno at the wall and looked down once again at the harbor. He strained his gaze to the east, in the direction of Sicily.

Hanno watched him, adding, "Fortunately the battles rage far from us here in Carthage. You cannot see Sicily from here, and even if you could, it would lie there," Hanno pointed. "Behind the cape."

Carpathimos studied the large land mass jutting out into the sea east of the city. As far as he could see, heavy waves pounded the rocky shoreline, throwing up a mist that obscured the tree line along the cape.

Hanno continued, "You are a long way from Rome, gladiator." He sat down on the stone bench on which he sat earlier and stretched an arm out along the wall. He looked up to observe Carpathimos standing expression-less, still staring at the sea. "You and I have something in common I believe. Both of us want to see to Rome's destruction."

Surprised, Carpathimos glanced quickly at the older man then back to the sea. Hanno continued, "Much of Sicily has been under our control for many generations. The crops we grow there feed much of our population, including our navy and the armies we control. Now the Romans wish to rob Sicily from us. They are an emboldened and pompous lot, sparing nothing in their path."

Hanno's face tightened. "It is hard to see such savagery. Once we held a treaty with Rome, when Pyrrhus, the King of Epirus, claimed much of Sicily's northern shore for himself. The Romans needed our help to defend against him. Now that Pyrrhus has gone and Rome has grown, she attacks the hands that nurtured and protected her when she was small."

Carpathimos sat down on a nearby bench with a sigh, slumping down like a bag of grain as if he could no longer support the weight above him. He ran his fingers through his thick and curly dark hair, which reached his shoulders. Leaning forward and resting his elbows on his knees, he spoke at last, about Akragas. "The Romans will starve them out, then massacre the weak, young and old, and enslave the remainder."

Hanno nodded. "You are correct. Fifty thousand starve within those walls right now. The Romans did the very same across the eastern half of the island, first in Messina then Catana, Carmarina and Gela. Only the Syracusians were spared when their King Hiero traded honor for a place at the Roman's table. Now he supports Rome, providing them safe passage to resupply their army."

"It is done, then," Carpathimos said.

"No," Hanno growled. "It has been decided that we must make a stand at Akragas and, if not there, then at Drepanum. The Romans must not be allowed on the western half of the island." Hanno stood and faced Carpathimos. "As we speak, the son of General Hannibal marches at the head of a mercenary army to reinforce Akragas. Some fifty thousand Celts, Numidians, and Iberians, along with several thousand cavalry and sixty elephants, march together along the coast from Drepanum to relieve the people of Akragas from their siege. That, my young friend, is where you come in."

Carpathimos's eyes grew large as he looked up at the older man. He had sensed that Hanno must have some task in mind for him or he wouldn't have been sharing all of this information. Reflexively, Carpathimos stood to face him.

Hanno gripped Carpathimos's upper arm. "You and I share a common dislike for the Romans. Perhaps, even hatred. I need someone I can trust to provide me with information. Someone with the talents and strength sufficient for the task."

"What is this task?" Carpathimos towered over the older man.

"The more information we have of Rome's intentions, the better we can defend ourselves." Hanno pounded one fist into the other. "Akragas may be lost already, but if you can use your knowledge of Rome's military to gain access to her plans, then we may be able to thwart the next siege or even be in position to initiate an offensive of our own. You must find a weakness, Carpathimos."

Carpathimos spoke scornfully. "I will not be able to simply walk up and ask them their plans! There is no safe way to infiltrate a Roman legion."

"With your thick beard and long mane, you will blend in as a common migrant. You are a skilled and cunning warrior. I am confident that you will be able to find your way in and back out again." Hanno reverted to his more relaxed, confident tone. "I must remind you, Carpathimos, I never said this was going to be *safe*. I want to know where else they plan to attack and when. Where are they weak? Where can we trap them? If you do this for me, I will consider your commitment to us complete and you will be a free man once again."

Carpathimos avoided his eyes and paced back and forth along the wall. Hanno watched him closely, trying to decide how much leverage he needed to add in order to coerce the warrior to agree. "As you will see, Sicily's terrain is hilly and steep, and the cities are heavily fortified with high, thick walls. So far, we have been able to dictate much of the pace of battle, and the Romans sustain heavy losses with each long siege. Nevertheless, they march on and we continue to lose ground."

Carpathimos looked suspiciously at Hanno. "I will serve no man ever again," he stated defiantly. "How would you hope to keep me under your whip?"

Hanno smiled, knowing now what leverage he needed to influence Carpathimos to come to his side. "You are no slave. Our relationship can be one of mutual satisfaction. I know that you ultimately desire to return to Rome and why. I also believe that you will help me in exchange for safe passage back to Rome. After all, we share a similar goal, do we not?"

Carpathimos stopped pacing, contemplating Hanno's words. Hanno took several steps away from Carpathimos, then sighed before continuing, "However, if a whip is what you respond to, then I can provide that as well, for even a soldier's horse needs to feel the rider's foot at her side some of the time."

Standing now between his men, Hanno stared into Carpathimos's eyes and said softly, "Her name is Yzebel Gisgon, is it not? The daughter of a common farmer."

Carpathimos lurched toward Hanno. The abrupt movement was threatening enough. Within an instant, Carpathimos was surrounded by Hanno's guards, razor-edged spears pointing at him as they glistened in the sunlight. Hanno laughed, "Do not despair for the girl. She will be all right, I assure you. I think, though, you understand the agreement we have reached."

Carpathimos glared at the man for long moments before he asked, "How do I send word to you?"

"Let me explain," Hanno began. "North of Drepanum stands the Temple of Eryx. Go there to worship the Goddess Astarte. The high priest will hear you and relay your message to me. You must introduce yourself to him as *the gladiator who brings information for Hanno and the Council of Elders*. I will ensure that a small boat will be hidden on the beach below the temple, at the foot of the limestone cliff. It is yours to do with as you must." Hanno smiled. "Now, Carpathimos, you must enjoy yourself in my small oasis. Today you are my guest here. As you can see, I enjoy surrounding myself with marvels from the far reaches of our known world. Tomorrow, you leave on a ship bound for Sicily."

# PART II

# Chapter IX

———

TIRED, DIRTY, AND more than a little perturbed, Elijah arrived in the port city of Carthage to an absence of fanfare. This was not the destination intended when he boarded the merchant ship at Alexandria—or at least not the destination promised him at the time. He had been upset when he learned that he had been lied to, but he vowed to make the most of the situation and simply find a more trustworthy ship captain, one who would actually take him where he promised and not force him to labor against his will. In reality, he had every intention of lending a hand and working in exchange for his transport on board the ship, but when he learned that Carthage was the destination and not Greece, he was far less motivated to serve at the will of the captain.

Glad to be leaving this crew behind, Elijah stepped from the merchant ship and carefully made his way up the pier toward the city, which sat high on a hill overlooking the harbor. Its pale-colored buildings glistened in the morning sunlight. Weaving around crates of poultry and small herds of livestock being unloaded from another ship moored along the pier, he scanned the docks looking for someone who could inform him about any ships departing for Greece, Anatolia, or anywhere close to his final destination.

He was disgusted about the time he had wasted on a ship taking him in the wrong direction, but Elijah tried to shake the feelings and focus on the task at hand. Finally, he found a dockhand who could direct him to the man in charge. Without looking away from what he was doing, the busy dockhand grunted and pointed to a large building standing at the junction between the harbor and the city rising up the hillside behind it.

Elijah entered the building and found it bustling with activity. Just a few paces ahead of him, a number of men were apparently trading supplies and bickering over the prices of goods. Behind them, several more were stacking large bags of grain and crates of fruits and vegetables. Along one wall stood rows of small pens where a variety of animals were kept. Elijah was struck by the loud atmosphere, complete with the bleating of goats, mooing of cattle, and the yelling of laborers and merchants. The dust in the air was almost as thick as the noise.

Elijah sneezed and stepped back into the open doorway to find relief. He watched several boys, certainly younger than himself, pull and push carts overloaded with goods to and from the docks. Everything was either coming to or leaving from this building, to be loaded onto a ship or having just been unloaded off a ship.

Mesmerized, watching the boys persevere with their heavy burdens, Elijah stood off to the side of the building, trying to stay out of their way. Elijah studied the layout, estimating the opening in the front of the building to be at least four or five meters wide and roughly three meters tall. Then, a man striding through the doorway nearly plowed right through him.

Stumbling off balance, Elijah stepped behind a large barrel to avoid getting knocked down. He was back in the noise and dust, but at least here he would be out of the way. He tried to eavesdrop on the conversations taking place near him. He noted a statuesque man of perhaps six decades arguing with two men about a pile of bags that stretched nearly to the roof of the large building. Judging by the debris on the floor, the bags must have been filled with grain or something of small proportion. Putting an abrupt end to their argument, a cow charged into the building, kicking its hind legs off the ground and angrily throwing its head from side to side.

The young boys chased it through the building, trying to corner it and snare the rope that hung around its neck and dragged in the dirt between its legs. The animal swung its large head back and forth, no doubt trying to intimidate them. The tall man marched over to the boys, cuffing one behind the head and shoving another to the ground before lunging at the cow. He grabbed the rope and secured the animal to a timber in the wall before the cow realized it had been captured. Returning to the men with whom he had been speaking, the rescuer merely smiled and resumed their conversation. It seemed that they agreed on whatever it was that they had been arguing about, for soon afterwards, the two men walked off toward the docks. The tall man looked down at the ledger he was carrying and began making notes on it.

Sensing an opportunity, Elijah stepped out from behind the barrel and walked timidly to the tall man's side. He tried to swallow the heart pounding in his throat, but his mouth seemed too dry to accomplish it. When he remembered what he had endured on the ship from Alexandria, he felt more confident. He straightened up and announced himself. The man holding the ledger did not look up from what he was doing. In fact, he showed no signs of having heard Elijah speak, although Elijah was sure he had spoken loudly enough. Perhaps he wasn't familiar with Greek?

Elijah considered trying to communicate in another language but decided to repeat himself more loudly. "Good day! My name is Elijah and I seek passage to Greece on one of these ships. Can you help me?"

Elijah stared at the tall man studying his complicated ledger as he waited a response. The warehouse official had a commanding presence, tall and sporting a moderately protuberant abdomen. His arms were large and muscular and covered in a thick crop of dark hair, which seemed to rise over his knuckles and run contiguously all the way up over his shoulders before disappearing beneath the roll of cloak that clung just over the top of his rounded deltoid. His head seemed small for his height and his ears were set too far forward. His nose was large and bulbous, his lips thick and wide. Elijah decided that the tall man's facial features had been created too large for the space provided.

Irritated, the warehouse keeper looked up from his ledger and scowled at Elijah, furrowing his thick black eyebrows. "I am not deaf, boy," he growled before turning his back to Elijah and marching away, vanishing behind the large stack of grain in the center of the building. Elijah chased after him, around the bags of grain, and found him counting the goats in a pen nearby.

"Excuse me, sir. I would like to board one of these ships. Can you tell me which one is going to Greece?"

The man continued counting until he was done, made a mark in the ledger, and then moved on to another pen, ignoring Elijah. Elijah persisted until the man stopped his count and spun around to address him.

"Enough!" he shouted. "There is no room on any of these ships! Can you not see how we fill them? All day long the sailors come to protest to me about how full we load their ships yet fill them we must. Not one has room even for a scrawny boy like you. Besides, none of these ships are traveling anywhere today."

"Then I should come back tomorrow?" Elijah persevered.

The big man rolled his eyes and put a hand to his forehead, rubbing as if it hurt him. "Do not come back here, boy!" he shouted. "When these ships are full, they will leave together for Sicily and Sardinia, guarded by the birds of prey."

Pulling Elijah toward the opening so he could see the expansive harbor, the man pointed at three Carthaginian warships anchored just beyond the outer rim. "You don't want to go where they are going," he advised sternly.

"But surely a merchant ship will leave for Greece soon," insisted Elijah. "I know that this city trades with everyone on the great sea."

"That is true," the man said, seemly impressed by Elijah's knowledge of the trading prowess of Carthage, "but there will be no ships leaving for Athens, Sparta, Byzantion or even Alexandria for many days. Right now, the priority is to take the fight to the Romans."

Elijah looked down at the dirt and sighed. How difficult this journey was becoming. He realized that he should have stayed in Alexandria and waited for a ship that he knew for certain was destined for the north. He might even have gone with a caravan along the eastern shore. He watched the tall man walk away and continue his counting and directions for the boys who worked for him. Elijah sat down on a crate and allowed the sack slung over his shoulder to slide off onto the ground. He put his elbows on his knees and rested his face in his hands, gently rubbing dust from his tired eyes with the delicate ends of his thin fingers.

As he sat, he let the din of the world around him melt away. He prayed softly and thought about his family and his grandfather. This strengthened him. He always felt better when he focused his mind on the most important things in life. Suddenly, his focus was broken by a loud crash and shouts coming from the docks.

A knot of boys standing within the doorway of the warehouse ran down toward the ships. The warehouse official threw down his ledger and followed closely behind, his large body moving more quickly than one would expect. Elijah stood, pulling the sack over his shoulder and stepped to the doorway to investigate.

Looking down the docks toward the second pier, a small crowd was gathering near one of the nearby ships tied off at that location. From Elijah's position, he could see men in the middle of the crowd frantically moving supplies off what was now an overturned pile. These goods were intended to be loaded onto the ship and had been stacked along the side of the pier so people could move past. Elijah watched as three of the young boys ran up to the warehouse to fetch a wheeled cart. Elijah inquired of the youngest of the three what had happened.

"The ship's crew was busy securing some of the animals on the ship, so they fell behind as our men brought more supplies to the pier to be loaded. We stacked the supplies next to the ship so that the crew could finish loading as soon as they were able. The pile shifted and fell, pinning one of the sailors underneath," explained the boy quickly. Elijah nodded. "It was not our fault," said the boy. "Not our fault."

Elijah watched the boys guide the cart down the docks and out onto the pier, disappearing into the crowd when they arrived. Moments later, men pulled the cart back up the pier with the wounded sailor inside. The warehouse official walked behind them, speaking to a member of the ship's crew. Elijah suspected it was the ship's captain. As the cart wheeled by, Elijah could see that the sailor was just a young man, no older than himself. The young man lay motionless, with a trickle of bright red blood staining the side of his cheek and neck and pooling under his head and shoulders. He was not breathing. The young man was dead.

The ship's captain was also rather youthful, but he carried himself with all the strength and pride of someone with more years of experience. Despite his rank, however, his face was stricken and sad and he never took his eyes off the dead sailor. Elijah sidled a bit closer to listen to his conversation with the official.

"I promised his mother—my mother—that I would watch out for him. He was my youngest brother. What will I tell her now?" the captain lamented. "He had only been on two other voyages with me before today. He should have kept belowdecks taking count instead of trying to help load the ship."

"But he was eager to help you, so you could get underway," said the tall man, putting his hand on the captain's shoulder. "Well, perhaps you can wait until you return from the island and then tell your mother that he died fighting the Romans."

The captain broke his gaze and looked at the tall man. He appeared to contemplate the suggestion before shaking his head. "No, I must go tell her now. She lives not far from here and she must know. I must tell her. Please keep him on this cart and have someone clean him. After I tell her, I will wheel his body to a quiet place so she can see him." Turning to some of his men who had gathered around, he ordered, "Finish loading the ship. We must not fall behind the others and our escorts."

Elijah had already started cleaning the blood from the young man's face and neck, collecting straw from the numerous piles in the warehouse. He spread straw under the man's body, to hide the blood, and so doing, made the young man look as if he was resting on a bed of straw. As he worked, Elijah continued to listen to the warehouse official and the captain as they walked away conversing.

"I mean no disrespect," said the tall man, "but where will you find a man to fill his place on the crew when you leave so early tomorrow morning?"

The captain shrugged his shoulders and turned around to look back at his younger brother's body, watching Elijah brush the hair out of his brother's blank eyes. "I probably won't find anyone until we return from Sicily, but I would be very grateful if you find someone suitable before our return. We are scheduled to carry bronze to the east, are we not?"

"Yes, you may be correct," responded the man, looking down at his ledger. "That shipment has been delayed because of these supplies needed for Sicily." He gestured to the boats. "We will have the bronze and the other supplies ready to load upon your return."

The captain nodded. "I thought so. I was scheduled to carry those goods to Thrace before I was redirected to Sicily."

"What qualities do you require in the new man? In case I can find you one."

"Well," thought the captain aloud. "You won't be able to replace my brother. I just need someone to handle small tasks for me: to keep the ship clean and the sailors fed and—"

"I will go!" announced Elijah, feeling a frisson of excitement well up within his thin body. "I can do those things for you," he said confidently, catching the captain's eyes.

"Have you sailed before?" the captain asked kindly, while the warehouse keeper stood beside him with his mouth open in surprise.

Elijah hesitated, then he did what he knew he must. "No. Not really," he answered honestly. "I fished in a boat with my father once, when we visited his family on the coast, but I came here from Alexandria on a merchant ship. I did much hard work for that crew."

The tall man scoffed at the suggestion. "Who is this strange boy? A sailor he is not!"

Perhaps grateful for Elijah's kindness shown his brother, the captain walked closer and stared at Elijah. "What is your name and why do you want to risk your life sailing for Carthage? You must be running to or away from something."

"My name is Elijah. If I show you that I can do what you ask of me, can I earn passage with you to the east?"

The captain looked back at the warehouse official, who looked dubious about Elijah's proposal. He made up his mind. "Keep looking for someone with experience, but I will give him a chance," he told the official. "If he proves himself on our voyage to Sicily, then I may have found the person I need for the next voyage."

The tall man laughed and shook his head in disbelief. Then he turned and walked away, leaving the captain and Elijah alone together.

"I must go now to tell my mother of this tragedy. We leave here tomorrow morning just after sunrise. If you are late, I leave without you," warned the captain.

Elijah nodded and watched as the man pushed the cart carrying his brother out into the street. After they disappeared into the crowd, he went to inspect the ship. He wasn't sure what he had just gotten himself into, but he hoped the rest of his crew would be as kind as their captain.

In the evening, Elijah returned to the warehouse and found himself a pile of straw on which to rest. He nestled down next to a small pen of goats huddled beside one another on their own pile of straw. Nervous energy kept him awake, so he pulled the tightly bound roll of papyri from his leather sack and unwound it so he could read.

He selected one of his favorite passages and read aloud softly. When the remaining light faded away to nothing, Elijah settled back onto the straw and placed the roll in the sack. He closed his eyes and thought about his travels. He thought about his grandfather and the great city of Alexandria, with all its monuments and great structures. He wondered what Sicily looked like, but realized that he wouldn't see much of it from the port they would enter. Not until the wee hours of the morning did he finally fall asleep.

Hours later, Elijah woke to the sounds of snickering from the young boys who worked on the docks. When he opened his eyes, he saw them standing over him with broad smiles upon their faces. They scattered when the great booming voice of the warehouse official echoed within the building. Elijah listened to the man shout a list of orders to the children, signaling the start of another noisy day. Suddenly, Elijah realized it was morning. He sprang to his feet and leaped from the pile of straw. Running from the building while trying to sling his sack over his shoulder, he waved to the man as he flew by.

"You better hurry, boy!" the official yelled. "The captain already passed through here looking for you!"

Down on the pier, Carpathimos stood between several Carthaginian soldiers waiting to board a ship. He wasn't happy about his situation, nor about the idea of joining a Roman legion. Nevertheless, it might provide the means for getting to Rome, and he certainly didn't want harm to come to Yzebel. He looked out over the water and tried to picture Yzebel's face. The last time he had seen her she was crying. The thought made him angry.

Elijah hurried to catch up to the captain. He had slept later than intended and worried that his chance of getting to Greece might slip through his fingers. Running awkwardly through the crowd of sailors and dock hands, he was on a pace to catch up. In his haste, however, while nearing the end of the ship's pier, he leaped over a crate and caught his foot on one of the large ropes draped over the dock. Plunging forward, he scrambled to right himself, narrowly missing several sailors. He careened into the back of a man's legs, knocking him forward. Teetering at the end of the pier, the victim flailed his arms, trying to grab anything to stop his fall. Finding nothing to latch onto, he dropped into the water below. The men milling about on the pier broke into raucous laughter as the man bobbed in the water far below. Carpathimos, who had already been in a foul mood, swam to the large wooden timbers of the pier and scaled his way up.

Lying on his belly in order to reach out and assist the man, Elijah hoped to find someone with a grin staring back at him. Instead, Carpathimos's large menacing figure climbed toward him. Fearing the wrath of this unfortunate man, Elijah jumped back and squeezed between the sailors, seeking refuge. Carpathimos hauled his wet body over the pier's edge, then rose to his full height, a good head taller than any other man around him.

Carpathimos pushed the wet hair back over his head, combing through it with the fingers of both hands as he glanced about for the culprit. With only smiling faces staring back at him, he sighed with a huff and then pulled his tunic over his head to wring out the water. He grasped the garment in both hands and twisted it, squeezing the water out onto the wooden pier, where it quickly disappeared into the desiccated wood.

Moments later came the call to get underway. From the bow of each ship, horns sounded, alerting the sailors that it was time to take positions and cast off the lines. Someone from each ship sounded the captains' orders, "Push off!" Carpathimos donned his tunic and looked across the harbor as he scaled the wooden ramp onto the deck of the ship. Then he watched the warships' long rows of oars protrude from their hulls and splash down into the water. Driving hard against the sea, the oars swung in unison as they propelled the three Carthaginian quinqueremes from the mouth of the harbor. They took their positions ahead of the merchant ships that would follow.

Large mooring lines slid across the piers and slapped at the hulls of the large merchant ships as they drifted free of their holds. The thick ropes disappeared over the top of the rail and were replaced by long oars that slapped at the water, steering the heavily laden crafts away from Carthage. The oars churned the calm harbor waters into a frothy white swirl.

The rhythmic cadence of the rowing crew seemed to keep pace with the growing distance from Carthage, but when the open sea became the only thing in sight, the monotonous cadence sounded faster than the progress the ship seemed to make. As the days progressed, Elijah fell into the ship's routine, swabbing the decks, cleaning the animals' crates, and rationing the bread, fruit, and meat to the sailors.

The captain seemed pleased when he saw Elijah's work. Elijah didn't mind keeping busy with his duties. They kept his mind occupied and made the time move faster. Nevertheless, he was relieved when he could rest in the evenings as the sun's light faded away. Sprawling out on a pile of straw for bedding, Elijah fished for the knapsack he kept hidden between the cages of chickens and one of the many large timbers that supported the belly of the massive ship. Retrieving it, he opened the roll of papyri and read the words he had transcribed, each night reading a little further through its wrinkled, yellow pages.

Most nights, after the light dimmed and he could no longer read, he recited the remainder of the passage or story from memory. Then he gently rolled the leaves together and tightly bound them, using long strips of tanned rawhide, before returning the sack to its little corner for safe keeping. He drifted quickly off to sleep, seldom paying attention to the others who occupied the belly of the merchant ship.

Elijah recognized the powerful figure he had knocked into the water. The man spent many hours sitting quietly against the opposite side of the hull, alone with his thoughts. Occasionally, he ascended the narrow wooden ladder topside. There Elijah often witnessed him leaning on the side of the ship, staring off into the distance. Elijah surmised that he must be important cargo or paid well for his place on the ship, for he was left alone and had to do no manual labor.

Tonight, though, the man seemed restless, perhaps uncomfortable with his sleeping arrangements. Elijah watched the man shift and fidget. Feeling guilty about their first encounter, he stood and offered him more bedding straw and a partially emptied seed bag on which he could rest his head. The man merely stared back at him for a moment before shaking his head, refusing the gesture.

"I am quite serious," insisted Elijah. "I can get you something to ease your stay, if you would like."

"I am fine," Carpathimos said. "I ask nothing of you."

Elijah hesitated then his curiosity got the better of him. "Why do you sail to the island?"

Carpathimos grunted, "Leave me alone."

Unabashed, Elijah didn't move. Instead he asked, "Do you feel it? The men say the weather is changing. We are due to reach port some time tomorrow, but the ships are making less progress over the last few hours. The waves are getting higher and the captain ordered the sail put down."

"A storm is coming," Carpathimos said. "The call of the rowers has changed and the chop against the hull is more forceful. No one will sleep tonight."

The man was correct. Elijah spent the next several hours sliding around on the deck, trying to fasten down anything that was dislodged. Great swells tossed the ship like a tiny wooden toy, first lifting the bow clear into the sky and then dropping it suddenly into the water, making Elijah fear for his life. Crawling low on his belly, Elijah looked for cover from the wind that whistled over the deck, driving rain that pelted him with drops that felt like hard grains of sand.

In the middle of the night, the stars and moon disappeared and the sky turned as black as the water. Tossed around by the power of the sea, time seemed to move imperceptibly forward. Belowdecks, the merchant ship creaked and flexed. Water splashed and soaked everything in the lower level. Elijah couldn't be sure if it all came from the rain or from water leaking through the hull. Twinges of pain within his chest produced a fierce sense of panic. Elijah crawled over his saturated straw bed to find his knapsack. Pools of water formed where he placed his hands and knees. He felt around for it behind the crate of chickens that had long since drowned in the cold water. Pushing the crate away from the wall, he found the sack floating near the large timber. He lunged for it, his face and shoulders dropping under the surface of the water as he slid from the straw.

Clutching the sack tightly, he came up for air. At that moment, the great spine of the ship gave way with a mighty *Crack!* The many curved ribs of timber that lined the inner hull snapped repeatedly in succession as a long twisting void appeared along the center beam. Jets of water shot upward through the crack in the hull, spraying the upper deck with frigid seawater.

Someone grabbed Elijah by the back of his belt just as his hand snared the strap of his knapsack. Both Elijah and the sack seemed to fly through the air as he was dragged up the ladder to the deck above. He had no time to get his balance, for his feet entered the water before he ever set foot on the deck of the ship. Gasping, Elijah inhaled the cold water. It instantly choked him, sealing the panic within his chest. He tried to scream, but no sound came out. Only the knowledge that someone grasped his wrist consoled him as he sank into the blackness.

———

Carpathimos stared at the glowing embers at the base of the fire, transfixed by the heat's shimmering motion. Within his mind, he listened to Myridia's voice and watched their son play on the ground near his feet. The scene took place so long ago, yet her voice still sang to him as clearly as the day he brought her home. Home, he thought. Would he ever see it again? Did he even want to? As the questions mounted, his thoughts turned to the fateful day when Roman soldiers sent—he thought—to protect them, instead turned on them. His friends, his woman, dead at the hands of those men. Only three people—himself, his son, and his sister—cheated death. He wished he hadn't.

Lost within the images of long ago, Carpathimos did not notice Elijah's eyes blinking open and closed. He was starting to recover consciousness. Lying on his side near the fire opposite Carpathimos, Elijah began to shift, first one limb and then the other. He was taking inventory of his parts when Carpathimos finally noticed that he was stirring. In time, Elijah sat up and rubbed his head and then his arms and legs. He felt as if he had been beaten, but he couldn't remember that happening. Suddenly, he stood with a jolt and looked around frantically for his knapsack.

"Where is it?" he exclaimed. "No! Where is it?" Then he saw it. His knapsack and its contents were spread out neatly on top of a broad, flat stone, drying in the sun next to the fire. He knelt to inspect it for damage. The papyri seemed to be in good shape. It didn't feel very damp. He unrolled some of it to find the writing intact, although on some of the outer leaves, the ink had bled, making the characters look wider and less defined.

He glanced at Carpathimos who remained motionless, sitting on a large piece of driftwood and staring at the fire. His clothes were spread out next to him along the log, drying. Curious, Elijah stood and surveyed their surroundings. He and Carpathimos were alone in a small cove, surrounded by rocks on three sides and beach to the south. The shore was predominantly composed of large rocks and boulders. Waves crashed against the stones, sending spray high into the air, but not high enough to reach them in the cove. Elijah looked up and down the shoreline. No sign of their ship. In fact, no sign of any ships or other people. They were alone.

Clearing his throat, Elijah spoke at last. "Do you know where we are?" When the man did not reply, Elijah asked, "Did you see anyone else?"

Carpathimos turned his head toward his questioner and nodded.

"Does that mean, yes?" asked Elijah. "To which question?"

Carpathimos took a deep breath, let it out, and then reached for his clothing. Dry enough. He began to dress, but not before Elijah noticed the whip scars on his back.

Elijah introduced himself. "I don't remember much about the ship. Did you help me out of the water?"

"I helped you into it as well," answered Carpathimos with a hint of a smile, "though the sea would have done that on its own, eventually."

"Have you ever sailed in a storm such as that?" asked Elijah.

"Yes." Carpathimos hesitated, then decided to continue the conversation. "The Carthaginians are good sailors, but such a storm would be difficult for even the most experienced crew. I think they were trying to use three ships for the job they should have been doing with four."

"You mean they loaded the ships too full?" asked Elijah.

"Or built the ships too hastily," Carpathimos suggested. "Perhaps both are true."

"Do you think any of the ships survived the storm?"

"I do not know. I suspect that the wind scattered them over a great distance. All I do know, is that you are on your own."

"But did we reach Sicily?" Elijah asked, calling after Carpathimos, who was already climbing out of the cove. Hurriedly, he rewrapped the papyri and carefully slid the roll into the animal skins before replacing it in the knapsack. He was relieved that the books were unharmed. A thought struck him as he raced up the hill after Carpathimos.

"Wait!" he cried. "I wish to thank you for saving my life! How can I repay you?"

Carpathimos called back to him, "You can't."

"Then tell me your name and I will pray for you," pleaded Elijah.

"Where I go, you must not follow. Do you understand?" Carpathimos said sternly.

Trying and failing to keep pace with Carpathimos's long strides, Elijah attempted once more, "But where do I go? How do I——?"

Out of breath, he sat down on a grass-covered knoll while tears of fear and frustration welled in his eyes. "What is your name?" he called out, but the man who saved him had already disappeared.

# Chapter X

GALLUS AND CATO crashed through the underbrush of a dense Iberian forest, still linked together by a meter of chain. To Sorian, they sounded like a herd of panicked bovine rather than two starving, desperate men. Sorian carried his own chain close to his body, so it wouldn't catch on twigs and branches. He tried to maintain some distance ahead of his two lumbering partners. He disliked the ranting and complaining about their chain almost as much as he disliked his own chain, but he found it was possible to stay focused on his goal while ignoring them if he simply stayed at least twenty meters ahead of them at all times.

His two companions had made intermittent attempts to run in tandem, trying to catch Sorian, but each attempt so far had ended in failure, with one or both tripping and falling to the ground. Springing up from under Gallus's foot, a thin switch of poplar slapped Cato in the mouth, making him wince. Irritated, he put the back of his hand up to his mouth to temper the sting, and in doing so, he smeared bright red blood into the dirt caking his knuckles. He looked down at his hand and cursed.

"I can't take this anymore! We have to find some tools to rid ourselves of this chain," declared Cato angrily. "I cannot believe you left the ax in the tunnel!"

"We will find one, Cato," answered Gallus. "We would be free already if that mangy dog hadn't been so protective of his master's tools."

"I know." Cato sighed. "We have been walking for over two weeks. I am just reaching a point where I can take no more of this awful marching, lurking about in the wilderness, and hiding from every suspicious noise we hear. I think it means either someone is hunting us or an animal might eat us." Cato paused as he slid over a fallen tree trunk, dragged along by Gallus. "I will be free of this chain at the next home we come to," he declared. "That I promise you, Gallus. I will take on a whole village of angry people to be free once again. As long as we are connected by this chain, we are no closer to freedom than we were inside the walls of the mine."

"Look on the bright side, Cato," encouraged Gallus. "The sun is pleasing and we have been eating well. The berries and roots have been both fulfilling and a welcome change."

"Shut your mouth, Gallus!" cried Cato. "You may be stronger than me, but I swear I will beat you with this chain! Your optimism makes me sick inside."

Gallus turned and smiled at his older, shorter, and bitterly frustrated chain-mate. "It is agreed then. I will fight with you, if it comes to that, no matter how many villagers try to keep us chained together."

"That is wonderful to hear," replied Cato sarcastically. "Now, let's catch up to Sorian."

Approaching the western steps of the Pyrenees, the terrain changed once again, becoming steeper and more rugged. The men had crawled, scrambled, limped, climbed, and hiked over five hundred kilometers of untamed wilderness, much of it along the Duero River as it flowed out of the high country from the east. Passing over the divide, Sorian led the way across the headwaters of the Duero before turning to the southeast to follow the mighty Ebro, which flowed toward the Mediterranean. Here the terrain was easier. The hills slowly grew higher and the forests less dense.

So far, the prisoners had encountered only one village and had crossed the paths of only a few peasants. Now, with the tall spires of the Pyrenees looming large on the horizon, Sorian quickened his pace.

Struggling to keep up with Sorian, Cato and Gallus helped and encouraged one another to avoid falling behind. Gallus called out to their guide, "Sorian, do you know which way to go from here?"

Sorian paused in mid-step, put his foot down, and straightened. He stood still, staring at the horizon in the east. As Cato and Gallus approached him from behind, Sorian pointed to a high spot in the mountains. The two men stared past his finger to a high ridge of ragged and dark gray stone.

"That is the Aneto Mountain. It stands over three thousand meters high. Remember its shape," commanded Sorian. "From now on, it shows us the way."

Aghast, Cato exclaimed indignantly, "There is no way, Sorian! There is no way we can climb that mountain. Its peaks are ragged, and the indentions are packed with glacial ice."

Sorian shifted his hand southward toward an expansive and deep valley, some fifty kilometers from where they now stood. Atop the shoulder of a broad foothill, they could see the upper portion of the valley as its walls sloped inward under the watchful face of the Aneto.

"The Valley of Aran lies beneath the mountain to the southeast and, to the south of that, the waters flow toward the Mediterranean. We will keep the Aneto over our shoulder," Sorian said as he patted his left shoulder with his right hand. Cato and Gallus stared at him, mouths agape at his confidence and the breadth of knowledge he had acquired during his service to Rome. "I have heard the valley is rich with plants and animals that thrive in the warm sun and the fresh water flowing off the mountain."

He added reassuringly, "Our path through the valley will be good for us. Remember, where animals live, so too will there be people and tools." Sorian held up the end of his length of chain and shook it, implying what the tools were to be used for. Cato and Gallus smiled—skeptically.

The cool air stirring high in the foothills, pushed along on the back of a stiff breeze, made Cato shudder. "I hope the sun is warmer in the valley and the wind has fewer teeth," he said. "I can't wait until we are basking in the sun along the shore of the Mediterranean once again."

While the trio stood quietly with the western sun at their backs, the shrill cries of wolves rang out. Made uneasy by their numerous haunting howls, Gallus interrupted their brief rest. "Let us move onward. If we march through the night and throughout the day tomorrow, we should be able to make Sorian's valley with enough daylight left to make a decent camp for ourselves. Perhaps we might even be able to hole up for a few days to recuperate."

As predicted, the three men arrived at the lip of the Aran Valley late the next day. Exhausted, they stumbled into an area filled with deep green grass. Delicate alpine flowers dotted this sea of green in patches of yellows, whites, and pale blues. Rambling around the edge of a glacier-fed lake, they spotted a brilliantly white rock ptarmigan foraging for bugs and seeds along the water's edge. Aware of their proximity, the bird squawked and ruffled its black and white wings before darting into the grass ahead of them. Moments later, its calls drew their attention to a flat escarpment, on which it now stood.

The escarpment was set back from the edge of the lake, leaving a narrow passage of about ten meters between it and the water. This massive rocky table stood above the grass by roughly two meters, its flat top nearly large enough to host one of Rome's legions in formation. Toward the back of the shelf, the ground inclined, forming a long, tree-covered ridge that extended for several kilometers into the surrounding mountains. Looking along its length, Cato wondered if this was one of many fingers that stretched out into the valley from the mountains surrounding them, and how many of those they would need to climb.

Drawn back to the call of the angry bird, Cato and Gallus separated from Sorian. They made their way to the rock shelf while Sorian circled along the lakeshore, hoping to attack the ptarmigan from the other side. The irritated bird flapped his foot-long wings and croaked loudly as it hopped along the weather-worn lip of the rock escarpment. It had been successful at getting their attention, though the men were in search of something that could not be hidden by the raucous bird. Sidling near the bird along the stone wall, Sorian made a feeble dive for the male ptarmigan's feet as it took flight. It would have made a good meal, but chasing it took more energy than any of the three men could afford.

Quickening their pace, they began searching the ground around them in the shadow of the escarpment. Before long, Gallus spotted the dull brown plumage of the female as she sat near the base of the rock. As he and Cato approached her, she too took flight. Crawling on their hands and knees under the large lip of the escarpment, Cato and Gallus soon found the nest. In it were seven brown and black speckled eggs, each the size of a grown man's large toe. Gallus was the first to pick up an egg, press his thumb through the end, and suck out the warm, sticky interior. Sorian joined them. Each man selected two eggs before climbing up the face of the escarpment. Here, with the sun on their backs, they relaxed and enjoyed a meal of sweet yokes and gelatinous protein.

Far from satiated but satisfied by his good fortune, Gallus lay on the rock and closed his eyes to rest. Cato watched him begin to doze and said, "I think this would be an adequate place to make a camp for the night. Don't you agree, Sorian? We have fallen wood behind us and good water near our feet." Sorian nodded.

The next morning the three men stripped off their foul clothing and swam in the frigid lake water, trying to eliminate the lice from their bodies. Even if the relief was only temporary, since their clothing was lice-infested, washing away the grit and sweat of so many days felt like its own form of freedom. Dressed and refreshed, they set off across the southern flank of the valley, making their way to the southeast while keeping the great Aneto over their left shoulders.

With the chill of the morning burning away under the midday sun, the earliest and faintest whiffs of smoke caught the trio's attention as they walked abreast through the grass. The smoky smell became more pervasive and a focal point of the men's concentration. It heralded a distant fire, but the small column rising above the trees indicated a small fire. They all surmised that it was probably not coming from a village.

Turning eastward, they shifted their course toward the smoke, but when they entered the forest they lost sight of it. Trying to maintain the same direction through the tightly spaced trees proved rather difficult but, miraculously, upon exiting the opposite side of the tree line, they stumbled into the outskirts of a small village hidden in the shadows of the round-topped mountains.

The men hid in the thick forest until dark, scrutinizing the layout of the village and its people. Looking for a source of tools under the cover of darkness, Sorian made his way into the village by himself. He feared his partners would make too much noise and arouse the suspicions of every canine in the valley. He grinned warmly when he spotted the open workplace of a metalworker and his tools. The embers of the fire used to heat the metal were still warm.

Feeling his way along in the moonlight, Sorian studied the man's tools, which were scattered around the workplace in a disorderly fashion. Sorian felt disdain for the unknown blacksmith. Granted, he was not familiar with a common man's work ethic, but such carelessness would never be acceptable in a Roman army encampment.

Sorian spotted a thick wedge-shaped tool and picked it up. It was solid and heavy, weighing roughly five kilograms. One end was marred and scored from being beaten by a maul and the other end was more sharply defined, with an edge that could be used to split or hew wood. Clutching the chisel and his chain tightly in his left hand, he searched for the heavy maul that

could drive it. Scanning the ground to his right and then to the left, he spotted the handle and heaved the heavy maul onto his shoulder before slipping
out of the village and into the woods. Cato and Gallus greeted him with jubilant smiles. Before departing for the deep forest to the east, Gallus offered
to carry the maul while Cato took up the metal wedge.

Late that night, the men made camp. They had marched through the
darkness of the forest for several hours, putting as much distance between
themselves and the village as possible. Exhausted and hungry, the beleaguered travelers gathered firewood from deadfall in the understory. By luck,
they had reached a small clearing, a flat, round space with a diameter mea-
suring seven or eight meters and an equal opening above them in the canopy.
Sparse, knee-high grasses covered the ground. Near the center of the clearing stood a solitary spire, the thick trunk of a long-dead tree. Still upright,
the dead trunk stood several meters high while its broken and rotting top
lay across the ground. It reminded Sorian of a Roman column, its ornately
sculpted capital smashed and scattered on the ground at his feet.

They gathered the dry branches and fallen tree limbs, dumping most of
it on top of the fallen tree top. Before long they had a raging fire. Satisfied by
the magnitude of their fire, the three men could wait no longer to free themselves from their chains. Out of respect to Sorian, Gallus and Cato suggested
that he be freed first. He graciously accepted as he positioned himself on the
ground so the chain connecting the shackles around his wrists was stretched
taut over a flat stone embedded in the forest floor. Cato held the wedge over
one of the clasps and prepared for the first swing of the maul. Gallus lifted
the hammer over his head to make the first strike, only to be serenaded by
the night's first howls of the wolf pack. Gallus shifted uncomfortably, peering
into the darkness of the forest, dreading to see the creatures making such
terrifying sounds.

To Sorian it had seemed as though, over the course of the last week,
the pack had followed them up through the foothills. Every night they called
to one another and every night, while Gallus and Cato slept, Sorian stayed

awake, listening to their calls and imagining how and when they would make first contact with the three of them. Now, with their cries growing louder, it seemed that the tireless pack was at their heels and about to close in.

Caught between panic and the necessity of a well-placed throw of the maul, Gallus's first attempt at splitting the clasp of Sorian's left shackle nearly ended in disaster, missing the mark and striking the stone several centimeters from the hand that Cato was using to hold the wedge. Cato and Sorian glared at Gallus. He apologized profusely, promising to concentrate and ignore the wolves. Excited by the prospect of impending freedom, neither Cato nor Gallus noticed how close the calls had become. Sorian, however, focused on the call of the wolves to avoid the impulse to pull his hand away when Gallus swung the large hammer. Taking several swings, Gallus finally severed the joint of the shackle, springing it open and sending the short length of chain recoiling against Sorian's other wrist.

Sorian got to his knees and rubbed his freed limb with his right hand. He smiled at Gallus and then repositioned himself on his belly, holding the right hand over the stone and pulling at the length of chain with his left hand. Giving a nod to indicate that he was ready, Sorian prepared for the release of his right hand. Cato placed the wedge over the clasp of the right shackle while Gallus took aim and made his first throw. As with the other side, the first swing made little impact on the metal surface, forming a slight dent that only Cato could see by the firelight reflecting off the dark metal of the shackle. Kneeling so close to the fire, Gallus wiped the sweat from his brow with his forearm before lining up for the next swing. Cato was also warm. He could feel his face, knuckles, and the back of his fingers on the hand gripping the wedge grow warmer and slippery as he waited for Gallus to swing the maul. With their backs to the woods, neither man could see the yellow eyes staring at them.

They had been concentrating so intensely that none of them noticed the howls had stopped. Sorian once again prepared to disengage his mind from his hand. He stared into the darkness. The light of the fire failed to penetrate farther than the ring of pines surrounding them. Instantly, he spotted several sets of yellow eyes that seemed to hover above the ground. He watched them loiter in the darkness as he dipped his head low and backward with each swing of Gallus's maul. The clang of sprung iron spooked the wolves. Sorian was finally free. He sprang to his feet and rubbed his wrists together, exhilarated by the sensation of freedom. Cato grinned and asked, "How does it feel?"

Sorian looked at Cato and Gallus and returned the grin. "Wonderful! Freedom is wonderful! Who will be next?"

Crouching down on his haunches, he rubbed at his freed limbs. Sorian suggested they play a game to determine the next man to lose his irons. He proposed a guessing game in which he would pick a number and they would each try to guess it. "The man with the closer guess will be first." Cato and Gallus accepted the challenge, knowing that each of them would soon be free. Sorian stood and announced that he was ready to begin, but before they guessed, he would place more wood onto the fire.

"Soon you will both be free of your bindings and free of one another as well!" declared Sorian before slipping behind the tall column that now burned brightly under an undulating carpet of bright orange flame.

Cato and Gallus exchanged glances and started laughing, believing Sorian's statement was a literal truth. Casually, Cato pivoted and stared into the darkness, turning his back to the fire to cool his face. Suddenly his laughter ceased. Gallus glanced at Cato, sensing something was wrong. That was when he saw the wolves surrounding them. Six sets of gleaming yellow eyes stared at them over long, straight snouts. Gallus's large grin faded. Cato gasped in fear. On the opposite side of the fire, Sorian faced the same threat. Four more wolves stared at him from the darkened perimeter of the trees. Free or not, Sorian thought to himself, this will be a long and perhaps deadly night.

Sorian stepped around the burning tree trunk to check on his fellow Romans. The backside of the tree had not yet started burning, so Sorian took pause behind it, shielding himself from the heat of the fire. Observing the large blackened trunk, he concluded that the tree had once been struck by lightning. Bending to grab a stick from the pile of gathered firewood, Sorian put his hand against the trunk and felt it give under the weight of his upper body. Its subtle sway would have been imperceptible to the others, but under his palm it provided the answer to his current problem.

Maintaining his composure, Sorian threw several dead branches on the fire, building it up so Cato and Gallus couldn't see him toiling on the other side. Meanwhile, Cato and Gallus, still bound together by a meter of chain and standing with their backs to the fire, frantically waved burning branches at the snarling creatures. Cautiously, the predators drew closer, testing Cato and Gallus for an opening through which to attack. The men could now see the wolves in their entirety, as the light from the fire cast long shadows. Lips curled to expose razor-sharp fangs, the wolves snapped and growled as they advanced, spilling cascading strings of drool to the ground. Daring and perhaps overconfident, one of the large gray wolves darted in to nip at Gallus's leg.

Terrified, Gallus hurled his smoldering stick at the animal, striking it along the back and sending it reeling into the darkness. Recognizing the reduction in flaming defenses, the wolf pack closed in more tightly, pushing Cato and Gallus closer to the fire and inadvertently drawing the chain between them more perpendicular to the large standing trunk. That was the action Sorian was anticipating. Cato and Gallus were standing perfectly in range of the tall, flaming column.

Sorian leaped over the remaining firewood and circled around behind the fire. He grasped a large pine bow and thrust its brown needles into the fire, igniting the dry wood in a billowing plume of flame. The combusting sap sizzled and snapped. He held it up in the air to ensure that it would continue burning and then he lunged toward the four wolves on his side of the fire. The action forced them to huddle together and back reluctantly away. He lunged again. This forced them around to the other side of the fire, rejoining the pack.

Sorian selected another long tree limb, which he stirred and poked at the fire, scattering some of the burning sticks to make the fire burn down more quickly. Returning to the column, he saw Cato and Gallus too focused on the wolves to pay him any attention. Sorian could also see the wolves over the flames. The pack was circling around Cato and Gallus, pinning them against the fire behind them. The hot flames licked at the backs of their legs, curling the hair into singed mats against their skin, their sweat rising as steam.

Sorian positioned his body behind the tall timber and pressed his shoulder against it, rocking it back and forth. It would topple, but he needed more force. Straining hard, he pushed against it and felt the wood shiver beneath his palms as fragile fibers gave way to his effort. Gasping, he stopped, stepped back and then launched himself at the trunk a final time. The aged wood cracked and snapped as it gave way, sending an army of tiny orange embers into the night sky within a thick cloud of gray smoke.

The large trunk sliced through the air, catching the chain binding the two men beneath its girth as it slammed to the ground. The falling timber caught Cato's ankle, forcing him to the ground as it drove his foot into the earth beneath it. He squealed in pain as the cloud of embers showered over the top of him. Pinned against the opposite side of the trunk by the chain, Gallus pulled at it desperately as the wolves closed in around them. Gallus hollered loudly as he marshalled more of the chain from beneath the fallen log, pulling Cato's broken leg under the smoldering wood.

Although the wolves briefly scattered when the log collapsed, they quickly reorganized and attacked Cato in ravenous fury. Only Gallus's loud screams preserved him—for the moment. Backing away, Sorian picked up two smoldering torches from the ground and disappeared into the darkness. As he raced through the forest, Sorian listened to Gallus's high-pitched screams. The echoes lingered only briefly before Gallus's cries were consumed by the night. Laughing to himself as he ran, Sorian thought of Cato and Gallus only once more. They had agreed to a chance at freedom in exchange for providing help he would need to escape. They had honorably fulfilled their part of the agreement.

Over the next few days, Sorian traveled south toward the Mediterranean. By the time he reached the shore, he was significantly transformed. His path had crossed with other travelers. From them, he stole a new tunic and a woolen cape with a hood. Elsewhere, he absconded with a sharp knife and used it to shear his scraggly beard, matted hair, and the burden of lice that preyed continuously on his patience.

Traveling east once again, he moved quickly along the pristine beaches west of the port city of Massilia, where he hoped to find passage on a ship headed to Rome. Surveying Massilia from a perch in the city's foothills, Sorian made note of the ships moving in and out of port. He studied the people and their animals as they traveled through the city gates to trade their wares. It would be easy to blend in here and get access to the docks, he decided.

During his time in the prison, Sorian had learned Punic phrases and he had mastered the smooth, rapid cadence of the Iberians. This would help him gain passage on one of these ships. Eager to leave, Sorian wove his way down the steep slope of the hillside toward the city gate. Looking back, he spotted a large bearded vulture hovering over the landscape's short wind-blown trees. The dark gray bird circled gracefully and soared through the air, scanning the ground for anything that could serve as a meal. Sorian admired the vulture's keen ability to take advantage of opportunity and its quiet, solitary life. What more, he envied its ferocious power. "A good omen," he assured himself. Cackling with laughter, Sorian spread his arms out wide, like the wings of the vulture, pretending to soar through the air as he descended the hill and entered the city.

# Chapter XI

---

AKRAGAS SAT UPON an expansive plateau just four kilometers from the sea and Sicily's southern coast. The city's position on the southern tip of the island made her a trading center and a frequent resting place for travelers passing from the east or west along the main thoroughfare. Despite its convenient location, a steep ridge at her back and two rivers joining at her feet gave Akragas a commanding profile and made her a very difficult city to attack. Nevertheless, she had been attacked many times over the centuries by men seeking the right to control the movement and sale of goods on the island.

From the east, the Akragas River offered the Romans little resistance as they marched toward the city. The Hypsas, to the west, would prove more difficult. Over the eons, it had cut its way through the volcanized stone, creating steep cliffs at its edge. Rome's four legions, under the commands of consuls Lucius Postumius Megellus and Quintus Mamilius Vitulus, divided along the banks of the Akragas within the expansive Hypsas Valley. Eager to fight, these forty thousand troops spread themselves across the gently sloping shoulder of the plateau, setting up camps among the forests, groves, and meadows that separated the Akragas from the city wall above.

The soldiers were trained assassins, having fought their way west across Sicily one city at a time. In small towns and villages, where people were eager to oppose them, the Roman intruders demonstrated their dominance. The many who folded under Rome's thumb were sold into slavery and shipped back to Rome in the bellies of troop ships. The remainder—the injured, elderly, and the young—were slaughtered. Some of the small towns, seeing such wrath, pledged immediate allegiance to Rome. Larger cities, fortified with walls and defenses, took more time to convince. In such situations, the Roman generals exhibited patience, starving the people into submission. In Akragas, Consul Generals Lucius Megellus and Quintus Vitulus prepared for victory by siege. They were eager to fight, but knew this massive city required a more patient approach. While they waited, they harvested the local crops and controlled the traffic along the great road, starving the city of its lifeblood.

The gifted son of one of Carthage's proud fighting families, Hannibal Gisgo, commanded the Carthaginian garrison within the city of Akragas when the Romans arrived. Under his protection, some fifty thousand men, women, and children endured months of siege by the Romans outside their walls. Conditions within Akragas became dismal. The stench of death filled the streets. The city's fires were not sufficient enough to consume the dead or quell the rancid odor.

Early in the siege, Hannibal attacked the Romans, but after losing too many men in a pitched battle, he withdrew back into the city. Here he devised a series of small, cleverly executed surprise attacks on isolated Roman troops, aiming to frustrate his Roman counterparts into making a mistake. He also used these sneak attacks to provide time to send a plea for help to Carthage. Through similar means, he was informed that help was on its way. What he did not know was whether the city could outlast the siege.

———

Struggling against the tenacious web-like tendrils of a wall of asparagus horridus bushes, Carpathimos kicked his legs and swung his arms free, finally emerging onto a well-worn cart path running east to west, just a few kilometers inland. The uninhibited pathway surprised him. It was quite wide, yet he noted that the bushes and small saplings growing along the sides of the path had been trampled and broken. On the roadbed itself, the wild grasses and weeds had been crushed under the feet of what appeared to be thousands of men, compacting the soil where once green foliage thrived. Based on the heights of a few tender new weeds growing precariously along the path, Carpathimos estimated that troops had passed this way many weeks before and, based on the direction of the tracks and snapped branches, he knew the men marched west, perhaps in support of the Roman siege at Akragas. Carpathimos turned to the west in search of these men.

He moved swiftly and quietly, keeping his eyes peeled for any sign of the army. Nearing nightfall, he paused at a clearing over which the road weaved and dipped, following the rippled terrain of the high ground. To this point, he had seen no troops and he was growing weary. He decided to rest for the night and get up early in the morning to resume walking. Lying among the wildflowers covering the rounded domes of the ridge, he rested his head on his arm and watched the sun set behind the far horizon in the west. As its belly sank below the mountains, the large orange orb cast hues of light purple and dark pink against the few wispy clouds stretching far across the western sky. The soft colors seemed to calm him. He relaxed with a sigh and his eyelids fluttered shut.

Having nearly passed through that strange void in which men can neither dream nor stay awake, Carpathimos was startled by the high-pitched squeal of what sounded like a bear cub. He had heard this before when the Roman army was camped in the high country, but he had not encountered a bear since. Propping himself on his elbows, he listened for the call again. Within moments he heard the sound that confirmed his suspicion, the low-pitched guttural roar of an Apennine brown bear mother. Occasionally, when an army marched through terrain such as this, a cub would be cut off from its mother. This sometimes led to rare but serious altercations with the troops. This roar reminded him of just such an event when he had served in a Roman legion near the Dolomites. The ferocity with which that mother fought for her cub reminded him of his place in the world and that he was out of place in hers.

Listening to her deep rumbling growl, Carpathimos realized that the animal was close and she sounded angry. Carpathimos stood and turned his head so that the wind quieted in his ear. The next thing he heard sounded like a bear on the run. Straining, he heard the pounding foot beats of a charge and then a human voice calling out in terror. Without thinking, Carpathimos hurtled through the brush, running toward the cry.

Passing into the dim gray light of dusk as it enveloped the thin woods, he could sense the mother bear's presence before he saw her. She was on her hind legs, threatening the individual who had the misfortune of stepping between mother and cub. Sliding to a halt only meters from her, Carpathimos assessed his opponent. She stood two meters tall but even at a distance she seemed huge. He followed her gaze up to the large lower branch of a fir tree near the crest of the ridge near the path. Why she hadn't climbed up the tree he couldn't understand, for her adversary did not appear formidable. Carpathimos shook his head in disbelief. He clapped his hands loudly, shouting at the bear. She hesitated to abandon her prey, but as Carpathimos approached slowly, clapping and yelling at her, she dropped onto all four feet, beckoned her cub, and disappeared into the cover of the dark underbrush.

Carpathimos breathed a sigh of relief and stared up at the timid figure looking back at him from the tree. Mortified, Elijah dropped from the branch and gathered his knapsack, keeping his eye on the place where mother bear had gone. "Thank you for coming!" Elijah said, a large toothy grin stretching wide across his thin face.

Carpathimos stared at him without any expression. "Why do you follow me?" he growled.

Before Elijah could answer, Carpathimos turned and slid through the thick tangle of weeds and saplings on his way back to the cart path. Panic-stricken, Elijah hurried along behind him, hoping to avoid becoming a bear's meal.

"I had hoped that we could travel together," Elijah said, panting and hurrying to keep close to his rescuer. "Perhaps we can help one another."

Irritated, Carpathimos didn't respond. Determined to avoid spending the night with his young follower, he kept walking, but the reminder of a bear attack propelled Elijah forward. Carpathimos could not shake him.

By early morning, they came upon a hillside from which they could see a city on a distant plateau and the massive army sprawled beneath, across the valley. Tents, men, and horses dotted the landscape, filling in the gaps between groves of trees and small fields of crops. Moving off the path, Carpathimos led Elijah into the valley below the plateau, where the river flowed south to the sea. Cautiously they crossed the river valley, angling to the north of the city while keeping alert for soldiers. By midday, Carpathimos and Elijah had scaled back up the ridge along the river. Here, they discovered a small camp in the woods bordering the mouth of a tributary.

Carpathimos studied the men and equipment from the protection of a stand of poplars. These soldiers were Roman and they numbered one centuriae, roughly one-sixth of a cohort of troops. As Carpathimos squatted down to observe them, Elijah followed suit.

Throughout the night, Carpathimos kept watch. When the small camp became quiet, only one soldier stood guard, pacing back and forth between the small tents where the others slept. Carpathimos racked his brain for a plan to infiltrate the legions without getting killed in the process. As he did so, a dozen men appeared within the camp, all barefoot and dressed in dark clothing.

Only the flicker of the lone campfire provided enough light to alert Carpathimos to their presence. The Roman guard was killed almost instantly by one man who crept behind him and slit his throat with a long, curved blade. The knife flashed like a spark in the light of the fire before disappearing out of sight. Systematically, the stealthy saboteurs worked their way from tent to tent, killing the Romans while they slept. As quickly as they appeared, the men completed their task and disappeared into the darkness.

Carpathimos saw his opportunity. He pushed Elijah, signaling the young man not to follow him, then he rose and walked quickly into the camp. He knelt by the guard who had fallen near the fire. Carpathimos could see he had bled from a wide and deep gash across the front of his throat. Hearing a faint moan, he looked around to locate its origin. It came from the nearest tent. He crawled into it as Elijah looked on in horror, terrified that Carpathimos would be captured.

Almost immediately Carpathimos emerged from the tent, dragging the body of a Roman soldier into the brush near Elijah. Elijah watched as Carpathimos knelt next to the man, looking at his injury. The soldier was still alive, but barely. He also had a gash across the front and side of his neck, but the major artery must have been spared. Although blood poured from the wound, he was still alive. Even his airway seemed unharmed, yet his breathing was shallow and growing more irregular by the minute.

"I will report this attack to the general," stated Carpathimos, shaking the man's shoulder. "What is the name of the commander of your cohort?"

The soldier opened his eyes and grasped Carpathimos's arm as he struggled to suck in a breath. Even in the darkness, his wide eyes seemed to shine. He looked terrified. Carpathimos supported the soldier's upper body against his thigh and repeated his question. This time the soldier murmured a name before his eyes closed.

"Servios of the Fourth."

Carpathimos stripped him of his uniform and donned it. Though of similar weight and weave to his own tunic, the color was consistent with those worn by the Roman troops, where his was too dark. He walked back into the campsite and found a breastplate and helmet that fit him. An uneasy wash of emotion filled him as he placed the helmet onto his head and took up a soldier's long knife from the ground, placing at his side.

Striding back toward Elijah, Carpathimos prepared to tell the youth that he needed to be on his own and run from this dangerous place, but when he approached the young man sitting near the dead soldier, Elijah stared at him, looking both confused and scared. His expression made Carpathimos hesitate and then alter his plan. "You stay hidden near the river. I will come find you when it is safe to do so."

"But I—," Elijah protested, faltering. His mouth and throat were too dry to continue.

Carpathimos had already turned and walked away, leaving Elijah alone in the dark forest next to the horrific scene. Under scattered moonlight, Carpathimos worked his way down the embankment, across the river, and back up the other side. Using the river as a guide, he skirted the tree line, making his way slowly to the southwest away from the dead centuriae of men, until he finally located a larger camp. Perhaps this was another cohort or even the southern end of the last cohort, he guessed. Seeing it at night and not from the top of the hill, he had no way of knowing where one legion's perimeter stopped and another one started.

Fires burned brightly within this larger camp. Carpathimos walked right in, knowing from experience where the cohort commander's tent would be located. Nearing the tent, several soldiers stepped into his path, ordering him to identify himself.

"I am Remus," lied Carpathimos. "My cohort commander is Servios of Legion Four. I request to join you."

The soldiers held position while another went to the commander's tent to alert him. The commander looked out from his tent at Carpathimos and ordered him closer. Carpathimos walked nearer while the guards remained with him, their blades drawn and ready.

"What is it that you want, milite?" the commander asked.

"My name is Remus, Commander. I am here to report that the men of my centuriae are all dead. I humbly request to serve under your command."

"You wish to report that the entire centuriae is dead?" scoffed the commander. "How is it that you alone survived, soldier?"

"Our men were attacked tonight by soldiers from the city. I chased several into the river, but they slipped away in the darkness. There must have been twenty or more."

"You want me to believe that twenty men came down from the city and killed an entire centuriae of Roman soldiers? That is preposterous." The commander glared at Carpathimos as he considered the possibility. "Very well. What can you tell me of their methods? This was not the first of these attacks—only the first with a witness."

Carpathimos told his story, describing the attackers as he had seen them, barefoot and dressed like the night. He claimed to have been attacked in his tent as he was preparing to dress for his shift as sentry. Nearing the end of his discourse, before the commander could ask more questions, he was interrupted by a rider. The man leaped from his horse, landing near the tent.

"Commander, General Quintus calls an assembly of the cohort commanders at once. There is news about troop movements within the city."

The commander reached for his gear while one of his men prepared his horse. He glanced at Carpathimos, then ordered his horseman to prepare a second animal. "Get this man a horse as well." To Carpathimos, he asked, "You can ride?" Carpathimos nodded. "You will come with me. I want to hear more about the attack."

Riding quickly from camp to camp, the commander and Carpathimos made their way to the head of Quintus's legions, where the general's quarters were located. Quintus had spread both legions along the river in opposite directions, with his staff and headquarters in the center. When Carpathimos and the cohort commander rode into the central camp of Consul General Quintus, a large crowd had already gathered. It was still before dawn, yet so many large fires were burning that the crowd could be seen in detail. The general's staff, his legion tribunes, and most of the cohort commanders awaited them. The cohort commander and Carpathimos quickly dismounted, joining the crowd just as someone began to speak.

An officer stood on a boulder near his tent. This put his boots near head level of most men in the crowd. He was a formidable specimen with a commanding voice. Carpathimos and the commander listened intently with the others. Carpathimos surmised that the man must have been the general named Quintus.

"We have now entered the sixth month of our siege and the will of Hannibal is breaking. Until now, the people of Akragas have burned their dead, but as they fall behind, the bodies come over the wall, untouched by flame. Our spies tell us the starving men and women have resorted to consuming their horses. We have only to wait for Hannibal to decide if he wants to confront us like a warrior or die in dishonor behind his wall," shouted Quintus. "I ask you to prepare your men. General Megellus and I have compared observations. Hannibal is preparing his men for a full-scale attack. He will meet us in open battle on the flats below the city!" General Quintus jumped down from his stone pulpit, disappearing quickly into his war room.

The cohort commander grabbed Carpathimos by the arm, pulling him in that direction. "Whatever you have to say, tell me now," he ordered. Briefly, Carpathimos summarized the attack. "I think that Hannibal is preparing for more attacks like this one, not a battle on open ground."

The cohort commander looked closely at Carpathimos. "What is your name?"

"Remus."

"Remus, you must tell this story to the general. If not him, then to the tribune."

Carpathimos nodded and let the commander lead him toward the general's war room. The commander ordered him to stand by the large rock while he sought out a member of the general's staff. Brewing with excitement, the young commander returned shortly by himself.

"We are to wait here until we are announced," he said, looking uncomfortable.

Carpathimos stayed at attention while he ran through the story in his head. He needed to make certain he described the attack in the same way he told the commander earlier, although perhaps now he could add more detail, if necessary. Soon a member of the general's staff emerged from the tent and beckoned them forward.

"You will go in and wait for the general to ask questions," the soldier said. "He will get the information that he wants. If you want to retain your heads, do not waste his night by providing irrelevant details."

The commander and Carpathimos entered the tent and stood at attention. The general was stooped over his map table, staring at a map of the city and the surrounding river valley. Carpathimos scanned the map, mentally placing himself and the troops he had seen along the river on the map.

The *flats*, of which the general had spoken, consisted of a long, tapering hillside southwest of the city, a short climb from the river's edge where they now stood. The Hypsas River coursed around the plateau from north of the city to the south of the city before it joined the Akragas River near the sea in the distant spillway of the valley. Quintus looked up to find the commander at full attention while Carpathimos's eyes were busy studying the map. Too early in the day to be irritated by this insubordination, Quintus sat down to learn of the attack.

"Speak!" he ordered. "Why do you think this attack was strategic and not simply carried out by a band of marauders?"

Carpathimos straightened and looked straight ahead while the commander spoke. "The attack was well planned and unfolded very quickly, General. It was a surprise attack by men dressed to hide in the night, moving silently without armor, as if stalking prey. The centuriae was surrounded and unaware of their presence."

"Where were the sentries?"

"Killed first and silently," answered Carpathimos. "The men sleeping near the trees were next. I was in a tent near the center of camp, preparing to take my turn as sentry when one attacker entered. He ran when he saw I was awake." "How many do you estimate? And how is it that you are still standing?" asked Quintus.

"There may have been as few as twenty, but there could have been twice that many hidden in the trees. I chased after the men I saw, but when I slid down the bank into the river, I was separated from them. When I climbed back out of the river and up the bank, no one was left and the attackers had disappeared."

"What cohort and where?" asked General Quintus as he motioned Carpathimos to the map.

Carpathimos stepped closer to the table and followed the curving Akragas upriver with his finger, placing it on the map at the campsite where he had acquired his uniform. "The cohort of Commander Servios."

"And what time of night was this attack?"

"Very early morning. Still dark."

Quintus scrutinized Carpathimos. "You appear more seasoned than I would expect for a foot soldier. What is your name?"

"Remus, General. I have served before, under General Lucius Myridias. I have no family and wanted to fight for Rome once again."

"I also served under Lucius Myridias," said Quintus. "He was a good general, but he failed in the Dolomites. Now he wallows like a fat hog in the senate, growing old and useless. I don't intend to fail as he did." Quintus looked again at the map. "Where will they attack next, soldier?"

Carpathimos looked at the general, searching for a trap. "I believe they will not stray far from the city wall, at least not at first. They will attack only at night." Carpathimos drew a finger along the map, tracing the small camps marked between the river and the city. He paused as his finger reached a spot on the map where a cohort, camped among the trees, was indicated on the map. "Here," he said confidently, drawing the general's eyes to that point on the map.

"Yes, these are not tactics of honor. This Hannibal Gisgo will continue to poke at us until even he has no meat on his bones," Quintus said. "He seems willing to sacrifice his best men as well."

"May I speak freely, General?" asked Carpathimos before the cohort commander could put a hand on his arm as a warning.

"You may," said Quintus, waving off the commander's concern.

"Do you think this Carthaginian expects he will soon receive assistance and that is why he considers these tactics fruitful?"

General Quintus considered the idea and then nodded. "Perhaps that is true, soldier, but we are four legions of Roman troops. That is thirty-six cohorts—two hundred sixteen centuriae of highly trained Roman soldiers! Hannibal would need to slice away at us in this feeble and tedious way for a very long time before we would be whittled down enough to be defeated by whatever army he hopes will come to his rescue."

Carpathimos nodded. The general dismissed the two men, but called the commander back into the tent after Carpathimos had stepped away. "Keep a close eye on that man, Commander. If he runs or appears to be a man of Hannibal, then you have my permission to slay him."

Carpathimos and the commander mounted their horses to ride back to the cohort while the general stepped out of his tent to observe the weather. General Quintus watched Carpathimos ride off, studying his features and the way he carried himself. There was likely more to this simple soldier than he wanted the general to believe. As he pondered this, men began shouting in the distance. Again, and again, the same call was repeated, growing closer with each call. "Riders, riders!"

Closing the distance rapidly on horseback, two Roman soldiers rode into camp, dismounting in front of the general's tent. The soldiers started forward, but he stopped them. "I am here."

The riders saluted, fists over their chests, then one began speaking. "We bring information, General. An army of considerable strength has marched on, and taken, Herbesos to the west. The Carthaginians are headed this way, General."

"How strong?"

The other rider answered him. "Perhaps fifty thousand infantry and over five thousand cavalry. They fly the colors of the Celts and Spaniards."

Quintus nodded, putting his hand to his chin to ponder the information and imagine his newest opponent. "There is more, General," said the rider. "We counted sixty elephants."

The general paled. Members of his staff, eager to hear the news, had gathered around him and could sense the change in his demeanor. Realizing his error, Quintus straightened his back, held up his head, and folded his hands together to quiet them. "Carthage has taken Herbesos and next will be our supply line. Now we and Akragas starve together. Let those words echo in your ears," demanded Quintus. "You will finally get the battle for which you thirst, and now we fight for more than just Rome. We fight for our lives! Go spread the news to the legions. Apprise them of these cowardly nighttime attacks and begin training drills once again for open field battle."

To the horsemen, he added, "Ride on to the camp of General Megellus and inform him of what you have seen and what you have heard here."

During the night, Carpathimos took a turn at sentry duty. He was to patrol the river bank and the tree line next to where his cohort was camped. His partner throughout the night was to cover the territory on the other side of the cohort. Between the two of them, they would walk an ellipse around the sleeping soldiers. At roughly sixty-minute intervals, they would meet one another at each end of the ellipse. The first soldier to reach the meeting place would wait for the other for only a short time, the cumulative duration of a prearranged sequence of songs he would sing silently to himself, before alerting the stationary sentries, who stayed in camp, to begin searching for the missing man. As was customary, a sentry caught sleeping was immediately killed and replaced—a uniquely Roman way of encouraging vigilance while on patrol.

Carpathimos was reminded of that very fact by his commander as he started off into the woods. He made several winding forays through his designated patrol territory, getting the lay of the land. There was ample moonlight and, with it, he could easily identify the details of the riverbanks in both directions when he peered over the edge at the water.

While circling through the woods, he thought about Elijah, not knowing whether the youngster could find food for himself but suspecting not. After making the last rendezvous with his partner, Carpathimos moved quickly through the woods, following the river upstream until coming to the place where he had left Elijah. He softly called Elijah's name, then waited for a response. Hearing no reply, he moved further upriver and repeated the hushed call. Again, nothing. He tried several more times. Just before he turned to go, he heard a voice that spooked him. Was it Elijah or a soldier looking for him?

He stopped abruptly and waited for it again. He started to wonder if the voice had just been within his own head. When he heard it again, he breathed a sigh of relief. The voice came from somewhere below him along the water's edge, some four or five meters away. It was Elijah. Crouching low and extending his head and shoulders over the bank, Carpathimos asked, "Have you eaten?"

"Yes," came the reply in a distant and hushed sort of way. "I found some berries on bushes nearby. The birds seemed all right when they ate them, so I took a chance. I also trapped some small fry in a pool at the water's edge. They are not too bad if you swallow quickly."

"I must go, Elijah. I will try to bring you food soon, but I must be very careful." Carpathimos prepared to leave the edge of the river bank. "Stay hidden."

"If we get separated," asked Elijah, "where do I go from here?"

"West."

Carpathimos ran back to the rendezvous point, arriving just in time. Meanwhile, Elijah hunkered down along the base of the washed-out wall at the river's edge. This concavity sat along a natural bend in the river, which took on the extra water in springtime. The area had slowly enlarged over the years, as the water carved away the earth. It was well hidden from view from all sides, except straight across, but the brush was thick there, so it was unlikely anyone would come across it. Elijah hoped that the bear wouldn't amble down to the river here and that a sudden storm would not wash him out of his hiding place.

When morning came, Elijah woke to find half a chicken, cleaned and fire-roasted, tied to the end of a long, thin rope dangling in front of his little river house.

Carpathimos finished his patrol with the rise of the sun and was allowed to sleep briefly before the men began morning drills. He trained with the other soldiers in hand-to-hand combat, wielding long and short blades, javelins, and shields. In this situation, he functioned more like a teacher than another milite, his training far superior to those with whom he sparred.

The sun was still low when news of last night's attack trickled into camp. There had been another nighttime raid on one of the cohorts of General Megellus's legions. Carpathimos had guessed correctly. The men attacked had been camped nearest the wall on the opposite side of the city. Most had been killed or injured, they learned when one of General Quintus's staff rode into camp. He ordered Carpathimos to accompany him back to the general's war room.

The general was waiting for him at his map table.

"Your prediction was true, Remus," said Quintus. "Fortunately, our men were ready and the battle was not one-sided. The centuriae still sustained heavy losses, but they were able to take some of Hannibal's men as well." He paused, studying Carpathimos's large frame. "Tell me, Remus, in what capacity did you serve General Lucius Myridias?"

Carpathimos studied the question a moment. "I was a foot soldier only," he offered.

"Then where and for whom did you serve after leaving the Dolomites?"

Carpathimos thought quickly. "I served both within Rome and then in Ostia before returning to Brundisium to fish." These cities were forever etched within his mind. He would have to think quickly to provide any details, but he hoped he had offered just enough information to satisfy Quintus.

"And then you volunteered again to join us in Sicily," concluded Quintus. "We are fortunate to have you, Remus." Quintus could not yet decide whether the soldier who stood before him was just smart and experienced or if he should be put to death as a spy for Carthage. His responses seemed genuine enough, however.

Quintus made his way around the map table and to the door of the tent, where he began to strap on his chest plate. He grabbed his helmet and then asked Carpathimos to follow him. With one of Quintus's tribunes in tow, the men walked into the open and up the short incline where the base of the flats began stretching upward toward the city of Akragas. "We will take this city," Quintus professed, staring toward the city wall in the distance while shielding his eyes from the sun, "and then the next one and the next one."

When Quintus turned to face west, Carpathimos followed. Standing on the plateau with the trees bordering the river below, Carpathimos could see the horizon many kilometers away. Quintus decided to offer the fisherman some bait. "Soon we will encircle this island and Rome's new navy will control the sea. Carthage will not be permitted onto the island and her famous navy will no longer be strong enough to menace our shipping lanes to and from Rome."

Quintus turned to address his tribune, speaking freely to the other senior officer, pretending not to mind that Carpathimos heard the news. "We know Carthage has been building up troops on Sardinia. It is believed they will use it as a stepping stone from which they can invade Rome," he explained. The tribune nodded. "After we landed on Sicily, the Senate ordered the construction of warships to be ready to set sail once we take Lilybeaum in the west." Quintus turned again, setting his sights once more toward Lilybeaum, still too far away to see.

"The fleet will surprise the Carthaginians in the waters north of Sicily, where Carthage travels freely. Meanwhile, my friend Marcus Regulus is pushing the Senate to approve his plan to attack Carthage on African soil. He intends to supply his ships with troops from here before sailing for Africa."

The three men stood quietly for a moment before Quintus started walking back down the slope. He stopped suddenly, then turned, stabilizing his footing against the damp grass of the morning dew, one foot higher up the hill than the other. "I nearly forgot why I summoned you this morning, Remus," he said. "The men who were attacked last night have lost their commander and they need a new leader. I thought that instead of splitting them into separate centuriae, you might be ready for a command of your own. Go to them now. You already know where they are." Quintus pointed in the direction Carpathimos had pinpointed on the map the day before.

Carpathimos knew better than to protest. He saluted Quintus and set off down the hill before marching into the woods. He felt trapped between a watchful eye and a battle he would be forced to fight. Yet he now had information to pass along to Hanno. Granted, it may be false or misleading information and part of a trap to catch him spying for Carthage. The only way out of this situation meant Carpathimos either needed to win Quintus's trust in battle or run from him. The problem with both options was that they required fighting to save his own hide.

General Quintus watched him until he disappeared into the woods and then he spoke to the tribune. "Now we watch him. He will either try to abscond with that information or he will be emboldened to stay and fight with us. I want you to reassign two or three of our fastest headhunters to his centuriae. He is to believe that we are just giving him more men with whom to fight. If he tries to run, send those dogs after him."

# Chapter XII

———

THE ROAR CAME first, a continuous rumble of thunder that slowly crescendoed. It began so subtly that it was ignored until the amplitude and resonance finally provoked a state of surprise. The listeners were shocked, however, not by how loud the roar truly was, but by how such a noise could have been ignored in the first place. Trying to rationalize such an aberrancy, soldiers look to the sky, trying to spot a wall cloud or a squall from which such thunder could emanate. But with bright blue skies overhead, the men are stricken with the realization that such a rumble, growing louder by the minute, is actually caused by the advancing charge of enemy cavalry. Thus, it was fitting that such a flagitious sound should herald the pounding of twenty thousand hooves against the hard earth as animals and riders raced toward a destination where the thunderclap in history will ring for centuries to come.

The Council of Elders sent Hanno The Younger, son of General Hannibal Gisgo, to rescue the city of Akragas and stop the advancing Romans. He had eliminated the supply line of the Romans and was now within striking distance. He sent five thousand Numidians on horseback ahead, to smash into the Roman line with one initial blow, throwing them sprawling backward on their heels.

With due urgency, the Roman cavalry assembled quickly, long starved for a fight and wholly prepared. Charging forward, the eager enemies met on open ground just west of the Hypsas, where the trees give way to a natural opening, exposing open fields already harvested by the siege engine of Rome. The cataclysmic impact of thousands of galloping horses and their weaponized payloads made the earth tremble.

The Numidian cavalry spilled onto the scene with great velocity, their horses glistening in the morning sun from the sweat blanketing their coats. The horses and their experienced riders weaved back and forth as they approached, defending themselves against the Roman arrows raining down upon them. Each horseman, dressed only in a waist garment or nothing at all, carried one round shield, made lighter by using only leather and wood, and a long javelin, which he unleashed on the advancing Roman cavalry at the last possible moment.

These were expert horsemen, needing only a rope to guide their mounts and no saddle to weigh them down. The black sky created by five thousand wooden missiles filled the rapidly narrowing divide between the charging front lines like a fog on a fall day, making it impossible to anticipate the impact of horse and man.

The speedy Numidian raiders outmaneuvered the larger, more heavily burdened Roman horses, turning back on them once they broke through the advancing line, thereby creating an attack from both front and behind. The Numidians fought with smaller and shorter knives, trying to inflict as much damage as possible before riding just out of reach into the tree line to resupply with a fresh stock of new javelins.

Armored with helmets, chest plates, and heavily constructed shields, the Romans deflected much of the initial assault, losing only a few riders and horses to well-placed javelin thrusts or knives. Driving their mounts at full speed, the Romans gave chase. Reeling from the last attack, the Numidians gave only one more barrage of javelin throws before disappearing into the woods behind them. Rome slowed at the trees, but an eagerness to pursue propelled them forward. They kept just out of reach of the retreating Numidians' javelins.

Approaching the coast, the Romans lost sight of the Numidians when they disappeared over a hill, but once the Romans scaled that same hill, they not only found the riders, but encountered the main body of the army of Carthage waiting to spring their trap. The front line of Roman cavalry careened into a wall of armor-piercing weapons and a mass of men that quickly overwhelmed them.

The Romans sounded the retreat nearly as soon as they came over the hill, but it was too late for several hundred men who perished at the hands of Spanish and Celtic mercenaries. Trying to preserve a fraction of the cavalry, the Romans fell back to the river Hypsas while Hanno's infantry made camp on the top of that hill. From there the young general could see his father's city and the expanse of Roman encampments. For today, the Romans had been beaten.

With a city in peril and a Roman army near starvation, cut off from its only supply line, the desperation felt within both was palpable. The Roman soldiers endured nighttime attacks and frequent raids from both the city and the hill covered by a Carthaginian army. After two more months, struggling to outlast the city of Akragas, Quintus and Megellus requested a battle with the young Hanno. Initially he refused, turning the Romans away in an attempt to break them. Shortly after this, however, Hannibal sent word to his son from the beleaguered city that the end was near. Hanno was forced to accept the Roman's request for an open battle.

Carpathimos, already accustomed to miserable conditions, had taken it upon himself to try to catch fish from the Hypsas River with his men. The river ran foul with mud and the feces of so many soldiers camped along the course of the river. Birds had vanished, since anything edible had already been eaten. The trees dotting the valley had either died or been cut down and burned. Morale was the worst he had ever seen. Carpathimos had once been witness to a Roman defeat by the Gauls at the start of winter, but that paled in comparison to this, he thought. His men seemed to accept his guidance and appreciate his daily training, wrestling and throwing and working on sword and javelin tactics.

Even Kurush and Isingoma took advantage of the practice. Both men were among the fastest runners Carpathimos had ever seen. Both had joined his centuriae shortly after he took command. Kurush was Persian. His powerful legs, he claimed, were the result of running in the mountains, carrying water every day to keep his family and animals alive. Isingoma was a very tall man with black skin and long arms and legs. He came from somewhere south of Egypt and had been a shepherd for his village. Both men had joined Rome's army the same way Carpathimos had originally, as slaves.

Something seemed different about them, Carpathimos mused. He had seen men change in all sorts of ways while fighting in Rome's army against their will. Some accepted and adopted the way of life, while others struggled to conform to the will of Roman dominance. Carpathimos had done both, but somehow, he had acquired a discipline while training as a gladiator that served his new role in the infantry. Probably serving under the father of the woman he loved had tempered him, too, he thought. These two runners, however, gave Carpathimos a wide berth. They followed orders but did not go out of their way to help others in the camp. Their shared demeanor made Carpathimos uneasy—and he didn't like that feeling. What's more, he had not been able to check on Elijah for months and he worried about the youth.

Occasionally, Carpathimos led his men through the woods to hunt for game or to forage for edible berries and plants. Very occasionally, he spotted signs that the young man was still alive. Fearing the other men might notice those signs as well, Carpathimos always kept his distance from Elijah's territory. He never felt he could safely sneak away from their camp. His men seemed to watch his every movement, especially Kurush and Isingoma, thus spoiling his chances of getting food to Elijah.

One day, a man named Caius, General Quintus's senior tribune, rode into camp on his black stallion, looking for the man they knew as Remus. His unannounced arrival interrupted the soldiers' badly deserved rest period, following a strenuous morning of training. He seemed to unsettle everyone's nerves about the coming conflict.

"Prepare your men for battle, Remus," ordered Caius. "At sunrise tomorrow, we fight Carthage. After that, we put an end to this city."

Carpathimos saluted. Caius rode off to alert another commander of his same destiny. The men standing, lying and sitting around Carpathimos had gone silent. Open battle was always something the men claimed to want. They trained for it. They yearned for victory and the spoils, much of which trickled down to even the newest Roman soldiers. And yet, for those who had experienced such a battle before, there was always a time where the mind hears the words and must try to convince the body that it has good news.

By now, Carpathimos was commanding nearly three centuriae of men, three groups of eighty men in each. This was not even half a traditional cohort, but nevertheless, he was considered a cohort commander. His ragtag group was composed of soldiers who had come from other shrinking centuriae after their commanders and many soldiers were killed during raids. Somehow, Carpathimos united them into one cohesive fighting force, albeit often strained by the variety of personalities in so many young and invincible men.

After the tribune Caius left, the silence was uncomfortable but, one by one, the expressions on the faces of Carpathimos's men gradually evolved, changing from fear and anguish to confidence, hope and finally pride. Within the camp, there was a nearly ubiquitous show of relief that something was finally going to happen. The long and bitter standoff was coming to an end. Eventually, the men around Carpathimos cheered, singing out a battle cry together and unifying the three centuriae over a common cause.

Carpathimos couldn't help but feel some of that excitement himself.

He had prepared them, live or die, to compete with the others in the legion. As before, he had gotten to know some of these young men and learn about their backgrounds and their hopes and dreams. They shared a sense of camaraderie and so, naturally, he wanted to see them succeed. He didn't want to let them down. Many of the soldiers under his command were barely old enough to sprout hair on their faces and yet he had been responsible for preparing them for what could be the last fight of their lives. At first, thinking about it made him proud. And then, as his memories interjected themselves into his reality, it made him sick to the inner core of his being. He loathed what these men stood for—not the men themselves, but Rome. Where the others yearned for victory, he yearned for the destruction of Rome.

He hated being in this position. He hated the wasted time and being part of what might become a Roman victory. He needed to get back to Rome to inflict as much damage as he possibly could on those responsible for the murder of his wife and friends. Sensing that this ordeal soon would be over, and that he would be able to report what he knew to Hanno, thereby ensuring that Yzebel Gisgon would be safe, he allowed himself to share in the excitement with his men.

Sunrise found the Roman encampments deserted, the fires only smoldering embers and the lonely landscape a wretched wasteland. Shining green leaves and grass had disappeared, replaced by mud and human detritus. In perfect formation on the middle ground between the city of Akragas and the massive army of Carthage, stood Rome's four legions in Sicily. They were an awe-inspiring force. Each man held a large, colored, rectangular shield, curved over a frame of wood and metal. Their crimson and black colors matched the plumes of their bronze helmets. The polished metal of the helmets represented the top of a five-pointed star of bronze, created by the breastplate in the center, the arm guards to the sides, and the waist and hip armor at the bottom.

The light infantry in the front lines held the short hasta, a throwing spear short enough to be used as a close-combat weapon. The men of the heavy infantry gripped both the two-meter long pila, which was devastatingly accurate at long distances, and the short cut-and-thrust sword, or gladius, the principle weapon of close combat. Vastly outnumbered, Rome would depend on the training of every man and horse for success. The cavalry, eager to avenge their prior loss, stood ready near the front. The archers flanked the legions at both ends. They would support the infantry with a barrage of arrows capable of penetrating the Carthaginians' lightweight shields.

Hanno had positioned his infantry in rows across the front, forming a line that stretched well beyond the reach of the Romans. He filled the front line with his most elite warriors, the Spaniards. Their tunics were lined with a crimson sash to match the crest of their helmets. Spread across the front of the hillside overlooking the Roman army, the polished metal from their short thrusting swords glinted against the morning sun. Behind the Spaniards stood the Celts, who fought with long curved blades. Next came the slingers from the Iberian islands, who could fell a running soldier with a stone hurled from their spinning leather pouches. Those stones could fly over one hundred meters. Behind them, the willing mercenaries waited. They had been gathered from the cities and towns on the march toward Akragas, and they were eager to defend their homes and fields from Rome's forces. Centered in the back row, Hanno's small but formidable forest elephants towered over all of them.

When the sun cleared the distant hills and trees, war cries emanated from each side, spreading across both armies, attesting to their fortitude and will to proceed. The Romans, outnumbered and at a disadvantage on low ground, made the first move.

What fighting experience Carthage had acquired in years controlling the sea, Rome had learned by their conquest of land. While some fifteen thousand Roman infantry charged forward at full speed, their archers and cavalry attacked the Carthaginian flanks. The speed of the Roman milite was renowned and considered second only to his tenacity with the blade.

Carthage was caught flat footed. The fierce Romans pierced the center of the Carthaginian line, slicing through the gallant Spaniards and sending the less trained and ill-equipped mercenaries fleeing for their lives.

But Carthage would not be outdone. Their greater numbers fought bravely and the battle waged on, the dead of both armies staining the earth and mounting as fast as the minutes of battle. Eventually, the elephants at the rear, surrounded by chaos and unfamiliar with the notion of retreat, panicked as the Romans flowed through the line. The elephants scattered, trampling men with indifference and fracturing the main body of the Carthaginian army, splitting it in two. The Romans seized control of this wide fissure and poured through it to the back, fanning out in both directions and pinning the soldiers of Carthage between two hammers.

The experienced Romans kept slashing, their brutal past enhancing their present and guaranteeing them a future on Sicily. Bewildered and surprised, Hanno and a few of his elite guard vanished in the melee, leaving thousands of his men butchered and dying. Witnessing the fall of the Carthaginian army, the garrison from Akragas flooded out of the city to attack Rome's exposed rear in a desperate attempt to turn the tide of the battle. However, despite the added force from the city, the numbers lay in Rome's favor. This assault was also put down. Like his son before him, Hannibal escaped, leaving the army to perish on the field and the remaining population of Akragas to beg for mercy under Roman rule.

At the end of the day, the sun set over the horrific scene of blood and bodies, a tangled mass of limbs and weapons, of gaping mouths and cloudy eyes. Rome had lost nearly a legion of men, but Carthage, decimated and stunned, had lost ten times that number. The remainder of soldiers without significant injuries traded death for slavery at the hands of Rome. The wounded would not see the sun rise.

Carpathimos, covered in blood like the rest of his men, stood victorious and nearly impossible to recognize. Aside from some nicks and a few developing bruises, he was fine. So were nearly all his men, despite their blood-stained skin and clothing. Even the polished bronze was dulled by the umber cast of coagulated and drying heme.

Following the battle, Quintus ordered one of his legions into Akragas and when the infantry entered the city, Carpathimos hid within the mass of men, then ducked away. He crawled through an opening in the city wall and ran quickly into the trees before slipping into the river. Carpathimos waded up river, glancing back to see if anyone was watching. Confident that he had escaped successfully, he dove under the water to clean himself of the terrors of war. Pulling himself onto shore, he studied his tunic, finding it irreversibly stained and tainted. No amount of river current could free his tunic of the marks of battle. Far from any sign of soldiers, he scuttled up into the trees to find Elijah.

"Elijah!" he called. He ran to the hollowed-out site along the riverbed where he had last seen Elijah and called again. "Elijah!" This time louder. Again, nothing. Calculating the worst possible outcome, Carpathimos ran farther upstream. He had to leave Elijah behind if he couldn't be found immediately. Carpathimos's mind raced as fast as his sprint through the forest.

He wanted to believe that he wouldn't be missed by the army—after all, so many had been lost in battle. He hoped that days from now as the men of his centuriae scoured the hill, they would give up the search for his body. He tried to anticipate what Quintus would do next. Would he assume that his secrets died on the hill with Carpathimos? Or would Quintus send a headhunter out into the wilderness to hunt for him? Presuming the latter, Carpathimos forged on.

He splashed across the river and clambered up the opposite bank, shedding his arm guards, belt, and hip armor into the water. He turned west, keeping to the trees to avoid any of Carthage's fleeing men or any Romans still in pursuit. Alone on a strange island, wearing a blood-stained tunic and carrying only his short knife, Carpathimos set his sights on the mountains in the distance.

While Carpathimos ran, Quintus's soldiers poured through the streets of Akragas like water flooding a dry river bed, entering every building and probing every hole. There was little to loot and even less to eat. The able-bodied men and women who remained were rounded up, tied together, and escorted out of the city. They would be marched back to Syracuse and await passage to Rome. Some twenty-five thousand became slaves that day. Those who fought, died. The young, old, and infirm were burned along with Akragas's dead as Quintus attempted to eradicate the city of its former inhabitants.

Kurush and Isingoma, as much as any men in the army, relished the feel of victory and enjoyed the rewards of Rome's conquests. Like many captured before them, they had accepted their new rulers and adopted the Roman ways. At first, fear made them comply, but later, when they became part of something as successful as Rome's expansion, Kurush and Isingoma assimilated. Romans, both citizens and soldiers alike, shared the bounty won in battle, and this practice influenced many of Rome's conquered individuals to assimilate into the culture and adopt Roman ideals.

Their first taste of victory had come under the command of the Consul Appius Claudius Caudex, when Kurush and Isingoma helped defeat Hiero in Syracuse and establish Rome's first foothold on Sicily. From there, the two eagerly joined Quintus on his march to the west, knocking Carthage backward like a stumbling giant, again and again.

As Rome razed Akragas through the night and into the next day, Isingoma remembered his directive. Peeling away from the raucous and celebratory infantry, he sought his commander. Tapping Kurush on the back to get his attention, Isingoma asked Kurush if he had seen Remus. He hadn't. Kurush fell in behind Isingoma and the two proceeded to search the crowds of soldiers throughout the city. Everywhere they went, they found men celebrating in one way or another. Men drank and sang and carried on raucously, while others fought over the few treasures that still existed within the city walls.

The two men combed the streets, searching for the man they knew as Remus. Kurush climbed up into a lookout along the wall nearest the main gate and peered through the pungent smoke that hovered over the western portion of the city. Isingoma found most of the men from his cohort, but no one had seen Remus since shortly after the battle ended. That is, all but one. Isingoma had run into one of the men in his centuriae who thought he may have seen their commander after the battle, but he lost sight of him in the tightly packed group of men crowding through the gate. Canvassing the crowd, Isingoma spotted the tribune Caius, who had charged them with the task of watching, and, if necessary, killing their commander. He walked up to Caius and brushed by his shoulder. "We go hunting," Isingoma said. Their eyes met only briefly. Caius nodded. Isingoma marched out of the city, waving to Kurush to follow him.

Carpathimos moved quickly through the fir and scrubby poplar groves dotting the landscape. He kept his ears open for any unnatural sounds and tried to look for signs of Elijah while he scanned the horizon for troops. That was a lot to ask of his senses, given how fast he was moving. He skirted open meadows. Where he could, he ran, especially when he was forced to cross vast open areas. Nearing another nightfall, he came upon a small subalpine lake fed by a meandering creek bleeding slowly southward from the central highlands of the island. Here he paused to drink the refreshing water and catch his breath. Carpathimos glanced around and then sat against a large stone jutting out of the ground between two trees. It was a perfectly placed seat for someone to gaze at the lake and listen to the trickle of the brook while relaxing from a hard day's hike. If only he could relax, he thought. He wondered when he had last enjoyed such a moment, trying to forget the cries of pain and the sights and smells of death.

Exhausted, he allowed his eyes to shut as the running water lulled him toward sleep. He dropped his hands to the ground at his sides to stabilize himself and his fingers touched a curved twig, lying flat across the dirt. Nearly asleep, he ran his fingers around the curve, but it kept going, forming a complete circle. He grasped it between his fingers and drew it up to his face for inspection. This had been a small sapling, cut from the ground and wound around itself several times into a circle the size of his face. Whoever had done this must have been sitting here, enjoying this view. And then he saw a thin piece of string used to lash the stiffer end to the main circle, tying it securely in place. The thin piece of string had been a part of a larger rope. The rope from which he had hung the chicken for Elijah to find.

Carpathimos jumped to his feet, scanning the ground for tracks. The leaves from the sapling lay on the ground behind the rock where Elijah had stripped them. They were wilted but not long cast. He wasn't too far behind Elijah.

Carpathimos crossed over the creek and searched for more signs of Elijah's whereabouts. The sun was setting and it was getting darker, so Carpathimos moved faster, thinking that he might not see something important in the waning light. Stepping closer to the brush, he noticed a thin twig, broken and bent to the side, likely in the direction of someone walking that way. He passed forward through the void in the bushes created by the broken twig, slowly at first, looking for this sign to repeat itself, which it did. Faster, he moved through the woods following the subtle trail as a large blood-red moon rose above him.

Kurush and Isingoma searched their centuriae camp, finding some of Carpathimos's things, but no sign of his armor or weapon. Next, they scoured the river banks. Knowing that Carpathimos would not have gone south—there were not enough places to hide—they agreed that he either set off toward the mountains or went east or west looking for a ship to board along the coast. Rome controlled shipping to the east, so they decided he would not travel in that direction and chance an interaction. That left north or west.

The two briefly followed the river north before crossing the Akragas. Making his way up the bank, Kurush spotted a set of hip armor pinned behind a rock by the running water. Holding it up for Isingoma to see, he spotted the arm guards as well. A man had crossed here. It may not be armor from Remus, but there was a deserter, and either way, the men knew they would be rewarded for returning to camp with a head on a spear. Signs of crushed grass and broken twigs guided them west. Keeping their eyes open and running just a few meters apart, Kurush and Isingoma began their hunt.

# Chapter XIII

———

SORIAN JUMPED OUT of the boat and onto the docks in Ostia, happy to be near dry land and relieved to be in a Roman city once again. Ostia sat along the mouth of the Tiber, a short distance to his destination—Rome. On this late summer day, the stone streets of this port city were filled with farmers, sailors, peddlers, and all forms of marketgoers eager to sell, buy, or barter the goods going to or coming from the harbor. He thought about the ironies in his life. As a young boy, he never had the opportunity to escape to the coast and lay eyes on the sea. He had never set foot in Ostia, despite living in Rome. Sorian did pass this city once—while incarcerated in the crowded belly of a river transport ferrying prisoners to the harbor, where they were loaded onto a larger vessel. Before that, while serving within Rome's army, he fought in the landlocked northern territories, where the only waters had been frigid rivers flowing out of the mountains. In the end, it had been water that rescued him from the mines and carried him back to this Roman city. All he needed now was to find passage to Rome, either on another boat or in the back of a wagon. At this point, he didn't care which.

Moving slowly through the crowd, he blended in with the commoners, perhaps a bit dirtier and more disheveled in appearance than those able to purchase goods in the market and merchant shops. He needed money. His mind raced, trying to think of a scheme while he observed the passersby. Stopping at a fountain near the city center, he sat on the stone lip of the large round pool. Pigeons frolicked at the water's edge while children danced merrily in the ankle-deep water.

Glancing toward a fruit stand, Sorian noticed two women who appeared well off. Both were dressed in white robes and adorned with golden lace hairnets and gold bracelets. One appeared slightly older, but they had similar features. Sorian speculated that they might be sisters, probably the wives or daughters of a landowner or wealthy merchant. One carried an armload of new linens and colorful blankets, while the other carried a basket of freshly cut flowers and a variety of fruits. They paused briefly at the fruit stand, fondling some of the produce before moving on to the next vendor. Sorian stood and discreetly followed them, keeping pace just far enough behind to avoid suspicion.

He watched the elder of the two pull coins from a small leather pouch looped over her forearm. Briefly he considered bumping into her and taking the coin purse, but then thought better of it. One could lose a hand if caught stealing and troops were constantly patrolling the city to protect citizens like them from would-be thieves like him. Conviction only required one witness, one accuser, and the evidence. Such an attempt was too risky. Pausing between market vendors, Sorian let the sisters disappear into the crowd. When a thought came to him, he studied the vendors, paying special attention to the way they handled money.

Each vendor was busy and focused on possible patrons. The men shouted at potential buyers, to get their attention and entice them to browse, often inviting women and men alike to try on articles of clothing, handle the soft linens, or caress the vividly colored shawls and blankets. Money changed hands nearly as quickly as words between customers and merchants. What

Sorian needed was a diversion, something to capture the attention of every-one around him, freeing him to acquire the money he needed.

This unique street in Ostia featured fruit vendors and jewelry makers, textile weavers, and leatherworkers, all selling their wares. Soothsayers were foretelling the future, medicine men peddled earthenware jars filled with sweet-smelling potions, herbal remedies, incense, and honey. Fishermen and farmers offered fresh fish, poultry, geese, goats, and lambs for slaughter. Stacked high alongside Ostia's many permanent buildings was a large pile of bundled straw drying in the sun.

Smiling at the notion he concocted, Sorian entered a promising build-ing in the middle of the market and greeted the owner as he browsed the merchandise. When the owner was distracted, Sorian grabbed a lit candle burning in a wall sconce and quickly exited the back of the building. Protect-ing the small flame with his hand, Sorian approached the tall stack of straw. Making sure no one was watching, he squatted and held the flame to a straw bundle. The breeze moving through the alley whipped at the growing flame, igniting the stack and soon it was a billowing inferno. Sorian moved behind the penned animals and waited. Within moments, the fire engulfed the entire stack and began gnawing at the wooden building. Shouts from the people in the market resulted in the expected melee.

Sorian hurried into the crowd of scurrying and distraught shoppers and shopkeepers. One of the farmers he had seen earlier was moving his goods out of harm's way as fast as he could go, picking up animals and moving crates out of the alley into the street. Sorian carried a crate of noisy geese and accepted the farmer's rushed acknowledgement and thanks as he con-tinued his rescue of the animals. Sorian set the crate down next to a clothing vendor and then stacked as many linens and woven goods as he could carry on top of the crate. With a nod, the merchant accepted his help; his arms, too, were loaded with precious items.

At the jeweler's stand, Sorian paused, setting down the heavy crate on the makeshift display table in order to restack the items on his pile. Shuffling the textiles back and forth between his hands, Sorian took in the sight of the fire as smoke billowed out of the alley and from the building now entirely consumed by flames. Within the melee of hazy smoke, scurrying people, and bleating animals, Sorian went unnoticed. The jeweler was preoccupied with bagging his precious stones and jewelry. Reaching down to pick up the crate, Sorian slid his hand under the table, taking a large handful of coins from a small wooden box the vendor had carelessly left unattended as he hurriedly packed up his other items. Heaving the crate of geese and the reorganized fabrics, Sorian disappeared into the crowd. It had all been so easy.

He left the market in a state of chaos, but with a new tunic, a pair of sandals, and a small new pouch in which he stowed the remainder of the coins. He now carried a number of heavy bronze trientes and a few shiny, new silver didrachms, which were new to him since he had last been on Roman soil. In his new clothes, Sorian moved along the Tiber, looking for someone to take him to Rome. Eventually, he found what he was looking for. He offered two of his bronze trientes to a man in exchange for passage on his boat. When it was full of goods, they departed for Rome.

Passing near Portus, a city on the opposite bank of the Tiber from Ostia, Sorian stared in amazement at a massive construction project. Adjacent to the river was a large harbor, the dirt having been excavated from the bank, widening the Tiber at this location into a large manmade lake. Within the harbor floated rows of brand new Roman quinqueremes, massive warships as new as the silver coins in his purse. Behind these, on the north bank, twenty more ships were under construction. Adjacent to this new shipyard, a large field was covered in rows of men sitting on what appeared to be long wooden benches. They were rowing with long oars to the cadence of oarsmen, who dictated both the speed and the angle of arc in the oars. Leaning back and then pushing forward against the oars, which rested in oarlocks at the top of posts, the new sailors directed the paddle ends of the oars through the air in deep, swooping ellipses.

Sorian glanced at the captain of the riverboat with a curious look. The captain smiled and responded, "For the past forty days, they have toiled along that bank, building warships and training men to row them. Nearly one hundred have sailed out within the past week alone! I am told that hundreds of boat builders have been employed at this new shipyard."

As his oarsmen pushed the riverboat along, the captain pointed at another ship anchored in the harbor. It had been damaged and burned. "They are copying the design of that captured bird of prey from Carthage." Sorian noted the similarity between the shape and style of the new warships and the Carthaginian vessel. The captain added proudly, "Rome is building her new fleet!"

Arriving in the city of Rome with the setting sun behind him, Sorian climbed out of the boat with a renewed sense of duty to Rome. He was more eager than before to confront his old adversary, General Lucius Myridias. Ambling along the main thoroughfare of Capitoline Hill, he wandered by the Temple of Jupiter Optimus Maximus. He paused to observe the great structure before entering to look around. He marveled at a large golden crown sitting atop a pedestal within the temple, remembering how he saw it with his father when he was a small boy. Now that crown was one hundred years old and he had grown up to become an officer in Rome's army.

The crown appeared to be made of solid gold but was far too large to fit on anyone's head—yet it seemed smaller than he remembered. Bending slightly, to allow the light of a nearby oil-fed lantern to shine on an inscription, Sorian read the words carved in the stone under the crown. The inscription told of Rome's triumph over the Samnite army, this crown being offered to Rome from Carthage as a gift honoring Rome's victory. Back in those days, being recognized by the world's greatest sea power was an honor. Now, they were preparing for a naval battle with that great sea power. Sorian shook his head.

Across the hexagonal esplanade stood another temple Sorian vaguely recalled from his youth. Perhaps it had been under construction when he came here. Walking up to the central portico he gazed at the inscription, trying to make out the writing in the poor light. This was the Temple of Hercules The Invincible, and it held the artifacts representing Rome's relationship to Greece, acknowledging Rome's heritage and cultural connection to its older sibling. Exiting the Temple of Hercules, he looked back at the Temple of Jupiter and reaffirmed his desire to again serve the elite and ascend Rome's political order. To do this, he needed to reconnect with old partners. He vowed to do whatever he must to hurt Lucius and take back the time Lucius had stolen from him. It was time to find those old friends. But first he needed to acquire some information, and he knew just the place to find it.

Weaving through the streets of the sleeping city, Sorian made his way beyond Capitoline Hill, past the Circus Maximus, which now stood quietly, like a dormant volcano, to the foot of the Caelian Hill and the start of the Via Appia. Just within the city wall situated along the Via Appia, there used to be a small establishment that served food and drink to weary travelers and thirsty city dwellers alike. It had been run by a one-eyed man just a bit older than Sorian. What this man lacked in vision, he made up for with his powers of observation. Aemilius always seemed to know something about everything going on in the city, and more importantly, what was being discussed in the senate among the leaders of Rome.

Sorian approached the old building, hoping to find not only food and drink, but also Aemilius, alive and well and still peddling information. Sorian pushed at the heavy wooden door and peered inside. Only two people sat there, at a small round table near the back of the room. Three oil lamps provided the only light. Sorian slipped in and sat near the wall by the door. The old wooden chair creaked under his weight, but it fit his body well and as he allowed his legs and back to relax for the first time all day. He could easily fall asleep in that chair.

Moments later, one of the two people in the back got up and walked over to Sorian. Sorian did not initially recognize him, but the man was Aemilius. He was more haggard and aged in appearance, but his smile was unchanged.

"What may I offer you, my friend?" Aemilius asked.

Sorian reached out to put a hand on the man's arm. "A glass of posca and a bit of bread and fruits."

Aemilius nodded. "You will have to settle for a mulsum instead because I am out of vinegar. Honey with wine feels better in the throat of a weary traveler, anyway." He hurried to fetch the items.  When he returned, the other patron got up to leave and said his goodbyes. Aemilius set down the tray of food and a chunk of bread he had torn from the end of a larger loaf. A tall, deep-throated clay pocula held the mulsum.

Aemilius stood quietly while Sorian laid two bronze coins on the table for the food and drink and then he set five more round coins in the center of the table, all stacked in a single column. Aemilius cleared his throat and sat in a chair across from Sorian, eyeing the stack of bronze coins while he slid his hand across the table to confiscate the first two coins.

"I haven't seen you here before, have I friend?" asked Aemilius.

"I spent some time here years ago. I thought I would come back to see if the food was any better now," joked Sorian. Aemilius laughed, then sat forward, fingering the stack of bronze coins. Sorian nodded. "Tell me Aemilius, do you still claim to know who comes and goes and lives and dies in this city?"

Aemilius grinned. "Of course I do. I may have lost an eye, but I still have two good ears! Besides, this is not just any little tavern along the streets of Rome. I have many faithful patrons who have deep ties to this city. They enjoy drink as much as anyone. Even members of the Senate and Peoples' Assembly meet here from time to time to share in drink and camaraderie."

"Is that so?" Sorian asked the next question casually. "Tell me, Aemilius, does the former general by the name of Lucius Myridias find his way here?"

Aemilius studied Sorian's eyes then glanced at the coins under his fingers. Sorian reached for the coins. He slid the top bronze coin from the pile with his thumb, pushing it in Aemilius's direction.

Aemilius scooped up the coin. "Lucius Myridias comes in here about once every two or three weeks and stays most of the night. He sits alone and sips at the wine, picking at whatever I set in front of him to eat. He isn't particular, just likes his place in that corner." Aemilius, pointed in the direction of a dark corner far from the door. "These days he isn't very popular. He seems bent on trying to stand in the way of the Consul's vision for our future."

Sorian spun an olive on the table in front of him, staring at Aemilius and waiting for him to continue. Aemilius eyed the coins again, trying to secure more payment for what he had to offer. Sorian leaned in and asked, "What makes you think that our General Lucius is trying to obstruct our path?" Sorian slid another coin in Aemilius's direction.

"He hasn't been the same since his daughter left and never came back. Word has it that he is trying to gather the votes needed to obstruct the other members' desire to send an army to Africa. People say that he is trying to keep Rome small, keep Rome from expanding."

"What do you think?"

"I think he is a cautious and deliberate man. He was against Duilius fighting Carthage at sea, but still the ships are being built. He won't succeed now, either, and I suspect that he will continue to wither away until they oust him from the Senate. The current Consul is too popular with the people and most of the senate members."

"Who is this popular Consul of whom you speak?" asked Sorian.

"You have been gone a long time, haven't you?" Aemilius grinned. "Marcus Regulus Atilius. Do you know of him?"

A broad smile crossed Sorian's face. "I most certainly do, Aemilius. I most certainly do." Sorian swallowed the last of his mulsum and reached for the remainder of the coins on the table. He jostled them within his palm, stood to leave, and tossed the remaining coins into the air at Aemilius, who tried to capture them on his outstretched tunic.

As Sorian opened the door to leave, he briefly ducked back in. "Where does my friend Regulus live now, Aemilius?"

Aemilius smiled, pointing through the open window toward a dark street on Palatine Hill. "You will find his palace overlooking the Circus Maximus. If you need a place to sleep tonight, you are welcome to the back room."

Sorian accepted the offer, following Aemilius to the little room. Before retiring, Sorian walked over to the small table and chair that Lucius frequented. He sat in the chair, running his hands on the wood surface of the table, imagining how Lucius might feel sitting alone in the darkness. The isolation was ideal, he thought. Lucius had been alone for a long time now, even within this large city. Sorian ran his fingertips over the wavy grain of the wood table, picturing Lucius doing the same. How he would enjoy taking even this experience away from Lucius. Sorian grinned.

Lying down to rest in the storage room, amongst an array of fruit baskets and the unmistakably pungent odor of vinegar, which evidently was not in short supply after all, he smiled and shook his head. He could scarcely believe his good fortune. In the morning he would catch up with a childhood friend and fellow soldier. He and Marcus Regulus had grown up on the same rough streets of the Aventine Hill and had trained together for battle many years ago. He was certain there was an alliance to be made. With that in mind, he would rest easily.

The dawn of a new day found Sorian up early to meet it. Cruising past the Circus Maximus, Rome's massive arena, Sorian stopped and gazed at the top of Palatine Hill. The rising sun behind him left a looming shadow from the Circus across the face of the Palatine, but the majestic palaces that lined the top were well illuminated by the morning rays. He recognized most of the structures from years past, but there was a new one, modest in comparison to some, yet still impressive in its own right. Its gleaming white walls and stone columns stood out from the others, whose luster had dulled over the years. Hiking the winding street to the top, he hoped to find his old friend receptive to his plan.

———

Marcus Regulus rolled out of his large bed and stretched, stiff muscles giving way to the strain and relaxing on his lean torso and wiry limbs. One of Rome's leading generals, his warrior's body remained tight and toned from daily exercises. He had vowed never to let his body fall to the passions of Rome's elite. He resisted the rich foods and rampant liquor consumption that led so many into a dissipated lifestyle. Returning to the bed, he leaned over the woman who shared his passions and kissed the small of her back, careful not to wake her. Then, stepping softly around to the end of the bed, he ran his long fingers down the back of her leg, over the gently curving muscle of her calf before ending his caress at the soft skin of her heel.

Quietly, he walked onto the massive stone balcony that overlooked the arena far below and stretched his muscles again. The morning sun warmed his face. He breathed in the fresh air, the sweet scents of myrtle, oleander and crocus flowers circulating in his nares and settling on his palate.

"It looks like you won our bet," came a voice behind him. Regulus swung around, surprised, his fists raised and feet spread defensively as two of Regulus's elite Red Guard came running, swords drawn.

"Marcus! Calm yourself. Surely you remember our little bet—who among us would be the first to erect a palace on the top of this hill," said Sorian, leaning against the balcony railing.

Marcus Regulus dropped his fists and relaxed his posture. "Sorian! Where did you come from? Wait! Have you been released from prison?"

"In a manner of speaking, yes, I have," Sorian tried to see his friend between the bodies of the Red Guardsmen taking position between them. Sorian studied the menacing figures standing before him. Both soldiers wore knee-length crimson capes, ornate bronze breastplates, and high crested helmets symbolizing their position among Rome's elite fighting force. Their task was to protect the consuls and highest-ranking officials in Rome, sometimes travelling to the furthest reaches of Rome's territory with their charges. Considered an honor, the guardsmen were handpicked from thousands of soldiers for their loyalty, bravery, and skills. Their sworn allegiance to the consuls or emperor, when there was one, was absolute.

"Release! This man is a friend to us," Regulus ordered, waving off his guards with a flip of his hand. "What are you doing here, Sorian?" he asked.

"I thought, now that I had some time, it would be nice to re-tie some of the bonds that I made in the past. Perhaps to better understand where I went wrong." Sorian stepped toward Regulus with a grin on his face and a gleam in his eye.

"Then welcome, Sorian, and yes, I did win our bet," replied Regulus, moving to embrace his old friend.

"Perhaps some clothes first," suggested Sorian, halting Regulus's forward progress with an outstretched arm.

"If you insist, my friend." Regulus entered his room and pulled on a tunic before stepping back onto the balcony. "Tell me, Sorian. How long have you been back in the city?"

"Long enough to know that you are assembling the troops necessary for a campaign in Africa." Sorian said. "Will you be able to convince the Senate that another fight is necessary when Duilius is building a massive fleet for his own campaign?"

Regulus stared at Sorian, momentarily considering the question, and then moved to the wall of the balcony to look over the city below them. Sorian followed, standing next to Regulus as the two surveyed the Circus Maximus and the people now filling the streets of Rome. "These people are eager for more," Regulus said. "They will do the convincing for me. Rome has grown used to success. The island of Sicily is coming under our control. Duilius will surprise them on the water and turn Carthage back to the southern shore of the great sea. We need to bring the fight to them at home as well." Regulus spoke firmly. "Besides, it is already approved by the majority. We will sail for Africa very soon."

"Very good, Marcus! I was led to believe that you had encountered some resistance, but it sounds as though everything is well underway," said Sorian, trailing off at the end to invite the general to respond to his suspicion.

"There are a few in the Senate, as well as a few in the Peoples' Assembly, who feel that we are spreading ourselves too thinly and looking for fights where they need not occur," Regulus said. "It is only a matter of time until they see reason and accept what is true—that we must strike now, while Carthage is wounded and on the run."

"Honestly, who leads such an inane resistance? There can be no reasonable argument against this campaign." Sorian probed for more information.

"Senator Lucius Myridias." Sorian could hear the disdain in Regulus's voice. "He tries to counter each and every debate with something sinister—always some conservative ploy to intimidate the remainder of the holdouts from moving forward. He is always speaking of risk and loss and hardship. He plays to the hearts of the oldest and most reluctant, those who are too comfortable in their dull and easy lives."

"As is he, I presume?"

"That is the strange part, Sorian!" Regulus threw his hands up in frustration. "He seems miserable. Everyone can see it. He lives alone and has nothing left to lose." Regulus halted, remembering why Sorian had been found guilty. "But you know Lucius, don't you, Sorian?"

"Indeed, I do. But I do not tire of hearing about his misery."

"First you must tell me exactly what happened to you, Sorian. Everything about that incident was kept very quiet. There have been rumors, but I never really knew how you were implicated in his daughter's death."

"I merely followed the orders of our great emperor, the late Tiberius, brother of our dear General Lucius."

"Go on," prompted Regulus.

"Tiberius felt that Lucius's daughter was running with a spy, a former gladiator who had been victorious in that arena." Sorian gestured to the arena below them. "Tiberius was also irritated by Lucius's lack of success against the Gauls in the north and believed him to be distracted by his daughter. Lucius had accepted their relationship and had even arranged for their escape to the islands in the east. Lucius considered me his right hand, but he did not know that I was also Tiberius's eyes and ears. The Emperor ordered me to slay the gladiator, thereby removing his brother's source of distraction."

"And you achieved this how?"

"I handpicked a detachment of soldiers that Lucius sent to protect his daughter and her lover." Sorian smiled at the memory.

"Handpicked for Tiberius?"

"Absolutely. They did what they were sent for. Unfortunately, Tiberius was later killed within his palace, so he was not able to protect me when Lucius came hunting for the truth."

"It is not a coincidence, then, that I find you standing on my balcony, is it, Sorian?"

"Perhaps there was another motive for coming here this morning. We can help each other, Marcus, like old friends."

Marcus Regulus smiled back at Sorian, nodding. "What do you need?"

"An opportunity and a place to go afterward." Sorian searched his body in vain for something. "I also seem to be without a weapon."

Regulus laughed. "We have come a long way since our childish days filled with simple crimes, like stealing food and clothing!"

"Well, at least you have," Sorian said, joining in the laughter.

Regulus became more serious. "I can get Lucius alone, Sorian, then, afterward, you can join me in Africa. How would you like to be a soldier again?" When he saw the somber look on Sorian's face, he added, "Do not worry, Sorian. You can serve on my personal staff. I wouldn't put the man who helped me conquer Africa on the front line."

Sorian grinned broadly. "You must not make it look like you had anything to do with his death, Marcus."

"I know. I will ask for a private meeting but arrange for another gathering publicly so I will be with others at the time Lucius dies," Regulus said. He again walked into his bedroom and a moment later returned, holding something in his hands. "This is a small gift for you in honor of your return, Sorian. I took it from a Samnite after I slit his throat with it. There are many like it, so it cannot be tied to me. Use it proudly, my friend."

Sorian accepted both the gift and the place at Regulus's side, happy to be back on top once again. Marcus Regulus would soon be free of his tether, sailing for Africa and destiny.

Accompanying Sorian to the street, Regulus offered a few parting words. "The moon will be full again in just over three weeks. Will you be prepared for your task that night?"

"Must I wait that long, Marcus?" asked Sorian facetiously before patting his friend on the back and departing.

"Stay well hidden, Sorian," Regulus called after him. "You never know who may recognize you in this city."

# Chapter XIV

———

ON THE EVENING of his third day on the run from the Roman army, Carpathimos slowed his forward progress, impeded by the sensation that he was either being watched or followed, close to running over someone, or all three. Looking at the bushes and undergrowth where he paused, it appeared that someone or something had relieved the bushes of their soft berries. Bears and birds usually fed on these plants, but generally with more care and discrimination, leaving unripe and overripe fruit behind. Whoever ravaged these bushes was either extremely hungry or didn't care what condition he left them in. Carpathimos assumed that this damage was caused by Elijah, and not long ago. He hesitated to call out to him, feeling that with each day that passed he was closer to some inevitable interaction with one of Rome's headhunters.

It was customary for the Roman army to hunt and kill deserters as much as it was for them to kill a sleeping sentry. This harsh treatment was well known and served to both treat the disease and deter its recurrence.

Carpathimos knew he had taken a huge chance by leaving, but he could wait no longer. His desire for revenge drove him more with each passing day. He felt no ill will against the men, women, and children of Akragas and could not bear to be a part of their final dispositions. Also, the confusion resulting from the carnage, wounded and dead soldiers, and whole cohorts in disarray after the battle seemed to provide ample cover for his disappearance—or so he hoped.

Carpathimos moved quietly along the edge of a long, tall patch of mulberry trees until he heard someone foraging on the other side. He slipped to the end of the patch, where he found a large plane tree, behind which he could hide. Peering over the massive trunk's shaggy and scaling white bark, he waited for the person to step back from the bushes. As anticipated, Elijah appeared, walking toward a fallen poplar tree. Evidently, he had made a resting place out of the upturned root ball. The dislodged roots formed a shallow hollow in the dirt at the tree's base and provided a roof for this earthen domicile. Elijah had apparently made himself a home, probably reluctant to leave this place with its ample food supply.

Carpathimos settled back behind the tree, trying not to rustle any of the dried leaves that covered the ground from last year. Realizing his own hunger, he reached for a handful of the juicy black thumb-sized berries for himself. He sampled a few and then took aim, landing one near Elijah's feet. Startled, the young man looked about, wondering about its source. The next one caught him in the side of the face. Carpathimos leaned forward, catching Elijah's attention. Both men smiled.

"I hoped that you would come," said Elijah. "I prayed to Yahweh each day for it." That was the second time Carpathimos had heard the name Yahweh. Yzebel had also referred to this god.

Carpathimos walked over to the fallen tree and sat on the mat of tall grass which Elijah had used to cover the dirt in the hollow. "You are no longer afraid of bears?" asked Carpathimos, pointing to the mulberries just a few feet away.

Elijah smiled. "I made much noise when I came upon this place. I think I scared away all my competition."

Carpathimos looked at Elijah, examining his slight frame. He looked very thin, the bones of his face and small arms seemed more exaggerated now than they had when Carpathimos last saw him. "Perhaps you should have tried to kill and eat the bear instead, Elijah. You could stand more meat on you." Elijah did not respond to the comment until Carpathimos put a hand on Elijah's shoulder. "I am sorry that I left you waiting for so long. It must have been hard to live this way on your own, but you never should have followed me."

"I had nowhere else to go. I could not go back the way I came, could I?" asked Elijah. "And what is your name, anyway? I never heard it!"

Carpathimos sensed the frustration and irritation in Elijah's voice. "My name is Carpathimos."

The two listened to the palmate-lobed leaves of the large plane tree wobble and shudder in the breeze. Songs of the warblers and black-headed buntings filled the air surrounding the mulberry trees as their owners challenged one another for a chance at the ripe fruit. Elijah pulled open his sack and pulled out the books of Moses, to read from them before nightfall. Carpathimos watched him unroll the document, admiring the young man's care of the delicate parchment and his ability to make sense of the strange writing. Unsettled, Carpathimos shifted slightly, turning away from Elijah and gazing out of the hollow.

"We need to keep moving, Elijah," said Carpathimos. "We should pick what berries we can and leave as soon as possible. We must not linger here for too long."

Unfettered, Elijah didn't stir or acknowledge him in any way, continuing to read from the pages. Carpathimos sighed, deciding that perhaps he, too, should allow time for rest. He adjusted his position so he could lie back and rest his head against the back of the shelter. Closing his eyes, he thought about his son, probably walking and talking now, and his sister Parma. He hoped they had a good place to rest their heads each night. Drifting into slumber, he thought, *Soon. Soon I will be with them.*

---

Early in the morning, Kurush and Isingoma cautiously made their way through the small forested area they had reached late in the evening the night prior. Having run a great distance during the day, they stopped to catch their breaths and collect their thoughts on how best to proceed. Several of the other forested groves they passed might have harbored their prey, and Kurush and Isingoma searched through them in a systematic way. Based on the tracks they followed yesterday, the men knew that the deserter they believed to be Remus had passed into this weald. Whether he remained was unknown. At this location, they agreed that Kurush would move slowly through the center of the woods and Isingoma would flank the more southern edge, since the wind was coming from the north.

Very deliberately, Kurush took his time, scanning the stand of trees and allowing Isingoma to get farther ahead. The footprints on the ground reassured him that their commander was just ahead. The plants' condition told him when Remus had come by this place. Kurush was an expert tracker and yet what had confused him was the second set of tracks, one small and one large. The larger was following the smaller for some reason. This was not typical behavior for a hunted man. Kurush was certain that the elder and more experienced commander would certainly know that he was being tracked.

Carpathimos stirred slightly, feeling a chill from the ground penetrate his flesh and spread over his bones. For the first time in many weeks, he had slept soundly, but now he felt the dull ache in his back and shoulders from spending the night with his large frame curled into a roughly hewn hole in the ground. Elijah breathed softly, still asleep. Something prodded Carpathimos to wake Elijah so that they could get moving again.

Elijah ignored the command, opting for a few minutes more rest. It was that time of morning before the sunrise when the darkness seems at its deepest. Feeling the urge to relieve himself, Carpathimos struggled to find a comfortable position. Frustrated in his efforts, he rolled out of the shelter and took several steps into the damp grass, his knee and shoulder both cracking as he straightened.

After passing his water, he listened to the birdsong, which was just beginning in earnest under the faintest light illuminating the structures around him. It was then that he heard *Crack!* A substantial weight had been placed upon a dead twig. Silence followed. He squatted low, scrutinizing the shapes of objects in the dim light and listening for any additional sounds. The birds had quieted. Carpathimos moved imperceptibly toward the fallen tree, crouching low along its trunk. Waiting, he drew the short knife from a scabbard he had fashioned from wood vine and wrapped about his waist.

Out of the brush stepped a man of moderate build and thick thighs. He was carrying a gladius, a standard infantry cut-and-thrust sword. The man moved quietly forward, careful not to repeat his mistake. He did not see Carpathimos. As he stepped closer to the root ball on the other side of the trunk from Carpathimos, he turned his head to peer into the mass of branches that stuck up from the other end of the tree, trying to search the cobweb of limbs and twigs for his prey. Carpathimos recognized him. It was Kurush.

Carpathimos gently palpated the ground near his left foot, feeling for a small object to toss over Kurush's head. His fingers found a small stone. Digging under it with his fingernails, he pried it from the ground and drew it up into his palm. It was only the size of a duck egg, but it would do. Watching Kurush, Carpathimos flipped the rock into the air with a quick snap of his wrist. It sailed over the man's head and began its descent. Carpathimos's muscles tensed for the impact and the sudden response to follow. The stone collided with the ground behind the man, who snapped his attention to the rear.

Carpathimos shot into the air, leapfrogging the trunk. With the muscle memory developed from his intense training and the athleticism of a lion in the arena, Carpathimos wrapped his big arm around Kurush's face from behind, pinning the man's mouth within the fossa of his elbow and stifling even the slightest gasp from his chest. Into a space just under the right scapula, the gladiator plunged his two-decimeter blade into Kurush's right lung, rupturing the spongy parenchyma and spilling the warm air into the cavity surrounding it.

Reflexively, Kurush twisted his body with his powerful legs, but Carpathimos's grip on his head was too strong. Lifting up on the knife, Carpathimos tipped Kurush off his center of gravity and pushed him to the ground. Kurush collapsed in a heap, writhing. His burning body silently screamed for one more breath to fill the collapsing lung, but panting could not calm his throbbing heart. While his heels dug into the dirt repetitively, Kurush's arms flailed around him seemingly without purpose. Suddenly he reached out and gripped Elijah by the arm, startling the young man from sleep. Elijah lifted his head and met the wild eyes of a man he had never seen before. Terrified, Elijah screamed. Pulling his arm free, he shot out of the shelter, running away as fast as he could. Briefly, Carpathimos stood stunned by the unexpected development. He replaced his knife in its scabbard, claimed Kurush's short blade as his own, then leaped over the fallen tree to chase after Elijah.

Isingoma heard the scream. He turned into the woods at his right, running toward the sound, then turned to follow the sounds of someone crashing through the brush. Picking up speed, he knew he would overtake that person.

Carpathimos, running full speed, reached forward for Elijah's shoulder, grasping the thin bones in his powerful hand. Sensing the hand belonged to Carpathimos, Elijah slowed, stopped, and faced him. His expression changed from fear to panic as another man crashed through the brush behind them.

Elijah shouted, "The Septuagint!" He pushed past Carpathimos and disappeared into the trees, back in the direction from whence he had come. Confused, Carpathimos followed him, unaware of the man Elijah had seen. Ducking under the pendulous coriaceous leaves of a willow tree, Carpathimos found Elijah, feet off the ground, held in a death grip by the long arms of Isingoma. Isingoma pressed his long knife to Elijah's side, the tip piercing the skin at the boy's flank. Elijah whimpered as Carpathimos walked forward to face his captor.

"Let the boy go, Isingoma," Carpathimos commanded. "He has nothing to do with this hunt of yours."

Isingoma smiled wryly, but did not heed the command. Instead he twisted the blade back and forth to irritate Elijah's flesh. Elijah grimaced, staring imploringly at Carpathimos. His fear chilled Carpathimos to his core, spurning a mental image of the fear he saw in his own mother's eyes when drunken Roman soldiers assaulted her.

"It is a head that you need to bring back to Quintus, is it not?" Carpathimos roared. "Then you can have mine in exchange for the boy's life. Let him go, Isingoma. I am tired of running."

As he knelt to the ground, Carpathimos pulled his knife from its scabbard and tossed it into the bushes behind Isingoma. The warrior smiled, relaxing his grip on Elijah, who slipped free and darted away into the bushes. Isingoma walked toward Carpathimos, who hung his head low, crossing his arms behind him. The tall black man stood in front of Carpathimos, his long yellow teeth growing in number as his smile widened.

"I have been hoping for this since the day Caius placed me under your control, Commander," stated Isingoma. "I will end this quickly. Do not fear. My people are compassionate." His smile changed to a sneer.

Carpathimos, face down, watched Isingoma's feet and lower legs approach him. He could tell how the man was standing, how much weight he placed on each foot, and how he shifted that weight from one foot to the other as he spoke. At the top of Carpathimos's line of sight, two more feet appeared behind Isingoma. Elijah was standing silently, just a meter away.

Carpathimos dug the toes of his feet into the ground, preparing for the blow. Isingoma began to move toward Carpathimos's left side when Elijah shouted, startling Isingoma. As he turned in surprise, he shifted his weight to his heels. Carpathimos lunged forward, careening into Isingoma's hip and knocking him off balance into the bushes. Isingoma flailed his gladius, swinging the long knife at Carpathimos. The sharp blade sliced into the skin of his shoulder, shaving away a superficial layer. That would be the only chance Isingoma had.

Carpathimos continued his forward progress like a boulder set loose upon a steep hillside. Drawing Kurush's knife from the small of his back in the wood-vine belt, he rolled toward Isingoma. As he landed on top of him, he drove the thin blade through Isingoma's upper abdomen just beneath the sternum. He angled the blade toward Isingoma's head, piercing the meat of his beating ventricle while pinning Isingoma's right arm under his knee.

Isingoma tried to throw a punch with his left hand, landing his fist against Carpathimos's torso. The swing only served to drive the tip of Kurush's blade more deeply into his own heart. Carpathimos reached for the hilt of the gladius, pulling it away from Isingoma, who struggled under his weight. Isingoma threw steadily weaker throws with his free arm until they merely slapped at Carpathimos in an almost playful manner. Carpathimos rose to his feet after the life drained from Isingoma's eyes.

Carpathimos stepped back and looked down at his attacker, wondering if there would be more than two. He turned to find Elijah sitting on the large poplar trunk, cradling his knapsack in his arms and rocking back and forth as tears streamed down his cheeks.

Instead of feeling remorse or empathy, Carpathimos felt anger. Reaching out for the sack and gripping it, he growled at Elijah, "What is this thing that consumes you? What could it be that calls you back into harm's way? It nearly killed us both!"

Elijah twisted and wrenched himself and the sack away from Carpathimos. He hurried away from the tree trunk, unable to speak.

"I must go," said Carpathimos more gently. "There may be more men coming and I must get to the coast." He paused, staring at the back of Elijah's head then he bent over the dead soldiers, gathering two short knives and one gladius before he faced Elijah. "I thank you for shouting and drawing his attention, Elijah. It was the distraction I needed."

Carpathimos frowned, regretting his anger but unable to admit it. Slowly, he walked through the woods toward the west. Elijah lifted his face and watched Carpathimos walk away. He took a deep breath and wiped his face with his arm, drying his eyes on the sleeve. Throwing the knapsack over his shoulder, he set off after Carpathimos.

The disparate pair walked silently, the warrior in the lead, for many kilometers before Elijah moved up to flank Carpathimos. Elijah answered the question Carpathimos had asked him earlier in the woods. "I carry the laws of Yahweh, as told to us by Moses, and others." Carpathimos glanced at him, looking puzzled, so Elijah continued, "I carry the books of Moses. My grandfather and I transcribed them from the old language into Greek so our people could have the laws of Yahweh to guide them."

Carpathimos stared at him for a moment and then glanced at the knapsack before looking back at Elijah. "Why do you and your grandfather know these books and the old language while the rest of your people do not? Could it be that your people choose not to use it to guide them yet your grandfather cannot let the old ways die?"

Elijah answered eagerly. "No! You see it is this way. I will tell you." He proceeded to explain how the Jews had been dispersed over the centuries, often against their will, while at other times they followed new rulers across the lands. He spoke of Nebuchadnezzar, who had enslaved the Israelites in Babylon, and Cyrus, the great king of Persia, who brought them back to Jerusalem. He continued with the story of Alexander, the son of the great diplomat King Philip II, who came down from Macedonia with the language of Greece spreading out behind him like the wake of a ship. Next, Elijah told the story of Alexander's rival generals, who divided the young conqueror's territory, dispersing the Jews yet again.

"After all these centuries, the stories and laws given to Moses by God teetered on the brink of a vast abyss," Elijah said. "They contain the world's forgotten cultures and histories, and they are at risk of becoming lost forever."

Gradually, he explained, the Word had been lost too many times, and only the learned elders could remember and recite the ancient texts. "Through the benevolent wisdom of King Ptolemy II Philadelphus of Egypt, one of Alexander's generals and the new pharaoh in Egypt, the books were rewritten by men such as my grandfather," Elijah said, and Carpathimos saw the pride in his face. "They wrote it for the Greek speakers among them in Egypt." Elijah described how he and his grandfather had worked by night to create another copy of the Torah for the Greek speakers scattered throughout the known world.

"You see what it is now, and how important it is that I give this to them, don't you?" Elijah implored. "This is Yahweh's gift to his people."

Carpathimos stopped walking, pausing at the side of a treacherous void, the sound of rushing water echoing from far below them. "Does your god's gift give instruction on how to get around this?" he asked facetiously, while contemplating Elijah's story and their new dilemma.

Carpathimos and Elijah gazed across a rough river gorge, cut sharply by the Platani River. The waters coursed far below them, churning an almost black water into a cascade of white ragged caps and spray. The Platani drained the jagged summits of the Sicani Mountains in the north, creating and delivering an almost continual supply of fog and humidity to the crystal-clear turquoise-colored sea to the south.

Elijah didn't comment, his mouth agape at the chasm. Carpathimos pointed to the mountains. "We must follow the river north into the hills and try to cross up there. The Temple at Eryx is northwest of those mountains anyway."

"That seems far." Elijah sighed.

"It will take many days and the terrain is rugged, but we should find ample food in and along this river, food we both need." Carpathimos squeezed the boy's shoulder sympathetically. "Come, we will walk until dark."

"Do you think you will make a fire tonight?"

Carpathimos shook his head and sighed. "If we get high enough and the fog comes in to hide us, then I think that would be all right."

———

Carpathimos blew gently at a wisp of smoke that rose slowly out of the crumpled grass he wedged under the split timber, the ends of which rested over a circle of small stones. After a few more puffs, the smoke began to rise, and then a tiny flame erupted out of the grass, consuming the fibrous strands as it licked at the log above. Elijah could not contain his excitement as he watched the wood ignite. He had been dreaming about a fire to warm his bones for weeks, but had been ill-equipped and too fearful to start one. Carpathimos piled more sticks onto the fire, feeling his uneasiness about the past few days start to melt away with the chilly air around them. The sap trapped within the fallen fir sticks crackled and snapped, sharing their stored energy with the two weary travelers.

Carpathimos and Elijah had climbed more than one thousand meters during the day, following the eastern rim of the Platani River into the rugged caps of the Sicani mountain range. Passing over the shoulder of the first of several tall spires, the men descended into a highland meadow littered with irregular blocks and shards of limestone that had been shed by the overlooking peaks. Ascending again to the second summit, they had found this high ledge, a good location on which to camp for the night. The fire burned at the base of a wall over which the second summit loomed. Within that wall, a triangular gap, created by the slough of fragile limestone, allowed refuge for the two men and their fire. Outside their small triangular space, a cool breeze whipped at the wall before sailing over the ledge and turning to course down the southern slope of the range.

"Carpathimos?" Elijah spoke quietly, without looking away from the fire. "Where is it we are going?"

Carpathimos stirred, similarly mesmerized by the same flames and lost in thought. "We go to the mountains in the north and west, toward a place known as Eryx. There I must relay what I know of Rome's plan to build a navy and attack the Carthaginian fleet north of Sicily and that they intend to invade Carthaginian lands in Africa."

Carpathimos picked up a stick and probed the glowing embers deep within the base of the fire, shifting some of the unburned wood deeper into the mass and sending tiny sparks into the night sky. They glowed and danced on the wind like hundreds of tiny fireflies.

"Will we then be able to travel toward Greece?" Elijah asked. When Carpathimos didn't answer immediately, Elijah said, "Perhaps I should first ask where you planned to go after that, Carpathimos. I should not assume that you would be going that way, but—" His voice trailed off. He did not know how to continue.

"They promised me a boat to use after I fulfill my duty. I hope to travel east to Rome and, after that, I need to reach Anatolia. My sister and son are somewhere in Lydia," answered Carpathimos.

Elijah thought quietly for a moment about Carpathimos's answer. He wanted to ask many questions, but he was unsure how to ask them without irritating his friend. Elijah had been told he asked too many questions. "Can you tell me more about your sister and your son? What are their names?" he probed cautiously.

After a quiet moment, Carpathimos offered more information. "My sister is named Parma and my son is named Lucia. The rest is just for me. My stories of them are for me alone."

Elijah nodded, pretending to understand. He suspected that Carpathimos knew many stories he would refuse to share. He hoped that he could learn at least something about the man who had saved him so many times.

"Perhaps you can explain more to me about the bundle that you carry so carefully, Elijah," Carpathimos said, trying to change the subject.

Pleased at his sudden interest, Elijah unbound the rolls of papyrus from the leathers and cleared his throat. "May I read to you?"

Carpathimos nodded. He settled back onto his elbow, pushing his legs out to the side, waiting for Elijah to begin. Elijah cleared his throat again and started to read, eager to share his knowledge and passion. He knew of no better way to repay the kindness Carpathimos had shown him.

Stopping only rarely to feed the withering flames, Elijah read for many hours. At one point, Carpathimos wondered how Elijah could read in such darkness. And then he realized that the boy wasn't reading at all. He was reciting with his eyes closed. Carpathimos studied the young man, trying not to disturb him. Elijah continued until he noticed that Carpathimos had drifted off to sleep.

That night, Elijah had shared the creation stories as well as those of the ancestors, of Abraham and his travels between the river Nile and the great river Euphrates to the east; of Isaac and Rebekah; Jacob and Rachel; and finally of Joseph and his ascension to the most powerful in Egypt under Pharaoh. Hopeful that Carpathimos had heard most of the stories, Elijah carefully rewrapped the rolls of papyrus in the protective leathers and replaced them in his knapsack reverently. Lying on his back, he rested his head on the knapsack and watched the light from the glowing fire dance against the stone above him. It had been a hard day but a good day, he thought.

Early the next morning, Elijah woke to find a moderately sized forest creature stripped of its skin, roasting on the smoldering coals of last night's fire. He abruptly sat up, fearful that he was alone in the mountains. Rubbing the sleep from his eyes, he crawled from the opening in the wall to find Carpathimos standing near the cliff edge. Carpathimos turned when he heard Elijah shuffling in his direction.

"The meat should be cooked enough to eat," Carpathimos said. "I woke up early to find a number of the black creatures moving through the stone pines and oaks just below us. When I surprised them, the boar separated from the rest to charge me. I hit him with a stone."

Elijah stared at the smoldering animal roasting in the steaming coals. Its legs were spread wide from a crater left by its missing entrails and the clear juices of its meat bubbled up out of cracks forming in the blackened crust. The unexpected aroma of cooked meat made his stomach growl, but Elijah held back, concerned about consuming a cloven-hoofed animal. Disheartened, he studied the foot nearest him and was surprised. It had a small hoof like a donkey. It wasn't cloven at all. Certainly, this was a different type of swine from what he was accustomed to. He hesitated no longer.

Elijah's hunger overtook whatever reservations he had for consuming this small boar. He picked at the limb of the roasting animal, trying to tug some of the meat free. Carpathimos slid in beside him, brandishing his short blade and offering it to Elijah. Elijah stared at it pensively. "You should do it."

Carpathimos smiled and proceeded to cut large chunks of the juicy meat from the bones, separating the warm tissues and setting them aside in a pile. "Eat, Elijah. We have a long day of walking before us," insisted Carpathimos, "and, while we walk, I would like you to tell me more of these ancestors of yours." Elijah briefly stopped chewing and smiled.

# Chapter XV

—

FOR MANY DAYS, Carpathimos and Elijah crossed the ragged Sicani range, heading toward the windswept lowlands in the northwest quarter of the island. The terrain was difficult to navigate, with deep gorges and impassible escarpments frequently forcing them to alter course. Passing the time, Elijah read from the books by night while Carpathimos absorbed what he could. By day, Elijah shared his understanding of the material they had covered the night before. He answered almost every question Carpathimos could throw at him. Though small of stature and meek, Elijah kept pace with his stronger traveling companion, driven on by both his passion and desire to share God's lessons with Carpathimos.

Only fifty kilometers from the mountains from which they had descended, the men felt the heat of midday. From this location, the man and boy couldn't see Eryx in the distance. It would be a lone and isolated peak near the coast. Weaving through a maze of sunbaked stone and windswept outcroppings, they spotted golden eagles circling overhead on a seemingly endless supply of wind. Small, brilliantly colored kites darted back and forth, picking off the insects that hovered over the arid landscape. In Elijah's estimation, the only interesting findings were the winding pig trails criss-crossing the landscape, preventing the usual vegetation from growing. Left to his imagination, Carpathimos felt the pattern on the ground created by the winding pig trails resembled that of the destruction left behind by a giant fishing net, under which no plants could thrive. The image of Neptune, carelessly casting his net aside onto Sicily, and later returning to retrieve it, brought a smile to Carpathimos as he lumbered along one of these dusty pig trails. It seemed altogether more ludicrous having now listened to Elijah's stories about his god. Elijah's stories about the creation of the earth made Carpathimos regard the majestic scenery surrounding them with new appreciation. He marveled at the power of a being who could create such mountains with a spoken command.

Carpathimos had been intrigued by the notion of a single godlike being, one who could create all things and rule over that creation. Throughout his life, Carpathimos had been told of many gods who dominated both the seas and the earth, a hierarchy of figures with powers to control aspects of everyday life and to interfere with the plans of others, like jealous siblings. For Carpathimos, listening to the stories of men like Abraham, Joseph, and Moses, stories told with so much detail, the idea of one true god began to seem possible, even desirable. Navigating his way across this desert-like lowland, Carpathimos felt even more isolated, caught between two worlds of gods and histories. He did not know what to believe, what to accept.

As they hiked and climbed, the hours turned to days. To pass the time, Elijah taught about the ascension of the great kings, Saul and David and Solomon. Of particular interest to Carpathimos was the relationship of King Solomon to the Phoenician King of Tyre, the one named Hiram. Yzebel had explained that her father's family had come from Tyre. She, like Elijah, was a believer in this one god, the same god, Carpathimos reminded himself.

Elijah explained how David's son Solomon expanded upon the treaties and territories acquired by David, using his diplomatic prowess to obtain a treaty with Hiram. Through the treaty, Solomon could obtain cedar from Phoenician-owned lands and he used the mighty cedars to build a temple in Jerusalem. He then began the business of trading by sea, creating a fleet of ships and hiring experienced Phoenician sailors to man them. "Some cedar seedlings brought to Jerusalem with this lumber, had been planted there," Elijah told his listener. "My grandfather said that the offspring of those cedars still grow to this day, each several hundred years old!"

Finally, they left the lowlands and began the uphill climb once again. The mountain of Eryx appeared on the horizon at last. Its solitary peak towered above the relatively flat territory surrounding it. Seeing it now, Elijah began to wonder what they would encounter at Eryx. The possibilities gave him pains in the pit of his stomach. "Carpathimos, what must we do when we get there?" he asked.

Carpathimos kept moving, but he looked back at Elijah, sensing the young man's growing concern revealed by the rising tenor of his voice. "We must find the high priest and pray to the Punic god Astarte."

"Astarte!" exclaimed Elijah. "But we cannot! She is the abomination. It is forbidden, Carpathimos. The Israelites were condemned for the very same!"

"What do you know of this Astarte?" Carpathimos chuckled. "We must only perform a ceremony in some way and then we can move on. It will mean no more to you than it will to me."

Elijah stopped in his tracks. "King Solomon, of whom I have spoken, built a temple to this Astarte just outside of Jerusalem, but it was destroyed hundreds of years ago. He did this to honor his arrangement with the Phoenicians of Tyre. He was criticized for doing it. The Word of Yahweh forbids worship of Baal, the storm god, or Melquart, the protector of Tyre, as well as any of their consorts—including Ashtoreth, or Astarte, as you call her. It says so in the stories of the judges. I read it to you, Carpathimos!"

Carpathimos glared at Elijah. "I must do what I must do, Elijah," he said sternly. "Praying to this god, or any god, means little to me, but I will do it if it protects those dear to me, if it can possibly help me reach my family. The ceremony does not need to have meaning to you, either, but if you would rather hide in the wilderness and wait for me, then so be it. Otherwise, do what I do and close your mouth."

Elijah stared at his feet. Humiliated, ashamed, and unable to speak, he let his knapsack slide from his shoulder onto the ground. To Carpathimos, it looked like a gesture of defiance. Irritated, Carpathimos resumed walking, pausing momentarily before adding a recommendation. "If you choose to wait for me outside of the temple, then use care. I suspect there will be soldiers of Carthage about." Elijah's eyes widened at the notion of more troops. He couldn't watch Carpathimos walking away. He shouldered the sack and hurried to catch up.

The temple was an expansive structure that sprawled across the top of the mountain in an orderly and impressive fashion. Here and there, surrounding the ramparts, were remnants of the temple's past, ruins of a once larger structure torn down by invaders. Stone columns and broad walkways of varying ages had been built atop the fallen walls, indicating the temple had been sacked and reconstructed numerous times over thousands of years.

From their position, Carpathimos and Elijah surmised that the main edifice of the temple stood to the south, at the far end of a long concourse that ran along the center between the temple walls. Three similarly shaped smaller buildings were spaced along the concourse, one at the center, while two stood side by side at the north end. The grounds were filled with gardens lush with flowering plants, fruiting trees of a number of species, and small stone-rimmed ponds.

The totality of the complex, including the four temple buildings and the central concourse, was surrounded by a stone wall of limestone, the blocks of which were stacked three, and, sometimes, four high in places. Each block was roughly a meter tall by a meter wide and hewn to a slippery smooth surface. Carpathimos eyed the area like a warrior. Scaling such a wall at the shorter sections would not be insurmountable, he told himself, but an approaching army attacking from the steep slopes of Eryx would have a difficult time moving quickly over the wall. Although the Carthaginian garrison at Eryx appeared small, it would be able to defend itself against such a slow-moving attack, wounding and killing many before it could be overrun.

Under the cover of a dense fog rolling in from the sea, Carpathimos and Elijah slipped slowly along the outer wall, moving quietly and staying low, to avoid being seen. Presently, they reached one of the low sections. Carpathimos jumped to grasp the top of the wall and pull himself up so he could inspect the layout. From here, it was a short distance to one of the gardens, where high bushes and fully-grown olive trees could hide him from view. Carpathimos hung from his fingertips for several minutes, observing whether any soldiers patrolled the grounds nearby. At the north end, he spotted two soldiers walking together from one small temple building to the next. They briefly disappeared within the second and then came back into view several minutes later, followed by a young couple and a small child, who was carried on the woman's hip. Five other children, all older than the first, walked closely behind.

Looking back at Elijah, Carpathimos gestured for him to come near to the wall. Carpathimos hoisted him to the top before pulling himself over as well. Pointing, Carpathimos nudged Elijah, indicating he should follow him into the garden. Together they quickly crossed a narrow walkway before disappearing into the thick foliage. Crawling on their bellies through the tall tussocks of grass between the many bushes, Carpathimos and Elijah stopped within ten meters of the central temple building.

Narrow columns, equally spaced in the shape of a circle, formed the walls of this round structure, and the pale-colored limestone columns supported a thick stone roof on which were carved cherubs and reliefs of Phoenician sailing vessels. Lying next to one another, Carpathimos and Elijah peered through the limbs of a high bush, studying the people inside the cylindrical building in front of them.

They could see two men dressed in what looked like topless tunics stretching from their waists to the ground, covering their feet. They wore headdresses covering their ears and the backs of their necks. One of them, likely the older of the two, also wore a long necklace made with bronze amulets and seashells; a shiny red talisman hung from the bottom of this necklace. That man was holding a rooster and speaking, but Carpathimos and Elijah could not hear what was being muttered. The other man was tending a large fire burning within a stone cauldron in the center of the temple. While Carpathimos and Elijah looked on, the younger man handed a large knife to the man with the necklace. He proceeded to slaughter the rooster, eviscerating the bird over the flames and showering the cauldron with spilled blood.

Carpathimos leaned toward Elijah and whispered, "Those two must be priests. I suspect the man with the necklace is the one I must engage." He was about to add something else when the two Carthaginian soldiers appeared inside the wall of columns, flanked by the family and their small child. Oblivious to the newcomers, the priest with the necklace continued chanting, rocking back and forth, making his tunic wave with his movements.

The younger priest stepped to the parents and accepted the child when the woman held it out to him. The child was nude and female, not more than two years old, and she was crying. She reached back for her mother, who stood expressionless next to her family. Moments later, as Elijah and Carpathimos looked on from the bushes, the young priest held the child over the cauldron, his hands wrapping around her chest below the child's arms, stifling her cries. Elijah's mouth opened in a silent scream as the elder priest slit the child's throat with the knife and her blood poured out from the gash into the fire.

Elijah gasped as the priest eviscerated the child as he had the bird. Elijah started to run into the temple, but Carpathimos tackled him from behind, dragging him to the earth. He fell upon him and wrapped his large hand over Elijah's mouth to quiet him. Lying on top of Elijah, Carpathimos could feel the boy's muffled scream within his own chest and the heat of the heavy breath in his hand. Elijah swung backward at Carpathimos with his free hand, trying to free himself and lash out at anything he could hit. Carpathimos kept his eyes focused on the guards and priest.

When the young priest dropped the limp body of the child into the flames and raised his hands as if in prayer, Carpathimos nearly retched, sickened to be a witness to the pagan ceremony. When he felt Elijah's body relax under him, he knew the young man's resistance had died. He slowly let go of Elijah after watching the family depart with the soldiers.

The elder priest left the temple, walking south toward the main edifice alone. The younger priest busied himself tending the fire and arranging items on the altar before he, too, set off toward the main temple building.

Carpathimos stood and then bent over, pulling a white-faced Elijah to his feet. Elijah's eyes stared forward, unblinking. Carpathimos clutched Elijah by the wrist and pulled him along behind. "Come, Elijah. We must follow the priest," he hissed, pointing to the large structure at the south end of the concourse. Moving quickly but cautiously, Carpathimos dragged Elijah along by the arm toward the building. Elijah tripped clumsily behind.

The temple's largest building was constructed much like the central smaller building, except for its ringed wall composed of three sets of columns arranged to obscure a view of the interior from the outside. The roof of this epic monument was twice as high as the other three, although similarly sculpted cherubs and vessels edged its roof, too.

Standing between two columns of the outermost ring, Carpathimos grabbed Elijah by the shoulders and gazed into his eyes. Elijah was breathing fast, but his face was expressionless. Not knowing what to do for him, Carpathimos pushed Elijah down to the ground into a seated position, resting his back against the rigid stone of one of the columns. "Wait here," whispered Carpathimos. "I will do this on my own and then together we will go find the boat." Elijah said nothing in response, his gaze fixed on a far-off point. Carpathimos shook his head sympathetically and then slipped through the network of columns into the temple building.

He discovered that the structure beyond the columns was one massive room where four huge black cauldrons sat upon the stone floor. Each cauldron marked one of the cardinal directions and all had a fire crackling within. Above each cauldron hung a metal pot from which steam rose toward the ceiling, filling the enclosed space with the aromas of incense and floral spices. In the center of the circle formed by the four cauldrons stood a tall stone sculpture. Try as he might, Carpathimos could not identify what the sculpture represented. It had the legs and feet of a woman, but there was no body above the thighs—unless the rest of the body protruded through the ceiling. The copious steam emanating from the four pots and gathering around the waist of the sculpture prevented Carpathimos from seeing any opening in the center of the roof.

Near the inner circle of columns, Carpathimos spotted stairs leading up to what must be a second story of the building. He quietly ascended the steps and found the top half of the stone woman. There was no roof just above her. The rising fog of incense from the lower level, which leached through the floor around her waist, swirled around her torso and head before escaping through the hole above her. It seemed as if she was ensnared by a writhing ribbon of sweet-smelling perfumes and the volatile gases of hot, fragrant oils.

The figure had been sculpted from marble. She wore a long robe that twisted tightly around her bodice and fell to the floor. On her head, a crown of flowers rested over two curled horns stretching from her head. One arm reached out before her, palm up, with her fingers extended. Perched on her outstretched arm sat two large sculpted doves, gleaming white and looking off in the same direction as the woman's eyes.

Moving along the inside set of columns toward what must be the front of the temple, Carpathimos studied the woman's face. She gazed into the distance past the doves, in the direction she was pointing. Considering the cauldrons and the direction the idol faced, Carpathimos realized that the sculpture of Astarte was looking toward Carthage.

As Carpathimos descended the steps to the lower level, the two priests were standing on the other side of the sculpture. They had not seen him. He watched them quietly from the stairs as the elder read from some papyrus scroll while the younger knelt on the floor arranging a variety of flowers, fruits, and branches at the foot of Astarte. Walking down the remainder of the steps, Carpathimos shuffled his feet and cleared his throat. Both men stopped what they were doing and turned to face him.

Carpathimos walked within several meters of the men and knelt to the floor, his hands extended forward at knee level with his face down between his upper arms. Neither man said a word, so Carpathimos lifted his head slightly and spoke softly, staring forward at Astarte's marble foot. "I am the gladiator. I bring information for Hanno and the Council of Elders."

The priests stared at him, mouths agape. Carpathimos glanced quickly at their faces and returned his own to its position of prayer between his arms. Both priests seemed surprised or alarmed, judging by the looks on their faces, which made Carpathimos suddenly anxious that he had erred in some way.

Abruptly, the high priest smiled. "It was some time ago that we were warned of your coming. I did not expect that you had survived the journey. Clearly, I was mistaken. You have proven yourself a most worthy partner." After speaking, the high priest moved to his altar. The younger priest took Carpathimos by the hand, pulling him up to his feet. From the altar, the high priest said, "You must pray with us to the goddess of the heavens, the queen of the stars, then you will tell me what you know of the Romans."

Directed to kneel in front of the stone statue of Astarte, Carpathimos resumed the position while the two priests walked in a circle around him and Astarte. When the high priest's assistant approached a small wooden box near the altar, he carefully opened the top. Reaching in, he pulled out a live dove and held it gently within his cupped hands. Meanwhile, the high priest stepped in front of Carpathimos and knelt before him, holding a knife out for Carpathimos to see. He looked at Carpathimos while he chanted something that Carpathimos could not understand. Nodding reassuringly, he took one of Carpathimos's hands within his own. Holding the blade's tip lightly against Carpathimos's palm, the priest gently drew the blade over the thenar eminence at the base of the thumb, spilling a few drops of blood from the cut onto the flesh of the palm. He did the same to the other hand. When he finished, his assistant held the dove to Carpathimos. The high priest guided Carpathimos's hands into position around the bird so that the head faced away from Carpathimos and the blood from the cuts in his hands stained the feathers of the soft, white wings. The priests then guided Carpathimos up the stairs to a gap in the columns through which Astarte stared at the horizon, directing him to release the dove into the air.

As if by a miracle, the dove darted up and over the sea, heading southwest toward Carthage. Carpathimos watched the bird fly away until he could no longer see it. He looked down to see the waves of the great sea crashing upon the rocky shore far below his feet. The sounds barely reached his ears. A gentle breeze climbed the alabaster cliff, tussled his hair and tugged at the fabric of his tunic. For the moment, he felt at peace.

There is magic here, he thought. It would be so easy to fall from the sky and put an end to his mighty struggles. Just then, however, the priest's assistant grabbed his wrist and guided him back into the temple. He departed, leaving Carpathimos alone with the high priest.

Carpathimos related what he knew of Rome's intent to attack Carthage's fleet north of Sicily and of its plan to invade Carthage's territory in northern Africa. He also told him what Quintus had said about the Roman fleet taking troops from Sicily before sailing south. He knew that such talk may have been a ruse, but he provided it anyway, hoping that Carthage would somehow use the information to its advantage. When he concluded, the high priest escorted him out of Astarte's temple and he was greeted by the young priest, now accompanied by two soldiers. Carpathimos scanned the columns as he exited the temple but did not see Elijah.

"Do not be alarmed, Gladiator," said the high priest. "These men will escort you down to the beach. There you will find a boat for your use. No one was to touch it until you came, and I am confident no one has. I am afraid, however, that it may now be overgrown by thorny plants and tangled vines."

Carpathimos nodded and said sternly, "Before I go, I would like to know why the young girl was sacrificed."

The young priest stared at Carpathimos blankly until he realized that the gladiator had witnessed the event earlier that day, before he joined them in the temple of Astarte. He looked to the high priest for assistance, but the older man only smiled at him before disappearing through the columns back into the temple.

"Very well, Gladiator." The assistant explained patiently, as if to a child, "Nearly every day families make the journey to Eryx to offer their youngest child to Astarte and to honor Carthage. Their sacrifice is pleasing to the gods, who in turn strengthen Carthage and her armies. These sacrifices also ensure the wellbeing of our people continues, unhindered. By such sacrifice, parents bring good fortune to themselves, their neighbors, and their communities—which is more beneficial to all of us than the life of one small helpless child. It is, Gladiator, as it must be."

Carpathimos then asked the young priest about Elijah. "I came here with a young man named Elijah. I left him near the columns. He must travel with me."

The priest closed his eyes and nodded. "The guards have him, but do not worry. He did not resist, so he is unharmed. You may take him with you."

The guards led Carpathimos along the concourse and they descended out of the temple area down a long and undulating stone path that wound along the steep western slope of the mountain before turning sharply in switchbacks to the low ground. The guards entered a small stone building at the base and returned with Elijah in tow. The youth still looked dazed. He didn't acknowledge, or even seem to notice, that Carpathimos was present.

To Carpathimos, they handed Elijah's knapsack, and directed him to a cart path leading to the north and west. "The boat is three kilometers away. Follow the path—and only the path. At the end is a pier extending out into the water from the beach. Your boat is hidden in the brush that grows at the base of a tall outcropping at the north end of the beach. The sail is rolled and stowed within. We looked at it not too many days ago. It is seaworthy. We will be at the beach in the morning. Do not be there."

Carpathimos nodded as he reached for Elijah. He gripped him gently by the arm, pulling him toward the cart path. They traveled the short distance in silence, striding among tall, wispy grasses growing precariously out of the white sand. The embankment was short but steep. At last they reached the beach. Carpathimos directed Elijah to a large rock resting in the middle of the beach, but Elijah didn't stop there. He walked into the water up to his knees before he stopped. As Carpathimos looked on, Elijah tipped his head and gazed into the shimmering blue water as he began to sob. He yanked the knapsack from his shoulder and hurled it onto the dry sand, then screamed. Off balance, Elijah dropped to a sitting position in the water, drew up his knees, and cradled them as he continued sobbing. Carpathimos ran into the water and sat next to Elijah.

"What is wrong with these people?" Elijah screamed as he fought back tears and slapped at the water in front of him. "I have witnessed more death on this journey then I was prepared to face. How can you keep going, Carpathimos? How can you be so strong when you face it . . . when you even cause it?"

At first, Carpathimos did not have an answer. Death had been a part of his entire life. He had cheated death to survive. Death chased him from his home and death lured him back to Rome. "Perhaps I am not the strong one, Elijah. You are facing death in the eyes right now. You are asking how to fight it. I, like so many, have used it for my gain, to stay alive. It doesn't mean that I like it any more now than I did when I saw it for the first time." Carpathimos sighed. "The image of my father's body, slain by Romans on a beach like this one, haunts me to this day. Holding my wife's body after she was slain—" Carpathimos paused, then confessed, "I just know that I must go on. I have more to do before I can rest."

Elijah nodded and washed his face in the water. Carpathimos patted him on the shoulder and then walked back to the beach, angling toward the high escarpment to search for the boat. A short while later, he called for Elijah to help him. They dragged the boat down to the water and Carpathimos rigged the sail to the thin mast and pushed off. Elijah grabbed his knapsack and jumped in, taking a seat in the bow.

Driving an oar into the earth, Carpathimos shoved the boat forward and began rowing. He directed the small craft through the mouth of the bay, then turned it northward. The small craft skimmed around the tip of the cape and approached the dark blue depths of the sea below them. Carpathimos opened the sail and the wind caught it, billowing the fabric and spinning the bow toward the east in a path that would carry them along the north coast of Sicily.

Carpathimos leaned back and peered under the sail at Elijah, who turned his face into the wind. When he glanced to the back, he found Carpathimos staring at him. "I am glad to be leaving this place, Carpathimos."

Carpathimos smiled and nodded. "We will stop along the way to stretch our limbs and find food before we cross over to the mainland. In the meantime, tell me more about the book of the laws, Elijah."

Elijah grinned, eager to let the teachings erase the cruelty of the day.

# Chapter XVI

———

LUCIUS TOOK A seat on the stone ledge, letting the pool's hot water envelope him up to the neck. A drop of perspiration formed over his right eyebrow, then migrated through the patch of short dark eyebrow hair before sliding to its eventual demise off the tip of his lashes and tumbling imperceptibly into the steamy waters of the large bath. He opened his eyes and gazed around him, the way one does when resting in a place created for solitude, yet anticipating the arrival of someone who would destroy that peace with small talk or annoying introductions. Finding no such person, Lucius relaxed and closed his eyes.

The density of hovering steam created a calming peacefulness; steam drifted from the warm water and gently circulated about the room. Lucius rested his head against the rounded lip of stone tile protruding from the edge of the bath. He breathed in and exhaled a heavy sigh, trying to escape, even if only momentarily, the past, present, and future of Rome's political scene. It was dirty and corrupt, despite the republic's short lifespan.

He came to the baths almost every morning, awakening particularly early each day to avoid the masses of people in the Forum. He was also able to avoid the throngs of people who used the baths throughout the middle of the day when the streets of the city became sultry and uncomfortable. Lucius took advantage of the protected halls leading to the baths; these were reserved for Rome's upper-class citizens, who seldom rose this early. His goal was to avoid acquaintances and strangers, alike.

Rome's baths were yet another facet of life within an exceptional city. Its vast structure was divided into a network of both cool and heated pools and lavatories with continuously running water for cleansing rinses. On its stone walkways and in its gloriously maintained gardens, one might find peace with the gods. Fresh water stolen from the highlands entered the Roman baths via a large aqueduct and temporarily circulated over large stone furnaces set beneath the heated pools before gradually cooling once again as it flowed into progressively larger pools. Eventually it spilled into the Tiber River.

The massive wood burners were stoked by slaves permanently blackened by the soot and smoke that escaped through shafts in the great columns supporting the roof. Elsewhere within the bastion of this oasis, Romans of fortune mingled while sipping herbal teas or wine, conducted business while ingesting cleansing concoctions, and shared the latest gossip while enjoying massages with fragrant oils.

Lucius seldom enjoyed those added touches. He came and went every day, avoiding conversation or social interaction whenever possible. He wasn't a cold man, but since his daughter died, people found him withdrawn and aloof. In the past, his place within the Senate hierarchy was firm, owing to his ancestry. His own brother, after all, had been Consul and then, briefly, Emperor. Lucius, too, had been held in high regard for his service to Rome as a masterful general and military strategist. Yet his merging affiliation with more conservative senators had strained many of the relationships he had woven over many years, and with that strain came a dwindling number of supporters and friends.

Lucius's best friend for decades had been a man named Tacitus, who became Emperor after Lucius's brother Tiberius was killed. Tacitus, too, had died, succumbing to an illness of the lung that left him feeble and ghastly as he coughed and gagged upon foul-smelling and bloody purulence. Ultimately, he drowned beneath what became an unstoppable hemorrhage. His death reinforced Lucius's reclusive habits, to the dismay of a few lingering and true friends. Only a few men truly knew the real Lucius Myridias, yet now he seldom shared his feelings unless they probed for answers.

Slipping into an unusual state of profound relaxation, Lucius's mind floated gently along a winding course, drifting carelessly between the places of dreams and the narrow doorway of awareness. For brief moments, images of his daughter Myridia appeared in his mind. First, he saw her as his little girl, gentle yet precocious, loving yet headstrong. Then she transformed into a beautiful woman, precious like the delicate petal of a young rose, eager to follow her own path. He saw her again within his tent in the Dolomites, where he had staged a battle against the Gauls, Rome's enemy to the north. There she had told him of the man she had grown to love, a gladiator.

The gladiator was a man of incredible power and wisdom, but as innocent as a small boy lost upon the sea. This was a man he would honor. Lucius pictured them together, the soft, winding curls of her long, dark hair blowing in the breeze as she stood happily on an island somewhere far away with Carpathimos, strong and tall, a beast of burden yet quick, cunning and agile as a lion. In his mind, Lucius reached out to them, but the more he tried, the farther away they seemed. His heart quickened. He grew anxious as they slipped away from him, disappearing behind the smoke that clouded his mind's eye.

Staying long beyond his usual time of departure, Lucius did not notice the approach or hear the murmurs of the men who joined him in the water. Senators Domitius and Faustus neared the same ledge on which Lucius was sitting. They kept their distance, fully aware of the ways a man can strike out when suddenly alarmed. They saw Lucius's weapons and his muscled physique, still impressive despite his age.

These two men were all that remained of the part of Lucius that still clung to life; to friendship, kindness, and trust. They remained devoted friends and colleagues, eager to support Lucius through any battle or tragedy.

Nearly five years older than Lucius, Domitius was a gifted orator who, in earlier times, had served under Lucius on the battlefield. His military prowess and his skills on the Senate floor could have made Domitius consul general, leading legions of his own into battle, but timing was never in his favor. Now he was too old to desire such an ambitious career. Nevertheless, he found what fulfilled him, both as a friend to Lucius and as a representative of the Roman people.

Faustus, on the other hand, had a different beginning. Several years younger than Lucius, he was the brilliant nephew of Lucius's dear friend and former emperor, Tacitus. As a young man, Faustus became a household name while in the Peoples' Assembly, a Roman governing body responsible to the common man and the endeavors of the city instead of affairs of state. He was a strong advocate for the weak and oppressed, fighting to ensure that Rome's victories were shared with her people. When Tacitus became Emperor, replacing the fallen Tiberius, he nominated Faustus to fill his seat in the Senate. Nearly everyone agreed, though for different reasons. Many supported the family line and followed the recommendation with blind faith, while others felt that keeping Faustus close at hand would be a better way to control him. Therefore, he won the seat with a healthy majority.

Sensing the proximity of the men, Lucius let his mind drift back to real time. He blinked and directed his head away from the tile behind him, to identify the faces jutting above the water near him. With a subtle smile, he tried to hide his embarrassment as he greeted his friends. As he noted the scattered chatter now filling the open air of the vast building, he lifted a hand from the water to stare at his fingertips. "It seems I have overstayed my time in here today. I will be wrinkled like one of the many shriveled and neglected grapes in Faustus's garden."

"Yes, but unlike Faustus's bad grapes, we have not been able to find you. At least the grapes stay where they are planted, so we know where to look," Domitius said.

"Can we leave my garden out of this discussion?" Faustus suggested. "Lucius, Domitius is right. We have been worried about you. Where have you been hiding? You have not been at home for two days."

Lucius put his hand on Faustus's shoulder. "I thank you both for your concern, but I am fine, I assure you."

"Then where have you been, Lucius? If it is a woman, then just say so," Domitius joked, "and we will leave you alone."

"Unlikely!" Faustus said, grinning.

Lucius snorted, "There is no woman. I need no such complication in my life, Domitius." Lucius looked down into the water and reflected upon the last few weeks. "I needed time to think about what we are try-ing to accomplish. The other night I went to that old tavern I mentioned before and I listened to the talk of some young soldiers who were home on leave. They sounded proud of themselves, so eager for victory."

"They sounded like us a long time ago," reminded Domitius.

Lucius nodded. "I thought, perhaps, we were being too steadfast in our obstruction of Regulus. In any case, I left there and started walking along the river out of the city. Yesterday morning I decided I had better turn around, come back here, and stand up for what I believe in."

"And that is?" asked Faustus.

Lucius continued, more solemnly, "I reached this point in life, mak-ing many decisions. Some were bad, but most were good. I decided that I feel this way because I have been through the battles and have seen what it means to fight and lose. I have felt hunger and pushed my men over mountain passes with supplies stretched as thin as the clothing on their backs. We do not need to conquer for the sake of conquering. Tak-ing Sicily alone will fortify us for generations. I see no reason why we must slaughter Carthage at home as well. One day we may need their help to defend ourselves from those who now fight in the east."

"Do you truly believe that Carthage would accept the treaty that you outlined before the Senate last week, Lucius?" Faustus asked. "The treaty still calls for Carthage to pay significantly for many years to come, which is above and beyond that which they will lose by relinquishing Sicily."

"After all," broke in Domitius, "they still rule the sea and there is no guarantee that losing Sicily will be enough to spoil their aggression."

Lucius took a deep breath, sighed, and shook his head. "I am not certain, my friends. Perhaps if we can stall Regulus long enough to see Duilius to victory on the water with his new ships. Maybe then they will concede without more battle, for they already know we are dominant on land."

"I will try to reiterate those words at the next gathering, Lucius, but you may need to speak to the Senate as well. In fact, you should speak to the members from your heart as you did for Faustus and me today," Domitius said.

"I am not a gifted speaker as yourself, Domitius." Lucius ran his hands through his wet hair. "Besides, the Senate has grown weary listening to my feelings about war, and—"

"Still, the Senate has many impressionable young members who need to hear the opinions of the men they once worshiped as heroes," Domitius interrupted. "You need to use your voice, Lucius."

Lucius stared into Domitius's large brown eyes and then at Faustus before looking down again in contemplation. Finally, he nodded.

"So, we can count on you to stay close at hand and avoid disappearing again?" asked Faustus.

"Yes, like Faustus's bad grapes!" Domitius spoke loudly, prompting snickers from Lucius. Faustus slapped water at the two men before marching off for his clothes.

"I thank you, Domitius," Lucius told his old friend. "Even if we cannot sway the whole body of the Senate, at least we may touch a few of the men."

"I am hungry, Lucius. Let us go put Faustus back together and talk him into feeding us."

---

In the glistening blue waters west of Rome and stretching north in an arc from Mount Etna to Mount Vesuvius, a series of emerald islands form the stepping stones by which the gods cross the Tyrrhenian Sea. Life flourishes on these Aeolian Islands, fed by the fertile volcanic soil and warmed by the steaming fumaroles and hot springs dotting the lush green landscape.

Sailing east, Carpathimos directed his craft between the beaches of two islands belonging to the Aeolian chain north of Sicily. Nearing nightfall, he began to veer to the right, directing the boat toward a gray sand beach. The two islands stood erect, like two opposing giants emerging out of the water. Trees and foliage clung to the steep cliffs with relentless tenacity. High above them, a volcanic plume billowed into the darkening sky before tipping and riding the prevailing wind to the east. Far below the peaks of these islands, Carpathimos and Elijah stared over the plank-sheer into the crystal-clear water.

"I can see all the way to the bottom, Carpathimos!" Elijah exclaimed, gripping the side of the boat as if he were preventing a free fall to the sea floor. "And look at all the fish!"

Carpathimos guided the boat onto the beach until it slid to a halt. He leaped ashore and hurried into the forest as Elijah clambered out more cautiously. Soon he came back out with a long stick, on which he had carved points out of a division of its branches. Entering the water slowly, he moved deliberately and stepped carefully, trying not to splash and scare away his prey. Once up to his chest, he began to breathe deeply and quickly as he had learned to do as a child when his father took him diving. Elijah watched, his head tilted like a confused dog. With nary a ripple on the water, Carpathimos disappeared below the surface. Elijah stumbled closer to shore. He could see Carpathimos swimming slowly near the bottom. His movement seemed effortless, reminding Elijah of driftwood. For the moment, time stood still as Elijah watched Carpathimos crawl steadily forward and out of sight.

Elijah grew anxious. He began to hold his breath too, but when he could no longer stand the ache in his chest and the burning sensation behind his eyes, his mouth blew open, expelling the old air to make room for the new. He gulped in a new breath and still Carpathimos did not resurface. Terrified, Elijah sprang into the water and ran along the beach, waving his arms and shouting. Realizing the futility, Elijah charged the boat, crashing hard against the bow and backing the vessel into the water. He jumped in as it floated away from the island, peering over the side into the darkening water, straining to catch a glimpse of his friend.

In an eruption of water and air, Carpathimos's upper body shot out of the water. He grabbed hold of the wooden hull behind Elijah, showering the frightened young man with seawater. Elijah stared at Carpathimos, his mouth hanging open. He couldn't speak.

"That felt good." Carpathimos lifted a large fish into the boat with the wooden spear he had fashioned. The blue-and-silver saddled bream flopped and banged against the wood floor of the boat until its tail slapped against Elijah's foot, stealing his attention away from Carpathimos. "Come back to shore and we will cook him over a fire, Elijah."

Carpathimos sank back into the water and swam leisurely to the sandy shore. Elijah shook himself from his stupor, took up an oar, and paddled clumsily back to shore. "How can you swim like that?" he called after Carpathimos, who once again disappeared from view, this time into the thick brush of the hillside. He didn't get an answer.

Later that afternoon, resting next to a crackling fire and satiated by the large meal of fish he had caught, Carpathimos studied the islands in the distance. The sky to the north was so clear. Even the sliver of moon above him provided contrast to the islands, which seemed to float above the calm, silver surface of the sea like dark green clouds. He and Elijah had scaled the central peak of this island, finally reaching the source of the noxious plume of foul spray that escaped from within its core. They found a place out of the wind, yet with a view to the north. Up here, they could barely hear the gentle waves lapping at the shore.

Carpathimos spoke quietly as he stared beyond the fire toward the black islands. "I grew up on islands much like these. My sister and I played amongst the trees and on the beaches. My father taught me how to fish and how to dive for sponges and mollusks." When he paused, Elijah stared at him, hoping for more. "After the Romans released me, I returned with my woman and my sister. I had missed home so much. All I could think about while I fought with the Roman army was how to get back to Leros. I longed to swim once more in the clear green-blue waters and fall asleep on the warm, soft sand."

Elijah stirred, eager for his friend to dig deeper into his past. The words had trickled out of Carpathimos like water from an urn long assumed to be dry. Elijah wanted to hold the urn upside down and shake it for every last drop. "Then you are on your way back home, Carpathimos?"

"I will never go back. I cannot go back there."

"But why not?"

"I have lost so many I loved there. I cannot bear to face Leros again," replied Carpathimos solemnly.

"Yet you have many fond memories of the island, do you not? What could the island have done to your family?"

"It was the Romans!" snapped Carpathimos. "The Romans killed my father and mother. The Romans enslaved my sister. The Romans forced me into battle and trained me to kill. I was just a boy like you, Elijah. I knew nothing of violence and warfare. I was just a fisherman's son." Carpathimos shook his head in disgust. He sat back against the rock that had been supporting him, gaining control over his temper. More calmly he continued, "The Romans came to Leros one final time, to take Myridia away from me."

Elijah opened his mouth to speak but thought better of it, not wanting to open wounds any deeper. Instead he sat back against a large stone, facing the islands. The small fire glowed between the two travelers. Carpathimos spoke again, wanting to apologize to Elijah for snapping at him, but doing so in the only way he knew how. "Elijah, explain to me how this god, Yahweh, as you call him, can take his chosen people from Sinai to an oasis near Kadesh, just short of the Promised Land, and force them to wander in the desert, condemned to death, in hopes of teaching the next generation about faithfulness and trust."

Elijah accepted the opening as a means to help his friend, understanding that Carpathimos was not angry with him but troubled all the same. Opening the sack and pulling out the Septuagint, Elijah began, "You must understand. The people were not obedient. They did not have faith in Yahweh. They sent spies into Canaan who brought back large clusters of grapes showing all the bounty that existed in the land, but still the people of Israel hesitated, fearing the people of Canaan. They chose to shun faith and the protection of Yahweh. For this, the people chose death."

Elijah continued speaking unimpeded as he thumbed through the papyri looking for the appropriate place. He described how the people assembled on the Moab near Jericho, waiting for the next generation to be prepared by Moses to enter the Promised Land. He explained how Yahweh chose Aaron to lead them through the priesthood and how they conquered the Kings of Sihon and Og on their migration into Canaan. Yet, once again, the people of Israel faltered when they worshiped Baal. "Yahweh must intercede, putting down the idolaters, before helping Israel defeat the king of the Moabites," he said.

Carpathimos listened, absorbing the story. He was intrigued by the young man's unwavering devotion to his god. Elijah continued speaking into the night, reciting the last book of the Laws of Moses while he circled around the fire, recounting the ways to worship Yahweh that Moses taught. "Yahweh must be obeyed. His followers must not worship false idols and fall into the ways of the people of Canaan," Elijah explained. He reviewed the commandments given at Mount Sinai and emphasized how Yahweh chose the people of Israel because he loved them and they were expected to love Yahweh in return. He explained how Joshua became the successor of Moses and why Moses could not to enter the Promised Land himself.

Before retiring, Elijah taught Carpathimos the song that Moses taught the people of Israel before they left him on Mount Nebo to die. The song was to remind them always of Yahweh's love for them and the dangers of disobedience. Elijah sang in a rhythmic melody, the way that Alexander had taught him. It was more musical than intended, but the best that Elijah could do, turning the Hebrew words into Koine Greek with an Aramaic tongue. Before long, Carpathimos joined in, moving around the fire, clapping in unison, singing into the night.

That morning, Elijah woke up alone. Rubbing his eyes and face, Elijah smiled as he thought about the night before. He felt as if he had finally broken through the hard surface covering his friend's life, learning more about his past while they shared Elijah's passionate commitment to his Yahweh and his faith. He hoped they would be able to discuss the books again, as they had almost every day. He knew that learning an entirely new history of mankind was a hard thing for anyone to accept, especially by way of trust and faith.

Standing, Elijah looked down toward the beach to see if Carpathimos was back in the water. As he did, he caught sight of what appeared to be large ships travelling north in a line from a point west of Sicily. Smaller ships accompanied the larger ones. Just then, Carpathimos clambered out of the dense forest behind Elijah and walked up beside him. Elijah pointed to the ships.

"Yes. I noted them earlier, when I awoke this morning," Carpathimos said. "I think they are merchant ships sailing to the island of Sardinia. Carthage has troops there."

"And the smaller ships?"

"The Romans always spoke of Carthage's Birds of Prey, their fighting ships. I suspect they accompany the merchant ships to protect them from attack." Carpathimos clapped Elijah on the shoulder. "Come. We must go now. We have a long voyage ahead of us across open water. I would like to get underway before the sea gets rough."

Pushing off the island, Carpathimos rowed into the wind. It was favorable, heading in the right direction. After tucking the oars behind the planksheers, he unfurled the lone sail. It captured the wind and jerked them forward. As Carpathimos sat, Elijah pointed to the east and shouted, "Look!"

Several kilometers ahead of them, sailing north and west, a wall of ships too numerous to count crawled over the sea. "There are many columns of ships, all in lines!"

Carpathimos nodded. "We will steer clear of them. They may be Roman." Carpathimos wondered if the information he had given the priest may have been too late, at least as it pertained to Rome's plan to attack the Carthaginian fleet north of Sicily. Perhaps, though, a battle between the two forces now would validate the rest of his story.

# Chapter XVII

———

A STUBBORN HEADWIND pressed against his ship's wide bow like the fangs of an adder, its body twisting down from Mount Etna through the aged chestnuts and towering pines, then over the coastline and out to the water, where it slithered into the Straits of Messina, gathering strength as it fought through the narrows. Fighting against this boundless serpent, Giuias Duilius compelled his men forward, demanding the best their bodies could offer, to push him and the rest of the fleet into the calmer waters of the Aeolian island range.

Duilius listened to the drumbeats sounding the rhythm and setting the pace for the oarsmen and the cries of the crew masters calling out the strokes required to move such a massive fleet forward as it sliced through the difficult waters. Within the belly of each ship, rows of oarsmen swung their long, straight timbers over and over, again and again, into the salient azure water, churning the Tyrrhenian Sea beneath them into swirling eddies. The crews of hardened oarsmen pushed against the sea under the whip strikes of their officers while the weaponized portion of the crew, the Roman soldiers, looked on ahead for the enemy to the northwest.

The prey they hunted were the massive merchant ships of Carthage, slung low in the water, en route to Sardinia. The bellies of these ships would be laden with food and supplies for the islanders and the military garrison at the outpost on Sardinia. This citadel had been strategically placed to defend Sicily and to launch an offensive, if necessary, against the Romans on the Italian peninsula. The shipping lane over which the Carthaginians sailed, a lifeline and supply route between Sardinia and Sicily, was two hundred kilometers north and west of the island of Lipari, in the southern limb of the Aeolian range. Much of the equipment and military supplies destined for Sardinia were carried by troop ships sailing from Carthage, while grains and animals came from Sicilian fields. To hinder or obstruct this steady stream of food and fuel for Carthage's army would be a major coup for Rome's first large-scale naval endeavor. The man to lead it was Duilius.

Duilius stood on the deck of his flagship, staring at the wake of a nearby ship, mesmerized by the rolling blue water capped with foam. He was leading one hundred twenty new warships toward the supply route, hoping to catch Carthage unaware. Success would be measured simply by seizing a few of the merchant ships and perhaps destroying some of Carthage's infamous birds of prey. Duilius was thinking about his diffident and callow sailors in their new ships. Rome's confidence on the water paled in comparison to her confidence on the battlefield, so planning a short intrusion into the waters west of the Italian peninsula seemed most appropriate. For this initial experiment, Duilius commanded his whole fleet, hoping to provide all his men valuable training on the open sea.

Periodically along the way, Duilius stopped his fleet to practice maneuvers with the new wooden ships, to give their crews the experience necessary to engage the enemy in close combat. Each captain was learning the abilities of his men and growing more confident in the soundness of his craft. Sailing in close proximity, the crews practiced with grappling hooks and ropes, catching paired quinquereme to draw them near enough to deploy the corvus, the hinged, narrow bridge made of beam and plank over which a ship's soldiers could board the deck of another ship.

During these friendly trials, the hooked beak of the corvus was not attached, preserving the decks of the fine new ships for the battle to come. Therefore, the soldiers were hesitant to cross. They crawled on hands and knees over the corvus, worried about slipping into the sea between two drifting vessels. Before long, the practice emboldened the once timid crew. The men grew sure-footed, pouring over the deployed corvus as if it were just another land bridge they had crossed hundreds of times before.

Rome's new warships were built to exacting standards by some of the finest ship builders of the time, commissioned by the Senate to complete the construction of the navy in short order. In fact, the number of ships built in such a small period of time was staggering, and yet their quality was second to none. Modeled closely after a Carthaginian bird of prey the Romans confiscated after it ran aground in bad weather, these ships were designed to achieve speed, strength, and reliability. Every slab of wood, every cut and curve, was painstakingly copied. The Roman quinquereme, like her enemy's counterpart, was built for maximum maneuverability without sacrificing strength.

The Carthaginian warship, much like the falcon, did its damage at high speed, ramming into an enemy vessel and fracturing its hull, opening it to the sea. Each Roman ship was built around one great wooden keel running longitudinally from bow to stern. The old-growth timber was hewn from great evergreen trees harvested from the foothills of the Dolomites far north of Rome. It provided stability as the craft hurled forward into its target like a battering ram. As most prototypes are enhanced or upgraded, these Roman ships sported a unique addition: the corvus.

Standing over ten meters high upon the foredeck of each Roman warship, the bridgeworks of wooden beams and planks rose into the air ominously. At their base was a system of hinges and swivels attaching each unit to the deck, allowing the corvus to rotate and collapse upon the enemy ship. At the peak of the corvus, a sharp iron spike resembling a bird's beak was fastened; it would penetrate the wooden deck on which the corvus was deployed, holding the enemy ship tightly in place. The corvus also served as a gangway for Rome's other unique adaptation to the Carthaginian design: foot soldiers.

On board all of Duilius's ships sailed one hundred heavily armed infantry soldiers, seasoned and eager for battle. The corvus, in reality, was born out of necessity, a means to an end. Rome knew it needed soldiers to win a sea battle and they needed to deploy those soldiers onto the opposing ship as quickly as possible. The soldiers and their corvus would even the score. The quinquereme could now ram its target and deploy the corvus, allowing the soldiers to pour across to the enemy's ship for hand-to-hand combat. Carthaginian sailors stood no chance against trained Roman infantry. This was how Duilius would prevail.

After clearing the eastern promontory of Sicily, just beyond the shadow of Mount Etna, the Roman fleet slid past the embattled port city of Mylae. This aged Sicilian seaport had been standing inconspicuously for hundreds of years atop the rocks of a long, narrow peninsula protruding into the sea. Shaped like the dorsal fin of one of the sea's feared hammerheads, this peninsula marked the location where Duilius's men would rest, eat, shift positions, and again practice boarding maneuvers over the corvus.

Enjoying their respite, the men fed on dried deer and pork, along with smaller animals like poultry and goats. These were slaughtered as needed to feed the large crews. Nuts were fed to the oarsmen while they rowed, to provide continuous nourishment. Because of the dearth of fresh water, each man was periodically given wine for hydration. Little else but these meager rations fueled the men on Rome's ships—save for their fear of harsh punishment and their growing eagerness to confront Carthage at sea.

The temporary pause near Mylae was the last pause until the engagement with Carthage. Each day, the men hoped for calmer seas, growing more confident and prepared. On the fateful day of battle, as it should occur for Rome's navy on its first major sea offensive, the men filled their bellies while their captains reminded them of their duties. Every oarsman was relied upon for his strength and endurance, the men charged with operating the corvus were relied upon for speed and accuracy, and the soldiers were trained to brandish their weapons with deadly accuracy. These duties had been drilled and rehearsed over and over again to ensure success, to no lesser degree than what was expected of Rome's forces on land.

Duilius moved about his flagship constantly, supervising the maneuvers as his ship sailed through the fleet, weaving between and around the other vessels while they engaged one another in tactical drills. His fleet stretched far and wide, so the flagship seldom reached the perimeter. Satisfied by what he had witnessed, he and his first officer moved belowdecks to inspect his own oarsmen and gauge their preparedness. "Not too much meat or too much wine," he warned his first officer. "Be sure to keep the men slightly hungry, for we cannot afford to have them tired and listless. Take this time to practice the corvus and allow the oarsmen to rest their muscles."

Then the horns blew. Duilius's men exchanged glances, wondering if what they heard was real. Duilius and his first officer charged up the steps to the main deck to identify the source of this unexpected commotion. They found their men, as well as the men on the ships surrounding them, all gazing into the bright sky to the west.

Duilius hurried to the side of the ship, clear of any obstructions, and stared hard toward the horizon. Squinting into the white light reflecting off the water, he held out his hand over his eyes to block the most intense rays. That is when he saw them. A massive flotilla of warships bearing down on them at incredible speed. Carthage was patrolling these waters. The confrontation would come a day earlier than he had expected.

Carthage did not merely protect her merchant ships with warships sailing in convoy, Carthage sent other ships patrolling the waters through which the merchant ships crossed. The Carthaginians sailed a sprawling armada stretching toward the west as far as the Romans could see. Seemingly outnumbered, the Romans would need all their skills and courage. The time for practice had ended. Duilius's men were either ready to defeat the enemy or die. He hoped this fear might compel them to perform herculean tasks.

"Sound the horns again! Make ready for attack!" Duilius shouted. "Attach the spike to the corvus. Our battle begins!"

From ship to ship, the horns blew in succession, spreading across the water like ripples on a pond. A preordained combination of horn signals transmitted Duilius's orders throughout the fleet. Duilius moved to the bow of his flagship, staring at the birds of prey flying toward him, closing the distance rapidly. These were Carthaginian waters, but what confused him was the size of the attacking force. It seemed much too big and cumbersome for warships on patrol.

As the enemy advanced, the large Carthaginian force divided, widening the distance between themselves in order to optimize the angles for ramming. At Duilius's call, the Roman oarsmen accelerated, narrowing the closing gap more quickly, hoping to throw off the timing of the charge. The Roman captains prepared their oarsmen for the next set of maneuvers, which would come when the birds of prey flew by, missing their targets.

On the first pass, the Romans lost several ships when the Carthaginians punched into them, penetrating the bellies of the quinqueremes, crushing man and timber under the mass and momentum of these colliding vessels. Many of the original targets, though, had been missed, forcing recalculations by the Carthaginian captains. They needed to select new targets as they moved through the divided fleet.

With every collision, men fell into the sea, thrown by forces impossible to resist, although with each contact, many of Rome's soldiers managed to board the Carthaginian ships, harassing their attackers like enraged hornets. The soldiers did what damage they could before being overpowered. Then they were slain and cast into the water. However, this unexpected chaos accomplished what was necessary to shift the balance of the battle. The Carthaginian ships had been hindered long enough to allow the Romans time to respond.

The quinqueremes leading Rome's fleet advanced into the middle of the mass of enemy ships, spinning around to the north and south to ensnare the ships skimming passed them. Duilius's flagship was among the first to split through the enemy's center, swinging about to the south to come alongside a Carthaginian warship. As his quinquereme raced through the water, the oarsmen drove hard, their long oars slicing at the water, pushing the ship onward ferociously. The drum beats quickened. The cries of the crew masters pierced the air.

Duilius's ship careened against the hull of the speeding bird of prey, splintering her portside oars into ragged chaff. They were now close enough to see the whites of the enemies' eyes. Duilius's soldiers hurled the grappling hooks into the air, the ropes unravelling from their neat coils as they followed the hooks onto the deck of the enemy ship. The men then pulled hard at the ropes, marrying the two vessels in a wicked dance upon the water.

Duilius's soldiers sprang into action, dropping the hooked bridge onto the harnessed bird of prey. The iron spike slammed down into the deck of the ensnared vessel, splintering wood and catching her fast. The soldiers raced over the corvus and spread across the enemy's deck like a wave of water washing across a floor, slaughtering the ill-prepared sailors attempting to halt their advance. Before long, the Romans disappeared into the belly of the raptor to exterminate the oarsmen who, despite their ineluctable destiny, never ceased their efforts, rowing to the bitter end.

Duilius looked on proudly as his men took control of the captured vessel, his heart pounding vigorously with the drums below him. He spun on his heels to look across the water at the individual battles waging. From one ship to the next, his men were prevailing. By numbers, the two sides had been evenly matched but, in the end, Rome won the day. Even the Carthaginian flagship had succumbed to the corvus. It was tethered by the grapples and pinned down. The Carthaginian leader, however, managed a hasty escape, boarding another vessel while Duilius ravaged his remaining fleet.

After losing more than fifty ships to Rome, Carthage retreated with a sizeable force still intact. Rome sank over a dozen birds of prey and captured four times that number, securing the supplies and confiscating what amounted to a great source of unexpected wealth. Rome had not gone unscathed, however. Before withdrawing to find safe harbor elsewhere, Carthage managed to sink almost twenty of Rome's new war machines.

Giuias Duilius considered giving chase but thought better of it. This was a clear victory for Rome, yet something kept his confidence in check. Something held him back. His mind wandered to the thought he had pondered earlier in the day. The number of ships patrolling the sea had been the giveaway. He surmised that Carthage knew about the Roman fleet and was prepared to meet them on the open sea. Perhaps, given the attack near Mylae, they even intended to sink Rome's fleet in the Strait of Messina.

The aftermath of the battle, widespread and horrific, floated atop a now calm cerulean sea. Surveying the carnage, Duilius gazed across the water at the scattered remains of ships and crews, contemplating his next move. Pontius, the next in command, reported the tally. "We have lost only seventeen, and for the rest, the damage is minimal, Consul Duilius."

"And what of Carthage?" asked Duilius, not taking his eyes from the corpse of a man floating face-down in the water near the side of his flagship.

"Based on the reports coming back from our ships, we have sunk or captured nearly half the enemy fleet. The men are dividing powers in order to bring the captured vessels home."

Duilius nodded, his affect flat, his face void of emotion.

"Consul Duilius," Pontius added, "several of the captured vessels are carrying precious metals. The men are reporting slags of gold and silver worth hundreds of thousands of sesterces!"

"Likely still carrying this from one of their last raids," Duilius suggested.

"All the more likely that these ships were diverted to our location to intercept us. Somehow they knew our intentions."

"Do you mean there may be an emissary of ill intent among us in Rome?" asked another officer.

"More likely one of our brothers in Rome," said Duilius quietly. "It was no secret that we were constructing a fleet of warships, for we searched for experienced boat builders from all across the great sea. We did not, however, disclose our intentions."

"Should we chase the remainder of their fleet and try to capture their officers to interrogate them?" Pontius asked.

"No," growled Duilius. "They have scattered and would ambush us among the islands. They still number nearly eighty. I don't want to risk losing all that we have gained. We will uncover the one sharing our information with Carthage once in Rome, I assure you."

"Do we then return home?" Pontius asked.

Duilius looked around at his attentive crew. They seemed eager for another confrontation. "Divide the ships," he ordered. "We will take half of the fleet to Segesta with all the soldiers and liberate the city from Carthage. They will finally lose their last foothold on the island. The remainder of the ships and sailors will return home with our captured vessels and the bounty."

"Rome will insist that you march through the streets in a victory parade upon your return, Consul Duilius!" Pontius said, with a toothy grin. "They will honor your success with a Triumph and erect a monument in your name within the Forum!"

Duilius marched over the deck of the flagship to its highest point, stepping up to address his men. He scanned the proud faces of the many simple men staring back at him. "We will take our place among the greatest of Rome!" Duilius shouted to his crew, who crowded the deck to hear their leader's words. As he spoke, his message was relayed from ship to ship. "We have met Carthage on a new battlefield, in her territory, and we have prevailed!" His men cheered loudly until he raised his hands to calm them.

The cheering diminished gradually as it moved across the water, spreading from boat to boat in ever increasing waves. "What's more, we have shown our fellow Romans what we are capable of doing on the water. This is the first of many more sea battles we have yet to fight, but now, on this day, Rome may know that her power truly has no boundaries, for wherever we may sail, we will conquer!"

His men stomped on the deck, cheering his name, chanting in unison to create the most noise possible. Carried by a gentle wind, his words and the trailing chant spread quickly across the fleet, just over one hundred ships and a legion of warriors drifting closely together over the open water of the Tyrrhenian Sea, victorious under the setting sun.

# Chapter XVIII

———

"WHAT END DO you hope to find by confronting this Lucius man—General Lucius? What do you hope to achieve, Carpathimos?" Elijah struggled to keep up with his large companion while being jostled around within the large crowd milling about along the Via Appia near the west gate of the city. Carpathimos and Elijah had come ashore south of Rome and walked the remaining distance nearly in silence. Elijah had inquired about finding transportation to Greece but had been told that that would have to wait until Carpathimos could meet with Lucius.

Prancing quickly across the cobbled stone road, Elijah wove around the peasants, villagers, and farmers who made their way to and from the markets within the city walls. As he got within arm's reach of Carpathimos, he repeated his question, only to have it ignored again.

"Do not use my name here," warned Carpathimos. "I do not wish to invite more attention to us then what may come on its own."

Elijah didn't understand the connection Carpathimos had with the people of Rome as a legendary gladiator. His name would still have meaning to some the games' steadfast fans. Those events had been held within the great arena called the Circus Maximus, the top of which Elijah could now see as he squeezed after Carpathimos between a cattle-drawn cart and the wall at the city gate. "Fine," responded Elijah, frustrated by the mounting delays he had experienced on his circuitous route to Greece. "I hope that this meeting with the general will be quick and soon arrive."

"It will be soon." Carpathimos scanned the many buildings, warehouses, and shops over the heads of the bustling crowd.

"Do you know how we will find him among all of these people?" Elijah stepped quickly out of the way of passing soldiers marching along the side of the road. He stared at their armor and weapons and felt a chill run down his spine. He noticed Carpathimos had taken shelter in a market shop, pretending to look at the merchandise. Elijah guessed that his companion probably had a similar reaction to the soldiers. Leaving the shop, the friends made their way down the hill toward the city center. The crowd grew less confining as they put more distance between themselves and the cramped confines near the city gate. At least now they could walk side by side.

"The soldiers marching by the store back there gave me an idea, Elijah," Carpathimos said. "We need to split up for a while."

"What do you mean?" Elijah shot Carpathimos a look of concern.

"I mean that I need to seek out General Lucius and find out when I might speak with him alone," Carpathimos said. "Meanwhile, you can find us safe passage to Greece. Furthermore, if you find a ship that is departing soon, you should take it and not wait for me."

"But we are—"

Carpathimos interrupted his protest. "Go now, Elijah. Do not wait for me," he ordered. "I cannot guarantee that I will be able to join you, and you should not risk getting detained further. If everything goes as planned, I will be on the next merchant ship sailing east. Perhaps our paths will cross once again."

Elijah stared back at Carpathimos in silence, unable to overcome the shock of separating so abruptly with the friend who had shared so many adventures and close calls with him. Carpathimos sensed the fear and bewilderment in his young friend. He, too, felt sick in his belly, but he was confident he was correct. Putting a hand on Elijah's shoulder, Carpathimos spoke softly, "Go, Elijah. You will be all right. I know that you are strong enough to fulfill your promise to your grandfather. I thank you for sharing your passion with me, for teaching me."

Elijah swiped at a tear as it teetered from the tips of his dark lashes. "I wish to thank you as well, Carpathimos. I would not have survived this far without you." Elijah spoke slowly and deliberately as he tried to maintain his composure. "I am very grateful as well."

Carpathimos smiled and patted Elijah's shoulder several times before turning to leave. Elijah reflexively took a step to follow him, then stopped, calling after him instead. "But where do I start?"

Carpathimos glanced over his shoulder and pointed toward the open market farther down the hill. "Find someone to take you to Brundisium on the coast. Find a ship headed east." Carpathimos took a few steps before hesitating. He looked back at Elijah again. "And Elijah," he added lightly with a smile, "try to avoid getting tricked onto the wrong ship again." Carpathimos put his fist over his heart, saluting the young man. Then he turned away.

Elijah watched Carpathimos until he disappeared around the corner of one of the many mud and stone-walled buildings. He stood in place for what seemed like many minutes before realizing he wasn't really breathing. He took a deep breath and glanced around at the people and buildings surrounding him. He was utterly lost within this large city. He felt incredibly lonely. Gradually, he began to walk toward the market. His whole body felt numb and his feet felt as heavy as the heart beating in his chest.

As Elijah navigated through the crowd, someone walked too closely behind him and bumped the sack that he carried over his shoulder. He clutched the strap tightly and remembered what it was he carried. He thought of Carpathimos and the hardships his friend had overcome in his life; they made him humble. Elijah stood up straight and took another deep breath. "I can do this," he said out loud.

Carpathimos climbed the steady incline of Quirinal Hill toward the home of General Lucius Myridias. Without really paying any attention to the structures around him, he walked quickly through the central Forum and over the piazza before starting up the hill. He thought about Elijah, hoping the youngster would stay safe and find his way to his people in short order. He disliked parting with Elijah in that callous way, and so he spent the time walking, trying to convince himself that it had been the best thing to do.

Nearly two-thirds of the way up Quirinal Hill, Carpathimos recognized the home immediately. As he approached the front entry of the large villa, images of Myridia flooded his mind. It seemed like it had been such a short time ago when he had hurried up this street on his way to meet Myridia after his return from battle in the Dolomites. He could still smell the rose and lavender in her hair and see the golden snake she wore around her elbow. He tried to focus his memory on her face, but the precious features wouldn't come. His mind could only conjure quick flashes: her straight white teeth, her playful green eyes. The harder he struggled and failed to visualize her, the angrier he became.

Before he knew it, Carpathimos was standing at the threshold of the entry, between two massive columns. Startled, he looked about for anyone watching him. Seeing no one, he took a few calming breaths. With slight hesitation, he held up his fist and pounded on the thick wooden door. He waited for a moment and then pushed the door slowly open. Carpathimos peered in, calling out, "Is anyone here?"

A young woman entered the hall and stared at him. "May I assist you?" Judging by her simple attire, she was a servant in the house.

"Yes. I am an old friend of General Lucius. Does he still live here?"

"If you are looking for Senator Lucius Myridias, then, yes, he does live here," the woman answered, adding, "but you will not find him here now. He comes and goes throughout the day and is often away until late in the evenings. He did not tell me how long he would be away. May I tell him who stopped by to see him?"

Carpathimos smiled at the woman. "No need to bother him. I will come here at another time and announce myself then." He nodded goodbye, exited, and closed the door. Leaning against it, Carpathimos thought about what he would say to the general when he saw him again. Perhaps it had been for the best that Lucius had not been there now. Carpathimos had rehearsed what he wanted to say over the preceding months, but he was dissatisfied with the different versions. He hoped that the next time he approached this home, his anger would return, so that he would be able to say the words he needed to say.

Walking back down the street, Carpathimos considered his next step. Certainly, he would return to confront Lucius. With dusk approaching, Carpathimos felt he needed the span of night to consider the pending confrontation. Perhaps he should return tomorrow night. Over the hillside, the moon was rising, large and orange and nearly full. Surveying the strangely shaped spots and smudges on the moon's face, as he had done hundreds of times before, Carpathimos thought about Lucius's home and its quiet neighborhood. In the past, Lucius had kept only one or two servants. If necessary, Carpathimos could handle them.

Approaching the Roman baths, Carpathimos remained vigilant, in case he encountered Lucius along the way. He moved quickly through the streets on his way to the Forum, which was still busy at this late hour.

---

Moving about the market, Elijah was growing weary and was about to give up his quest. The heat, the bustling crowd, and their constant chaffering made his head buzz like the sound of flies gathering on a south-facing wall. He had spoken to nearly every peasant, farmer, and merchant within and around the market who had acknowledged having at least some Koine Greek. None of them, however, knew it well enough to understand what he wanted. He tried Aramaic but didn't find anyone who answered to that in a friendly way. He knew Hebrew wouldn't elicit much of a response, either, so he had not bothered to use it. At one point, Elijah tried to draw a picture in the sand covering the street, attempting to draw the likeness of a ship sailing toward the sunrise. Apparently, the man for whom he had drawn the picture thought his ship was a pig, because he kept trying to sell his sow to Elijah. Now, in frustration and reaching a point of despair, Elijah sat down on an empty wooden crate and stared at the people before him.

A thought occurred to him. Did Rome have a synagogue where he could go to pray and study the books? He assumed not, but had he dismissed the thought too quickly? What if there were Hebrews who, like his grandfather, had come this way from Jerusalem instead of going to Egypt long ago? He sighed. It didn't really matter anyway, for he had no means of finding it, much less asking for directions. What he really wanted to do now was to return to the temple in Jerusalem, the only true temple, the only legitimate place to sacrifice and be close to Yahweh. Unfortunately, he was here, stuck in Rome and utterly lost. All he could do at this point would be to make his way east, eventually finding his family again.

Tired of the same scenery, Elijah cast his sack over his shoulder and walked in the direction of the Forum. At least he had learned something about the city while trying to speak to the people in the market. He probably would have ended up near the Forum anyway, since there seemed to be a natural ebb and flow of people between the markets here and the happenings there. Perhaps he would have more luck interacting in the Forum with people who travel farther from Rome than the farmers in the market.

Nearing the temples of Castor and Pollux and Saturn, Elijah slowed his pace, gawking at the structures, turning from one to the other as people shuffled around him. Nearby, music was playing, and people were chanting or singing along with it, though Elijah wasn't completely convinced of either activity, based on the talent represented. Trying to tune out the din, Elijah studied the intricate carving of the stone on the temples before breaking away to join the crowd forming around the noise.

A short walk led him to the foot of the Temple of Jupiter Optimus Maximus. This Etruscan structure was more grandiose than the other two he had seen, with massive columns and ornately carved capitals. In order to see over the crowd assembled, Elijah climbed the steps ringing the massive temple and peered around one of the columns at the front corner.

To his amazement, he could see the massacred remains of a bovine in the middle of the crowd. Like the animal and the ground beneath it, the people kneeling nearest the animal were covered in blood. A man dressed in long black robes, his head covered with a veil, examined the entrails of the dead animal, spreading the guts loosely across the ground while repeating phrases, as if chanting. The people in the crowd repeated the chant or song. As Elijah watched the activity curiously, one man noticed Elijah's confused expression. He stepped close and asked what could be the matter with him. Elijah shook his head, for he did not understand the language of Latium. To Elijah's surprise, the man spoke again, but this time, in Greek.

"They sacrifice a heifer to Zeus in preparation for a battle," he explained. "The high priest inspects the innards for any faults. If he finds one, they slaughter another. In years past, I have seen this go on for days. Once he finds a perfect specimen, he will burn it at the altar in the temple."

Elijah nodded. The scene made him uncomfortable, so he turned his attention to the man speaking. He was tall and thin. A coarse, dark beard covered most of his face. He wore something resembling a uniform, a short two-shouldered tunic and tall leather boots. His soft round cap was purple and from the center hung a short tassel.

"Why do you watch this sacrifice?" asked Elijah. "You are not from here either, are you?"

The man shrugged. "I grew up here many years ago, but I joined a shipping crew from Rhodes when they once stopped here to trade goods. As a young man like yourself, I joined them for adventure, and I have been sailing with them ever since."

"Why are you in Rome today?"

"Because I am looking for a boat builder to fix our ship. It was damaged during a storm on the Adriatic. Only by the mercy of Neptune did we make port in Brundisium. Oddly, there are no boat builders to be found there. I was told that Rome had been building ships, so I came here to hire someone to help us."

"Brundisium!" Elijah exclaimed. "Do you think your captain would let me sail back to Greece with you?" In his excitement, Elijah gripped the man's elbow.

The man smiled. "I am the captain, and, yes, you can join us as long as you work for your place on board."

Elijah grinned. "I will work hard! When do we leave?"

Again, the man shrugged. "That I do not know. First, I need to hire the builder and then we must travel back to the coast to fix the hull. If you make your way to Brundisium, where we are anchored, within the next two moons, you will find me again, I am certain."

"Two full moons!"

The captain laughed. "It takes several weeks to walk there from here, my friend." Before he could continue, there was movement within the crescent-shaped crowd in front of the temple. As Elijah and the captain looked on, another heifer was led into the center. Elijah watched intently as the young bovine, trying to resist its bonds, was held in place before the high priest. Without warning, the priest drew a long blade and slit the deep throat of the anxious animal, spilling its blood onto the stone steps in front of the temple. The creature's stocky legs wobbled and gave way under its weight, and the yearling fell to the ground. The priest sliced open the belly, spilling the entrails onto the ground.

"What happens now?" asked Elijah. When he got no response, he spun, scanning the crowd for the purple hat, but the captain had disappeared. Nauseated by the show of blood, he desperately wanted to find the captain. He had no idea how to reach the port of Brundisium. His mind was racing and his heart was galloping in his chest. He looked back upon the carnage of the heifer, to see a young slave couple being led into the center of the circle. Their hands had been tied together and they were pulled toward the priest by a rope tied around their necks. They had been stripped bare. The male appeared beaten. Elijah looked closely at their faces. They appeared to be his own age.

Once in front of the priest, two soldiers pushed them into kneeling positions on the blood-covered ground. Their faces were anguished. Elijah stared at them in horror, realizing their fate would be the same as that of the calves. Elijah panicked. His heart pounded in his dry throat and he felt his mind go blank. As his breathing quickened, he found he lacked the ability to scream and yet he could not look away. The crowd closed in on the scene. Pressed against the cold stone of the column beside which he had been standing, he awakened from his frozen terror and he started to act.

Deeply troubled by this scene of idol worship, false gods, and human sacrifice, Elijah pushed passed the people nearest him and ran down the steps toward the high priest. Skipping several steps at a time, Elijah slammed into the man's back, knocking him over onto the greasy plat of blood-stained stone. Elijah shouted above the dying chants of the crowd. Stunned by the unexpected interruption, the crowd watched Elijah sprint back up the steps to the massive portico of the Temple of Jupiter. Withdrawing the books of Moses from his knapsack, Elijah held them over his head while reciting words long committed to memory. He spoke of how Yahweh, the one true God, condemned His people for worshipping fake gods and making egregious offerings.

One by one, members of the crowd started to absorb what Elijah was doing. They shifted about uncomfortably, turning to one another with questioning looks. What started as a sudden and unexpected aberration in the middle of a common ritual had quickly degenerated into a major incident capable of enraging the once lackadaisical Romans. Nearly in unison, the crowd became an irritated mob yelling back at Elijah. Their solemn rhythmic chants turned into calls for his death. Several young men raced up the steps toward Elijah. As he stumbled backward to avoid capture, the first man to reach him grabbed Elijah's tunic, but his blood-covered hand made for a slippery hold. Frantically, Elijah pulled himself away and ran into the street on the other side of the temple.

Pausing briefly to look over his shoulder for pursuers, Elijah glimpsed the angry crowd sweep around both sides of the temple in pursuit of him. While stuffing the books of papyri back into his sack, Elijah started running, the young men just paces behind. Running for his life, Elijah headed back toward the shops and central market. He now understood that interrupting the ceremony was a grave mistake, but he dared not stop to ask for forgiveness.

Fear propelled him on his way. Elijah raced into the disarray of the market, trying to use the disorder to his advantage. Hardly slowing his pace while weaving and dodging around man and beast, Elijah burst through the other side of the market. His pursuers had started to fall away, but before long several of the young men were hot on his heels. Turning up a side street, he ran in front of one shop and then another. Running uphill and gasping for breath, Elijah's legs were about to give out. He was about to fall into the hands of the hunters when he suddenly felt the presence of a large man flying out a shop doorway as he ran past it. The collision of bodies as the man plowed into the young men trailing behind Elijah, frightened him all the more. He couldn't look back, he didn't dare.

Then, as if the large man had dropped from the sky, Elijah sensed he was being chased by a new predator. His pursuer sounded heavy, based on the sound of the footsteps. His stride was longer than Elijah's and yet the frequency of the steps was increasing, not decreasing. The man was picking up speed as he ran and closing the distance between them fast. Elijah could push no faster. He felt the man at his side and an arm wrapped around Elijah's chest, lifting him off the ground. Elijah struggled against the grasp, but the powerful arm was squeezing the air from his already burning lungs. Feeling faint, Elijah sensed a sudden change in direction. His body went limp when he realized that he and his captor were racing between two buildings.

The sensation was other-worldly. Elijah felt his body was floating over a narrow dirt path lined on both sides by scant grasses and tenacious weeds lining the base of the passageway walls. Elijah's sight was growing dim and dark curtains seemed to impede his field of vision. When they turned again, Elijah lost touch with consciousness. His captor was ascending a wobbly wooden ladder near the back of one of the shops.

The man pulled Elijah over his shoulder as he struggled up the old wooden structure. Hanging head down, Elijah started to regain consciousness. He was dizzy from the run and the rapid change in direction, but he tried to focus on the feet below him. He knew those feet!

It was Carpathimos.

Clearing the top of the ladder, the gladiator kept running. Across the roof of one building, with Elijah bent over his shoulder, he leaped across to the next, and so on. After three or four rooftops, Elijah lost count. Suddenly, Carpathimos stopped and dropped Elijah gently at his feet before collapsing down next to him. They lay silently in the darkness on the rooftop, listening to the sound of the mob as it made its way up the street and beyond.

His mouth dry and his heart still pounding, Elijah thanked Carpathimos for saving him again. Carpathimos, out of breath, sat up and shook his head. "I looked out of the doorway to see what all the shouting was about and there you were, sprinting up the hill with a mob of angry young men in pursuit. What did you do?"

"I lost control, Carpathimos. I looked on as that crowd sacrificed animals and prayed to one of their gods in a false temple. They were going to kill two people! I tried to stop them," Elijah gasped.

"If they had captured you today, you would be a burnt offering right now!" Carpathimos said sternly.

Elijah said nothing, grateful beyond words for Carpathimos. He knew that his friend was right. He ran his fingers through his hair and then covered his face with the crook of his arm. Carpathimos ran his fingers through his own thick dark hair, pushing it out of his eyes and off of his forehead, and then he said, "These people are not ready for you yet, Elijah. Come. We had better go to a quieter part of the city."

———

The air within the Senate House was alive with chatter, its members hurriedly departing the morning meeting, anxious to move on with their days. Most had already gone, yet a few small groups of senators still lingered on the expansive voting floor, conversing about various topics not yet sufficiently argued. Consul Marcus Regulus sat between several of his closest friends. He made jest of something which made them all laugh boisterously. Across the floor, Lucius had been saying goodbye to his friends Domitius and Faustus as he was about to leave for the day, when the raucous laughter of Regulus's entourage stole their attention. Faustus glanced over Lucius's shoulder at Regulus and then murmured, "Those idiots would laugh even if he told them they were to be fed to the animals in the arena."

"Easy, Faustus," Domitius said. "We will have our time as well. Today Regulus won his right to assemble an army, but we may still be able to tighten his purse strings after he has gone."

Faustus nodded, then smiled at Lucius who was looking rather glum. "Domitius is right, Lucius. We have not lost completely. As we witnessed here today, there are many members who are apprehensive about Regulus invading Africa, only to slog down in an endless campaign against Carthage, draining our city dry of man and money. Many were compelled by your voice today."

Lucius nodded, but he did not share his friends' positive assessment of the morning's events. Nor did he believe that the members who had voiced dissent had been sincere. That morning, the Senate members had voted overwhelmingly to grant Regulus control of an invasion force to Africa and they had agreed to support his need for ships, sailors, and troops. Duilius's victory at sea had inspired the members to support another offensive. All Regulus required was to assemble his legions and set sail. Lucius thanked his friends for supporting him. As he reached the top steps outside the senate building, he heard Regulus calling his name. Lucius could only imagine that Regulus wanted to gloat.

"Lucius, wait!" yelled Regulus, running to catch up. "Lucius, please, I want to speak with you a moment. May I walk with you?" Of course, such a request from a consul was not to be rejected. Lucius nodded as Regulus joined him on the outer steps.

"Lucius, I would like you to know that I understand your apprehension about attacking Carthage and I did appreciate your words today," Regulus said. "But the Senate has spoken. I hope I can trust that you and your delegation will support Rome's continued progress while I am away."

Lucius said nothing, but slowed his pace, as if in protest to the condescending display of patronage. Regulus continued, "Is it not wonderful to hear of Duilius's success on the water? Is it not splendid to see another victory column raised in the Forum to honor Rome's first major battle at sea?" Regulus grabbed Lucius by the arm. "Duilius will come home soon and be celebrated with a Triumph! Should we not honor him by continuing where he has left off? You were one of the greatest generals Rome ever knew. Why won't you share these victories with us?"

Lucius glared at Regulus. "Because, my Consul Regulus, with respect, I have grown older and wiser. And along the way I have lost what I would wish upon no other man, including you. Rome is happy and healthy, yet I fear your ambition will stretch her beyond her means. One day soon Rome will tear down the middle and what little remains will falter. Men will lose daughters and sons, but," Lucius paused to calm himself, "I don't expect you to understand."

"Well Lucius, I do understand this," growled Regulus, "someone in our midst warned Carthage of Duilius's plan. They were more prepared for his attack than they should have been. As you well know, someone performing such an act of treason would be stripped and dragged through the streets of Rome before being beaten and beheaded by the very *happy* Romans you cherish. Don't make me point my finger in your direction, Lucius. For once you are my enemy, my enemy you will stay."

"How dare you threaten me!" Lucius roared, his anger turning his face umber. "You won your vote. Now try not to fall off your horse."

Regulus stepped back from Lucius and let go of his arm, intimidated by the older and more experienced warrior. "Of course," he said. "You are correct, Lucius. I am wrong to make such an accusation without proof." Regulus continued, "I would like to visit with you more about this matter before I leave for Africa. You are an honest man and I trust your integrity. You may be able to find out who leaked the information to the Carthaginians." He asked if Lucius would be home on the evening of the next full moon, only days away.

"Of course," responded Lucius dryly. "As you wish."

# Chapter XIX

———

I T WAS THAT time of morning when a chill still exists in the air and droplets of dew cling to the leaves and stones and the cooler things, not yet obliterated by the heat of the bright white sun. The sun too had yet to rise over the hills in the distance, though the grayness of night had already gone. The crowds that normally filled the streets by day had not yet assembled. Within the hour, merchants and migrants would gather to wait for the market to open. Their laughter and the confluence of many voices would radiate throughout the low areas of the city, rising like steam toward the heavens.

Walking briskly, Sorian crossed the empty street, making his way to the Tiber. He enjoyed walking the streets of Ostia before the onslaught of this punishing cacophony stole away his solitude. Yet, today, he walked with a different purpose. Thinking deeply, Sorian hardly noticed the peace and tranquility afloat on the cool morning air as he rounded another corner on his route to the docks to find Regulus.

Sorian had paid a boy to watch the docks, and he had come early to wake him. Eager to collect the sum Sorian had promised, the boy announced with excitement and a tooth-filled smile that troops were assembling and great ships were being loaded. They filled the harbor and the sea beyond. Patiently waiting for the boy to conclude his discursive announcement, Sorian handed him a silver coin and patted his head before jumping out of the wooden bunk where he had slept for the past few weeks. This bunk sat among piles of straw above a livery stable on the outskirts of the city. Hoping to catch Regulus at the docks this morning, Sorian hurried down the ladder at the back of the stable and set off in the direction of the harbor.

Ever so cautious, Sorian had kept to himself since his first appearance in Rome. After all, he had enemies there and this was not the time to be spotted carelessly milling about the city. Since his arrival a few weeks prior, he had made only rare contact with his friend, Consul Marcus Regulus, biding his time until he could carry out their plan. They had agreed that he should lay low in Ostia until the time Regulus would arrive with his men.

Sliding straight fingers through his dark hair and then over his body, Sorian shook off the strands of straw and dust that lingered on him and his clothing. He pushed back the longer strands of gray hair on his temples, tucking them behind his ears. He plaited the mass of black and gray at the back of his head, securing it with a short length of string. Full of vigor and confidence, Sorian approached the docks and was surprised by the chaos and multitude of men that surrounded him. Admixed with the usual odors of seawater and fish, the pungent scents of animal manure and horse sweat mingled in the air. The usually placid atmosphere of the harbor in early morning had been replaced by a maelstrom of activity. The boy had been correct: Regulus had called in his troops and was preparing to set sail.

Man and beast filled the docks and the adjacent harbor streets while sailors and soldiers loaded the ships that filled the harbor in this still sleeping port city. Sorian worked his way through the crowd toward the center of the action, occasionally jumping in place to try to see where Regulus might be standing. This early in the morning, he wasn't even sure that Regulus would be present, but he suspected that the consul was eager to get under way. Sorian continued the search.

Sorian had been a member of several legions during the course of his career, but never one that was about to set sail. Having marched into every conflict, the whole notion of ferrying legions of soldiers over the great sea seemed foreign to him, but he understood what great impact such a feat would mean to the empire. If Rome could deliver her legions across the sea and conquer just as effectively as at home, then she could expand her reign as far as the fleet could carry the troops. Sorian was hesitant to take another sea voyage, but he was also eager to be a part of Regulus's victory. For that opportunity, he would tolerate the open water.

Pushing his way through the myriad soldiers, Sorian came up next to a horse-drawn cart that was also making slow progress toward the docks. He climbed onto the back of the cart and stood as tall as he could, craning his neck to search for the gaggle of officers he knew would be gathered somewhere in this mess. Scanning the mass of humanity, he finally spotted Regulus's head and free-flowing waves of hair.

Regulus was also standing on something, perhaps a platform or maybe even a cart of his own. His chest plate gleamed in the morning sunlight while his crimson cape rippled in the slight breeze at his back. Regulus was looking out across the sea of soldiers while barking orders at his soldiers or perhaps scolding his officers, who were crowded around him. Establishing distance and direction in his mind, Sorian hopped down from the cart and began to push his way toward Regulus.

Nearing his friend, Sorian took pause at the sight before him. Regulus had since joined the melee, his face vermilion with anger. The veins of his temples and neck pushed out through the skin as he whipped the back end of a horse laboring to drag a block of alabaster stone up the gangway from the dock. At Regulus's command, his soldiers pulled and pushed the animal and the stone, helping it slide the square-cut stone up and over the threshold onto the deck of the ship. As the horse struggled to deliver the stone across the deck to its destination, the next horse and its stone arrived in front of Regulus.

Sorian looked on with a subtle grin as Regulus joined his men, encouraging each horse and stone up the slanted timbers of the gangway. As the men gave out cheers with each small victory, Sorian made his way toward the center of the half circle of soldiers and sailors observing the activity to wait for Regulus to step back and notice him.

Once it became apparent that his men were able to manage the horses without him, Regulus handed the whip to a subordinate and stepped back to observe them. Wiping his brow with the back of his hand, Regulus took a position in front of Sorian without noticing who the man was behind him.

"Why stones?" asked Sorian, surprising the consul with the odd question. Regulus turned, glancing angrily in the direction from which the voice had come. He laughed as he recognized Sorian's face.

"These are blocks of salt," Regulus said, with a glint in his eye. "For some reason they have been stacked under a roof in Rome for years. I decided that I would take them with me and sow them into the dirt around Carthage when I flatten the city to the ground."

Sorian glanced at the long row of horses coming down the pier from far beyond the reach of his vision. "There must be hundreds of these blocks!"

"Over one thousand," confirmed Regulus. "I had to secure more ships for them and I wanted to ensure they got loaded while the legions were still here to assist. The men can see these blocks and touch them with their own hands, knowing that each is destined to poison the ground where we march. This, too, can be used as their motivation to march on Carthage."

"I have heard talk of armies doing this in the past, but we never destroyed the lands of our enemies after any battle in which I fought before," said Sorian. "Does it really work?"

"The elders state that some eight hundred years ago, within the Syrian lands, a king named Abimelech salted the land of his own city, called Shechem, after he put down a revolt there. Crops would not grow after for many generations," Regulus said with a grin.

"And you intend to do the very same to Carthage." Sorian gave him a nod of respect.

Regulus turned from the parade of horses and salt, grabbing Sorian by the arm to lead him away from the others. "I think that this is where you come in, my friend."

Sorian dutifully walked with Regulus to the end of the pier, where they could speak privately. "You want me to command blocks of salt?" Sorian joked.

"I want you to complete your task with our dear friend Lucius," the Consul ordered, "and then come join me in Africa. These ships will be anchored here waiting for you. I must first move on ahead to gain control of the mainland, but when I have the port of Aspis in my grasp, I will send word for you to set sail."

"How can I possibly hide here for so long after killing Lucius?" Sorian looked quizzically at the consul. "I will be hunted like a wild dog."

"Rest easily, Sorian. No one knows you are here. Lucius will be dead in Rome and you can hide out here in Ostia until I send word to you. The only other man to know of your existence will be Amelius, the captain of this ship." Regulus pointed to the first ship loaded with salt blocks. "My men and I will set sail tomorrow for Ecnomus, on Sicily, to collect more troops and supplies before we cross the sea. Lucius has agreed to honor me with a private meeting at his home when the moon is again full."

Sorian looked at Regulus, curiosity written on his face. Regulus completed describing his plan. "No one will be there except you and Lucius. Therefore, you will complete your mission, come here, and wait here for my instructions to sail."

"Won't Lucius know that you left for Ecnomus with your fleet the day before your scheduled meeting?"

"No." Regulus held his index finger in the air, "I have thought of that already. I am sailing with the fleet but leaving my flagship behind for some repairs. I will make mention that I am sailing later with her once the repairs are made, so people assume I am still in Rome. My captain will sail her the day after Lucius is dead, and by the time anyone realizes that I am not with her, they will simply believe that I had a change of heart and sailed with my army."

"Then I could sail on the flagship?" Sorian felt excited at the prospect.

"Again, no," said Regulus, causing his friend's face to turn cloudy with disappointment. "Think Sorian! Lucius's friends will scour Rome, and even this ship in Ostia, looking for me. Everyone knows that Lucius and I are enemies. You must stay well hidden. Once they realize that I left before he died, they will turn their attention elsewhere."

"Very well." Sorian, stared down at the dock. "Thank you for your patience with me, Marcus. I guess I am just eager to join you and eager to pay Lucius his due."

"I understand, my friend." Regulus patted Sorian on the shoulder. "Soon you will get the revenge we both so much desire. After that, I assure you, the waiting will be easier."

---

Jugurtha smiled warmly as he looked at Yzebel. He had known her since she was small, and even though she had grown up to become a strong and independent woman, her uncle still cared for her much like one of his own children. Working side by side under a blistering, late-summer sun, Jugurtha and Yzebel busied themselves binding armfuls of wheat near the edge of one of the fields.

Yzebel worked as hard as any of the laborers. Her long, toned arms gathered piles of grain that often were as wide in girth as those Jugurtha could pull together. It often seemed, to Jugurtha at least, that Yzebel was competing with him. In the prime of his life, Jugurtha had been a very powerful man, full of vigor and vitality, but now, entering the latter half of his sixth decade of life, he could no longer keep pace with Yzebel.

Taking a short rest to wipe sweat from his head, Jugurtha looked upon Yzebel and recalled the many times she had joined him and the other laborers in the field, often bringing water to drink or food to eat. She was indeed part of his family, as he had been a part of hers. The bond they shared through her late mother remained strong.

Catching up to the men who had been cutting the grain and had stopped briefly to rest and drink water, Yzebel and Jugurtha stood and stretched, pausing in their labors. Standing together, they all heard the hoofbeats of horses approaching. Kanmi and his men were riding toward the main house, which was only a short distance away from the edge of the field. Kanmi was evidently making his monthly visit to the farm to check on their progress and tally the grain and fruit that could be supplied to Carthage's Army.

The few visits with Kanmi during the summer had been fairly uneventful, for there had been little to report other than the progress of the crops. Nevertheless, Kanmi generally had a way of making every visit unpleasant. Yzebel managed to avoid him much of the summer. This time, however, Yzebel knew that Kanmi had seen her working in the field.

Yzebel looked toward the main house, where her father was awaiting Kanmi's arrival. Scanning the land between the buildings, she saw Kanmi and Jabnit walking together into the orchard next to the main house. Meanwhile, Kanmi's men were spreading out, looking in the buildings to ensure no laborers loitered on the landowner's coin.

For the most part, Kanmi's men offered no difficulties, except under the direction of Kanmi. More than once his men had whipped a laborer when Kanmi felt he or she had been guilty of some crime in his imagination. Jugurtha, trying to stay out of trouble as Kanmi's men approached them in the field, kept his head down, continuing to gather armloads of the long, golden grains. He paused when he heard the call of Jabnit from the orchard, beckoning Yzebel to join him.

Yzebel put a hand on Jugurtha's back and said, "I think you had better join me, in case Kanmi wishes to ask about the oils from the nuts. I don't know the answers to those questions as well as you, and we shouldn't keep him waiting."

Jugurtha acknowledged her request by setting down his armload of grain and falling in behind Yzebel as they approached the orchard. Kanmi smiled at her while Jabnit continued to explain something about the fruit trees. Irritated, Kanmi interrupted Jabnit. "I do not care to hear your excuses, Jabnit. I think the yield of your fruits will be less than that from the other farms, yet the fruit here is at the same stage of development. That means your laborers, or you—" he poked Jabnit in the belly with the short stick he was carrying, "—have been eating the fruit! Your trees are less full and when you weigh the harvest in a few weeks, you will find that I am right. You will have to make up the difference to Hanno."

"I assure you, no one has been eating these fruits!" Jabnit insisted. "These are Hanno's trees, and we do not eat from them."

"Very well," said Kanmi, "but when the time comes to harvest them, I will send one of my men to ensure that you are weighing them correctly. We must have the numbers. When I find that you have been lying to me, there will be consequences, Jabnit Gisgon."

Jabnit stood quietly and bit his lip, afraid to argue with Hanno's young inspector. Yzebel, however, spoke freely. "Perhaps you should look at the yield from last year, Kanmi. I believe you will find that these trees yielded more than anywhere else. And, as fruit trees often do, they are recovering this year. No one has been eating the fruit," she said sternly.

Kanmi smiled at Yzebel and spoke condescendingly to Jabnit. "Perhaps your lovely daughter is correct, Jabnit. If she is, then your yield next year should be equal to that of last year. If that is not the case, then you will make up the difference from what is expected!" Kanmi barked. Fuming, he began walking toward his horse in the main yard.

Jabnit caught up to him in front of the house and begged Kanmi to allow him to show more of the farm. "Perhaps you would like to see the supply of oils from the nuts or see the quality of the grain, Kanmi," Jabnit pleaded.

"I have seen enough," growled Kanmi. "We must be on our way." He climbed onto his horse and waved his arms to beckon to his men to join him. Jabnit stood quietly, wringing his hands nervously. Kanmi glanced at Jabnit and then his eyes settled on Jugurtha, who had trailed Yzebel throughout. As he stared at the man, Kanmi's men began to assemble around him, coming in from the buildings and the fields. Startling every-one, Kanmi pointed at Jugurtha and shouted at Jabnit, "Why is this man not working? Why is he standing here on the same level as my men?"

Yzebel stepped forward and responded, "I brought him with me in case you had questions about the oils or the laborers. Jugurtha is very knowledgeable about these things and he is very important to us."

Kanmi scoffed at Yzebel. "Your father knows all that is needed of the oils and how the process works. Your laborers are both expendable and re-placeable. Get back to the field!" he yelled at Jugurtha. Before he could act, two of Kanmi's men rushed Jugurtha, knocking him to the ground while the others laughed. Kanmi grabbed the reins of his horse and redirected it toward Jabnit. He pointed his finger and said, "You are all replaceable! Be sure you reach your targets for this harvest, Jabnit."

Jabnit nodded, acknowledging Kanmi's order then Yzebel spoke up again. "We do everything you ask of us, Kanmi. You would not find a more loyal manager as my father!" She glared up at Kanmi.

"Perhaps you're right, Yzebel," Kanmi said, "but to test that theory, perhaps we should see how far your father will follow."

Swinging down from his horse, Kanmi directed two of his men to grab Yzebel. Instinctively she fought, trying to pull away as they held her by the arms. Jabnit looked on in disbelief. Kanmi came up to Yzebel and grabbed her jaw with his thick hand, then pressed his body closely to hers and kissed her on the mouth. Repulsed, she pulled away, spat at his face and kicked at him with her foot.

Casually, he wiped the spit from his cheek and licked his finger as she glared at him. Kanmi nodded to his men. They forced Yzebel to the ground. Kanmi glanced at Jabnit, who was frozen in place. Yzebel screamed angrily, daring Kanmi to go any further. Kanmi got down on his knees, squatting on top of Yzebel's legs to press them against the ground, then he slid his body over her and kissed her mouth as she wiggled beneath him.

Jugurtha pulled loose from the men who had knocked him down and lunged at the men controlling Yzebel's arms. He knocked one of them to his side onto the ground near Yzebel's head while Yzebel swung her free hand at Kanmi and scratched his face with her fingernails, leaving a gash that stretched from his temple to the fleshy part of the cheek just over the cheekbone.

In reaction to the biting discomfort of the scratch, Kanmi jumped up, out of the reach of Yzebel's legs, while his two men struggled once again to ensnare her. Kanmi put the palm of his hand to his face and glared at them all, one by one. As drops of blood began to drop onto the dust at his feet, Kanmi ordered his men to beat Jugurtha.

Despite the burden of two men, Yzebel struggled to her feet, aiming to help Jugurtha. As she struggled, one of Kanmi's men hit Jugurtha in the back with a long stick, knocking the man to his knees. In vain, Yzebel continued to fight with her captors as Kanmi's men beat Jugurtha with their wooden rods.

Kanmi mounted his horse and smiled at Jabnit as he dabbed his bleeding cheek with a soft square of linen he had pulled from his tunic.

"You are indeed loyal, Jabnit. Yzebel was right." Kanmi directed his horse near the unconscious body of Jugurtha and spat on him. Then he looked at Yzebel over the top of his horse's head while he spoke again to Jabnit. "Hanno and I have an understanding, Jabnit. You may rest easy. Soon Yzebel will be mine. That should help you keep your place among Hanno's land managers."

He looked again at Yzebel, who glared at him, held by his men. "I will see you again soon, Yzebel," said Kanmi, "I hope to finish what we started today—with your father's permission, of course." He smirked as Jabnit hung his head in shame at the suggestion. Kanmi circled his horse around the others and then made his way to the road.

The men holding Yzebel threw her to the ground and quickly mounted their own horses, leaping over Jugurtha, who lay immobile on the ground, a bloody mess. Yzebel sprang to her feet and ran to Jugurtha, kneeling by his side. Tears of anger and fear flowed freely as she ran her hand over the stellate wounds on his scalp and back.

After Jugurtha had been carried to the longhouse and Yzebel tended his wounds, the young woman stormed out of the laborers' longhouse. Her dark eyes were fixed on the door of her father's home. She had spent the entire afternoon tending to Jugurtha's injuries. She left him still unconscious and perhaps fighting for his life. Enraged, Yzebel mounted the steps and flung open the front door, behind which she knew she would find her father quivering like a cold and feeble lamb. Bitter and resentful, she could no longer control her frustration at her father's cowardice.

Jabnit had grown into a timid old man, unable to stand up to Kanmi and incapable of defending his own daughter's honor. In Yzebel's heart and mind, she knew that Yahweh wanted her to respect her father, but right now Jugurtha was hurting and so was she—and it was her father's fault.

Yzebel stormed through the door and found her father sitting at the table alone, his head resting upon his forearms, which he had crossed on the tabletop. He didn't look up when she came in, but to her surprise, he spoke the first words. "Yzebel, I am sorry. I did not know what to do. I—"

Recklessly, she interrupted him, "You are a weak man, my Father. Jugurtha has been more of a father to me then you may ever be! Kanmi pushes you around and you do nothing! He threatens harm on our family and our workers, and you let him. One day he will drag me from this place, and you will do nothing to stop it. I am ashamed of you!"

Yzebel stood, her breath jagged and labored as she stared at him. The heart that pounded loudly in her throat became the only sound she could hear within her childhood home. The daughter stood so close to her father's arms, yet she stood alone, a wide chasm between them. Jabnit would not look up. He could not look his daughter in the eye.

Abruptly, she turned to leave. She drew the door shut behind her, slamming it. With tears cascading over her cheeks, she walked slowly toward the longhouse, where she planned to sit with Jugurtha through the night and coming days, until his wounds healed. Together, she and Jugurtha would fight.

Tremulously, Jabnit stood up from the table and pulled open the door to call out to his daughter. But no words were spoken. His jaw trembled as, without a sound, he watched her walk into the longhouse and out of his life. His timidity through the years had dug a hole within him dark and frightening. He crumpled to the floor, his legs too weak to bear the burden of such a vacuous space. Devastated, he leaned his head against the wall near the doorway and sobbed.

# Chapter XX

<br>

———

SORIAN SLID ALONG the row of tall green spires of cypress trees that bordered the street stretching up the hill toward Lucius's house. Evening had come and the moon was full, lighting his way under a soft white glow. He paused to study the back of his hand, which he stretched in front of him, to observe how strong the moonlight had become. He could now easily see the dark veins as they roped through his skin, coursing over the dorsum of his hand and across each tendon like rivers drawn on a map. He wiggled his fingers, as if tapping at the air, and the veins of his hands writhed in place, jumping with the flexion and extension of each finger. The sight reminded him of the tails of the many rats that consumed the corpse of his fellow prison inmate, the man who had shared his chain.

Sorian had made the short trek from Ostia earlier in the day. Having made good time, he found that he had plenty of time to proceed cautiously forward, making each step toward his target with deliberate care. Tonight, was the night. He had been anticipating this night for years—an age, really, imagining how it would feel to plunge his blade into Lucius over and over again. By slowing his pace, he allowed the excitement to build within him. With each step toward the home, he savored the growing anticipation.

In his mind, Sorian rehearsed what he wanted to say to Lucius. He reviewed the mechanics of the attack once more. He would easily gain entry to the home. He would find Lucius awaiting his guest, Consul Regulus, and surprise him with his own appearance. Lucius would be alone; that much he was sure about. To Sorian's knowledge, only he and Lucius knew of the meeting planned by Regulus.

The air circulating about him as he climbed the hill was still warm. There had not been much of a breeze until recently and now the cypress trees he passed filled his airways with their semi-sweet, astringent perfume. Sorian fingered the blade Regulus had given him. Stopping by a corner, he examined the weapon under the moonlight. He knew the curve of the handle and the slope of the blade. He had held it lovingly and studied it thoroughly for weeks. Under the light of the moon, he could see the scratches in the metal of the blade, left behind like scars from the battles in which it fought. The blade was strong, hard. Sorian wished it could speak to him and share the stories of its own experiences.

Silently, Sorian moved toward the back of Lucius's home. Crouching low and bending forward, he hurried along the side of a stone wall that formed a perimeter between the home and the gardens beyond. Reaching the back, he quietly slipped over the waist-high wall and into a large central garden that merged with the rear entry of the house. Here the fruit and olive trees offered cover from the moonlight. He knelt down to rest for a moment and observe for any activity within or around the home. He reflected on how easy it was going to be. A single door stood between him and the man he hated so passionately.

At the front of the home, Elijah and Carpathimos chatted quietly as they walked up the same hill Sorian had climbed moments earlier. They had spent the day discussing their journey to Greece. They would travel to the harbor and reach the ship by October. Carpathimos had insisted they stay in Rome one more night, so he could meet with his old friend and take care of some unfinished business. Beyond this insistence, he had remained silent. Elijah, on the other hand, easily filled the void in their conversation. Because he had spent many such days with Carpathimos, he no longer felt annoyed or intimidated by the silence. Excited about the end of his journey, he rambled on incessantly about whatever thoughts he had, not concerned with whether Carpathimos would reply or even care about the content of his conversation.

Ever since his near disaster at the hands of an angry mob, Elijah remained apprehensive about being left by himself. As a result, he insisted on coming along with Carpathimos tonight, despite his friend's better judgment. Carpathimos had tried to insist that Elijah would be more comfortable waiting for him elsewhere, but, in the end, he knew Elijah would follow him anyway, so he gave up trying to convince him otherwise. They ascended the hill toward Lucius's home. Nearing the front door, Carpathimos halted and asked Elijah to wait for him outdoors. Elijah looked around and begrudgingly nodded.

"It should be safe under the cover of those tall cypress trees, and it will be easy to see anyone coming in the light of this moon," Elijah said, trying to sound unafraid. Failing to convince himself of the lack of danger, he sidled more closely into the shadows of the trees.

Carpathimos reassured him one last time. "You will be all right, Elijah. The only people walking around up here at night are both old and weak."

"But you won't be long. Is that right, Carpathimos?" His friend could hear the pleading in his voice.

Carpathimos ignored the question and strode to the front door. He stood motionless there for a moment, taking a few deep breaths before advancing. Pushing firmly on the handle, the heavy, wooden door eased open. It was not locked. Quietly, Carpathimos slid into the home, disappearing from sight, but leaving the door ajar, to Elijah's surprise. He had expected Carpathimos to knock on the door. Not doing so seemed curious behavior.

Elijah grew even more uneasy and he moved closer to the front door, still trying to stay within the shadows. Presently he heard voices coming from down the hill. In the moonlight, he could tell that the noise was coming from a small unit of troops or guards who were marching down the hill. He watched them from the shadow of a column on the portico behind. They marched onward, passing this street and then the next before disappearing. Feeling trapped between the chance of being spotted by troops or alarming someone living in the neighborhood, Elijah hesitated, then slid through the front door of Lucius's villa.

Crouching low, Elijah glanced to the left and then, not finding what he was looking for, he looked to the right. He spotted Carpathimos kneeling behind a waist-high wall that separated the entryway from a large central gathering hall near the center of the building. Carpathimos's position certainly resembled something that could be construed as nefarious behavior.

Elijah crawled up next to Carpathimos, who glared at him with disgust. Elijah sheepishly shrugged his shoulders. Carpathimos nodded, accepting the silent apology. He put a finger to his lips.

Together, they knelt on the floor, side by side, for what seemed like a very long time. Impatiently, Elijah shifted from one knee to the other to relieve the discomfort created by pressing his bony knees against smooth marble. Silently, a man entered the room from across the large hall. Carpathimos grabbed Elijah's arm in warning. Carpathimos then peered over the low wall and stared at the man, watching him walk across the hall toward them.

To Carpathimos, the man appeared older than Lucius should look. Yet this man appeared physically fit and dignified. It was indeed Lucius. He still wore a close-cropped mat of gray hair, but his face was careworn, with more deeply furrowed wrinkles than before. He carried his large, muscled stature with easy grace and his hands held a small plate of food. When he stopped in front of a small table set against the wall, he delivered the plate and leaned over the table, appearing to study something. It was a document, Carpathimos realized, hearing the slight rustle of papyrus. As the senator read, he put his weight on two straight arms. His knuckles pressed against the stone of the table top, like the hooves of a massive war horse.

Carpathimos remembered him standing just this way when he studied the maps on his war room table in the Dolomites. Another flood of lost memories careened into Carpathimos's mind, like a tidal wave smashing against a rocky shore. They all finally came back to Carpathimos as he studied the man's features. He remembered a night long ago, sitting on horseback on a high plateau overlooking a meadow filled with Roman soldiers. He and Lucius had discussed the stars, his childhood, and the love of both of their lives, Myridia.

Immediately afterwards, for the briefest of moments, Carpathimos could finally see Myridia's entire face in his mind once again, something he had not been able to do for a long time. Then, and just as briefly, he caught a glimpse of his son. He tried desperately to cling to the image, but it faded from his mind, replaced by another image: two men, friends he had made under Lucius's command.

Then, like an unexpected lightning strike within his mind, he thought of the men who tried to kill them all. The rage he had carried for so long began to boil within the confines of his body. He once again felt the anger and anguish he had felt so many times before. The life force within him, placed there by a higher power for the purposes of good, withered under the heat of a searing rage. His blood began to seethe within his vessels. He clenched his fists and stiffened his back as the muscle memory from years of battle and fight training flooded back into his torso and limbs. His body remembered why his desire for revenge had brought him to this place.

He had hoped Lucius would be able to give him the answers he sought, but whether or not he did, in the end it would not matter. The outcome would be the same this day. The burning question that drew Carpathimos away from his sister and his son on the shores of Anatolia was not really a question at all. The reason why Carpathimos and his friends and his woman had been hunted by soldiers Lucius sent was not the point. Revenge had driven Carpathimos over so many leagues and through so many challenges. Revenge consumed him. It acted like the thing that pulled migrating birds back to the same places every year. The gladiator didn't want an answer. He wanted an end—and that end stood just a few feet away. The time had come. At last.

Elijah shifted, every muscle tensing. Unconsciously, he sensed the tension growing within the man by his side. He glanced over at Carpathimos and found him staring at the Roman as if looking right through him. The muscles of Carpathimos's jaw tightened, rippling within his cheek. Elijah could hear Carpathimos grinding his teeth, although he did not yet understand the reason for his friend's behavior. The realization had dawned on Elijah that they were in this home for more than a mere meeting between acquaintances.

Firelight caused something to shine in Carpathimos's hands. Elijah looked down to find the knife Carpathimos had taken from one of the headhunters he had killed in Sicily. Carpathimos had been spinning the weapon without thinking, and the blade's tip had bored a hole in his palm. A drop of blood welled up around the rotating tip. Elijah swallowed hard, his throat dry, trying to comprehend the bizarre situation he now found himself in.

Mustering the courage to speak, Elijah whispered, "What are you planning to do with it?"

The question, though immaterial, accomplished what Elijah had hoped. It shook Carpathimos from his eerie trance. Carpathimos shook his head and looked at Elijah warningly. Elijah glanced from the knife to Carpathimos and back again. The warrior glared at Elijah, but the glare was met by an equally intense look of disappointment. Carpathimos's gaze softened, but he could spare no words with his companion.

Elijah whispered again. "Why, after all this time, Carpathimos, do you come here with hatred in your heart?"

Carpathimos stared at his friend for a long moment. His anger lessening, he sighed quietly, and prepared to push himself off the floor, stand, and announce their presence. But the sound of another person entering the room stopped him. Carpathimos peered carefully over the wall at the man approaching from the opposite side of the room. He did not recognize him—at first. The disheveled-looking man sauntered into the room, apparently without a care, as if he belonged, though his appearance stood in stark contrast to that of the home. Hearing this intruder, Lucius spun on his heel. His face registered his surprise.

The man practically growled as he approached. "Lucius, my old friend! Dear General Lucius."

Lucius took a step forward, straightening. "Visitors are to present themselves at the front door," he barked. "Who are you and why have you come?"

"To deliver a message from Consul Regulus," Sorian answered, his voice now smooth and even pleasant sounding. "You are waiting his arrival, are you not?"

Lucius nodded "But, again, I ask you: who are you and what is your message?"

Sorian looked around him leisurely, expansively, as if admiring the adornments and tapestries furnishing the opulent home. After his eyes danced over the rich furnishings, they came to rest on Lucius's own set of piercing eyes. "My message is that your meeting with Regulus has been changed. You will instead meet with me."

Growing impatient with this man's impertinence, Lucius retorted, "Very well. State your business and then be gone!"

Sorian laughed loudly. "Perhaps I will make this easier for you, dear Lucius." He pulled his hair behind his head and placed it under a rag, letting it fall like a horse's tail. "Perhaps now you remember your faithful right-hand man."

Lucius looked at him closely. His mouth opened in disbelief. "Sorian," he growled once he recovered. His muscles tensed and his hands closed into fists. "Sorian," he repeated, "you filthy dog. How did you get here?"

Sorian laughed again. "I have journeyed far, of course. You sent me to the mines in the west, but I grew tired of such toil. I decided that I needed to occupy my mind in far more industrious activities, so I set out on a very long and arduous journey, just to thank you!"

"Thank me?" repeated Lucius, suspicion in his voice. "Why would you want to thank me?"

Sorian began to pace back and forth. His smile disappeared and a furrow formed between his brows. He stared at Lucius as he crossed from one side of the room to the other. "You see, Lucius, you and I are related in an interesting way. We both served a higher power. I just served it better than you did, and for that you punished me."

"What higher power? What game are you playing, Sorian?" Lucius sounded impatient.

"We both served at the pleasure of your brother, the Emperor. You disobeyed his orders and ignored his decree to push over the Dolomites and smash the Gauls, I kept him apprised of all your misguided plans."

"Yes, you spied on me. You spied on your commander. And then you did far worse than that—as if I should need to remind you."

"Once again, I did what was asked of me. Your brother knew you were a traitor. He also knew that you would never conquer the barbarians as long as you were distracted by your daughter. He commanded me to do what you could not do—dispose of the distraction that kept you from serving Rome and her Emperor."

"We have been over this, Sorian," reminded Lucius, "at your trial in front of the Senate. You interpreted his orders to you as a call to murder my daughter and her lover. For that, you were sent away to rot in a cold, dark mine on the Iberian Peninsula. Tiberius gave no such orders."

"I did exactly as I was ordered, Lucius. I served my emperor—and I served him well," Sorian contradicted. "Now I've come to do what even he couldn't do, what he should've done. I am here to remove the real problem. It was never the distraction over your daughter. The problem has always been you, dear General. Why even now you stand in the way of Marcus Regulus's certain glory."

With that said, Sorian drew his blade and drew near Lucius, backing the larger man against the table. Having heard every word, Carpathimos leapt over the wall and rushed to a position between the two men. Lucius was stunned at the sight of this second intruder. He recognized the young man immediately, but he was shocked by his sudden appearance. Meanwhile, Carpathimos stared down at the man ultimately responsible for the death of Myridia and his friends.

Sorian burst into laughter, "Well, General, it appears you hide behind your daughter's lover! Judging by the surprised look on your face, you must have assumed he was as dead as your daughter. No matter. Soon you both will join her on the Elysian plane. My goal tonight is to reunite you—one happily dead family!"

Carpathimos held up his blade and twisted it back and forth. The firelight glimmered on the shining blade he held in Sorian's face. "Your only goal tonight," said Carpathimos, as he maneuvered around the room, "should be to die quickly."

The two men faced each other with knives in hand. They slowly began circling one another. As this treacherous dance unfolded before him, Elijah clumsily tripped out from behind the stone wall, approaching the two men. Carpathimos glanced over at his friend, witnessing what appeared to be anguish and fear upon the younger man's face. Then Carpathimos stopped moving. He stared again at Sorian, sizing up his opponent. He glanced again at his dear friend and then began to speak to Elijah as he turned his attention back to Sorian.

"I am sorry, Elijah," said Carpathimos. "I confess to you that I came here tonight to do a terrible thing. Instead, I have been made witness to a truth that has opened my eyes. The man I came here to kill was never the evil man I had believed him to be. My hatred has driven me unjustly. You, Elijah, throughout our time together, have been trying to show me a better path to follow, but until now I had been too simpleminded to understand."

The three men surrounding Carpathimos stared at him, seemingly dumbfounded by his revelation. But there was more. He continued, "I am tired of fighting and I am tired of running, Elijah. I want to have meaning in the things I do, no more lies. But if this cannot be, then I choose to walk with Myridia on the Elysian plane, perhaps in the light of your god, if he will accept me."

With those words, Carpathimos looked at Elijah and dropped his hands, letting the knife fall to the floor. As it bounced off the stone tile, it rang out within the room like the clang of gong inside a bronze bell. The sound echoed within the large, open room.

Sorian shook his head in disbelief at his good fortune. He lunged at Carpathimos with the point of his knife leading the way. Elijah sensed Sorian's attack and was prepared to move. In the lingering melody of Carpathimos's vibrating blade, Elijah cried out, "No!" As if shot like an arrow from a bow, Elijah leaped forward, sailing into the path of Sorian's attack. The polished blade pierced Elijah's chest, driving deeply between the ribs over his left nipple. Elijah expelled a gasp as the blade penetrated his lung. The sound of the impact filled the room like the thud of an arrowhead smashing into a tightly woven shield.

Elijah fell, stumbling backward out of control as his hands grasped feebly at the knife, the force of the blow propelling him toward the wall. His torso collided with the legs of one of the lighted pyres standing near the corner of the room. The pyre wobbled then tipped, spilling its flaming oil in a cascade of glowing heat onto Elijah and his knapsack before flooding around him in a pool of dancing flames.

Lucius raced to the wall, tearing down one of the large tapestries that hung between the columns at the side of the room. He tossed the free end at Carpathimos, who caught it between his hands as they raced to Elijah's side. As he slid into position near Elijah's limp body, he threw the fabric over the young man and the flaming pool, trying to deprive the fire of its air. Lucius came behind, carrying the other end of the tapestry, covering the expanding pool of oil. Furiously, he tamped down the flames chewing away at the knapsack. Carpathimos knelt near Elijah's body, dragging his head and torso onto his shoulder. He cradled the youth, pleading with him not to die. Lucius looked on as the color quickly faded from Elijah's face.

In the confusion, Sorian found Carpathimos's abandoned knife and moved swiftly into position behind the defenseless gladiator. With the knife held high above his head, he continued what he had started just moments before, aiming the blade toward the soft meat of the neck in the triangular space behind the collarbone, intending to sever the head from the shoulder.

As rapidly as the knife began its descent toward its target, a large, muscular arm wrapped around Sorian's neck like a python, twisting around its prey with unforgiving proficiency. The muscles in Lucius's arm bulged and folded as he crushed the air and blood from Sorian's neck. Sorian's blade halted halfway through its arc, searching instead for a new target along Lucius's arm. Suddenly that knife toppled from Sorian's hand toward the floor as Lucius buried his own blade deep inside Sorian's back, twisting the weapon in his mighty hand and forcing it higher and deeper into Sorian's upper flank.

As the rigid blade within Lucius's firm grip ground past bone and sliced through liver, Sorian's feet came off the ground until only his toes danced upon the stone. Lucius withdrew his arm and launched Sorian into the air with his knife hand. Sorian's body crashed onto the floor, limp, while a river of blood and foam drained from the corner of his gaping mouth. And then his dead eyes stared forward, captured in a look of surprise.

Lucius approached Carpathimos and the body of the young man still in his arms. He stared silently at him for many minutes, unsure of what to say. Unexpectedly, Carpathimos broke the heavy silence, speaking in a soft but monotonous timbre. "What day is it?"

Lucius hesitated, thinking the question was simply rhetorical, but then Carpathimos looked to him expectantly, waiting for an answer. "Well, it is near the middle of Mensis, September," answered Lucius. "This is the third day before the Ides. Rome will hold the Epulum Jovis, the festival of Jupiter, in just a few days."

Carpathimos nodded and then said, "It is as it is written in the books, then. I never thought that it would be Elijah sacrificed this day."

Lucius stared blankly at him. "What books, Carpathimos?"

Carpathimos gently laid Elijah's body on the floor and reached for the charred knapsack, grasping the smoking material in his blood-stained hands. It had been heavily damaged. With great care, he opened the brittle sack, peeling away the charred outside to find the books within. He withdrew the tightly rolled papyrus and examined the contents carefully, under the bemused gaze of his father-in-law.

"Oh, no," he groaned, as he paged through the documents. Much of the last book was unrecognizable. Part of it had fused to the material on the inside the charred sack. He carefully, reverently, rolled the rest of the documents together, tucking them into his tunic. Carpathimos stood, staring down at Elijah's body. He did so for many minutes.

In time, Lucius cleared his throat and whispered, "Carpathimos." Again, "Carpathimos."

Carpathimos turned and looked blankly at Lucius, as if he were staring straight through him. Lucius could see the pain on the man's face. He sensed the magnitude of his loss. "You were his teacher?"

"No," responded Carpathimos solemnly. "He was mine."

Lucius nodded. "Carpathimos, what will you do now?"

Carpathimos did not answer at first. Instead, he looked back down at Elijah. "I must finish his work," he replied. "What he has done for his god is bigger than I am. It is bigger than any of us. It must be finished. I owe it to him."

"Tell me: why you believe in his god?" Lucius was more than curious. He was trying to sift through a lifetime of emotions.

Carpathimos studied Lucius's face, accepting the sincerity of the inquiry. "I want to believe in something. As he did." Carpathimos couldn't take his eyes off Elijah.

"Where will you go?"

"I must travel to Corinth. His family and many of his people fled north. I must bring the books of Moses to them."

Lucius looked at Carpathimos and rubbed his chin with the palm of his hand. "Carpathimos, listen to me. You must be very careful travelling there. That territory is very unstable now. I fear that the land from which your father came may be nothing like the memories you carry."

Carpathimos looked curiously at Lucius, and then recalled how he had described his father and his home to Lucius long ago. "What am I walking into?"

"Let me explain. Come, sit with me." The two men, both warriors, one young, one older, moved across the room and sat facing the bodies of the fallen. "Our runners and many merchants fleeing the east have kept us abreast of the events unfolding there now."

Carpathimos shook his head in confusion.

"You see, Carpathimos, many years ago the King of Epirus, a man named Pyrrhus, attacked us here on the peninsula. He was driven out, but he invaded Macedonian land to the east. He and one of Alexander's generals, the one named Lysimachus, drove out the ruling family. They were once again beaten back, but this shift in power left the territory to the north ripe for invasion by a horde of barbarians. You must remember them from our days together in the mountains."

"The Gauls."

"Precisely," said Lucius. "The torrent of Gauls ravaged the lands, sacking their way across much of Macedonia, Greece, and into Anatolia, until a young leader by the name of Antigonus Gonatas turned them back. I am told he is a descendent of Alexander's greatest general; the man known as 'One Eye.' Do you remember hearing about him?"

Carpathimos nodded.

"Antigonus turned the barbarians back at Thermopylae and Delphi and then again at Thrace."

"Then this is good news," responded Carpathimos wearily.

Lucius nodded. "He did reclaim the lands of Greece and Macedonia, but now he faces a far worse challenge. The city-states of Athens and Sparta have united and have risen up against him."

"United?" Carpathimos looked surprised. "What could force them together?"

"We believe they want to strike while the armies of Antigonus are tired and war-weary. And, they are supported by another."

"Who?"

"Egypt. The Senate believes that Ptolemy is supporting the Athenians and Spartans in order to keep Antigonus weak. The Ptolemies have always desired to control far more territory, as far north as Macedonia and Thrace."

"Are they in battle now?"

"Their war has gone on for nearly five years already, but Antigonus has Athens pinned against the sea while Sparta is under siege after their defeat near Corinth," explained Lucius. "Perhaps the people you seek will have perished or moved on, Carpathimos. You must be careful."

"Still, I must find them and deliver the Word to them." Carpathimos touched the roll within his tunic. "I owe it to Elijah, if for no other reason than to prove his death was not in vain."

Lucius nodded. "Very well."

The men stood. Lucius embraced his son-in-law, gripping his upper arms and scanning the face of the younger man, taking in each feature before ending with his eyes. "Do what you must do, my son, but before you go anywhere we have much to discuss. You must tell me where you have been and where the son of my daughter lives. Your son, Carpathimos."

Carpathimos seemed to relax under the gentle words spoken by Lucius. He nodded. "Lucia lives with my sister Parma in Lydia. They may be near the capital, Sardis. I sent them to find our mother's family and I intend to go find them after I finish Elijah's work."

"I strongly wish to see the son of Myridia, this grandson of mine," Lucius said. "Tell me, when you look into his eyes, do you see her, Carpathimos?"

Carpathimos smiled for the first time that day. "They are much the same. His eyes are her eyes. His smile is her smile."

For the moment, Lucius looked sad, then his face hardened into an expressionless mask of stone. "I cannot see her face anymore. I try, but nothing comes," said Lucius. "Sometimes I remember bits and pieces, like her mouth when I remember her laugh. Sometimes a smell of rose petal will come to me and I will remember the feel of her hair under my nose."

"Go with me, Lucius." Carpathimos suggested. Hearing Lucius describe the same difficulty seeing Myridia's face that he had been having, affected Carpathimos in a way he hadn't expected. He hoped the answer would be affirmative.

Lucius searched for his next words. "I have work here that I must do, Carpathimos. Consul Regulus has sailed for Africa. He intends to raze Carthage and destroy all of her fertile lands. I must try to slow him down before he eviscerates the people of this city instead. We are not prepared for such an advance. He is leaving our backsides open to attack."

Carpathimos looked stunned. "Where is he landing? When?"

Lucius was surprised by Carpathimos's sudden interest in an African invasion. He watched the younger man's eyes as he spoke. "I know that he has already left. Sorian said as much before he died. He will be there in a matter of days, once he has assembled the rest of his troops at Ecnomus. From there he will most likely make landfall along the coast, near the port at Aspis or Sabratha." Lucius added, "Why do you ask?"

Carpathimos was staring at the floor. "Someone who saved me lives there. I must go help her."

"You stand no chance against four legions by yourself, Carpathimos. Besides, you will never make it in time. Every available ship heading in that direction is occupied."

"What can be done?"

"I fear not much, but I am going to stay here to try to convince the Senate to recall some of his fleet and troops, perhaps limit his supplies and reinforcements. If I have my way, he will spend the winter season in Africa, his advance stalled and his ego spilling onto the sand with his blood."

The two men stood quietly for a short time before Lucius made a suggestion. "I believe you have already elected to travel to the east for another of your friends. Perhaps you can tell me more about Elijah and this woman who saved your life while I help you with his body. Then you can join me for something to eat, yes?"

"It is the tenth day of Tishri," said Carpathimos. "The Day of Atonement for the golden calf, as it is known in his people's sacred calendar. I must not eat tonight."

"Is this also written in those books of his?" Lucius pointed at the thick roll of parchment protruding from Carpathimos's tunic. "I do not understand this god of his, Carpathimos—yours," he corrected with a smile. "Come, I have a leather satchel that you may carry those in."

# PART III

# Chapter XXI

---

THE SURF POUNDING the scattered stones along the shoreline near Aspis was swelled by the breadth of nearly three hundred ships anchored just offshore. Almost one hundred of these were confiscated Carthaginian birds of prey that Marcus Regulus captured when the Carthaginians failed to stop his advance off Sicily.

With his head held high, Regulus stepped ashore from a small boat, his feet sinking into a sand so white it forced him to shield his eyes. He bent down to take up a handful of this fine sand, mixing it in his palm with seawater he scooped from a pool accumulating near the toe of his boot. Clenching it within his fist, he watched his army come to shore.

By the hundreds, small boats ferried men from the anchored ships to the shore of the African coast. Patiently observing his men coming to shore by the thousands, he opened his fist and smoothed the sand against his palm with the pad of his index finger. Within that sand, he traced the first letter of Carthage. Then he crushed it once again within his fist. Throwing down the sand, he climbed the short beachhead and moved into a tree line of tall, waving palms. Throughout the rest of the day and into the night, this army came ashore, followed by boatloads of weapons, gear, horses, grain, and crated chickens, goats, and pigs. Here at Aspis they met little resistance. But they were not alone.

The city stood a kilometer away. Its residents watched with horror the growing mass of invaders spilling onto the shore. Aspis was a port city southeast of Carthage, a perfect starting point from which to launch a Roman offensive. Though its harbor was too small to accommodate all of Regulus's fleet, it was situated along an expansive beach, which made unloading the ships easy. The walled city was set far enough from the shoreline to free Regulus's troops from any need to defend themselves from an attack as they came ashore.

Regulus had wanted to land in the center of Carthaginian territory so he could ravage its farmlands while cutting off Carthage's major cities from their food supplies. From here, he could also supply his own troops through a secured harbor and eventually march on Carthage, a short distance away. He had not, of course, planned on a naval battle off Ecnomus, but by destroying and capturing such a large contingent of Carthaginian ships, he assured himself an easy landing at Aspis.

Late that night, Regulus and his legion commanders met in his tent to review the coming morning's offensive strategy. Regulus's dark hair surrounded his face as he leaned over his map table. His officers, lined along the opposite side, watched in silence as he ran his finger across the map, tracing an imaginary line over the cities to the west of Aspis all the way to Carthage.

"At sunrise, the men will begin their siege of Aspis. Its walls are not tall and the gates not strong. The city should fall to us in a matter of days, not weeks. Once the city falls, I want your legion, Thracius, to travel east. Destroy every village and field you come to and do not stop until you take the city of Sabratha."

"It will be my honor, my Consul," Thracius responded.

Regulus continued, "After Aspis falls, we will march on Adys, sacking every city in between. We will leave one garrison here to defend the harbor and protect our ships." He fielded questions before dismissing his men, but before they departed he reminded them of one thing. "We do not feed the old, we do not feed the young, and, most importantly, we do not feed their wounded."

His officers nodded and quickly departed, leaving Regulus alone with his thoughts. The consul sat on the high-backed chair, resting his elbows on the map table and combing through his thick black hair as he scanned the map before him. His eyes followed the coastline drawn to the promontory where the city of Carthage stood. Glory was just sixty kilometers away from him. Sitting back, he slung his feet up on the table and rested his head against the magenta-colored cushion on the back of the chair, tipping the whole frame so the front legs hovered above the makeshift floor of the tent. On the map, he followed an imaginary line back to Aspis from Carthage, pausing briefly over the city of Adys. He felt a knot of anxiety form in his stomach as he looked again at the name Adys on the map. He suspected that Adys would be the place where Carthage would concentrate their greatest resistance to him. As he envisioned his seasoned army decimating the less experienced army of Carthage within the river valley near Adys, that knot of anxiety unraveled and was replaced by a glowing ember—its energy would keep him awake all night.

The next morning, his orders were carried out in the smooth fashion one should expect of such a well-used and proficient war machine. The siege engines were put immediately to use. By the time the city fell, construction of a palisade to protect the ships near the shoreline was well underway. The only resistance Regulus's men met during the siege consisted of a few hundred poorly trained skirmishers scattered along the top of the wall and throughout the city. Their cheap weapons and lack of armor did nothing to hinder the advancing cascade of Roman troops.

The city gates were forced opened and a chaotic scene was revealed. Men, women, and children were fleeing in all directions, scurrying like mice from the steady advance of soldiers. As Aspis quickly fell into Roman control, there were no smells of roasting food in the streets. There were no fresh fish on the tables in the market. There was no music for dancing. There had been only a feeble resistance and the chaos of a confused and desperate people. The people of Aspis had known the siege and assault were coming, for they had witnessed the arrival and assembly of a massive army outside the city. They had no possible way to prepare for such carnage. Faced with certain death, the terrified people of Aspis folded under the Roman boot.

On the afternoon Aspis fell, under a clear blue sky, Regulus stood atop a small, wind-worn berm near the south wall of the fallen city. Surveying his legions, Regulus breathed the cool sea air and let the sun warm his face. He was about to address his victorious troops as they eagerly awaited his next command. He could feel their excitement and sense their desire to march onward toward Carthage. Having lost only a few ships and men to Carthage during their feeble attempt to stop him south of Ecnomus, and after an easy siege here at Aspis, Marcus Regulus was invigorated and confident. He shared his men's desire to move on.

To his men he shouted, "You stand with me on African soil at an open gate to Carthage! They could not stop us on the great sea and they will not stop us in Africa. Soon Carthage will surrender to me and relinquish the islands of Sicily, Corsica and Sardinia to the Republic. As her people kneel before you as subjects of Rome, they will watch the Carthaginian fleet burn before their eyes!"

The legions of soldiers chanted, "Regulus! Regulus!" as his words passed quickly to the men at the rear. The cheers grew louder and louder as row upon row of jubilant warriors added their voices to those before them.

"From here we will divide and begin our march toward destiny. We will advance our assault to the west, city by city, before pouring into the river valley of the Bagradas. To the east, we will destroy the lands of Carthage all the way to Sabratha!"

Again, the men cheered and chanted. He could feel the power of their collective voices as the noise flowed up and over him. He scanned the troops fanned out before him as far as he could see. He raised his fist high above his head and pounded the air, shouting, "Burn it! Burn it all!"

---

Carpathimos took a deep breath and smelled the cool mountain air as it filed smoothly past his nostrils and filled his lungs. The air was heavy with the smell of aspen and pine, but the dew-covered moss on which he had slept was more pervasive, carrying notes of damp earth and spongy rhizomes into his nares. He shivered as the cool air touched his lungs. Without opening his eyes, he pushed his foot forward to stir the ashes of the fire that burned in front of the cave where he spent the night. He caught a whiff of smoke, but no warmth, so he opened his eyes, looking past his torso to see what, if anything, was left of the fire. This was his third night in the Pindus Mountains and he was growing eager to reach his destination.

The trip across the Adriatic aboard a merchant ship bound for Epirus had been largely uneventful. Once in port, he helped unload the ship at Orikos, in the gulf of the same name, and then he climbed into the Pindus Mountains, heading south and east. Along the way, he learned that these were rugged mountains hiding even more rugged people—people he hoped to avoid.

By now, he wasn't exactly sure where he was, but he knew that he had already crossed the Aoos River and was descending toward the Corinthian Gulf. He couldn't yet see it, however. He had been delayed when climbing the mountain, forced around a massive gorge with limestone margins that he estimated to be several hundred meters deep. He could find no good way down through the great divide, so around the rim of the gorge he went, adding two days to his journey. Here, at the higher altitude, the forest had been easy to travel through, in part due to a dearth of underbrush. The weather had been cooperative—thus far.

Carpathimos sat up and looked around at the quiet forest surrounding his small cave. He heard the sounds of a few curious birds and he had stoned a small rabbit the night before, but he had not seen larger animals. He thought again of his lost friend, Elijah, and tried to imagine what he would have said about the rabbit Carpathimos had killed. Smiling, he pulled at the remaining meat barely clinging to the bones of the roasted animal and wiped the blackened coal from his fingertips on the stone beside him. The sweet meat was now cool, but it felt good in his belly all the same. Satisfied, he stood and repositioned his tunic, then reached down for the leather bag Lucius had given him. Pulling it over his shoulder, he checked the sun and rounded the stone wall of the cave, making his way once again to the south. One more night in the foothills of these mountains, he thought, and then he would emerge somewhere near the gulf.

The next morning, he entered the small city of Nafpaktus, lying along the north shore of the Corinthian Gulf. This Aetolian-held walled fortress stood near the mouth of a natural channel connecting the Corinthian Gulf to the east with the Gulf of Calydon to the west. Deep enough to allow merchant ships to pass, the channel was a major shipping route from the Ionian Sea to the great cities in the east, such as Delphi and Corinth. Anticipating an opportunity to board a ship to Corinth, Carpathimos walked toward the harbor and the markets, following the chatter of bright white gulls which sored effortlessly in circles above the buildings and the street where he walked.

The markets were bustling with people and, although he was taller than most, he did seem to fit in well. There were many others in worn and dirty clothing who, he hoped, stunk as much as he thought he did. All around him people spoke in different tongues, but he did hear some people speaking in his familiar childhood language. Spotting a table displaying a variety of foods, he approached it, and dug for the coins he had been paid by the captain of the merchant ship that carried him across the sea. Standing behind the long wooden table, a young boy was selling breads, spice cakes, dried meats, and an assortment of fruits. Lying in baskets near his feet were at least three different species of sea breams and another basket of sea bass.

Curious, Carpathimos tried his Koine Greek. "Are these fish caught out here?" he asked, pointing toward the gulf.

The boy started to answer, but then stared back at Carpathimos, surveying him up and down. He nodded. Carpathimos smiled and showed him some of his coins.

"How much for three pieces of dried meat and one of the bread?"

The boy reached for the bread as he looked at Carpathimos's hand. "Would you like wheat instead of this heavy barley?" he asked. As Carpathimos considered the matter, the boy reached into a small basket behind him, pulling from it a wheat loaf smaller than the barley loaf. The boy had far fewer of these wheat loaves.

Carpathimos was hungry. "How much for the barley?"

The boy held up the wheat and smelled it with a smile. Carpathimos smiled and pointed to the wheat bread. The boy collected the coins from Carpathimos and handed him pieces of dried meat as well. As he did, an old man seated next to the table spoke for the first time. "Enjoy the wheat bread, Traveler. It is rare these days."

Carpathimos moved closer to the old man, realizing he was blind. Studying the open and scarred orbits, Carpathimos identified the marks left by the knife that had been used to extricate the man's eyes. This had been a trademark of fighters from Epirus. He had seen it on old men in Rome and he had seen it on the docks in Epirus.

"You have taught this boy well," said Carpathimos. "He knows how to make a sale."

"He knows who he can push around," said the old man. "You must have a forgiving face, Islander."

"How do you know I am an islander?"

"By your tongue and your feet." The spry old man grinned. "Your tongue is from the islands and your step is too light for a herder. You have been a sailor, yet you came by land—I know by the smells of fir and pine on your tunic. You are taller than I would have expected, however."

Carpathimos winked at the boy, who smiled and shrugged his shoulders.

"Why do you come to Nafpaktus, Islander?" The old man asked.

"I am looking for some people. I hope to catch a ship to Corinth." Carpathimos gathered his bundles.

"A fool's task," the man said sharply. "There is no one left to find in Corinth. The city has fallen to Antigonus. Athens will be next. The Spartans have retreated but approaching them would be like stumbling into a nest of angry hornets."

Carpathimos stared at the man, considering what he should do next.

"These people of which you speak," the old man continued, "are they islanders like yourself or are they much further displaced?"

Carpathimos shifted on his feet then rubbed his hand across the leather pack that hung at his side. "They have been further displaced than I," he said at last. "They may be in Thebes, Athens, or on Cyprus. We were headed to . . . I was told to seek them out in Corinth."

The old man nodded, then responded, "And they too speak Greek by now. These are many people, not few. You carry something for them at your side, do you?"

"I do," answered Carpathimos. "It is important for me to find the elders. The people of Moses and Abraham."

The old man smiled and reached out to find and place his hand on Carpathimos's arm. He slid it down the forearm and grasped hold of the warrior's hand. "These are the Yevani you seek. They do speak some Greek now. They once travelled through Lydia and Byzantion on their way here. Some came by sea. Many have come this way over recent months." The old man added, "They peddle their woven baskets and their silken garments. The boy's fish baskets were made by the Yevanic speakers." He jerked his head, gesturing to the baskets on the ground.

"These people are lost among us. They drift this way and that, as if blown like fallen leaves by the wind. Many came to the north to fight for Antigonus and others have been sold here as slaves, only to be educated and released as free men. In the past, they followed most of Alexander's generals to the limits of his territory, but now they wander without purpose." Abruptly, to Carpathimos's surprise, he added, "Perhaps it is purpose you carry in that leather sack of yours?"

Carpathimos did not answer, but he held the man's hand more tightly. He glanced at the boy who was busy at his table, selling what he had left of his food.

Again, the old man spoke. "Most of the people you seek have fled the fighting in the south. They are now more concentrated in Thrace. Perhaps they are returning to Byzantion, near the Black Sea, through which they once passed. If that is the case, you will surely catch up to them."

Carpathimos asked, "What is the fastest route?"

"The fastest is not always the safest, Islander," cautioned the old man, sententiously. "I suggest you pass by Mt. Olympus to the north after cutting across Thessaly."

"Inland from Olympus is peak after peak of rugged terrain," Carpathimos said. "This much I do know of my family's history. It would take me weeks to make my way over that range."

"Very well," said the man, "then you must cross Thessaly, making your way through the Vale of Tempe on the River Peneus, which bleeds into the eastern sea. If you make it across, head east along the gulf. A well-worn trail will carry you through the Kumli Valley and up over a narrow pass that runs between the mountain called Kerdylion and the high cliffs of the Chalcidice peninsula. From there, you will descend into the valley of the great Strymon. If the air is not wet and gray on the day you look out over the Strymon Valley, you will see eight other roads converging at a bridge spanning the Strymon River."

"And this is the *Bridge of Nine*," said Carpathimos. "I have heard stories of this place."

"You must cross this bridge to reach Amphipolis, but beware, for those who hold the bridge are wary indeed. That is the place where I lost my eyes to King Pyrrhus's men."

Carpathimos reviewed the warnings and directions in his head and then pressed the old man's hand once again.

"Be careful and be wise, Islander," said the old man. "Tell me one last thing. Who was travelling with you?"

Carpathimos started. "I am sorry," he responded. "I do not understand."

"You said 'we' earlier. I was curious who had once joined you on your travels."

Carpathimos paused a moment and then stated dolefully, "He was a friend I lost along the way." The old man nodded but said nothing. Carpathimos thanked the man and caught the boy's attention. He gave him another coin for another loaf of the wheat bread. The two shared smiles and Carpathimos turned to go. Before taking a step, the old man spoke one last time to Carpathimos.

"Remember Islander, as you cross the Nine Roads Bridge and throughout your journey, choose your path wisely."

# Chapter XXII

---

CARPATHIMOS LOOKED OUT over the fathomless Strymon River Valley through the low clouds, tracing the few roads that he could see toward their eventual confluence over the river far below. Some roads seemed wider and more heavily travelled than others, like the road from the north, on which much timber was carried toward the sea. Carpathimos guessed it would be destined for the construction of ships. From where he stood, along the western lip of the valley, Carpathimos could see hundreds of people divided among the many roads, some heading toward the bridge, others working their way back out of the valley. Those roads wound upward along the numerous switchbacks carved into the steep sidewalls of the great chasm.

Carpathimos had met several groups of people along the east-west road over which he had been travelling. He suspected they were mostly peasants or drifters looking for another home. Only once did he meet soldiers along the trail. He gave them a wide berth and, luckily, they had not paid him notice.

While considering the large, wooden bridge, Carpathimos observed soldiers marching over the bridge and turning to the south toward the Aegean. They took pause along the bridge to interact with the men guarding and patrolling it. The soldiers seemed orderly and carried on freely with one another, seemingly all in good attitude. When they departed, Carpathimos decided he had better take advantage of their good spirits. He began the climb down the steeply sloping face of the valley toward the river crossing. He briefly considered crossing the river further upstream but thought better of it after seeing how the churning brown water chewed away at the steep walls at either side as it rapidly tumbled toward the sea. No man, not even he, could withstand such a rough passage across a wild river and still have the endurance required to scale the opposing side.

Nearing the bridge, Carpathimos moved off the path and stood under a broad sycamore to let a large family pass him. They had oxen pulling a cart that must have been filled with all their belongings, for the teetering pile was stacked so high that portions of it shifted and slid with each dip or rise of the cart over the rough terrain. The cart had low side walls sticking out at an angle over the two tall wooden wheels, one on each side. Five children of varying ages sat within the cart. Four adults, two men and two women, walked alongside the cart and in front of the two oxen. Bringing up the rear of the family procession, was a long line of goats, all tied together with a long, thin rope about their necks.

Carpathimos watched them as they passed him and then he checked the soldiers at the bridge. Figuring that he might have a better chance successfully crossing in a group rather than on his own, Carpathimos jumped back on the road and took a position alongside the goats. While walking, he watched the children in the back of the cart who had been watching him as well.

The children had thin, dirty faces, perhaps too thin for their age, he thought. One at a time, they began to smile and snicker at him. He made a face at them, trying to get them to accept him, but soon he realized they had not been giggling at him so much as at the goat next to him, which was chewing a loose fragment at the bottom of his tunic.

Carpathimos lengthened his stride and quickened his pace. The goat broke into a trot, pulling tirelessly on the rope that bound it to the goats behind it. Eventually, Carpathimos reached the back corner of the ox cart, and the goat abandoned its unrelenting assault on his clothing. The children stared curiously at him over the rim of the cart, but did not seem afraid. One of the women, however, noticed Carpathimos walking behind her and alerted the two men. They stopped the oxen and confronted Carpathimos.

"What do you want with us?" the older of the two men asked firmly.

Carpathimos smiled at the men and nodded to the women. "I mean no harm. I saw your children and I wanted to give them some bread and some pieces of my dried meat. May they have it?" he asked, pulling both from his leather pack. The entire family stared at him, their faces like stone.

"You may," said the older of the two men.

Carpathimos handed the food to the oldest of the children, who took it from him quickly and began dividing it among them all.

"I was hoping that I might cross the bridge with you," Carpathimos said, watching the children feast on the small portions of food they clutched in their small hands. "I haven't travelled so far before without company and someone to talk to. I don't bring harm." Carpathimos studied their faces as the travelers looked at one another, as if tallying a vote on the question without requiring language.

Without answering Carpathimos's question, the older man took up the rope hanging from the ox on the right and began to pull on it, urging the beast forward. The women resumed their walking, leaving the younger man alone to speak to Carpathimos. This man had similar facial features to the older man, but they appeared too close in age to be father and son. He was perhaps older than Elijah had been, but still younger than Carpathimos.

"You may join us. My brother, sister, and my brother's wife are very nervous about the crossing. If there is trouble, they will not admit that they know you." he warned.

"And you?"

The young man shrugged. "I do not know you either, and there is little time to form a friendship. My name is Dositheos."

"God gives!" exclaimed Carpathimos unexpectedly.

"That is correct!" Dositheos said. "Not many know this name here."

"My name is Carpathimos. I had a friend who once told me stories about a boyhood friend whose name was Dositheos. He told me what the name meant."

"Where is your friend now? And what is his name?"

"We had to part ways some time ago. I haven't seen Elijah for a long time."

"Do you know what Elijah's name means?" asked Dositheos with a smile.

Carpathimos thought for a moment, trying to remember if Elijah had ever told him, and then he shook his head. "I do not."

"The name Elijah means 'My God is Yahweh.'" Dositheos grinned.

"The name fit him well, then," said Carpathimos softly. "What is your brother's name?"

"That ox is Theodorus. He is a bricklayer. He works hard, but as you can see there are many mouths to feed among us. We were working in Thebes, but tensions there are too high, so we agreed to move back to Ionia, where our parents grew up. We have heard that there may be work in Miletus or Smyrna along the eastern side of the Aegean."

Carpathimos at once felt closer than ever to a reunion with his sister Parma, and his son. He knew, however, that they were still a long way off and he had more challenges to endure before he would find them again. As the roads on the west side of the river began to converge into one wide thoroughfare, the trampled ground became more firm and less mottled with potholes and stony knurls. Streams of people walked alongside them, and they met others travelling in the opposite direction. Dositheos touched Carpathimos on the shoulder. "I will run ahead and tell the others about you before we reach the soldiers. I will return."

Carpathimos watched him catch up to his older brother, Theodorus. Ahead, some of Antigonus's soldiers spread out across the bridge in front of them, stopping travelers and talking to them, perhaps inquiring about who they were and where they intended to go. Occasionally, one soldier or another might get into a cart to look through some of the belongings or he would help herd some of the loose animals toward the side of the bridge. Nothing seemed terribly ominous until the family with whom Carpathimos traveled was stopped. Two soldiers spoke only to Theodorus and one of them climbed into the cart. When the smaller children started to cry, Carpathimos reached over the back of the cart and picked up the two smallest children. He leaned against the side of the cart and a third child crawled out onto his shoulders. The other soldier was looking squarely at him and the crying children. Theodorus also glanced back at Carpathimos before resuming his conversation with the soldier, who nodded and waved to his compatriot to join him. To the travelers' surprise, the soldiers indicated they could pass and proceeded to another group of people. Theodorus started the oxen moving once again.

Dositheos relieved Carpathimos of his burdens. He returned a little girl to the cart and grabbed a second little girl from Carpathimos's left arm. Carpathimos made no attempt to dismount the three- or four-year-old boy from his shoulders. He seemed content to ride so high off the ground. As they proceeded, Dositheos described the interaction with the soldiers.

"They are mostly looking for soldiers, I believe—either those willing to join them or those belonging to the enemy, who may be trying to sneak away. The one soldier did ask about you," he said to Carpathimos. "He knew that you didn't belong in our family and he offered Theodorus a reward if he was willing to tell him that you were either a deserter or a combatant. Theodorus gave your name and said that you were my friend from Thebes. He said that you were a bricklayer like himself. You aren't, by chance, are you?"

"I am a fisherman," responded Carpathimos. "I have never set a brick in my life."

"Well, then I am glad they didn't ask you to make bricks for a demonstration," said Dositheos with a smile.

Carpathimos realized how close he had been to being captured, killed, or jeopardizing this kind family. Had the soldier suspected that he was deserting from Sparta or his own army, he would have faced an entirely different fate, especially if they had stripped him and seen the scars across his back. The scars would have testified to the fact that he was not a simple bricklayer. Carpathimos knew the soldiers might have punished Theodorus and the others severely for not telling the truth. Then they would have either killed Carpathimos or beat him mercilessly before enslaving him. Either way, the crossing would have ended in disaster. Carpathimos wiped his brow. He was more nervous now than he had been before stepping foot on the old bridge.

The family marched on in silence until nightfall, when they stopped along the roadside to make camp in a small clearing in the woods.

That night Carpathimos sat with Theodorus and Dositheos as they spoke of family matters. Carpathimos tried not to pay attention to their conversation. A small fire crackled at their feet, burning the wood that Carpathimos and Dositheos had gathered from the forest floor outside the river valley. He felt badly for risking their safety and grateful for their help. He wondered how he could thank them. The women joined them when the children were finally asleep in the cart under a few blankets and the star-filled sky.

When a break in the conversation allowed, Carpathimos said what had been on his mind. "Theodorus, I am very sorry for risking your family's safety at the bridge. I never should have put you in that position. I should not have joined you and forced you to lie to the soldier. I should have tried to cross the river farther upstream."

Theodorus's wife spoke first, "That is nonsense! You might have died in that riv—"

"Carpathimos is right, woman," interrupted Theodorus, "but what is done is done."

Dositheos spoke. "It was indeed a risk, but we all took it. There is no way they would have let Carpathimos cross the bridge alone and we didn't turn him away. There must have been a reason for us to come together on the cart path leading to the bridge."

Theodorus scoffed. "Brother, stop! You always believe there is some meaning behind everything that happens whenever you have no idea. There was no special purpose for Sparta and Athens to rise up against Antigonus. There is no special purpose behind the capture of our father and mother and the way they were taken to Thebes as slaves and killed. There is no purpose for the children to go to bed with little more in their stomachs than cold bread. And there is no purpose for this man to meet us along a dirt road near an old wooden bridge!"

The group remained silent and solemn. When Dositheos shifted his position so he could cross his legs, he leaned against Carpathimos's leather pack. Carpathimos reached for it instantly, startling Dositheos and the others.

"Carpathimos, why do you travel this way? And what happened to your friend Elijah?" Dositheos asked.

"Why do you ask about Elijah? Why do you think something happened to him?"

"Before we came to the bridge, you said his name *fit* him, as if he no longer lives."

"I owe you my story—or at least part of it," Carpathimos said. He told the family about his friend, starting from their first meeting, when Elijah knocked Carpathimos off a dock in Carthage. He described their journey together and how Elijah died trying to save him. Then he revealed what Elijah had been carrying all the way to Rome from Alexandria. When he finished, he pulled the tightly rolled books from his leather sack.

The men and women gathered around the scroll, gazing at the tiny handwriting. "What does it say?" Theodorus's wife asked.

Carpathimos opened the Shemot. "This is the second book and Elijah's favorite," he explained. He read them the story of God's revelation to his people of Israel through Moses, who led them out of Egypt. Through a combination of reading and memorization, Carpathimos recited the story. When he finished, four sets of eyes stared at him against a background of the deepest darkness, at the point just before the night turns to dawn.

Theodorus spoke to his wife, his sister, and his brother Dositheos. Then he turned his attention back to Carpathimos. "I think we may know someone who can help you, Carpathimos," Theodorus said. "Our father's cousins may still live near Byzantion, by the large Black Sea. We will travel through there on our way. They may have mothers or fathers still alive who may know where you should take those books."

———

Regulus's troops under the command of Thracius spread out behind a wall of flames driven by a strong wind. As instructed, they had been ravaging the countryside since Aspis, leaving no village, farm, or domicile unharmed. Within a few days they acquired several thousand able-bodied prisoners, dragging them in chains. The Romans had destroyed crops on the verge of harvest, setting ablaze every field, orchard, and farm building along the way. For the innocent living in the path of this destruction, there had been little warning—yet no amount of time could prepare them for such a rapidly moving wall of inferno and armor.

On a late summer day much like all the others, Yzebel's eyes flickered open to the early morning light that squeezed through the slats in the porous shutter that covered her window. It spilled onto the stone floor in a long, narrow stream of bright white. She lay under her blanket, not yet interested in moving from its warmth. She thought about the sun as its rays moved across the floor and she idly studied the shutter, made of four vertical boards that covered the only window in her room. Earlier in the season, the sun peeked through the crack between the boards on the left side and, as the year moved along, the location of the sunrise had moved, and the light with it. The laborers on the farm were nearing the end of harvest and today they would once again be in the fields. She would go with them. Soon.

Crawling out from under her warm blanket, Yzebel stretched her arms and legs and reluctantly placed her feet upon the stone floor. Instantly she shivered, as she did every morning because of that wretched cold floor. She pushed open the shutter and sniffed the air. It was cool and moist and yet there was something altogether different about its quality this morning. Besides the usual aromas of sea foam and palms, primrose and thistles, she detected a faint whiff of smoke. It was barely perceptible. She sniffed again and again before convincing herself that it was real. She hurried to dress and ran outside to find Jugurtha awake and standing in the yard with his wife. They turned to look at Yzebel when she walked up to them.

"Do you smell it?" she asked with a shiver, clutching her upper arms, trying to warm herself in the early morning air. Jugurtha nodded. They continued to stand and wait for the dimness of dawn to clear. They could see no smoke and they could hear no alarm. They spoke briefly and then dispersed to begin their days. They would be joining the other families of laborers in the field to help harvest the grain. It was a large undertaking and all hands were needed today. Most of the laborers had already walked there yesterday to make camp, so that they could begin laying down the barley early in the morning. That way, it could dry in the late morning and afternoon sun.

As Yzebel reached the top step of the entrance to the main house, she heard feet pounding behind her. She turned on her heels. A small boy, the son of one of the laborers, was running as fast as his young legs could carry him. He sprinted into the yard along the long dirt path that ran parallel to the shoreline. By the time he reached Yzebel, he could barely speak. He panted to gather air into his heaving lungs.

"Shhh." She gathered him in her arms and carried him inside, offering him a wooden cup filled with clean water to drink. He forced down the water, some of it spilling over his cheeks as he poured it into his mouth faster than his mouth could accept it all. Yzebel knelt beside him and wiped the sweat off his forehead and neck as he drank, watching her father enter the room.

"Yzebel," the boy choked against the dry dust in his throat. "Soldiers are coming! The fig trees are burning!"

Before he finished speaking, she heard the pounding of hooves on the same path that the boy had taken. She hurried to the doorway and peered down the path. She could see the smoke now, climbing high in the sky. The wind was pushing it inland and eastward, toward them. She could detect the shapes of three men on horseback galloping hard toward the yard. It was Kanmi and two of his men. Yzebel's father joined her at the doorway. He gasped.

"Kanmi is not due here yet," he mumbled. Then he noted the smoke. "Oh! He is burning our fields! Yzebel, he is burning the fields!"

By the time Kanmi and his men reached the main house, Yzebel had become furious. She too had realized what Kanmi had been doing. She strode out on the porch and raced down the front steps to confront him. Her father tried in vain to slow her progress.

"How dare you!" she shouted at Kanmi as he sat atop his horse, which was still breathing hard from the ride up the path.

Kanmi shouted back at her. "We did not start that fire! Roman troops are headed this way! Gather your things, Yzebel. You are coming with me."

"I most certainly will not go with you!" she shouted. "I need to go help them!" She pointed to the laborers, who were moving in their direction. When she darted between the horses and started to run, Kanmi spun his horse around and rode after her. Near the opposite side of the central corral, he leaped from his horse and knocked her to the ground. She swung at him, but he caught her by the wrist and straddled her at the waist to hold her down. His men joined him. "Carry Yzebel back to the house!" he ordered.

Under a barrage of flailing fists and feet, the beleaguered men carried Yzebel into the house, with Kanmi following closely behind. Jabnit stepped aside, dismissing the small boy who had brought the news. Kanmi slapped the boy on the head as he ran out the door.

"You have no choice, Yzebel," Kanmi said. "Those Roman soldiers will be here any moment and they will slaughter you along with the rest of your kind. They have already murdered your precious laborers!"

Yzebel collapsed into tears, abandoning her resistance to Kanmi's men as she imagined the laborers' undeserved fates. Jabnit, meanwhile, scurried about the house collecting his most cherished items and the log books and documents that Kanmi inspected at every visit. Kanmi ordered his men outside to watch for the soldiers they knew would surely be close behind them.

"Gather the horses and be prepared to leave," he ordered.

As Kanmi watched his men run out of the house and chase his horse, he saw the wall of flames advancing in the distance. The wind created by the rapidly rising heat whipped at the palms around the yard. Ash was drifting on the air, settling to the ground all around the small house. The burning embers would be next. Kanmi poked his head through the doorway and listened carefully. Moments later he could hear the rhythmic pounding of marching soldiers over the rustling of the wind and the roar of flame. He saw them through a break in the smoke as the wind briefly shifted. Hundreds of soldiers were marching in a long column extending down the road. They were shouting or chanting something, but Kanmi could not understand the words.

Frightened, he turned his attention back to Yzebel. Grabbing her roughly by the arm, he hauled her to her feet. She slapped at him, so he hit her across the head just above the ear, knocking her off balance. Somehow, she managed to break free. She ran toward her bedroom and slammed the door in Kanmi's face as he raced to catch her. She leaped over the bed and was nearly out the window when Kanmi caught her and dragged her back by her hair. She landed hard against the floor. Before she could get her bearings, he picked her up again, slamming her onto the bed in front of him.

"You wish to die, Yzebel?" yelled Kanmi. "Then it will be by Roman hands, but not until I am finished with you." He was purple with rage. "You had your chance to escape with me, but you wasted it!"

Kanmi tore the neck of her robe while she kicked and scratched. She managed to take a slice out of his cheek before he swung at her, knocking her back with a fist against her cheekbone. As he crawled on top of her and ripped at her underskirt, she moaned out for help. Her father was now standing in the doorway, once again frozen with fear. Kanmi struggled against her will and gradually he subdued her. She screamed one last time and then the fight abruptly ceased. Yzebel felt her attacker leave her body and her eyes sprang open. She jumped onto her feet, astonished by the sight before her.

Kanmi was curled up on the floor near the foot of her bed, clutching at his neck as blood poured over his fingers onto the floor. If he moved even slightly, bright red blood shot out toward the near wall in crimson arcs across the stone. Her father stood over Kanmi with a blood-stained knife in his hand, the very knife he kept hidden in a small candle box in his bedroom. That knife and candle box had travelled with their family from Tyre long ago, but Yzebel had never seen her father take the knife out of that box.

"Father," Yzebel said, averting her eyes from the gruesome scene on her floor. "Father," she said again. "Are you all right?"

He didn't respond. He seemed mesmerized by the sight of Kanmi bleeding. She reached out for her father but stopped when she heard the boots of Kanmi's men rushing up the steps to the front door. She lunged for Jabnit to get his attention and he too became aware of them entering. Jabnit pushed Yzebel to the window and helped her down to the ground. He smiled so warmly, lovingly, at her that she felt once again like a cherished child, wrapped within the protective hands of the father she loved. She reached for his hand, but he had already turned to meet Kanmi's men as they closed in on him within the bedroom. The three men struggled, yet the battle was over nearly as fast as it had started. Jabnit's body slowly sank to the floor and out of sight of the woman beyond the window.

In shock, Yzebel raced toward the tree line behind the house. When she found shelter, she spotted Jugurtha walking toward the column of troops entering the yard. Briefly, he scanned the area. She knew he was looking for her. For an instant their eyes met. Jugurtha nodded to her in the way he always did, confirming that everything would be all right and he could manage the task. Yzebel was terrified but knew she must not delay. Jugurtha was about to die to distract the soldiers from her movements.

Her heart pounded in her throat as Yzebel ran toward the orchard. In its center a cellar had been dug deep into the earth long ago, the perfect place to store ripening fruit until it could be hauled away once all the trees were picked. She raced between the broad apricot trees to where she thought the entrance should be. Slowing to a stop and spinning around, she searched the ground frantically. She was aware that the main house was now entirely engulfed in flames and smoke was billowing high above the trees. The farm buildings had all been torched. Desperately she kicked at the ground in a broad circle, trying to find the opening. The long grass had matted during the last rain, making it harder to see the ground beneath.

She stomped at the ground as she worked her way first in one direction and then the next, trying to hear the sound of the wooden door of the entrance. She knew she had very little time to save herself. If she couldn't locate it immediately, she would have to run again. Her heart pounded fearfully. And then she found it. Her foot hit a flat board that announced its presence with a dull sounding clunk.

Yzebel dropped to her knees and scraped away the dried grass, clearing off the door. She pulled at the handle and the door wiggled free of the ground. As she tipped the door open, the smell of damp soil and cool air wafted up and around her. The earthen steps led down into a darkness she hoped would be empty and safe. She jumped down through the doorway and briefly looked back toward the melee in the farmyard before she dropped the door behind her. She had not seen Jugurtha. Gasping and wracked with sobs, she would wait near the doorway, craning her ears for the sound of any soldiers.

At the edge of the orchard, five Romans watched as the woman disappeared into the ground, drawing a wooden door closed above her. They waited for the soldiers to advance from the farmyard. One by one, the five hurried into the orchard from their hiding place within the tree line and found Yzebel's hiding place. Four men hid in the grass under a fruit tree.

One crawled over to the wooden doorway and rapped on the door with his fist, while keeping vigilant if any soldiers appeared in the distance.

"Yzebel Gisgon," he whispered softly. No reply. He knocked against the door again and this time he used his regular voice. "Yzebel Gisgon! I will not harm you. If you want to survive this day, then come with me."

Yzebel leaned against the cold earthen wall of the cellar, terrified and disgusted that she had been seen. She made not a sound, but could only imagine that the man calling her name must have heard her heart beating.

Again, the man spoke, this time more urgently. "Yzebel Gisgon! You must come out and follow me if you want to survive. The Romans will burn you alive in this hole. They are bringing torches now to light this orchard on fire. The flames will consume the air you breathe, and your blood will boil. Come out now, Yzebel!"

Yzebel thought quickly. If he was one of the Roman soldiers, why didn't he just march down and kill her on the spot? It might be a trap, but on the other hand he was probably right about the flames. This had not been a wise spot to pick to hide.

Slowly she pushed up at the door until it opened easily. The man was assisting her. He held it open and peered in at her, saying, "Crawl out and follow me."

Yzebel did what he said. He dropped the door. She flattened herself on the ground and waited for him to crawl past her. She followed his lead to the first fruit tree. Then he rose to his feet and started to run toward the tree line separating the orchard from the beach. She followed him, and they ran together, hunched over so that they would not be spotted. By now, the smoke produced by the advancing line of flames was spreading throughout the orchard, and they hoped it not only obscured their view, but also that of the soldiers.

As they neared the tree line, Yzebel was surrounded by four other men racing along beside and behind her. They all wore Roman uniforms and each carried short swords, except for the man leading her. Once into the trees, the group turned to the east and ran full speed, hopping over downed logs and ducking under low-hanging branches into a field of ripe barley that twisted in the breeze.

Yzebel canvassed the golden-brown field for soldiers, but all she could see was the smoke. At the corner of the field, a natural rise extended into the sea like an earthen pier. As the group fled over the ridge, the man she had been following directed her toward the water, where a small boat was beached on the sand. The men collided with the boat, grasped the hull and plank-sheer, and pushed the boat into the water before leaping in to grab the oars. The leader reached out to Yzebel and yanked her over the side. She collapsed in an exhausted heap on the floor of the boat.

"Stay down!" he ordered. She obeyed. The men rowed fast, in perfect harmony. Yzebel could feel the waves pounding against the hull as the men headed the boat out to sea. Within minutes, they approached a small one-masted galley. The men helped Yzebel on board. She found herself standing among thirty men, all staring at her.

Yzebel's rescuer called out an order and the men of the galley scrambled to action, pulling up the anchor, raising the sail, and taking positions along a central rowing bench. Twenty-four men forced the ship through the waves and into the great sea. The leader beckoned Yzebel to follow him down a small passageway and into a small room over the stern. He directed her to sit on a narrow bench built along the wall. He slid out of his Roman uniform and pulled a ragged and worn tunic over his body in its place. Yzebel stared at him and then peered through the passageway at the men rowing the ship.

"Men in Roman uniforms from an Illyrian galley rescuing a Carthaginian woman from Romans?" she asked.

Her host smiled broadly.

"And you must be the captain of this ship."

"I am Cyprian and, yes, I am the captain of these men." The man's voice and bearing were proud.

"You are a pirate?" Yzebel was surprised she didn't feel fear.

"We prefer the term *collectors*," quipped Cyprian with another smile.

"What will you do with me, Collector Cyprian?"

"You need not fear, Yzebel Gisgon," he said. "We mean you no harm. A fine Roman senator has paid us enough in gold coins to ensure that is the case."

Yzebel shook her head, confused. "How did you find me?"

"It wasn't as easy as it seemed," he confessed. "We have been watching you for several days, making sure we identified the correct woman. When we saw the Romans nearing the farm, we had to move more quickly than anticipated. I am sorry that we cut our timing rather close. That was not our intention."

"And you just happen to speak my language? Is that just a coincidence or did the Roman senator plan that as well?"

"I speak many languages." Cyprian thumped his chest. "It is quite useful in our adventures."

Yzebel smiled at him, appreciating the presence of someone capable and quick-thinking, someone who could rescue her from grave peril—regardless of whether the rescue was at the right price.

"Where will you take me?"

"Make yourself comfortable, Yzebel Gisgon," smiled the captain. "We sail to Byzantion through the Sea of Propontis."

"But who do I look for in Byzantion?" The story was getting more and more confusing.

"You will find a man who seems out of place there, a strong old man with short gray hair and a cunning mind. He speaks more with silence than he does with words." The captain seemed to hold this man in high regard, Yzebel realized. But that didn't quench her curiosity.

"Does he speak my tongue?"

"That I do not know. But the name Carpathimos does mean something to both of you, does it not?" Cyprian asked. Yzebel showed her surprise.

The captain walked away, leaving Yzebel with her thoughts racing along behind him. She had so many questions. She leaned back against the stern of the ship and took a deep breath, letting out the air in a long, slow sigh. She closed her eyes and pictured her father in his last moments. How proud she was of him now. Tears flooded her eyes and spilled down over her cheeks. Yzebel wept for a long time as she prayed for her father and Jugurtha and the many others who died that day.

# Chapter XXIII

---

“ARE YOU SURE this is what you want, Lucius?” Faustus asked with genuine concern. The serious look on his face was accentuated by the dim light within the large open rotunda of the Senate building where they stood.

"It is, Faustus." Lucius's voice was strong and confident. "I care for both of you deeply, but this I must do. I don't expect you to understand—but please do accept my wish."

"We certainly accept it, Lucius," Domitius assured him. "I, for one, acknowledge your desire to be with your family and I respect it. We will not stand in your way."

"For that, I thank you." Lucius smiled warmly at his friends, adding, "However I do fear that he may send more men after me." Lucius gazed into the darkness that surrounded them, alert for anyone who might be listening to their conversation, even though he knew they were alone. Lucius had asked his friends to meet him late in the evening to discuss his change of plans. The Senate building, despite its vital functions by day, was usually dark and quiet at this time of night.

"They will never find you," Domitius said. "Faustus and I will see to that."

"In fact," Faustus added, "we will simply notify the Senate that you are dead." The three friends smiled at the joke, but there was some truth to the comment. "In all seriousness, Lucius, Domitius and I will keep your secret forever. No one will ever find you." Faustus clasped his friend's hand tightly.

"Besides," Domitius jumped in, "do you even know where it is you will be going, Lucius? We certainly do not."

"No," Lucius admitted, shaking his head in mock dismay. "Not exactly. But I think I can find them. I am confident in that."

He turned his attention away from the men and focused on the quiet rotunda, studying the design and its character as best he could in the near absence of light. "I will miss this place," Lucius murmured. "I never thought I would say that." To Faustus, he admitted, "When your uncle, Emperor Tacitus, asked me to join him here, I thought he had gone mad. He knew that I loved leading troops into battle and I was content to spend my remaining years in the wilderness. He knew I couldn't stand the chaos of the city and the constant bickering and arguing that took place here week after week. Gradually, however, I learned to appreciate it as my father once did."

"And, you developed some wonderful friendships," Faustus reminded him, smiling happily, his voice reverberating within the stone theater that surrounded them.

"I also created some enemies," Lucius said quietly.

"Indeed," Domitius lamented, "I cannot believe that Sorian escaped from the mines and traveled so very far intending to kill you, Lucius. If I had not seen his body with my own eyes, I never would have believed it."

"Thank you both, again, for helping me dispose of his body the other night." Lucius said.

Both men nodded.

"You are certain that Sorian had been planning the attack with Regulus?" Faustus asked.

"Absolutely certain, Faustus. There is no doubt that Regulus wanted me removed from his path to Carthage and he took advantage of both the opportunity and the hatred that Sorian had for me." Lucius repeated what he had told them earlier. "Sorian said as much to me before he died."

"All the more reason to withdraw some of his troops and his fleet." Domitius spoke angrily, a scowl on his face. "I believe Faustus and I can make that happen, Lucius."

"Quite true!" Faustus said. "Most of the People's Assembly were apprehensive about the resources required for a full-scale land assault on Carthage. Many here in the Senate worry that keeping four legions in Africa over the winter is a grave mistake. We can sway some of the more conservative members to accept the fact that Rome cannot afford to fund Regulus's vast army for so many months. After all, winter is coming."

"Leave this to us, Lucius. Remember, most of Regulus's strongest supporters are with him now and the rest, who remain here, have cooled to him somewhat since he has been gone. We will be able to withdraw most of the troops and the fleet. In fact, I predict we will pull back three of his four legions," Domitius said.

"With any luck," Faustus growled facetiously, "the Carthaginians will capture him." Faustus grinned.

"Be careful," warned Lucius. "Don't trust too many in this city."

"Do you need anything for your journey, Lucius?" asked Domitius, quickly changing the subject.

"Your house has sold?" asked Faustus, breaking in before Lucius could answer.

Lucius nodded. "I carry only the clothes on my body and what valuables and coinage I can carry in the pack I brought with me tonight. I must admit, it feels liberating to not be tied down to anything anymore. I may grow to enjoy this humble life I have chosen for myself."

"Are we about done here?" asked Faustus. "We need to send off our friend here with a proper night of ample wine and good food!"

Lucius and Domitius stared at Faustus in disbelief, shaking their heads and mocking him before breaking into a laughter that filled the space around them, as if they were surrounded by the senate members themselves. The three men came together on the senate floor and Faustus and Domitius embraced their friend. To Lucius, Domitius said, "I will miss you, my dear old friend."

"And I will miss you," answered Lucius as he looked to each of them in turn, mustering only a faint smile.

"May we go eat now?" insisted Faustus.

As the three men stepped from the dark inner sanctum of the senate building into the tawny warm glow of a waning gibbous moon, they made their way down the broad stairs to the street below. They didn't notice the circumspective set of chestnut-colored eyes watching them as they departed. After the friends disappeared into the darkness of the city, the man with those chestnut-colored eyes stepped out from the shadows and into the moonlight. The light danced upon his ornately carved breastplate, while he placed the crested bronze helmet upon his head and unfurled the long red cape he had rolled over his shoulder to avoid detection. The crimson fabric dropped to its full length and shuddered in the breeze.

———

Carpathimos sat on the ground with his legs stretched out before him as he traced lines in the dirt with a short length of dried olive wood, trying to remember the outlines of territories he once saw on a map of the eastern Mediterranean basin. He found gaps in his memory, as evident by similar gaps in his map. He excelled at directions and he knew where he had to go, but he struggled to calculate the geography between the place where he sat and the place where his sister may be living. He had never before traveled this far to the northeast of the great sea.

Leaning back and resting against the wooden wheel of the ox cart, he studied the small, flat-topped mud building baked in the midday sun to what was now a very pale tan color. Along the edge of its roof, wrist-sized branches protruded, as if the house was capped by a crown of sticks. On top of these larger branches sat layer after layer of twigs and mud, which had similarly been dried to a smooth yet rigid surface. The house appeared to have only one room. Not even the ox cart would have fit inside it, had there been an opening large enough to accommodate its passage.

This house had been one of only a few like it along the dusty road to Byzantion, and they had stopped at all the others. So far, they had found no useful information about the whereabouts of their mother or father's relatives. Here, in the hills overlooking the city of Byzantion, Carpathimos waited patiently while Theodorus and Dositheos met with the people inside. He felt a growing sense of anticipation as he listened to the voices emanating from inside, hoping his travel companions were learning something about their relatives. Until now, he had believed it was unlikely, but his new friends had been inside this house for much longer than the previous homes. He looked down at the map he had drawn and shoved his stick in the dirt, observing the shadow that told the hour of the day. He was right! They had been in the house a long time.

Shifting on the ground uneasily, Carpathimos wanted to go inside to hear what they were discussing, but he knew that he should not. Theodorus had decided in front of the very first house they had approached that Carpathimos should stay outside because he feared that the man's intimidating size and appearance might make people too nervous to speak openly. Theodorus was right about that as well, thought Carpathimos. Strangers might indeed be reluctant to talk to such an imposing stranger. Carpathimos remembered the young boy who sold him bread in the market at Nafpaktus and smiled. He had not been scared of him.

With a start, Carpathimos felt straw falling upon him. Two goats had jumped onto the cart and were busy chewing the straw. As he stood up to chase the goats out of the cart, the door to the small house slid open and Dositheos rushed outside.

"Carpathimos! We have good news about our father's family!"

Carpathimos snared the last goat by the hind legs and hauled it over the rim of the cart, letting it drop gently to the ground at his feet. He grinned as Dositheos approached him. "These people left Ionia many years ago, when their parents died of illness," Dositheos told him. "They came here with their aged grandparents, on their way to the promised free lands in Thessaly. When the grandfather died of old age, they decided to live out the remainder of their lives here, where the grandfather is buried. They built this house and shortly thereafter the grandmother also died."

Dositheos continued relating his findings. "It seems that in Ionia, which sits on the far western shore of the Anatolian peninsula between Lydia and the sea, they had friends who were probably our relatives. Their parents' good friends would have been cousins to our father—and they may have even known our father!"

"This is wonderful news, Dositheos!" Carpathimos put his hand on the young man's shoulder. "Do we now go to Ionia?"

Dositheos nodded. "They are confident that their old friends still live in Ionia because only a year ago some people passing this way knew of them and said that their large family still lives and works near the coast."

"I am very happy for you and your family, Dositheos." Carpathimos instantly prepared to ready the oxen for their journey.

"Wait, Carpathimos!" interrupted Dositheos. "There is news for you as well."

Carpathimos halted and looked back at Dositheos who was smiling, his wide grin revealing his white teeth, a sight Carpathimos had never before seen above his host's scraggly brown beard. "You know of my family as well, Dositheos?"

Dositheos shook his head. "I don't have news that good, Carpathimos, but we have information that may prove useful for the purpose of your journey." Dositheos stepped closer and continued, "These people told us that they had traveled with another family until separating with them in Byzantion. That other family stayed in Byzantion, but they related their travels with several elders who were all brothers. The man of this house remembers listening to the brothers speak to one another using a different language. They never spoke the common tongue as we do, Carpathimos. They spoke the old language of the Jews—Hebrew."

"Do they still live in Byzantion?" Carpathimos felt a surge of excitement. "Will they know of the books of Moses?"

"I do not know, Carpathimos, but we know where to seek them. Perhaps the old men will remember the books like your friend Elijah's grandfather did. It is a good place to start, Carpathimos." Dositheos seemed genuinely happy at the good news.

Carpathimos was eager to get to Byzantion and Dositheos was equally excited to resume their journey to Ionia. The two men sensed the joy of the other. They embraced, patting one another on the back as they hugged. Theodorus poked his head through the doorway and announced that they would stay for a meal offered by their gracious hosts, and following that, they could be on their way. Carpathimos was invited to join them.

---

As the young family members traveled toward Byzantion that evening, Carpathimos reflected upon his splendid fortune and the kindness of the people who had shared their food with him. In all the years since his childhood, he could not recall a time in which he had felt so free. Even during the short time he lived with his beautiful Myridia and son Lucia on the island where he grew up, he had not felt the sense of freedom he felt now. He suspected that was because the Roman soldiers were stationed there with them. Their presence didn't make him relax, completely at ease, as he felt now.

In Byzantion, they found a dizzying mixture of people and tongues. This was a great thoroughfare for travelers along the natural land bridge stretching between the large Black Sea in the North and the Mediterranean to the south. Throughout the evening, the family walked through the markets and shops, trailing their cart and animals behind them in the street. Usually Carpathimos stayed behind to guard the family's belongings and mind the animals, especially the goats, which made every attempt to consume the local commodities from a close vendor's stall. Carpathimos couldn't wait to get out of the busy street, although he knew the family was doing everything they could to find the elders for him.

"Carpathimos!" shouted Dositheos from a short distance ahead of him. Carpathimos looked forward, scanning the crowd until he saw Dositheos waving to him. In a hurry, Carpathimos mobilized the cart and the animals and pulled through the crowd to catch up with Dositheos.

"Carpathimos, I just spoke to a man who knew the name of the family we are looking for. He told me the street and the part of the city in which to find them. It is not far," Dositheos said.

They waited for the others and then set out together on a side street, weaving down the narrow passageways, away from the busier center of Byzantion. Here, the neighborhoods of Byzantion were less well-kept and so were its people. Men fought and yelled at one another while others staggered and stumbled about as if in aimless pursuit of something, the control of their minds overtaken by the vessels of wine they clutched. Men were seen urinating on the sides of buildings and women lined the streets late in the day, fraternizing with men in ways that embarrassed the modest family of Dositheos.

Before nightfall, they drew up in front of a gray building that resembled all the others on both sides of the street. The breadth of the oxen and cart took up most of the narrow alleyway, so much so, that the family had to lift crates and piles of straw out of the way in order to pass between the buildings. The blank façade of this particular building was interrupted by only two small windows, one several meters above the other. Below, at ground level, there was a narrow, wooden door with a small loop of rope for the handle. No lanterns burned in the street, only the moonlight reflecting off the upper portion of the building provided light for the alley below.

Theodorus knocked on the door and waited for an answer. After a second knock, a voice called out from the lower of the two small windows. A man perhaps a bit older than Theodorus leaned through the window clutching a lantern, holding it out to the side so he could see below. "What do you want at this hour of night?" he inquired testily.

Theodorus introduced his family and Carpathimos and explained their story, what sent them from the road high in the hills. The man and the lantern disappeared, only to reappear in the doorway. He invited them graciously into his home. To Theodorus he said, "The animals and cart will have to be moved to the street behind this building where there is more room for others to pass."

When Carpathimos started moving the cart, Theodorus grabbed him by the arm. "No, Carpathimos," he said gently. "This is my cart and these are my animals. I will move them. You belong inside."

Theodorus got the oxen moving and disappeared around the corner of the building, the children fast asleep in the back. Carpathimos nodded at the man with the lantern and entered the building, ducking through the low and narrow doorway. The inside was nearly as stark as the outside of the building, although it was furnished with a short wooden table, four chairs, and a few shelves holding various sizes of clay pots, plates and cups. Near the back of the room, a bed was positioned alongside the wall. Near its head stood a long wooden ladder reaching through a square hole in the ceiling.

Dositheos and his sisters stood on the opposite side of the table from Carpathimos, while the man who let them enter stood in the middle of the ground floor next to a woman of the same approximate age. An elderly man lay asleep on the bed.

Dositheos began the introductions, stating his name. Nodding his head at his sister and the wife of his brother, he then gave their names. He saved Carpathimos for last.

Their host bowed and introduced himself. "I am Achim, and this is my wife Abby. You are welcome to stay with us, but there is only room on the floor. Our son and his family are asleep above us."

"And is this your father, Achim?" Dositheos inclined his head toward the old man in the bed.

Achim nodded. "His name is Yaakov."

Dositheos and Carpathimos exchanged glances. The man looked very old. "Does Yaakov have two brothers, Achim?"

"No longer, I am afraid." Achim sighed. "Yaakov's brother Yaal died a month ago. My father has been sick in bed ever since. Their elder brother, Alexander, died over a year ago."

Carpathimos felt hopeful. He knew Elijah's grandfather had also been named after the young Macedonian conqueror and they would have been about the same age. Theodorus came inside, having prepared the animals and the children for the night as best he could. He joined them around the table and Dositheos introduced him to their hosts. They stayed up late into the night, telling Achim the story of the books Carpathimos carried.

"Can your father read the Greek words?" Dositheos asked.

Achim shook his head. "I am sorry, but he cannot. He only speaks the old language that he learned as a boy in Jerusalem. The rest of my family speak the common language, but my wife and I speak Hebrew to him. I never learned to read Greek. I am sorry. You have traveled a long way."

Carpathimos stared at the floor, gripping the sling of his leather pack tightly in frustration. Dositheos looked at him sympathetically and then asked, "Achim, do you think your father would recognize the words if he heard them as the stories he learned as a child?"

"He may." Achim shrugged his shoulders and looked to his wife for confirmation.

Abby then spoke. "Yaakov was a follower. He always listened to his brothers argue and discuss matters of importance. Alexander was the most learned of the three and often spoke of the stories in the Torah, but the brothers did not leave Jerusalem with a Torah in hand. Now Yaakov has trouble remembering things. Some days he has a difficult time remembering our names. He can speak of places and events of his youth like they just happened yesterday, but the true events of yesterday he struggles to remember."

"Carpathimos, can you read and speak the words to Achim?" Dositheos suggested. "Perhaps he could then speak them to his father in Hebrew."

Carpathimos looked around at the people standing near the table and realized how hard they were trying to help him. "I can only read a few of the words. I have remembered much of the stories by listening carefully to Elijah. It might be a difficult and tedious process."

"Do you know anyone here who can read the Greek and translate the words to Yaakov?" Theodorus asked Achim.

Achim looked again at his wife, thinking, then he nodded. "Yes! There is a smart man who lives nearby. He keeps the records for the city. I believe he can help us."

"Go get him, Achim," Abby insisted.

Achim looked at his father resting quietly on the bed. "We will wait until morning. He will be fresh from a good sleep and I will catch Jacob before he leaves his house for the day."

In the morning, Carpathimos awoke to the voices of three small boys who were staring at him lying on the floor.

"Let us go, children," said Abby. "Leave the man alone. Come along." Abby escorted her daughter-in-law and mother of the children from the house, with the boys between them. It was early, but already sunlight shone on the street in front of the house.

Carpathimos stretched and crossed the floor to open the door. Sticking his head outside, he saw the eastern sun rising. In daylight, he could tell that the house was situated on the outskirts of the city.

"Good morning," announced a young man standing near the table behind Carpathimos. "I am Teman, son of Achim and Abby and father to the boys who woke you." Carpathimos smiled and bowed slightly to the young man. "You are the one they call Carpathimos?"

"Yes. Thank you for allowing us to stay here last night." Carpathimos was loathe to awaken Dositheos and his sister, who were asleep near the ladder. Theodorus and his wife had spent the night outside with the animals and the children.

"My father left early this morning to wait for Jacob outside his house. It was my wife, Ava, who left with my mother and the children just now. I apologize for allowing them to wake you," Teman said.

"There is no need to apologize. I was ready to get up for the day."

Teman said that his father had explained their guests' mission and what Carpathimos carried with him. "He should be home any moment with Jacob."

Dositheos and his sister joined them by the table under which Carpathimos had slept. When Teman's grandfather awoke, he was alarmed by the strangers standing in the house. Teman sat down with his grandfather on the bed and calmed him while the three strangers stepped out of the house and pulled the door shut behind them. In the cool morning air, they huddled against the wall as the sunlight splashed their bodies with a warm radiant glow. Theodorus and his family came around the corner. At the same time, Achim and Jacob approached from the other direction. They gathered in a large circle and made introductions to Jacob after they wished one another a pleasant morning.

"Let us go inside," Achim said to Jacob and Carpathimos. "Perhaps the rest should stay back, so we do not cause my father more concern." The others agreed and elected to walk down to the markets to find something to eat.

Carpathimos followed Achim and Jacob inside and the three men sat down at the table. Retrieving the leather bag from the floor, Carpathimos pulled out the tightly rolled books and flattened them out as best he could before sliding them over to Jacob, who sat across from him. Jacob began to read the parchment silently, under the effulgent light cast by tall candles Achim arranged the night before in preparation for this event.

After several minutes, Jacob observed, "This looks very detailed. The authors must have spent a very long time creating this. Do you think your father will be able to recognize whether or not this is real?"

"There is only one way to find out." Achim sounded nervous. "Perhaps there are other elders in these houses, too, who may be able to confirm this document." Carpathimos could hear the apprehension in his voice.

Achim stood and the others followed him to the back of the house, where Teman was sitting on the bed next to his grandfather.

"Father. Father," said Achim softly. "It's Nunee, Father."

"Nunee?" Jacob raised an eyebrow.

Teman rose from the bed to make way for the guests. "It's an old nickname my grandfather gave my father. They still use it after all these years. I have no idea where it came from and neither of them can remember either."

Yaakov stirred and called out, reaching for Achim, who was kneeling at his side. When Yaakov started to rise, Achim helped him to a sitting position on the edge of the bed.

"Father, it is Achim. My friend Jacob is here with me. He wants to read something to you. Will you listen?" Achim drew a blanket over the old man's shoulders. The old man didn't respond, but he sat quietly, perhaps waiting. Achim sat next to his father and put his arm around him. He nodded for Jacob to begin.

Carpathimos leaned against the wall, feeling weak with anxiety. Teman collected the books from the table and pulled a chair over to the bed. He set the chair down for Jacob, who rested the books on his lap. Teman then moved a second pair of candles to a small table next to the bed. With the light now pouring in through the windows, the lower level was sufficiently illuminated, so Jacob could read the written word.

Gently, Jacob opened the books to the beginning and started to read from the first of the books of Moshe – *Bereishit or* Genesis. Other than Jacob's voice filling the room with the stories of the Hebrews, there was nothing but absolute silence. Jacob read for an hour, until Achim held out his hand, catching Jacob's attention and making him aware of something extraordinary. The men looked at Yaakov's solemn face, watching the tears flow over his cheeks before disappearing into his long white beard.

"Father, are you all right?" Achim pulled his father close to him, with his arm extended over the old man's shoulders.

Beginning slowly at first, the old man spoke in his native tongue. Only Achim, Teman, and Jacob could understand him. Carpathimos had to wait for the translation, but he had a hunch the words were just what he had hoped for. "These are Alexander's words," Yaakov said. "These are the words he spoke so eloquently to Yaal and me for many years. Please continue, Jacob."

Jacob resumed reading as Yaakov listened intently. At one point, the old man asked him to stop so he could make water. He stretched out on the bed afterwards, but he insisted that Jacob continue to read.

"He has not been this calm for a long time. He has found peace," Achim whispered.

"The stories must bring him back to a time with his brothers," Teman said.

Achim nodded.

Several hours later, Yaakov was sleeping, and Jacob joined the men at the table.

"What do we do now?" asked Teman quietly.

The four men looked at one another and then three of them looked expectantly at Jacob, who rubbed his face in his hands. "I think we need to ask the elders to review this, as well. I have been thinking about this and I believe at least two elders may remember the old Hebrew text very completely. They both reside in this part of the city. With your permission, Carpathimos, I would like to take this to them. Like Yaakov, I will have to read it to them, for they do not read the common writing." Jacob asked his listeners, "Will you wait for me to return?"

Carpathimos raised his hand in acknowledgement. Achim then asked, "Carpathimos, I have noticed that the last portion of the books has been destroyed. The last few leaves are just flakes of ash," he said. "Do you have any more of the books? Or do you know how much is missing?"

Carpathimos ran his hands through his hair. "Most of the last book is gone. It was completely lost in a fire the day my friend Elijah died trying to save my life. He called that book the *Devarim.*"

"I am not sure if the document will be as important to the elders if the whole text isn't here, but perhaps they will be able to replace most of it with their combined knowledge and memory," Jacob said.

Carpathimos closed his eyes and then he started to recite the book of Devarim from memory. He began slowly at first and then gradually he picked up speed. Jacob and the others stared at him, their mouths held open in astonishment. Jacob listened carefully to the language until he interrupted excitedly.

"This man knows the last book! You know it completely, Carpathimos! Come, we must go together so that I can write this down as you speak it. Together we will take the text to the elders. If they agree, I will begin making copies for the people who have lost the old language. Once again, these lost people, our neighbors and friends, will have the words of their Lord!"

Days later, Carpathimos met Theodorus and his family at the home of Achim. They peppered him with questions, excited to hear what the elders had thought of the books. "What will happen now?" Theodorus asked.

"The elders have listened to Jacob read for hours," their friend told them. "He read from the books through the night and into the next day. Stopping him now and then, the elders asked Jacob to read from certain places." Carpathimos grinned at his audience, who could sense his relief. "They seemed pleased to hear exactly what they had expected to hear. Even the fifth book, as I recited it, was pleasing to them."

Jacob had been charged with creating complete copies of the text for distribution to the elders in Byzantion and for the leaders of the Jewish people throughout the north, so the people could learn the Word of God in their common tongue. The elders expressed their gratitude to Carpathimos. "These teachings will help us guide our people back to Yahweh!" they told him. "Our people will leave the wretched places many have gone, and they will unite once again in a common purpose."

Carpathimos told Achim that Jacob promised that his first copy would be a gift to his father.

"Teman and I will need to learn how to read," Achim said, smiling broadly. "A good reason indeed!"

Later that day, Carpathimos and the family of Theodorus left Byzantion on the long and winding road to the east. They intended to cross into the land of Antiochus, ruled by the Seleucid king, and then angle south and west around the Gulf of Propontis, toward the lands of Lydia and Ionia. They had been witness to a most amazing story, which each would tell for decades to come, passing that story from generation to generation. Carpathimos knew his journey had honored the life and work of his friend Elijah. He still felt the pain of this loss, but he believed that Elijah could rest in peace, his duty completed.

# Chapter XXIV

———

O N ANY GIVEN day atop a certain sun-soaked roof overlooking the docks and harbor of the city of Byzantion, men enjoyed drink and conversation while they watched the ships traveling through the Golden Horn, a natural harbor within the only passage between the Aegean and Black Sea. On this roof, men might trade goods with merchants or buy and sell commodities. In fact, it was not uncommon to find men making money selling people here. Throughout the northeast it was known as the busiest and most popular mercantile without walls.

One day, two merchants needed a place to store goods until a ship from Egypt came to port to haul it away. While they waited, they sat on stools on the roof. The owner had used the building as both a stable and warehouse for goods coming off ships or about to be loaded onto the ships. The owner of this simple little building had a penchant for drink, and he hid his liquor from his wife on the roof. That day, he shared his liquor with the two visitors. Before long, they were joined by the owner's friend, who ultimately purchased the men's merchandise. The enterprising owner soon realized that his squat little warehouse was a fine place of business, particularly because it commanded a fine view of the harbor. This would be Lucius's rendezvous point.

Lucius stood on the deck of a heavily laden merchant ship as it drifted toward the pier. He scanned the people along the docks and up the streets that stretched onto the hillside of Byzantion, eventually identifying the infamous little mercantile of which he had been told. It was a curious oddity in a city so diverse in culture and activity, yet to him, it seemed the ideal place to spend the next few days waiting for Yzebel to arrive. He was certain that he had arrived before her and Lucius was hopeful the wait would not be too long. His only concern was his reception. Lucius was Roman, after all, and he had not intended to separate her from her father. He had tried to make a deal with the pirates for the safe passage of both Yzebel and her father, but the captain had not been interested in extracting more than Yzebel. The price for her father was more than Lucius dared pay.

The sudden jolt meant his ship met the wooden pier. Crewmen rushed to secure the large ship in place, distracting Lucius from his thoughts. He gathered his things and waited for his departure. The usual assortment of deckhands and sailors busied themselves with the care of the ship and her contents; the few travelers, like Lucius, had paid for their passage on board. They left the ship uneventfully and made their way up the pier to the docks before disappearing into the city.

Lucius went in search of an inn where he could rest and clean himself after the long sea voyage. He had expected to find only a common room with a space on the floor and a shared area to wash, though with a bit of extra money he might be able to secure a private room. After establishing his quarters, he planned to investigate the mercantile, to see if it would be an appropriate spot to watch for Yzebel. Of course, for the right price, he knew it would be.

The inn Lucius found turned out to be only a few hundred meters from the mercantile. To his surprise, the innkeeper told him he had a vacant private room. Lucius followed the innkeeper through the common room, past a menagerie of Byzantion's finest, and up the stairway to the rooms that ran the length of the inn. The common room hosted a chaotic display of vagabonds, whores, sailors, and beggars. Its din was unsettling to Lucius. The innkeeper showed the Roman to his room and set down a pitcher of water next to a large bowl near the bed.

"The attendant will refill your water and collect the urine once a day unless you call for her more often. The excrement must be passed in the common bath on the main floor below," the innkeeper instructed. "As you can see, there is no lock on your door. When you leave, you should carry your things with you or you can leave them at my home. While you are in your room, the bolt will lock the door from the inside. I would recommend you use it or you may find a member of that rabble downstairs with you during the night."

Lucius nodded and paid the innkeeper. "I should be on the road in a few days," he said. When the innkeeper left, Lucius bolted the door behind him and looked around at his dark little space. Lucius lit the small candle on the table and poured water from the pitcher into the bowl, so he could wash the sea spray from his face and arms. A small square of old rag hung from a peg in the wall. He smelled it before soaking it in the water. Though stained, it wasn't foul. He used it to wash the rest of his body before lying down on the bed.

The bed was too short for his frame and not nearly wide enough to roll around on, but it didn't matter. He fell asleep as fast as his head could touch the bed. The sensation of rocking back and forth as if still on board the merchant ship lingered. He hoped the feeling would leave him by morning.

Lucius awoke later than he intended, but discovered the rocking feeling of being on board the ship had gone away. So, too, had most of the rabble in the common room. The sailors were probably back on board their ships or looking for new work. The beggars and vagabonds were probably moving on or moving through the markets. As it turned out, Lucius was glad to have awakened late. He could take advantage of the baths without the attention of others.

Unfortunately, the baths didn't compare to Rome's baths. These were simply a row of holes cut in a long wooden plank on which one would sit to defecate. Below the wooden seat was a long trough to catch the excrement; presumably someone was charged with cleaning it out occasionally. The stench was overwhelming. The air was thick with the smell of urine and feces. His eyes burned while he sat, trying to empty his bowels. He held the neck of his long tunic over his mouth and nose, but that made little difference. After completing his objective, Lucius hurried back to his room to make use of his water and bowl before leaving for the day. Closing the door to his room, he hoped that he would not need to return that night, although he knew that was merely wishful thinking.

Lucius found his way to the roof of the mercantile and spent time observing the people on the roof and the people below on the street that separated the mercantile from the docks. Nearly a dozen merchant ships were anchored outside the harbor and several others moored to the pier within. None of these fit the description of the ship he was waiting for, but one different type of ship sitting inside the mouth of the harbor caught his attention. It looked like a fighting ship and it flew colors he did not recognize. When he asked the owner of the mercantile about the strange ship in the distance, he was told that it was indeed a warship. "It sails under the colors of Ptolemy, the king and self-proclaimed pharaoh of Egypt," he said.

"Why so far north?" asked Lucius.

The owner shrugged his fat round shoulders. "It is not the only ship of Ptolemy in these waters. He has sent a fleet north to support the uprising of Athens and Sparta, but now I hear that Antigonus is smashing that resistance." The fat man tried to suppress the urge to yawn. "These bothersome sailors come here to resupply occasionally and then they bide their time until they are either sunk in battle or recalled home."

Lucius bought food and drink from the portly owner and chose a seat in a corner by himself. He watched and listened to the deals being made near him. He also watched the fat owner of the mercantile when there was nothing else of interest to watch in the harbor. The man was much shorter than Lucius and moved about the roof as if the forays were agonizing to his feet. Every errand required a series of quick rasping breaths ending in prolonged musical wheezes. Lucius observed him closely. The owner's appearance hinted that he had just run up to the roof from the end of the pier, though Lucius was fairly certain the man had never run that far in his entire life. His hands were large and thick structures, his fingers unusually short and round. He carried bowls and glasses frequently, but Lucius was skeptical if even half of the containers made it to their destination without slipping from the man's paws or crashing to the floor in the process. On his feet, the man wore something resembling woven sacks; they were as wide as they were long. Lucius surmised that he hadn't been able to wear sandals for years, for the man's ankles were too large to tie them. In fact, the bones of his ankles had been replaced with tissue that lay stacked in rolls over the top of his feet which was not unlike the roll of flesh that swung from the base of the man's jawbone. The skin on his legs was stained and spotted a dark brown and weeped tears of yellow fluid into the sacks around his feet. Periodically, the fat man sat and rested near the low wall that surrounded the roof. There he could lift his feet and rest them upon two wooden crates. As he rested, he slept.

Toward evening, the people dispersed, and the deals came to an end. Lucius found himself alone on the roof, enjoying the quiet of the city and the sunset. He sipped wine from the wooden cup he had used all day. The cool evening breeze soothed his lungs and brought a calm to him he hadn't felt in a long time. He dreaded going back to the inn, weaving his way through what he suspected would be another unpleasant gathering in the common room. He tried to put the foul thought from his mind and focus instead on the sounds of the breeze and the singing of birds, to ease him back to that calming peace. However, his thoughts were interrupted by booming rattles emanating from the fat man behind him.

The man was again sound asleep, his feet up on the crates and arms folded over his chest. His fat fingers were clasped at the center of his rotund body. His head had dropped back against the brick wall behind him and he drew in breaths that rattled so loudly the very building holding them up might come crashing down. Lucius watched him struggle for breath for several cycles, until the struggle stopped. Lucius waited, staring expectantly at the fat man and then rose to shake his shoulder. But the man had apparently died in his sleep—a death far more peaceful than those Lucius had seen during his years as a soldier.

Lucius scrutinized the man more carefully. He noticed the movements of the man's hands. The fingers still rose up and down almost imperceptively, thanks to the action of the man's chest. Yet no air was moving through the bellows until air did move once again. The man winced, and Lucius jolted, stepping back in surprise. As air rushed into the sonorous cavern of the fat man's chest, the booming rattles of his breathing resumed. The man had apparently not died or, as Lucius worried, he had died again and again, over and over.

Reassured by the repetitive nature of these pauses and subsequent recoveries of breath, Lucius shook his head and proceeded out of the mercantile, to spend another long night in the inn.

Two more days and nights came and went. Lucius began to question the logic of the routine he had established. He once again found his seat in the corner of the rooftop mercantile, where he examined the ships in the harbor as he consumed his daily breakfast of pigeon eggs, spice cakes, and an assortment of fruits. The fat man now joined him in his corner until the usual customers assembled. Lucius had grown oddly attached to the obese man, appreciating his company and discovering how much the man really knew about the goings-on in Byzantion.

On this particular morning, Lucius noticed that the warship of Ptolemy had gone, and a new ship sat in the harbor, flying another set of colors high above its deck. Lucius's companion confirmed it to be one of the few ships of Antigonus that ever sailed into Byzantion. Antigonus commanded a small fleet but he now controlled the forests north of the Strymon River Valley. "And his fleet is growing," his companion told Lucius.

The Roman senator continued to watch the small warship as his large companion left to mingle with the men now arriving for the day's buying and selling and drinking. The warship looked more weathered than a newly built warship should look. In fact, the timber planks lining its hull showed damages that could have only resulted from battles against forces wielding weapons that hurled flame, iron, and tar. Lucius studied the odd little ship, his mind considering its possibilities.

The warship was a small trieme, which was common enough among Greek, Roman, and Carthaginian navies. However, the more Lucius thought about it, the more he realized that this was no Macedonian ship. When the rowboat dropped into the water from the deck of the ship, Lucius knew precisely what this ship was—Cyprian's one-masted galley.

Lucius watched the rowboat slowly maneuver into the harbor. It carried six people toward the pier, four rowing the boat and two individuals facing one another in the bow. Lucius stood, leaving three coins on the table where he had been spending his days, paying both for his breakfast and the attention of his new fat friend. He left the mercantile and descended onto the streets of the city, making his way to the pier. When he arrived on the pier, he found a man and woman standing together near the end.

The man was indeed Cyprian. Lucius had once known him as a good soldier and loyal Roman, but he had been a young man then, with no family and few friends. He served his time under the command of General Lucius, but following the final battle, he had disappeared. Recently an acquaintance of the senator mentioned seeing Cyprian resurface upon the deck of a ship he had stolen from the Carthaginians off the coast of Sicily. He had been celebrated in Rome, initially, until he again disappeared with the ship and a crew. This did not sit well with the leaders of Rome, for they naturally assumed he had stolen it for them. Lucius had reserved judgment. When his need arose, he used his ample connections to get word of his mission to Cyprian.

The woman was at least two decimeters taller than Cyprian and nearly as tall as Lucius himself. She had light-brown skin and black hair pulled neatly behind her head, wound into a ball. Above high arching cheekbones, Yzebel's penetrating dark eyes probed deeply into Lucius's eyes as he approached her. Her confidence was in full display. She stood tall and strong, her feet spread slightly, and her fists clenched at her sides. She wore no smile, but her face seemed kind and gentle. Despite her defensive stance, Lucius hoped that she held no deep-seated animosity against him.

Cyprian initiated the conversation, as the tension on the pier was palpable. "General Lucius, or shall I say, Senator Lucius, forgive me. I present to you Yzebel Gisgon."

Lucius nodded to Cyprian, then smiled at Yzebel. He bowed his head slightly in her honor. "Please forgive the way in which you were brought here, Yzebel Gisgon. I mean you no harm. I had hoped to bring your father as well, but I was not able to arrange for the passage of—"

"My father is dead," interrupted Yzebel, her face expressionless.

Lucius glanced quickly to Cyprian. He explained, "Soldiers were already marching on her home when we extracted Yzebel, Lucius. We moved as quickly as we could to get the woman out unnoticed. Her farm and the rest of her people, including her father, were destroyed by the Romans."

Lucius sighed and spoke gently to the young woman. "I am very sorry for your loss, Yzebel. Losing someone you love leaves a hole inside you that will never again be full."

"What do you want with me, Roman?" Yzebel snapped.

"A man by the name of Carpathimos cares for you and worries about you. When I learned where you lived, I knew what fate might await you. I did what I could to remove you from the path of the Roman troops. I hope that you and I will travel together to find Carpathimos. We both wanted to bring you out of harm's way." Lucius hesitated, then added, "If that is not what you desire, then you are free to return, and I will pay for your passage."

"Why would I trust you, a Roman senator by the name of Lucius?" Yzebel asked. "And how did you get this information from Carpathimos?"

"I understand your confusion, Yzebel," Lucius said. "When you knew Carpathimos, he most likely wanted me dead. In fact, that was his intention when he came to Rome to find me. If he could not have been convinced of my innocence in his fate, then I would have accepted his anger and let him kill me. However, the truth came out, due to certain cataclysmic events that night, and he was witness to them. I am happy to say that he is my son once again."

Yzebel's fists relaxed. She shifted to a less confrontational stance. Cyprian looked back and forth between Yzebel and Lucius, and then said, "I have known the senator for many years. He has always been a man of honor, Yzebel. You can trust his word."

Yzebel studied Cyprian's eyes, then accepted the pirate's words. She nodded at Lucius, who gave a sigh of relief and smiled.

"Now, if you both will excuse me," stated Cyprian, "I would like to sail my ship out of this narrow harbor before I become trapped in it."

Lucius laughed and thanked Cyprian for his help. As the pirate captain descended to the rowboat, Lucius called after him, "Under which colors will you sail, Cyprian?"

"Whichever colors suit me this day, General Lucius! Whichever colors suit me!" He grinned and saluted his former commander.

Lucius chuckled before turning his attention back to Yzebel. She was watching Cyprian and his men with a charismatic smile. Carpathimos was right. She really is a lovely woman, thought Lucius.

The senator and the farmer's daughter walked together along the pier and into the city, heading toward the markets. Lucius was hungry and guessed she was too and he wanted to gather supplies before leaving Byzantion. Yzebel was quiet as they walked, so Lucius told her of his plan. When she did not reply, he asked, "I was not expecting you to speak

Greek, Yzebel. I had asked Cyprian to stay to help translate my words to you, but that was clearly not necessary. How do you know Greek?"

"My father was from Tyre. He taught me the language of his family," Yzebel said, her face showing grief at the mention of her father. "And you, senator of Rome, which colors do you serve?"

Lucius stopped moving. "Call me Lucius, Yzebel. I have shed my role and my allegiance to Rome. My only purpose now is to live out my days with Carpathimos and my grandson Lucia. I hope you will meet them both very soon."

Yzebel smiled and, in his relief, Lucius returned her smile. "Come, Yzebel, we have much to learn about one another and I am hungry. You must be, also. Let me feed you and then we can prepare for our long journey."

The pair broke bread together at a stall in the market, where they could find a private spot to relate how each had come to know Carpathimos. In time, they had shared enough to compare notes about the warrior and even laugh about his characteristic mannerisms. Later, Lucius purchased both of them another pair of footwear and another satchel to carry changes of clothing. He also purchased another leather vessel for carrying water. He looked over a pile of tunics, some with hoods. "Good for rain," he said. Yzebel nodded her approval of one hooded cloak Lucius held up for her to see. Then she turned her attention to the people in the street, intrigued by the mixture of races passing by in front of her. She had never before visited a city.

Neither one paid any attention to the man who entered the shop after them, and so neither noticed that he was watching Lucius while he casually moved about the shop, pretending to browse through the merchandise. The man wore a dirty brown tunic hanging nearly to the ground. The large hood was drawn over his head, so that his face was covered in darkness. Lucius sensed the presence of someone watching him, but he only saw a hooded figure bent over a table of colorful blankets. Lucius stared at him momentarily and then selected two hooded cloaks the right size for Yzebel and for him.

As he gathered his new items and prepared to find his coins to pay the

merchant, he listened as the store owner asked the hooded figure if he needed assistance. There was no answer. The figure left quietly, brushing quickly
past Lucius before hurrying into the street. Lucius sidestepped the man as
he moved by.

Perhaps it had been something instinctual or perhaps something more
primitive that still lingered inside him from his combat training so long ago,
but he moved out of arm's reach of the hooded figure. Lucius thought that
he saw a glint of polished blade in the man's hand, but he couldn't be certain. Perhaps the man had stolen something from the shop, although Lucius
didn't see anything resembling polished metal on the tabletops. The senator
watched the man as he disappeared into the crowd. That's when he noticed
the man's feet.

The man had been wearing thick-soled caligae, a heavy military san-
dal with a latticework of leather straps tied neatly around the ankles, each
joint of leather held together by brass tacks. These uniquely Roman and
expensive sandals caught Lucius's attention because of their contrast with
the worn and disheveled condition of the man's hooded tunic.

Yzebel looked over to Lucius and then followed his gaze through the
crowd, making note of his air of concern. "Is something wrong, Lucius?"
she asked, catching his attention as she approached him.

Lucius shook his head and then smiled at Yzebel. "Nothing. Come! Let
us begin our search for my grandson!"

# Chapter XXV

———

CARPATHIMOS AND DOSITHEOS stared in silence at the small wooden sign that marked the fork in the road. Although the sign was windswept and ragged, the names carved upon its cracked and weathered face were still legible. Others before them had apparently tried to refurbish the old sign, carving the letters deeper into the dry gray wood and spelling out the names of the old cities the sign represented. The word "Sardis" occupied the left half of the sign, marking the city's place along the eastern fork of the road, while "Samos" and "Miletus" had been inscribed on the right, indicating their place along the western coast of the peninsula. The sign had likely stood on this spot for decades, its post, a hardened and winding limb, buried deep into the arid soil beneath it.

Dositheos was the first to break the awkward silence. "Here our paths diverge, my friend. But perhaps within our lifetimes we will again meet and share new stories of our lives."

Carpathimos smiled at his friend as Theodorus and the rest of the family joined them in front of the sign. He held out his large, strong hand and shook the men's hands. He bowed to the women and tousled the children's hair before he thanked them. "I may never have been able to cross the bridge or deliver the books without your help," he said quietly. "I am forever in your debt."

"You have no such debt to pay, Carpathimos," Theodorus said. "I have come to realize that if I had refused you at the bridge, the books of Moshe may never have reached the ears of our people. Now we wait for that Word to spread. I am confident it will. I believe there was a reason we met that day at the bridge. Dositheos was correct in believing just that. I am proud to know you and to have journeyed with you."

Carpathimos smiled warmly and repeated his goodbyes to each member of the group. They felt like his own family now. He lifted the children into his arms, hugged them, and wished them all safe passage to their new lives along the shore of the great sea. With a backward wave, he started down the road toward Sardis, the great city of Lydia. He was alone again, but happy.

Founded by the Hittites one thousand years earlier, Sardis stood within the province of Lydia, but had passed into the subordinate rule of the Seleucids, the family of one of Alexander's skillful generals, Antiochus. This massive walled city overlooked the river Hermos and the expansive, fertile lands of the valley that stretched from the broad shoulders of Mount Tmolus as far as one's eyes could see.

A narrow bridge spanned the wide Hermos, but here the river ran calmly. Carpathimos stood at the side of the river and surveyed the broad valley toward the city nearly three kilometers away. Just above and behind the city, within the foothills of Tmolus, perched the citadel of Sardis, occupied now by the army of Antiochus. From their position high in the foothills, no invader could possibly enter the valley to surprise the city.

Golden sand and pebbles could be seen shining on the bottom of the river. Stripping off his sandals and dirty tunic, he slid into the cool water, which rose to his chest when he sat on the firm river bottom. Tipping back, Carpathimos dunked his head into the water, pulled in a breath, and let his face drop below the surface. The gentle current bathed his hair and covered his face when he plunged beneath its surface. Opening his eyes, he peered through the clear water at the blue sky above. He felt excitement building within him in anticipation of the reunion with his sister and son. He also sensed a pang of apprehension, fearing that he might not find them or that his son would not remember him.

He could imagine how imposing he might appear to such a small child. He was not the gentle man his own father had been, always smiling and humming away his carefree days. Carpathimos had been hardened by the things he had seen and by the wills of the men who formerly controlled him. He felt as battered and weather-beaten as the old wooden sign at the fork in the road. Like the post, his feet were cracked and hardened, made heavy over the years by the weight of soil heaped upon them as man tried to smother him. But enough of that.

Crawling up onto the bank, Carpathimos let the sun dry him and lull him to sleep, and he allowed himself the privilege of a much-needed rest.

When he awoke and started off over the bridge, the sun was still high in the sky. Approaching the aged city, Carpathimos strode among the many farmhands and families making their way in from the fields throughout the valley. Walking freely through the open gates, they entered a city that loomed large. As he entered its outskirts, Carpathimos soon realized that he was as lost as he had ever been.

Fortunately, enough light remained to allow him to wander through the city and get his bearings. He hoped that he could find the markets and learn more about the remnants of his mother's family. He didn't find answers before darkness descended, but morning in Sardis brought with it new hope.

Carpathimos had found a pile of wool stacked behind a market stall and slept there. He rose with the sun, before he surprised the merchant who owned the wool. He ambled through the central market area, which seemed as wide and long as the island on which he had grown up. Slowly, the people of Sardis began to populate the many streets that intersected the market.

Children ran about, playing games they seemed to invent as he watched them, their laughter distinct above the noises of the market, much the way sound travels unimpeded over the water. Gradually the many shops and stands opened for business. The din of bartering and trading, buying and selling, consumed the sounds of the children's laughter, along with any other sound once unique or identifiable. Surrounding the market were homes whose owners, too, were selling their wares: crafts and clothing, blankets and chairs, foods and cooking utensils.

The market's stands and shops were organized in concentric circular rows that extended outward from the center. Spaces were left between stands, so the streets could intersect the circles. This way, people could come and go from the center of the market with a cart and beast of burden, if necessary.

Carpathimos wound his way slowly around the circles, fascinated by the varied merchandise on display. He sampled fruits and plants he had never seen before. One merchant introduced him to something he called saffron. He ran his rough hands over intricately colored rugs and blankets, studied the clothing, and appreciated the fine leather goods. He even saw works of art, something that he had never appreciated before, thinking it impractical.

The women of the city, he noticed, were wearing the colorful clothes, which shimmered in the light as they moved. Brilliant shades of reds, yellows, blues, and purples were mixed and expertly arranged within each textile, such that when the fabric was wrapped over the body, it made the woman appear like a butterfly with folded wings.

Carpathimos was intrigued by the exchange of so many foreign goods. Customers were paying using coins he had never seen. Coins were both small and large, some dull and others shiny, but all of them made of gold. He did not recognize the heads on the coins, either, though he was never close enough to study one in depth. His pockets held bronze and a few bits of silver. He had not carried a gold coin for some time.

Listening to the merchants' conversations, he learned of a place in Sardis where these many coins were forged. The gold for these coins, he heard a merchant explain, was either mined in the mountain or taken from a river, perhaps the river Carpathimos had crossed. He couldn't be sure. He also learned that the women's dresses shimmered because gold had been woven throughout the fabric.

Catching a whiff of something more familiar, Carpathimos found his way to tables of brightly colored fish. Most were fairly large, about the length of his forearm, with greenish-gray bodies and yellow fins. He also saw small fish the size of his hand that had columns of vertical white stripes starting just behind their heads and extending all the way to the tails. On another fishmonger's table, he found a few very large fish with particularly tiny eyes. These were the size of the full length of his arm. Light gray, they had strange mouths, perhaps suited for feeding on the bottom. Carpathimos passed tables filled with small silver fish whose skin had a single row of black dots; these fish were more similar to the ones he had caught in the sea near his home. The sight of them was heartwarming. It drew him back to his youth and a much simpler time. He noticed the merchant was paying attention to him, so he asked from where they came.

"From the lake named Gygaean," the merchant said, while tending to a new patron. "The lake is named after King Gyges, who once reigned over this city long before the Persians."

Carpathimos smiled while he ran a finger down the back of one of the silver shads. "This one reminds me of the fish I once caught long ago."

"As it does me, Brother." A young woman had rushed up to him. Carpathimos looked in her direction, but he already knew the voice that had spoken. She launched herself upon him and his arms wrapped around her tightly as she buried her head in his chest.

"Parma!" he exclaimed. "Where did you come from? How—"

Parma sobbed into the cloth on his shoulder. "Oh, my dear brother," she choked. She pulled away to put her hands on his face. "I have come here every day for the past year, hoping to find you. I knew one day you would find your way to these tables!"

Tears trickled down over her cheeks as she once again pulled him close. Carpathimos wrapped his arms around her and pressed his cheek against the top of her head. They were reunited at last. For many minutes they clung to one another, both afraid if they let go, the other would disappear. They were too happy to notice the people pressing past them.

Parma was a tall woman with long curly brown hair. She had eyes the same color as those of Carpathimos—hazel. Her tender smile lifted her thin cheeks into soft pillows below those brilliant eyes. She was lean, yet very muscular, a feature she had not lost with the years. In time, she led Carpathimos to the edge of the market, where they could talk in relative quiet. She told him that she had learned a lot about the history of Sardis listening to the fishermen in the market every day. She had even started to help that man sell his fish once he recognized that she arrived at his stall every day, week after week, month after month.

"Are you here alone, Parma?" asked Carpathimos, anxious to find his son.

"I am, but Lucia waits for your return as eagerly as I did," Parma said. "We live near the Gygaean in a house that was once owned by Mother's aunt and uncle. We moved in with her cousin and her husband. They are watching Lucia for me."

"How far away is he?" Carpathimos could wait no longer to see his son.

"Come. I will show you." Parma grabbed Carpathimos by the hand and led him through the gates of the city. She pointed to the northwest, over the valley floor to a small ridge of hills. Just behind those hills, Carpathimos glimpsed a blue body of water. "Lucia is there, Carpathimos. The walk will take us two hours from here."

"And you come here every day?" Carpathimos asked in disbelief.

"I don't walk," she laughed, looking up at her brother before shoving an elbow into his ribs, "and I won't expect you to keep up with me."

Carpathimos laughed, then tapped his sister's foot with his own before running down the road toward the valley below. She caught up with and passed him in no time, making him laugh once again before he slowed to a brisk walk. She waited for him to catch up and they walked on together.

"We have much to learn about each other, Brother," said Parma. "Where have you been all this time?"

"I will tell you, but first I want to know more about Lucia." Carpathimos felt more nervous about reuniting with his son than he had ever felt going into battle. "Will he know me, Parma?"

"You are afraid of that, aren't you?" She touched her brother's arm. "I have been telling him about you every day of his life since you left. Every night when I come home, he asks if I found you. He gazes down the road, looking to see if you are following after me. He will know you."

"What made you decide to start looking at the market a year ago?" asked Carpathimos as he fought to banish the tears from his eyes, blinking repeatedly.

"I, too, have a child now, Carpathimos," Parma said. Her brother stopped walking. "She is fifteen months old," his sister added. Carpathimos stared at his sister with his mouth agape.

"What is her name? Who is her father?"

"Her name is Ligeia, but we call her *Bear* for fun, because she growls when she gets crabby." Parma laughed and Carpathimos heard the joy in her voice.

He chuckled, "Just like her mother, then."

Parma slapped Carpathimos playfully on the shoulder, then continued, "Ligeia's father is dead." Carpathimos felt her sadness as his own. "He was a soldier in the Seleucid army and he was killed while marching home from a battle in the east. He and his men were ambushed."

"How did you meet? When?" Carpathimos realized how many stories they needed to share.

"We met shortly after Lucia and I had arrived here. He was working as a runner in the mines when he ran into me—truly—in the market. He helped me find our family and from there we became good friends. One day we decided we wanted to be with each other forever."

"When did he join the army?"

"After I was pregnant with Ligeia. He decided he needed to provide more for us—how I wish he hadn't!" Parma's expression was somber. "He thought by joining the army he could earn more and protect us. Sadly, he never met Ligeia and he was never here to protect us."

The two walked on quietly for a while until Parma insisted on learning from Carpathimos what he had been doing and where he had been for the last two-and-a-half years. He told her everything he could remember about his accident at sea and then about Yzebel and Elijah. He described his journey to Rome and his peace with Lucius. He told her of the family he had met on the Nine Roads Bridge and how they helped him complete Elijah's work. Parma listened intently, interrupting only to ask him to describe the people in more detail.

As the road wound its way around the tip of the southernmost hills surrounding Lake Gygaean, the sun dropped in the sky and fog appeared as the cool air dropped out of the hills and mixed with the moisture over the lake.

"How much farther?" asked Carpathimos as he looked out across the still water.

"We are getting close, Carpathimos. Lucia is probably wondering where I am."

"We can run the rest of the way." Carpathimos was trying to picture his son and eager for their reunion to begin.

"Let me run on ahead," Parma suggested. She clearly had an idea. "You walk quickly but let me get ahead of you. Follow this road and you will find us."

Carpathimos nodded, confused. Until Parma disappeared into the fog, he followed her. For a while, he could hear her footsteps, but those were soon replaced by the sound of his heart as he felt it beating in his throat.

Parma slowed to a jog when she saw Lucia standing on the road in front of the small house. She slowed even more as she approached him. He asked her, as he always did, if she had found his father. This time she didn't shake her head or apologize. She stared into his dark brown eyes and reached out to tussle his hair as she passed him. He looked over his shoulder at her while she motioned behind her back up the road. Confused, the boy of nearly five years stared hard into the heavy fog descending over the road. He took one step forward. And then another. Out of the mist appeared a tall, dark figure. Lucia took another step.

The man's features were like those Parma had described. The man approaching him slowed his pace. He could see Lucia now. The father and son stared at one another for a brief moment, and then the man dropped to his knees. Lucia bolted forward. He lunged into his father's arms, clutching the man he hadn't seen since he was a toddler—but he remembered those strong arms.

Darkness fell upon them during their embrace. When a sturdy gale cut across the water and up into the hills, it wiped away the dense fog, pushing it over the land like a giant hand sweeping clear the view. The father and son looked up at the stars twinkling in the night sky. "Which one is my mother?" Lucia asked.

Carpathimos wiped the tears from his face and kissed Lucia on the forehead. Then he looked again at the sky. He found the star in the north around which all the others revolve. It twinkled at the end of the small ladle's handle. He pointed. "That one is your mother, Lucia. She will always be there to guide us."

———

"I don't care for the droll timbre the Etruscans use in these tragic performances," Domitius complained to Faustus as they departed from the play together. "They always carry on with such bathos that it makes me nauseous."

"Yes, yes, Domitius." Faustus tried to pacify his friend with a grin. "Just let it go and enjoy the day!"

The two men lingered along the busy Via Sacra toward Capitoline Hill, where they both owned homes. Faustus had talked his friend into joining him to partake of the activities along the sacred road after the Senate vote concluded earlier in the day. Domitius had agreed to join Faustus to celebrate their victory. They had procured the votes necessary to tip the decision the way Lucius had desired—to initiate a troop withdrawal from Africa before winter. The withdrawal would leave Regulus with just enough troops to hold the ground he had gained and defend against a Carthaginian response. Meanwhile, three legions would be sent home for rest and possible redistribution elsewhere.

All along the sacred road, Romans played games and enjoyed the fall weather. This road was often the setting for festivals and triumphal marches taken by victorious leaders returning from campaigns. Not so long ago, Lucius had been one of those victorious leaders. On days like this, the street was filled with throngs of people celebrating in their own ways: playing games or buying and selling everything from small trinkets to exceptional goods. Numerous women were selling themselves, for minutes at a time. Both bachelors, Domitius and Faustus observed these women, but never elected to spend their money or their time with common company. More to their style were the theatrical productions featuring renowned celebrities, travelling artists, or acting troupes from as far away as Athens.

Ascending Capitoline Hill, the men bid one another a good evening and went their separate ways, to their own homes. Faustus left the sacred road first, as he lived down the hill from Domitius and several houses removed from the Via Sacra. Domitius marched up the hill for another hundred meters before reaching his home. When he closed his door behind him, he was relieved to be alone and sequestered from the debauchery below. Removing his sandals, he rubbed his sore feet and then poured himself a glass of wine to enjoy before retiring to bed.

Sometime later, he entered his bedroom, removed his clothing, and washed the sweat and film of dust from his face and upper body over a large bowl of scented water prepared for him by his servant earlier in the evening. As he submerged his face in the cool water, he pondered the whereabouts of his good friend Lucius. Standing up and wiping his face, he realized that he was no longer alone.

The end came very quickly and from both sides. He never saw his attackers. The wounds they left were deliberate and effective. Domitius sank to the floor as the blood drained from the large vessels of his neck, evaporating his thought while extinguishing the light of life.

One street below and four houses to the east, Faustus was too exhausted to prepare himself for his bed. He rested in the small garden he kept behind his villa, sitting next to a small fire that warmed his feet while he sipped at a glass of mulsum, savoring the mixture of honey and spiced wine. The drink calmed him, and he drifted into slumber, but only briefly. His grip on the empty glass relaxed and it slipped from his hand, waking him as it bounced on the stone at his feet, cracking into pieces.

Faustus stirred and rubbed his face. As he rose to retire to his bedroom, he met two hooded figures on his path. The shadows cast upon their faces from the hoods of their capes hid their identities, but not their intentions.

Simultaneously they plunged short pugios into Faustus's chest, stealing his breath. The sharp daggers severed the tender tissues, collapsing both lungs. He dropped to his knees, clutching the sides of his chest as if to remove the daggers, but his widened eyes discovered them in the hands of his assailants. The knives were dripping his own blood onto the stonework at their feet. Slumping onto his back, the senator gulped at the air like a fish pulled from the water. His world became dark and cold and then it disappeared. Their brass-tacked military-grade sandals were the last things he saw.

# Chapter XXVI

———

LUCIA STOOD IN the bow of the boat, the fingers of his small hands wrapped over the plank-sheers, and studied his father, scrutinizing the muscles in the man's shoulders and the muscles that rippled along his back and forearms as he pulled at the net drifting behind them in the water. As the small craft rocked gently back and forth, Lucia put a hand on his own shoulder, running it over the muscles in his arms, trying to imagine how they might one day look.

Carpathimos strained to pull in the net hand over hand, until the last bit of it flopped onto the belly of their small, wooden boat. Only two small fish had come up with the net and they tossed and danced across the floor of the boat like drops of water in a scalding hot pan.

Carpathimos squatted down on his haunches and pushed his fingers through his hair to comb it back from his face. "I am afraid we must go farther from shore to find them now, Lucia," he said. "They must be gathering deeper in the water as the drought lengthens."

This had been an exceptionally dry year, as the native people had explained it to him, but the level of the lake had been receding each year for the past three. Carpathimos and Lucia had been fishing about fifty meters from the shoreline, where the water sat atop a shelf that only began to drop into deeper water another fifty meters from their position.

Carpathimos had ventured alone all over the large lake, but with Lucia aboard he didn't feel comfortable taking him so far away from shore. He remembered his adventures with his own father, although he wasn't certain how old he had been when they first left sight of the island where they lived. Here, on Lake Gygaean, Carpathimos caught more fish in the deeper water, but he had found this fishing more challenging, since both the net and the boat were small, and he hadn't yet begun to understand the movement of fish in this body of water.

When the waves pushed them closer to shore, tall reeds hindered the movement of their boat as it slid into shallow water. The tall fronds brushed against the fisherman's fingers as they ran along the plank-sheer of the boat. Suddenly Lucia stepped across the net on the floor and demanded his father's attention.

"Look, Father!" He pointed to shore.

Two people were making their way along the shoreline toward them, just down the slope from the long dirt path that ran in front of their house. Carpathimos stared at them, unsure of their identity until they got closer. Then his face broke into a delighted grin. Carpathimos took hold of the oars, twisted them into position in the oarlocks, and set the ends into the water.

Lucia looked intrigued. "Do you know them, Father?"

Carpathimos nodded.

"Who is the woman?"

"She is a friend, Lucia," Carpathimos said, rowing quickly.

"She is beautiful, like Parma." Lucia waved his arms at the strange couple approaching them.

"She is beautiful," acknowledged Carpathimos. "She is beautiful in many ways."

"And who is the old man?"

"That is your mother's father, Lucia. He is a great man. His name is Lucius."

"His name is like mine!"

Carpathimos laughed and rowed the boat eagerly to shore. As soon as it came to rest on the warm sand, Lucius came forward to grip the plank-sheer, steadying the craft. Carpathimos brought the oars over the sides glancing from his father-in-law to Yzebel. He was astounded to see them. Yzebel was beautiful, indeed. Smiling, she held out her hand, taking his as he stepped from the boat. They held each other close before Carpathimos turned to Lucius, keeping one hand on Yzebel's back and looking proudly at his son.

"Lucius, this is Lucia." Carpathimos didn't take his eyes off the general. "Lucia, meet your grandfather."

Lucius stared at the young boy, studying his little face. "I see your mother in your bright eyes, Lucia," Lucius said, his voice soft. "Did you know that she had the same nose and the same tangled hair as you when she was your age? In fact, I am quite certain that her face was just as dirty, too. Come!"

Lucius held out his hands and Lucia moved to him immediately. The grandfather lifted the boy over the side of the boat and hugged him tightly. Carpathimos and Yzebel observed the meeting between Lucia and Lucius with equal anticipation. While wrestling with, and losing, his emotions, Lucius reminisced about his daughter.

"I missed so much time with Myridia. I squandered her childhood, as you know, Carpathimos. I provided her with the best tutors and everything a girl could want. I sought to fulfill her every need, but one—me. I made a terrible mistake," Lucius admitted tearfully. "This is a second chance for me, and," Lucius gestured to Lucia, "this debt I owe your mother, I will gladly pay to you."

Lucius hugged the boy again and kissed him on the cheek before setting him down on the sand. He took Lucia's hand and they walked together along the beach toward the path home, with Carpathimos and Yzebel following closely behind.

Over the next few days, Parma and Yzebel became fast friends, as did Lucia and his grandfather. Yzebel and Carpathimos spent many hours together in the evenings discussing the things that Elijah had taught Carpathimos from the books. He liked to hear Yzebel's opinion on the stories and its teachings. By day, Carpathimos ventured into the deep water, trying to make the best of a marginal situation as the lake continued to suffer under the dry conditions. He also offered to turn Lucius into a fisherman, though it became rapidly evident that such an evolution would take much more time to accomplish. Lucius was quick to learn sailing and was exceedingly capable at tying and repairing the nets, but he lacked a certain degree of patience, a blessed quality for a fisherman. Unfortunately, as Carpathimos finally pointed out to him, fish did not follow commands like troops and were not necessarily eager to meet in battle like the enemy.

They met other fishermen on the lake, including the man from the market who told Carpathimos about the fishing banks. Even he, a life-long fisherman on Lake Gygaean, was having difficulty filling the tables at the market. In fact, he was using only one table each day now. He often fished at night too, which Carpathimos tried, but doing so reached a point of diminishing returns. Carpathimos even entered the water himself, diving like he had learned to do in his youth, to study the structure of the lake and its flora. Unfortunately, he found the lake water too murky, which meant light couldn't penetrate the deep water.

Diving into this nebulous basin was nothing like the experience of doing the same in the clear blue sea around the islands south of Greece where he had grown up. There, he would stay submerged for many minutes while he hunted for mollusks in shimmering warm water where the sun's rays reached clear to the bottom. Here it did not seem to matter how much strength the sun had, it could only illuminate the first two or three meters from the surface of the withering lake.

The winter season was coming soon, and their lake water was becoming ever more concentrated while the shore was enlarging practically every day.

More and more of the lake bottom was exposed in front of the little house and the walk to the water was getting longer and longer.

On one of these late fall days, Carpathimos and Lucius were walking back from the beached boat, trampling over the very lake bottom that Carpathimos and his son had fished over just weeks prior, when Lucius experienced that peculiar feeling seasoned soldiers acquire. Something wasn't right. Lucius scanned the beach in front and around them, from one dried clump of reeds to the next, for something or someone that didn't belong. As they approached the road, he did the same thing, scanning it in both directions. Next, he inspected the house and the small patch of territory on which it stood.

The little house was one of several, all perched on a small clearing between the ridge of hills and the road. The hills were sparsely wooded, with few scraggly fir and thin poplars. The underbrush, like the lake, was suffering from the drought, so it was not as dense as it might otherwise have been.

Reaching the house, Carpathimos ducked inside. Lucius lingered outdoors. He continued to scan the hillside behind the house. He could find nothing that hadn't been present before, but as he started to lower his head and shoulders and follow Carpathimos inside, his eye caught someone standing at the top of the ridge. Reflexively his head snapped back up. An individual wearing a hooded cloak was facing him.

Feeling for his knife, Lucius launched himself into the woods. He raced up the hillside as fast as he could. Nearing the top, he lunged from tree to tree, grasping the trunks to help pull himself along. Panting, he rounded a small escarpment and stepped onto a tiny footpath that ran along the back of the ridge. He ran to the east and then turned and ran back the other way, searching both slopes for the man he had seen watching them. He slowly spun around and around, vigilant, expecting an attack from behind. But none came. He waited. No one came.

Walking back down the hill, he tried to rationalize his behavior. Why did he keep seeing a hooded man and why did he suspect he was being hunted? Why was he having these visions? He did not want to raise suspicion in Carpathimos, so he kept his own anxiety to himself. After all, he had only experienced the hooded man once, in faraway Byzantion. And once here. Moving forward, he made a promise to himself to forget about the man in the brown cloak and enjoy his new-found freedom.

Several days later, on a clear night under the stars, Carpathimos floated upon the open water, searching for anything to fill his net. He was growing desperate, as was the fisherman from the market. They had agreed a few days before to join forces and share their catches. Both men would fish all night in their separate boats and then take turns during the day, when fishing was usually worse. That time off gave each man opportunities to rest and mend nets.

Parma and Yzebel offered to do the selling in the market so the fishermen could continue fishing without spending much time away from their boats. Parma sometimes brought her daughter and Lucia along to the market, although Lucia often asked to stay with his grandfather and the elder aunt and uncle of the house.

This morning was Carpathimos's turn to come ashore, rest, and make repairs, while the other fisherman stayed on the water. The oarlock on Carpathimos's fishing boat had cracked and loosened, so he took his time coming in, gingerly rowing the boat without applying undue torque on the fragile oarlock. He planned to remove it from the boat and heat the metal, so he could beat it back into shape before refastening it in place. He was tired and discouraged about catching only a few fish during the night.

Parma and Yzebel usually left in the early morning after he returned, so they could carry the fish with them to the city. Today, Carpathimos had told them, they could leave with the other fisherman's catch if he wasn't back in time. He didn't wish to hurry and risk ripping off the oarlock completely.

At the house, Lucia and his grandfather awakened and shared breakfast, then began their new daily ritual: learning to read and write and calculate problems. Lucius was far more patient teaching Lucia how to read and write than Lucia was about learning, but they both enjoyed their time together. Under his grandfather's tutelage, Lucia was reading and writing some Greek and he had started tackling more complicated words. Lucius even had him learning Latium, the language of the Romans.

The women left at dawn. About an hour later, Lucius looked out through the doorway, concerned about Carpathimos, since he would normally be off the water by this time of the morning on his free day. He peered over the water but couldn't see the boat. Lucius decided to give Lucia some math problems to occupy the boy while he walked to the water's edge.

Soon after stepping from the house, Lucius felt for his knife. It wasn't there. He remembered leaving it on the small table that the family shared for meals. He hesitated only briefly. Shaking off the foolish notion of being attacked, he continued walking.

Nearing the road, he heard footsteps on the soft dirt behind him. At first, he expected to see Lucia sneaking up on him, so Lucius didn't turn—until he realized that the footsteps were too heavy to be made by his grandson. He whirled around, braced for the blow.

The hooded figure lunged at him, knocking him onto the hard-packed surface of the road. He cringed as he rolled and leaped to his feet just as the knife cut across his shoulder. His shoulder and good timing saved his neck, or his lung.

As Lucius sprang onto his feet, the man lunged again. Lucius stepped aside at the last possible moment, knocking the man out of the way. However, Lucius was suffering from a gash on his chest. He winced at the burning sensation, which felt like a bolt of lingering lightning. But he flexed his torso, put up his fists, and prepared for his attacker's next move.

As Carpathimos rowed slowly through the calm morning water, he was unaware of the battle that raged on the road. Casually, he tipped his head to the side to listen for Lucia. What he heard didn't make sense to him. He twisted his head and then saw Lucius fighting for his life. Lucius was crouched defensively as a man wearing a hooded cape circled him, knife in hand.

Carpathimos spun back around and put all his power into the oars, driving them hard into the water and sending them back through the air furiously, for another slice at the lake. Several strokes were all the oarlock could take. It tore from the hull with a crack as the wood splintered. The inertia of his throw sent Carpathimos to the bottom of the boat. He stood and dove into the water, coming up a few meters away and grabbing as much air as he could hold. He threw his arms and legs into motion, driving himself through the water faster than ever before.

Lucius endured several more glancing blows before Carpathimos reached the beach. The older man had managed to rip the hood from the man's head, to look upon his face. Although he was not clean-shaven, he had maintained the cropped hair of a Roman soldier. He wore brass-tacked sandals, the long straps of which wound around the man's ankles to the base of the calves. Under the cloak, the man wore the same chest plate and bronze waist belt Lucius himself had worn for so many years. Lucius did not recognize him, but he identified him as Red Guard.

The younger soldier was fast and strong, but perhaps too eager. Lucius had decades of experience in combat and the patience to wait for a mistake, but he was wounded and tiring fast. As the two men circled one another, Lucia stepped from the doorway, calling out for Lucius. His voice fell silent when he saw his grandfather and another man on the road in an intensely vicious struggle.

"Lucia, get back in the house!" roared Lucius harshly, never taking his eyes from his assailant.

Lucia couldn't move. Fear gripped him and wouldn't let go. Just as Carpathimos splashed onto the sand, Lucia ran for the woods on the hill. Carpathimos slogged through the wet sand, picking up speed as the ground became firmer and dry beneath his long strides. His muscles burned like fire, but he pushed hard, driven by the fear of losing both his son and the man that he had come to know as a father.

Charging up the beach and then the bank to the road, he could tell that Lucius was out of time. He was bleeding and exhausted. Lucius had likely gotten in some hard hits of his own, but each one may have cost him a slash from the blade.

The other man was facing away from Carpathimos, who had to keep his momentum in order to win by surprise. Lucius hollered as if enraged, like a cornered feral dog. He did it not out of fear but by intent, for he was stealing both his attacker's attention and the man's ability to hear the approaching warrior nearing him.

Carpathimos dove after his foot hit the compact soil of the road and he slammed into the back of the man's legs, twirling the attacker's feet high over his head. Carpathimos rolled and skidded to a stop where Lucius had been standing. When he spun around, Lucius leaped through the air, landing upon his attacker only a blink of an eye after the man's head hit the ground. Lucius shattered the man's jaw with his fist. The force of the impact drove his knuckles through the bone of the ramus. His second blow smashed the man's windpipe.

Carpathimos spotted the bloody blade held tightly within the grasp of the man's right hand. With fingers and feet clawing at the ground, Carpathimos willed his limbs to pounce catlike while watching the hand force the blade through the air in a crimson arc. Its intended destination was Lucius's chest. Carpathimos dove in time to catch the man's wrist in a vice-like grip. The blade tip punctured the skin just below the axilla, but Lucius rolled away.

Carpathimos took control of the knife as Lucius threw himself onto the man's belly and gripped his ears in his hands. "Who are you?" Lucius growled through gritted teeth.

The man's chest billowed, sucking in a rasping, whistling column of air until there was enough force within the man's chest to drive that air back out through his crushed and swollen airway. In that same rasping wheeze, the man glared at Lucius and warned, "Your friends are dead and more like me will come."

Lucius stared at the young Red Guardsman and repeated the words in his head. He reached over and grabbed the knife from Carpathimos, then slit the soldier's throat, spilling his blood into the dirt. Lucius stared at the young man's eyes as his wheezing breaths came to a quick end. Panting fiercely, Lucius slowly rose to his feet, stumbling as he stepped clear of the body. He turned to tell Carpathimos to find Lucia, but Carpathimos had already gone.

Carpathimos ran in and out of the house, frantically calling Lucia's name.

"Come! Search the hillside!" Lucius ordered. Bloodied and battered, he climbed into the woods with Carpathimos at his side, but as Carpathimos moved up the hill ahead of him, the younger man looked back at Lucius. "What evil did you bring with you?"

At those words, Lucius fell behind and soon dropped to his knees, too exhausted to continue. He crawled to the base of a sturdy old poplar, praying for the safety of his grandson and wondering if his friends Faustus and Domitius were truly gone. His mind raced. How far would Regulus chase him? As the sun shifted into the western sky he grew weak from his wounds, which continued to bleed. He rested his head against the tree and closed his eyes.

In the cold darkness that surrounded him, Lucius thought perhaps that he heard voices. Did he feel Parma and Yzebel rush to his side and speak to him? He couldn't overcome the sleep that pressed down on him like a heavy stack of blankets. He could no longer move.

***

Lucius awoke from his sleep the next day, to find himself bandaged and clean. He ached all over and the slightest movement was instantly regretted. When he managed to crawl from his bed, he found the house empty. Shuffling toward the door, he heard someone approaching. Parma stepped into the room and smiled at him.

"You're finally awake!" she said, joy in her voice. "Lucia will be thrilled to see you alive and well." She helped him sit at the table and set a bowl of food in front of him. "You must eat to get stronger and heal those wounds, Lucius." She started to say something else, but Lucius interrupted her, his voice raspy and weak.

"I must leave here before any more soldiers come. I cannot let any harm come to any of you."

"Nonsense!" retorted Parma. "You are delirious from your injuries. You are a part of us here. You are a part of this family, Lucius."

"But how can we live our lives never knowing when the next storm will come?" Lucius covered his face with his hands.

"Whatever storm may rain down on this family, we will fight it together, not each alone," said a deep voice from the doorway. Carpathimos stood staring at his son's grandfather. "Parma is correct, Lucius. You are a part of my family. I recall you saying that you owed a debt to Myridia. I expect you to repay that debt to Lucia for many years to come."

Lucius sat quietly, staring through the doorway unblinkingly until Carpathimos nodded at him and left, his spot taken by Lucia. The boy jumped up on the stool next to Lucius and wrapped his arms around his warrior grandfather. Lucius winced at the pain but cherished the hug. His chest ached with his love for the child. He glanced up at Parma, who was watching him.

"You see, Lucius? I was right again," she announced.

Lucius and Lucia laughed together at Parma. They had learned she was a very competitive person. Then they followed her outside, to see Carpathimos standing alone in front of the house on a small knoll overlooking the lake. A soft breeze blew off the water and tossed his hair, blowing a few strands across his face and over his eyes. Parma and Yzebel walked up behind him while Lucius, who was carrying Lucia on his shoulders with a little difficulty—which he would not let the boy see—followed. Carpathimos sensed them standing behind him. He took a deep breath, sighed and said, "The water here has soured. Fish wash up on shore every day now. I don't think I can support us here any longer. I am sorry."

Lucius gripped Lucia's ankles. He thought he knew the real reason why Carpathimos wanted to leave this place, which was now stained by the blood of evil, but he was about to learn much more about the man he considered a son.

"Where do you want to go, Carpathimos?" Parma held Ligeia on her hip. She recognized the look in her brother's eye and understood that he had been yearning for something more for them.

"I want to fish in the Sea of Chinnereth." Carpathimos spoke with the assurance of a commander. "Elijah spoke in detail about the fishermen there and the lives they lead. He described fertile lands at the foot of majestic cliffs bordering the northern side of the sea. Wheat grows as high as a man's shoulders, fruit trees are plentiful and laden, fish swim in schools as large as a flotilla of boats."

"We would move there?" Parma considered the practical factors. "It is very far away."

"It would be a shorter walk to Jerusalem from there," Carpathimos countered, nodding to Yzebel.

"The City of David!" she exclaimed.

"I would like to know the city Elijah knew, but more than that, I would like to know the Yahweh Elijah knew," Carpathimos said. "I have traveled long distances over land and water and I have seen many things, but I want to see the temple and the massive cedar trees that were brought to the city from Tyre. We are all together now and we can be free of the hardships that haunt our past. Let us share a better life in *that* place."

Lucius looked up at Lucia and noticed the broad grin and excitement on his grandson's face, a grin void of two middle teeth. "Our trust is with you, Carpathimos." Lucius put his hand on the warrior's shoulder. "We will follow you anywhere the wind should carry you."

Carpathimos shifted his feet and a look of discomfort flashed across his face. "I do not deserve such trust. I am no leader."

"Brother, nearly three years ago, Lucia and I watched you sail away out of our lives," Parma said. "I never expected to see my beloved brother ever again. Someone new arrived home to us. He answered to my brother's name, but his body is very different, his tales are very different, and his dreams are very different. One thing remains the same, however—the same determination and love for his family. I recognize those qualities from our childhood. Your life's experiences have changed you, Carpathimos, but the brother I once knew, the father Lucia once knew, suffered many hardships to return to his family. He returned a better man, a wise leader. We will do what you say."

Yzebel took Carpathimos's hand and quickly glanced at the rest of the family before staring into his eyes. "We will follow you—not for the places you may lead us, but for the man you have become."